DAIMON
GUARDIANS OF HADES BOOK 6

FELICITY HEATON

THE GUARDIANS OF HADES SERIES

Book 1: Ares

Book 2: Valen

Book 3: Esher

Book 4: Marek

Book 5: Calistos

Book 6: Daimon

Book 7: Keras – Coming Fall 2020

Discover more available paranormal romance books at:
http://www.felicityheaton.com

Or sign up to my mailing list to receive a FREE vampire romance ebook,
learn about new titles, be eligible for special subscriber-only giveaways, and
read exclusive content including short stories:
http://ml.felicityheaton.com/mailinglist

CHAPTER 1

This wasn't going well.

Daimon slipped a throwing knife from the holster that sat against his ribs over his navy roll-neck long-sleeve, and funnelled his power into it before sending it flying at the daemon running right at him across the dewy moonlit grass of Hyde Park. The small blade hit its target, nailing the human-looking male in the chest. Ice immediately spread outwards from the point of impact and the male grunted and went down clutching his chest as glittering frost flowers rapidly covered it. His skin darkened, turning mottled in the low light, appearing almost black.

Beside Daimon, his older brother Ares unleashed a wave of fire at another two daemons, driving them back, and tossed a fireball at a third.

They had expected this.

What they hadn't expected was that it would take so long to close one of the main gates.

Behind him, Valen grunted and muttered a black curse in the mortal tongue. The scent of his brother's blood hung heavily in the damp autumnal night air. Worry ran through Daimon, and not only him. Ares flicked a concerned glance over his broad shoulder, the fires of the Underworld raging in his eyes, making them glow in the darkness.

Eva bit out something in Italian. She had stopped speaking English around five minutes ago, when Valen had announced the gate was resisting his attempt to seal it and had decided to spill more of his blood in the hope it would speed the process along since twenty daemons had descended on them.

"I'm going to need more," Valen gritted, his voice tight and speaking of the frustration Daimon could feel in him.

As well as the pain.

"Too risky," Ares answered as a whip made of fire appeared in his right hand and he narrowed his gaze on the trees that enclosed one side of the area around the gate. Daemons spilled from them, cutting across the paths and the grass, heading right for him. He grunted as he lashed out at the daemons with the flaming whip, driving them back and stopping them from reaching Valen. "You sure you're using the right wards? Or doing them right? I mean, we all know how shitty your wards are."

Valen chuckled, the sound out of place given the graveness of the situation. "Don't know what you're talking about. My wards are beautiful."

They weren't. Valen had never bothered to apply himself when it came to studying wards. Their father, Hades, the god-king of the Underworld, had gone as far as calling them bad. It took a lot for their father to admit to a fault in any of his sons, let alone point it out to the entire family.

"You're definitely using the right ones?" Daimon didn't take his eyes off the daemons as they made another attempt to get past him and Ares, breaking into four teams of four and coming at them in one wave.

The longer this war to protect the gates between the mortal realm and the Underworld went on, the more organised the daemons were becoming. He swore the enemy were training them, teaching them how to fight as a unit—turning them into soldiers.

He had to admit he'd preferred it when the daemons had been lone wolves, only a few of them reckless enough to succumb to the lure of breaching a gate and entering the Underworld—a realm they were forbidden to enter.

Just like Daimon and his brothers.

Only unlike the daemons, he could go home once this war was done.

He drew down a breath and threw his right hand forwards as he summoned his power. The dew on the grass became a thousand tiny ice needles that flew through the air and hammered into one of the daemons, taking him down. The female daemon who had been running beside that wretched male shrieked as she was caught by a few of the small spears of ice, her ear-splitting cry piercing enough that Daimon flinched and his next wave missed their target.

"Exactly as Cal told me." Valen huffed and water sloshed as he moved, a reminder to Daimon to keep his distance from his brother since standing in the Round Pond was the only way for Valen to get close enough to the gate to spill his blood on it. The last thing Daimon wanted was to accidentally freeze the small lake. Valen grumbled, "And Keras hammered home around thirty times."

His violet-haired brother wasn't embellishing that.

Keras, their oldest brother and self-appointed leader, had sat Valen down on one of the cream couches in the Tokyo mansion and gone over the wards at least three dozen times. In the end, Valen had stepped, a term they used for teleporting since it only took a single step for them to travel great distances, to escape another round of which wards went where.

It wasn't that Keras didn't trust Valen to get it right, it was that this was important.

Since the enemy had revealed they were in possession of two of the Erinyes, goddesses who had the ability to siphon powers and who strengthened that power by passing it between them in a cycle, and those Erinyes had gotten their hands on the ability to command the gates Daimon and his brothers protected, they had been on red alert.

The gates were the focus of their mission, the reason Hades had banished Daimon and his brothers to the mortal world two centuries ago, after the Moirai had foreseen a great calamity, one where an unknown enemy would breach the gates between the mortal realm and the Underworld, fusing the two into a new hellish realm.

It had come to light that he and his brothers were more than just protectors of the gates though.

They were bound to them in blood, a bond forged at the time of their birth, one gate created for each of them.

Cal had managed to close their twin sister's gate in Seville, and had gone over everything he had done, using wards, a sort of spell, to seal it and conceal it, stopping it from opening and rendering it safe from the enemy.

With the enemy able to open the gates thanks to the power the Erinyes had stolen from Marinda, Cal's girlfriend and the third Erinyes, and the fact the enemy seemed bent on breaching at least one gate before that power faded, Keras had decided they needed to act.

Closing the gates was dangerous, because it meant there were fewer gates to share the power that flowed between them all, and that would make them more unpredictable and harder to command, but it was a necessary risk.

And the only path open to them.

It would not only give the enemy fewer gates they could hit, but it would mean that the enemy couldn't split him and his brothers up as easily.

Valen had volunteered to seal the London gate, which was bound to him, and Cal had volunteered to close the main Seville gate. Cal was there now with Keras, Marek, and Caterina, Marek's *girl-fiend* as Valen called her because she was a hybrid, a human who had been given daemon blood by the enemy in an attempt to take down Marek.

Everyone had thought sealing a main gate would be as simple as closing the twin gate had been for Cal.

Apparently, everyone had thought wrong.

Ares took out another two daemons, bringing their numbers down but still not enough to satisfy Daimon. He imbued another two knives with his ice and let them fly. One of them buried to the ring-shaped hilt in the forehead of a female daemon, and the other slammed into the throat of the male behind her.

Valen bit out a ripe curse.

Daimon didn't take his focus away from the daemons charging towards him.

Ares looked back at their brother and swore too.

That didn't sound good.

Daimon risked a glance over his shoulder as he sent a thicker spear of ice flying at the closest daemon, cleaving the male in two at the waist.

"Shit," he muttered as he spotted what his brothers had.

More daemons, sprinting towards them from the other side of the Round Pond, a shadowy mass of them silhouetted before the elegant red-brick and sandstone Kensington Palace.

The new horde of daemons split into two groups as they reached the far end of the pond, coming at them from both sides.

Above the water, the flat disc of the gate shimmered in a rainbow of colours, chasing back the darkness. The thick rings rotated slowly in opposing directions, all of them chasing around the central violet circle. Glyphs encircled each band, smaller ones that filled the gaps between them, and larger ones inside the ring. The power of the gate hummed in the air, inside him, drew him to it with a promise that on the other side was home.

Home.

A place he wanted to go more than anything.

There, his power was under his control, would no longer shimmer over his skin in a way that felt like a curse. Here, he couldn't touch anyone, not even his brothers, without risking killing them with his ice, or severely maiming them at the very least. Here, he was alone, even within the circle of his brothers.

The blood Valen had spilled on the gate absorbed into it, the colours that danced across its surface and curled into the air like faint smoke brightening again.

It was beautiful.

Beautiful and vulnerable.

Daimon's stomach swirled as the daemons closed in, the foul coppery odour of them filling the air, drawing out his darker side. He wouldn't let them near the gate.

He closed his eyes, drew down a slow breath that filled his lungs, and focused his power, calling on it. His blood chilled and he shuddered, huddling down into the tall neck of his long-sleeved sweater and his ankle-length black coat, trying to keep that cold at bay.

It never worked.

It was always there, always part of him in this world, a constant presence that drained him emotionally.

He flicked his eyes open and swiftly raised both of his gloved hands.

Around him, his brothers and the gate, hundreds of clear shards of ice shot from the earth and the water to form a circular wall forty feet tall.

Daimon sagged forwards and Ares came to check on him as Valen muttered an oath.

His older brother ghosted a hand over Daimon's spine, the warmth that emanated from him giving Daimon a brief reprieve from the cold. Ares shared his problem. His brother's power over fire had manifested in this world, meaning he couldn't touch anyone without the risk of burning them.

Or at least he hadn't been able to until Megan, a Carrier with the ability to heal, had come into his life. Megan was immune to Ares's fire, and could withstand Daimon's ice, and he and his brothers had surmised she was closer to her demigod ancestors than most Carriers.

"Can you get it done?" Daimon pressed his hands to his thighs and ignored the way the frost on his leather gloves spread onto his black jeans.

"Give me a minute." Valen went back to work, holding his arm out over the gate and closing his eyes as his blood spilled onto it. Beside him, Eva, his brother's mortal assassin girlfriend, shifted foot to foot, concern shining in her rich blue eyes.

"I'll handle these guys." Ares straightened and broke away from Daimon, heading for the few daemons that had ended up within the ice wall.

Daimon wanted to help him, but he needed to focus on the wall. Where it touched the water, it was in danger of melting, was weaker and vulnerable. The daemons had already figured that out and were beating it with fist and claw, attempting to break through. He focused there, summoning more shards of ice to reinforce it.

Wishing Esher was here.

His brother would have used that water to his advantage, would have drowned all the daemons in a heartbeat.

Daimon looked at the gate and fought the urge that suddenly sparked to life inside him.

Esher was on the other side of that gate, in the Underworld, hunting for one of the enemy who had slipped through the gate in Paris. He was alone. Lost to his other side. Daimon rose to his full height and drifted towards the gate, pulled to it as his heart filled with a need to find Esher.

Pain bloomed inside him, searing his bones in multiple places where an injury didn't exist on his own body.

It existed on Esher's.

Daimon could feel them, the depth of the bond they had forged over the centuries relaying not only the pain his brother felt, but the anger and frustration.

The rage.

The other side of Esher, the savage and cold one that had been born in the darkest of times, was firmly in control. Daimon could feel that too. He needed his brother back with him, not only because he needed to know he was safe and because he was worried about him—missed him.

He needed him back so he could *bring* him back.

Esher had confessed to him once that he feared that other side of himself, that he loathed it. Daimon could only imagine how his brother was suffering now, a slave to his darker side, driven to hunt and not rest until he had secured his prey.

The wraith.

Eli.

If they could get their hands on him, they might be able to find out who was behind this attempt to breach the gates. Once, they had believed it was purely the work of daemons, but then they had discovered a Hellspawn, what he and his brothers called the species of daemons who had been allowed to remain in the Underworld after the last rebellion against Hades, was involved, and now there were goddesses on the enemy side.

Where did it end?

Someone was behind all of this, and all they had to go on was that it was a female.

Their father had sent them a long list of possible enemies currently residing in the Underworld, far too many for Daimon's liking. Discovering which of them, if any, were behind everything would take too long. It was quicker to get their hands on the wraith and make him talk.

An ominous creaking noise drew Daimon's gaze to his left. His eyes tracked the jagged fault line spreading up the ice from a point where several daemons were clawing at it. Was he imagining it, or were there even more daemons now?

"You guys got this?" Valen said.

"Sure." Daimon readied himself, shoring up the wall of ice but aware it wouldn't hold, not against that many sets of claws.

The daemons' black blood streaked the clear ice, the foul stench of it filling the air. Disgust rolled through him and he curled his lip.

Ares grunted in response from the right side of the pond as he slammed a daemon into the pavement that encircled the water.

"Good, because I'm not sure I can do this." Valen sounded tired now, and when Daimon fixed his senses on his violet-haired brother, he felt it too. "Not without a little more juice."

Daimon looked back at him.

Valen's golden eyes glittered, glowing in the light shining from the gate as he raised one of his blades.

"No," Ares snarled, pivoted towards him, and kicked off.

He wouldn't make it. Neither would Daimon, not even if he stepped.

All he could do was watch as Valen ran the blade across his wrist and blood gushed from the wound.

"Stronzo!" Eva barked and lunged for him, her short black hair flying out of her face as she reached for the blade.

Valen sagged as blood poured from his wrist, splattering across the surface of the gate and spreading outwards, and Eva grabbed him instead of the knife. She caught him as his knees gave out.

He breathed hard from between gritted teeth, his eyes rapidly darkening as they narrowed.

Eva muttered soft words in Italian, sweet chastising ones coupled with a few strong swear words that Daimon decided his brother deserved.

Valen leaned heavily on her slender shoulders, his arm shaking as he tried to keep holding it out over the gate. Eva took hold of his arm for him, helping him, and he looked at her, a hell of a lot of love in his eyes that was still strange to see. Valen's default setting for his entire life had been caustic, and it had only gotten worse in the centuries after their sister had died and Zeus had punished Valen for his insubordination by removing his favour from him, leaving a ragged scar down the left side of Valen's face and neck, a permanent reminder of what he had done.

So it was weird seeing his brother looking at someone with genuine warmth in his eyes.

With love.

The blood Valen was spilling onto the gate seeped across the surface, muting the colours.

"I think it's working," Valen slurred.

Eva struggled to keep him on his feet.

Daimon wasn't sure how their youngest brother, Calistos, was going to be able to handle closing the main gate in Seville if closing London was draining Valen this much. Cal had been out of sorts since they had lost the chance to discover the location of his twin sister, Calindria's, soul and Esher had disappeared. Cal was blaming himself for both of those things. Daimon doubted he was strong enough to handle closing Seville on top of all that.

"Think I'm—" Valen cut off as he suddenly dropped, his knees hitting the bottom of the shallow pond, and Eva yelped as she was dragged down with him.

Daimon looked at the gate as he called on his power, summoning one last wave of ice. It rose up around the inside of the wall, the shards only seven feet tall but enough to keep the daemons at bay while Ares checked on Valen and the gate.

A gate which Daimon could no longer feel, not as he could before. The power that flowed from it now was muted, barely there. Had Valen done it?

The rings slowly began to shrink, the innermost one winking out of existence as it touched the central violet disc.

It was closing.

"Is he good?" Daimon hollered, keeping his focus on the wall of ice, aware the daemons were still there and still trying to get to them.

Ares looked up from his position crouched next to Valen and nodded. "Think so. He's out cold though."

Daimon didn't like the sound of that.

Closing the twin gate had been taxing on Cal, but he hadn't passed out.

Ares pulled a phone from his pocket, the screen casting white highlights in his overlong tawny hair and across his face as his thumb danced over the device. "Calling in a retrieval."

Because neither he nor Daimon could teleport with Valen without harming him.

Eva tore the hem of her T-shirt and bound Valen's wrist, muttering obscenities in Italian under her breath the whole time.

Beyond Ares, Valen and Eva, the last ring of the gate shrank into the central disc. It shrank too and then disappeared with a violent flash.

Gone.

For now.

Once the enemy was dead and the threat over, Hades would want the gates opened again. Their father had sent a Messenger to Keras to say he had stopped all traffic through the gates, but had made it clear he couldn't keep the Underworld closed for long.

Gods, goddesses and Hellspawn didn't appreciate being caged in that realm, having their freedom taken from them. Hades's staff were already dealing with hundreds of complaints.

Considering the alternative was them all losing their home and being ruled by whoever was behind this uprising, Daimon figured they could put up with their freedom being impacted a little.

Daimon kept an eye on Valen as Eva tended to him, worry a constant weight in his heart as his senses remained locked on the daemons. They retreated into the night, but he kept his boots firmly planted where they were, resisting the urge to follow them and eradicate them all.

Valen needed him here.

The ice walls surrounding them were beginning to crack as Marek appeared, black ribbons of smoke curling from the shoulders of his torn charcoal linen shirt and onyx daemon blood streaked across his face and darkening his wavy brown hair.

His earthy eyes shimmered with green and gold flakes as he looked down at Valen where he lay in Eva's arms. "Cal suffered the same fate."

Daimon cast a glance at Ares. Concern etched hard lines on his older brother's face, unease that ran through Daimon too as he thought about not one but two of their brothers out cold with no sign of coming around.

If he had known closing a gate would cause this to happen, he would have spoken out against it rather than going along with it. The look on Ares's face said he wasn't sure what he would have said, and Daimon didn't envy him.

Marek looked just as conflicted as he stooped and lifted Valen into a fireman's carry over his shoulder.

Daimon was glad he wasn't one of the oldest of their group. He felt the weight of responsibility enough as it was. He couldn't imagine how heavily it weighed upon Keras, Ares and Marek's shoulders.

Keras was under enough pressure as it was, without having to order them to close the gates knowing full well they would end up like Valen and Cal.

Closing the gates was something they needed to do, but Daimon feared the cost of shutting them down was dangerously high.

He only hoped he was wrong about that.

Marek held his hand out to Eva. Her blue eyes reluctantly shifted away from Valen and landed on it. She placed hers into it and they both disappeared.

Ares was quick to follow them.

Daimon lingered, waiting for the ice walls to break because he wanted to be sure all evidence of their existence would be gone by morning, when mortals would enter Hyde Park. He didn't want them seeing anything out of place.

That was the only reason he hadn't teleported.

It had nothing to do with the sorceress who was probably waiting in Tokyo to give him hell.

He scrubbed a hand over the spikes of his white hair, watching the ice begin to crumble.

The ancient Edo period mansion felt far too small with her staying in it, but when he had suggested she bunk elsewhere, Cass had been quick to launch into an argument with him. Her ward, Marinda, was staying in the mansion with Cal since the London townhouse that was his home had been breached by Eli and the enemy, which meant Cass had decided she was also staying in Tokyo, right under Daimon's feet.

Daimon rubbed the back of his neck and huffed.

The sorceress had a bad habit of just deciding things, and no one got a say in them.

Daimon had been staying in Tokyo to take care of the mansion, which was primarily Esher's home now although their father had built it for all of them, and so he could be there for Aiko. Aiko was devastated by Esher's disappearance, and Daimon needed to look after her for his brother.

He was doing his best, but some days were harder than others.

Some days, Daimon's dark thoughts and fears about his brother weighed too heavily on him and he couldn't face her, or anyone.

His phone vibrated and he didn't bother to check the message that had come in. It would be from Keras, asking him where he was.

He focused on the wall, raised his hand and curled it into a fist. When he squeezed it, the ice shattered, and Daimon stepped. Darkness whirled around him, cool and comforting, a connection to the Underworld that he savoured, and then his boots hit gravel.

He opened his eyes and looked at the mansion, aching inside.

It felt empty without Esher in it, even when all his brothers and their women were there, crowding the long main room of the single-storey horseshoe-shaped building. Morning sunlight reflected off the glazed grey ribbed tiles of the roof and brightened the white panels that filled the spaces between thick dark wooden beams. It warmed his back, casting his shadow out before him, across the gravel and the steppingstones, to the base of one of the large stone lanterns that were dotted around the front garden.

From inside, voices rang out, a cacophony that had him wanting to teleport to his own home in Hong Kong to get some peace and quiet.

And avoid the owner of the angry female voice that for some damned reason he picked out from the blur.

"You should have taken me with you. Now look what happened. I could have helped," Cass snapped, her words harsh and clipped, bringing out her Russian accent as they rang with the fury he could sense coming from her.

Keras didn't respond to that. He carried Cal towards the right side of the mansion, disappearing from view with Marinda hurrying behind him. Cass turned, her pale blue eyes tracking her ward, a worried edge to them that almost made him feel there was a warm heart somewhere beneath that irritating, haughty exterior of hers.

Daimon forced himself to walk to the front porch, stepped up onto the raised wooden deck as he toed his boots off, and steeled himself only a little before entering the house.

As expected, Cass's eyes immediately leaped to him.

He cursed when he realised they were alone.

She strode towards him, the thigh slit in her long black dress flashing a lot of creamy flesh at him. He swore she never took the damned thing off. Would it kill her to wear something less revealing, less figure-hugging? The soft black material embraced ample breasts and a small waist, and flared over curvy hips. It flashed every inch of her and made it impossible not to notice things about her.

Things he didn't want to notice.

Before she could open her mouth to launch her first salvo, he held his hand up and strode past her.

"Not interested."

Daimon made a beeline for the garden nestled between the three sides of the house, needing air and some space because he felt as if he was drowning.

Had been feeling that way since Cass had come crashing into their lives.

He couldn't get a moment alone, and gods he needed a moment to breathe.

Cass stepped into his path, the flare of anger in her ice-blue eyes rapidly fading into something far worse—concern.

She gave him a once-over. "Those wounds need looking at."

She pointed to his chest and then his legs, and he had never been more aware of his own body as he was whenever she was gazing at it.

"I'm not in the mood for you, Cass. Just leave me alone." He stepped past her, heading for the garden and the air he badly needed.

Space to rein his riotous feelings back under his control.

Needs he had no right to feel.

"Daimon, wait…" She started after him again.

Wanting to be sure she got the message and left him alone, he turned on her with a growl as his feet hit the wooden planks of the covered walkway that ran around all three wings of the house.

"I don't have time for this right now. Esher is still missing, I'm tired and injured, and we don't know when or where the enemy will attack next and I need to take care of Valen."

Cass inched back a step with each harsh word he threw at her. It wasn't like the sorceress to shrink away from someone, especially him.

"I just want to help," she bit out, a little too sulkily for him to not feel anything other than like a royal dick. "Let me help with Valen."

"Fine," he muttered, and took some of the bite out of his tone as he added, "I'd appreciate that."

He turned to his right, towards the southern wing of the house where Valen's quarters were.

Cass murmured, "It wouldn't kill you to let me help you too."

He knew that, but he couldn't. He needed to keep his distance from her.

He'd made a promise.

He drew his long black coat back and slipped his right hand into his pocket, and clutched the pendant hanging from his phone.

A promise he intended to keep.

CHAPTER 2

Cassandra could feel Daimon withdrawing, pulling away from her as he turned his back to her and strode towards the wing of the house where she had been sleeping in Keras's room. She wanted to push him, wanted to know why he did that. He changed so frequently she couldn't keep up.

One moment he would be lashing out at her verbally, as scathing as could be, and the next he softened and accepted her presence, would even go as far as speaking with her as if she was a normal human being.

Not something he wanted to wipe from the face of the Earth.

She remained where she was on the covered walkway, staring after him, trying to make sense of him and feeling as if she would never understand him. The temptation to follow him was great, especially when rather than entering Valen's room that was directly in front of her, he banked right and headed towards the garden instead.

Cass held herself back.

Because he needed space.

It hadn't taken her long into her study of him and his brothers to notice that he was closest to Esher, and it had taken her less than a second to see how deep that love ran when Esher had leapt into the gate in pursuit of the wraith.

Or perhaps it had taken her longer than that.

In the short time since Esher had been missing, she had witnessed a dramatic change in Daimon.

It was as if he was slowly falling apart before her eyes and there was nothing she could do to stop it.

There was nothing anyone could do to stop it.

He wasn't going to be whole again until Esher returned.

What happened if he never came back?

It wasn't any of her concern, and neither was Daimon's state of mind. The reason she had studied these gods, and the reason she was here now, was for Marinda's sake and to keep the vow she had made to Marinda's father, Eric, who had been murdered by the brothers' enemy.

A promise to keep Mari safe.

That was her priority.

Daimon was just a nice distraction, a bit of eye-candy that brightened things up while she was keeping an eye on her ward. He was nothing to her. Just some harmless fun.

He couldn't be anything more than that.

Her gaze drifted after him and she idly tracked him as he crossed the arched vermillion and black wooden bridge that spanned the koi pond at the start of the lush rolling garden. He paused at the apex of it and gazed down into the water, his profile to her, too far away for her to make out any details.

Not that she needed to be close to him to know how he would look.

Lost. Adrift. Hurt.

Lonely.

It was none of her business. These gods meant nothing to her.

Daimon meant nothing to her.

She had to remember that, had to remember her duty, even when it felt like a sword hanging over her, ready to fall and sever her from her life, throwing her into servitude that grated and had her mood blackening whenever she thought about it.

Cass pulled down a breath and purged it, and all her feelings. When she was calm again, as empty as she could manage, all her worries and desires washed from her, she padded barefoot towards Valen's room.

Eva looked up as Cass entered the sparsely furnished room, her blue eyes filled with concern and fear. It was strange seeing the assassin afraid of something. Cass shifted her gaze to Valen where he lay on top of a pile of blankets in the centre of the golden tatami mats that covered the floor, his violet hair in disarray but his face peaceful.

Beside him, Eva tightened her grip on his left hand, clutching it as if she feared he would slip away if she let go.

Cass eased down to kneel on the other side of him and looked him over. Someone had bandaged his right arm from his elbow to his palm. Crimson spotted it, a rather nasty patch of it over his wrist. She started there, holding her right hand over it as she closed her eyes and formed the words in her mind, a powerful incantation that would speed his healing process. Heat bloomed in her hand and Eva's soft gasp rang in her ears as light shimmered from her palm.

As she was funnelling the healing spell into Valen, she probed a little, using another incantation to study his vitals.

There was nothing out of the ordinary on the surface, but as she summoned stronger magic to delve deeper, she wanted to bite out a rather unladylike curse.

This wasn't good.

She needed to speak with Mari.

Cass withdrew her hand and met Eva's blue gaze. She wasn't sure what to say to the mortal, just as she was never sure what to say to Daimon, or to Aiko, Esher's lover. She stared at her in silence, searching for the words that wouldn't come.

When the silence began to grate, she pushed onto her feet, and forced a smile and a slight nod. "He will be fine."

Did those words ring with the hollowness she felt in them?

It was the right thing to say, but it felt wrong of her to utter those four words, offering hope where she wasn't sure there was any. Perhaps that was the reason she never knew what to say to Daimon or Aiko.

She couldn't bring herself to lie to them to make them feel better.

She hurried from the room, striding straight across the front of the main living area of the house to the other wing of it. She turned right at the end of the corridor, passing the TV area, and her pulse picked up as she neared Cal's room.

Mari was quick to stand as she entered, her blue-green eyes bright with unshed tears and her golden hair falling down from the twisted plait that arched over the top of her head. She ran her hand over it again as she hurried to Cass, hope surfacing in her eyes.

Cass caught her arm and pulled her towards the door, aware of the other two gods in the room with Cal, standing over him.

Keras and Ares, two men she had discovered were formidable in their desire to protect their younger brothers, and in their ability to fight.

What she wanted to tell Mari was liable to spark both of those things in them.

"Mari," she whispered, hoping the gods wouldn't hear her. "I think Cal is going to be sleeping for a while."

"How do you know that?" Keras's deep voice was calm, emotionless.

Dangerous.

When the firstborn of Hades sounded like this, he was a step away from unleashing hell upon someone.

In this case, her.

She looked at him, refusing to let him see that what she really wanted to do was mutter her strongest barrier spell and distance herself from him.

Because he wasn't going to like what she had to say and, like his father, he had a tendency to shoot the messenger.

"I used a spell on Valen to probe a little into his physical condition." She braced herself for his reaction.

But it was Daimon who was suddenly beside her, his voice a black snarl as he advanced on her.

"You did what?"

She stood her ground, stoked her courage and squared up to him. "You said I could heal him. I just wanted to see what damage I was dealing with so I could find the appropriate spells."

She didn't take her eyes away from his icy blue ones. They were rapidly brightening, turning white ringed with navy, sparks of silver lighting them as the anger she could sense in him mounted.

"Did you hurt him with that little probing spell of yours? Because I didn't give you permission to do that," Daimon snapped, and Cass wanted to bark right back at him, but she kept her temper in check.

Because she had been wrong about these brothers, had judged them without knowing them, but if she had been quick to do such a thing, it had only been because she felt protective of Marinda.

Now that she had seen Cal with Marinda, she could see that Eric had been right to trust the god and that Cal clearly loved her, and she knew it must have been a comfort to Eric in his last moment. He had seen a vision of the future, and in it he had seen his daughter would find someone who loved her as deeply as he had loved her mother.

All the brothers were like Eric in that way.

When they loved, they *loved*. No half measures. It was a forever kind of love. Whether it was for their family or for a woman.

Gods, she was being sentimental.

Love was just love.

There was nothing magical about it.

It wasn't necessary.

She stared into Daimon's icy eyes, feeling nothing. Not fear. Not love. Not hate. He was just a distraction. A pleasant diversion.

One who looked ready to throttle her.

16

She risked a glance at Keras and Ares and found them looking the same way.

"Listen," she bit out, before they could turn on her or Daimon could get ideas about attempting to drown her in the pond again. "Valen is in a deep sleep. One might call it a coma. He sealed a gate. Did you honestly think there wouldn't be consequences from tampering with something bound to you all in blood? Created *from* your blood?"

Ares scrubbed a hand down his face, his deep brown eyes filled with fatigue and worry. Keras actually looked concerned for once as his green gaze dropped to Cal where he was tucked under the covers on the floor.

"Check him," Keras said. "See if they both feel the same way to you."

She kneeled beside Cal, took hold of his wrist and closed her eyes as she summoned the spell again, pushing past her own fatigue to make it as strong as the one she had used on Valen.

Her strength drained from her as she funnelled it into him and waited.

He was hurting, so she gave his healing a little push as she had with Valen.

And then she felt it.

That same feeling Valen had given her.

"He's asleep," she murmured, holding the connection between them open. "A coma-level sleep. He's still functioning normally, but I can feel this isn't a normal sleep."

"When will he wake up?" Mari's voice trembled and Cass broke her hold on Cal and looked up at her.

For once, she didn't hide her feelings, let Mari see them all. She knew what Mari was really asking but was too afraid to voice.

Would he wake up?

She pushed onto her feet and gathered Mari into her arms, holding her close. "I'm not sure. It might be a few days, sweetie, it might be a few weeks."

She refused to say it might be never.

She couldn't do that to Mari.

"At worst, he might not wake until the seals are removed from the gate," she said.

"I don't like the sound of that." The sense of dark power Keras constantly emanated grew in strength and Cass had a hard time withstanding it in her weakened state.

She leaned on Mari, hoping her ward wouldn't notice it or if she did, wouldn't mention that she was weak from using her magic on gods. She didn't want these gods to know that she had her limits.

"I don't like it either," Daimon muttered.

"We can't afford to leave the gates open, but we can't weaken our side by having two more of our team out of action." Ares folded his arms across his broad chest, causing the tattered remains of his black T-shirt to stretch over his muscles.

Mari whispered, "Cal closed the gate. How can anyone else open it?"

Cass smoothed her hand over Mari's fair hair, hoping it would comfort her.

"We could probably use their blood," Daimon offered from behind her. "It might be enough to allow another of us to undo the wards."

"We should wait." Keras levelled a dark look at Daimon. "Don't give me that look. I am only talking about waiting a few days to see if their condition changes. Valen and Cal will need to recover from the blood loss of sealing the Seville gate anyway. A few days, and then we shall decide what to do."

Cass hoped for all their sakes that Cal and Valen awoke.

The air in the room remained dark, oppressive as the three brothers stood in silence.

They were already missing one brother, having another two out of action was an understandable cause of worry.

Daimon broke the silence. "If we're going to be out of action for weeks, weakened by draining our blood to close the gates, then we're going to be vulnerable to the enemy. Maybe this is all part of their plan."

She pulled back from Mari and looked at him, catching the concern in his ice-blue eyes as he ran a hand over the spikes of his dirty white hair. Concern that echoed inside her too.

"What if they're forcing us to close the gates, so we're concentrating the power of them into only a few, making them harder to manage? They could be setting us up for a fall." Daimon exchanged a look with his brothers, one that chilled her blood.

What he was saying made a dreadful sort of sense.

They had planned to close four gates as quickly as possible, but with this new turn of events, that would be too risky.

As it was, there were still five gates in need of protection and only four brothers to do it. If the enemy attacked now, her side would be at a disadvantage.

"We'll have to be on our guard." Keras lifted his green gaze from Cal and settled it on her. "Can we count on you?"

Daimon's gaze drilled into the side of her face and she suppressed the urge to point out they could have counted on her tonight, when they had gone to London and Seville. Rather than throwing it in their faces again, she nodded.

Looked at Keras and Ares.

And then right into Daimon's eyes.

"Whatever you need from me, you've got it."

CHAPTER 3

Daimon trod the well-worn path that trailed through the garden in the gap between the north wing of the mansion and the white wall that enclosed it, enjoying the cool shade and the peace.

And maybe the escape from the gloomy air inside the house.

It had been three days since Cal and Valen had sealed two of the gates, and in that time, Daimon and his remaining brothers had been fighting daemons away from the gates each night. The Erinyes had targeted two or three gates a night, starting the opening process using the power they had stolen from Marinda, and then disappearing just as he and his brothers reached the gate, leaving them with hordes of daemons to deal with as they closed the gate again. Everyone was tired and beaten down, and he wasn't talking about just his brothers.

Caterina, Eva and Cass had been on the frontline with them, battling the daemons, working as a team to help him and his brothers in the absence of Cal, Valen and Esher.

Daimon had the feeling that the enemy was trying to weaken them. Or maybe they were testing the limits of their powers.

His side was testing the limits of the Erinyes' powers in return.

Keras had asked Marinda to avoid touching Cal so they could see whether her power over the gate would weaken, and could discover how long a furie could hold on to a power they had siphoned from another.

Whenever Daimon went to check on Cal, he could see how difficult this was for Marinda. Cal was still sleeping, and it was clear she wanted to hold him, to touch him and offer comfort, and she couldn't.

He could understand how that felt.

He couldn't touch his brothers to give them that either. His touch would only cause them more pain.

Daimon neared the front garden, tipped his head back and stared at the endless blue sky.

Gods, he was tired.

Bone-deep tired.

Whenever he tried to sleep, he saw visions of Esher in the Underworld, terrible things that plagued him when he woke, stayed with him through the night as he carried out his duties until dawn came and sleep beckoned again.

He had woken two hours ago in a cold sweat and had been walking the garden ever since, seeking some respite, trying to purge what he had seen in his nightmares. Desperate to sleep and get some rest this time.

As he rounded the corner and the path opened up again, shaded by a beautiful old maple tree on his left and bushes on his right, his gaze landed on the two motorbikes Cal had brought with him from his home in London after Keras had declared it a loss and ordered him to move into the mansion in Tokyo.

The lime-green and black one was sleek and sharp, built for speed, just like his little brother. The gold and black one beside it looked closer to a normal road bike.

Esher was going to flip his shit when he came home and found them parked on the gravel of the front garden.

He shook his head, could easily picture it playing out, and how Cal would attempt to defuse the situation and probably only make things worse. Daimon would be the one to talk Esher down, and in the end, his brother would reluctantly agree to the bikes staying, but would want them moved to a place where they wouldn't ruin the aesthetic of the garden he loved so much.

Daimon paused on a steppingstone, his eyes drifting over the front of the mansion, tracing the line of the roof where it swept over the porch and the contrast of the slate-grey tiles against the blue sky.

The single-storey house was enormous, but it felt too small with Cass in it. He couldn't seem to escape her. The only time he was safe from the sorceress was when he was with Aiko, trying to keep her spirits, and his, up. Cass didn't seem to know how to respond to Aiko, usually made herself scarce when it all became too much for the young Japanese woman and she broke down.

If it weren't for the fact Daimon had seen how much Cass cared about Marinda, he would have thought Cass was the one with a cold heart.

But it was him.

He knew that.

21

He had closed it off long ago, had hardened himself and pushed away everyone except his family.

He didn't want to feel anything. Not anymore. His heart was ice now. No trace of feeling left in it.

It *was* ice now.

He told himself that as Cass appeared on the porch, drawing his gaze to her. She wiped her hands on a cloth, looking like a bizarre combination of housewife and glamourous jetsetter. Her long black dress that hugged her curves like a second-skin, her polished onyx nails and perfectly preened tumbling waves of her jet hair, were all at odds with the dirty rag she held.

Her aquamarine eyes settled on him. Not piercing, nor probing. Not anything.

But her presence still rankled him.

"What's your problem?" he snapped, unable to keep the bite out of his voice or stop himself from reacting to her.

She arched a fine black eyebrow at him and tipped her chin up in that haughty way that made him want to snarl at her.

"Good morning to you too," she said, her tone whisper-soft, her words lashing at him.

He hated it when she did that, responding to him in a civilised manner when he couldn't bring himself to be the same towards her. He couldn't help it. He was constantly on his guard around her and it was her fault. She had made it clear more than enough times that she was determined to strip down his walls.

And he had made it clear he was determined she wouldn't.

So now they were at war, locked in a battle he was going to win.

She lowered the cloth to her side and smoothed her glossy black hair, luring his gaze back to her face. He cursed her.

And then cursed her again when she spoke.

"Aiko made some food for those of us who sleep eludes, and I just wanted to tell you." She looked down at the rag she held. For a moment, he thought she would leave it at that and leave him alone, but then she lifted her head and locked gazes with him. "You need to eat."

Those words were stern. Commanding.

Irritating.

"I don't need to eat." His stomach grumbled, calling him a liar.

Fine, he did need to eat but he had no appetite.

He stood there, a thousand thoughts and feelings colliding inside him, and the weight on his shoulders felt too heavy to bear.

He was drowning again.

He tried to hold back the tide, looked away from her thinking that was a good place to start, but he ended up staring at the mansion.

The weight on his shoulders dropped right through him, tore a gaping hole inside him as he remembered all the good times, before everything had gone to hell.

He absently lifted his hand and rubbed the aching spot above his heart.

"If you need to talk—"

He cut Cass off with a vicious snarl, baring emerging fangs at her. "If I need to talk, it won't be you that I'm talking to. I'm fine."

"You're not fine." She took a hard step towards the edge of the porch, her eyes glittering like ice as she narrowed them on him. "I haven't known you long, but it's obvious you share a bond with Esher, and with Esher—"

"Esher is coming back," he cut her off again, that hole inside him filling with acid that scoured his insides, with darkness and pain—and despair. His voice dropped to a whisper, losing all strength as it all crashed over him. "He'll come back. He has to come back."

Cass was mercifully silent for a moment.

But then she softly murmured, "What if he doesn't?"

He stepped, darkness swirling around him for a heartbeat before he appeared right in front of her. Her breath hitched, her entire body tensing as if she anticipated a strike against her.

As if she believed he would hit her.

A low growl curled from him, birthed by the thought she believed him capable of such a thing.

He drew a steadying breath to calm the raging torrent of his feelings, lifted his right hand and hovered it over the front of her throat. He stared at it, at the smooth, pale column of it that was stark against the black of his gloves.

"You're playing with ice, koldun'ya," he whispered low, his gaze transfixed on her throat and the frost forming on his gloves, fascination rolling through him as he felt the warmth of her against his palm despite the gap of air between them. "If you're not careful, one of these days, you're going to find out what it's like to be touched by me."

She murmured sexily, "Is that a promise?"

His eyes leaped to meet hers, shock rolling through him as he saw in them that she wanted it to be, that she wanted him to touch her. Need flooded him, a fierce hunger that had him close to inching his hand forwards to make contact.

He shut it down.

Backed off.

Disappointment flickered in her eyes.

For some damned reason, it echoed inside him too.

He was disappointed with himself. That was all it was.

He had promised his heart to another, and Cass was just someone the Moirai had sent to test him. She was nothing to him. He didn't want her. He didn't need her.

He backed off another step, ignoring the cold abyss that opened inside him as he distanced himself from the sorceress.

This was what he wanted. This distance between them. This coldness.

This was what Penelope would want from him and what he owed the woman he had loved and lost. She deserved his faithfulness. He was devoted to her, and nothing would change that. He didn't want another female.

He would always be loyal to her.

These needs growing inside him were inconsequential. All that mattered was remaining true to Penelope. He didn't need a woman.

He didn't want one.

A growl rose up his throat when an image flickered in his mind, his brother Ares softly touching Megan's cheek, a wealth of love in his eyes as their skin made contact.

He shut it out.

He didn't need that.

He didn't want that.

It was a blessing that his touch was ice, liable to give pain rather than pleasure. It was a blessing.

It was.

His heart was constant. Forever Penelope's. He was constant.

He was.

Marinda appeared behind Cass, her tropical blue eyes shimmering with tears. "Cal's awake."

Cass's face warmed as she turned to Marinda, her soft rosy lips curling in a smile as her aquamarine eyes brightened with love and happiness.

Gods, she was beautiful.

That thought hit him like a gorgon, striking so hard and fast out of the blue that he actually took a step back to brace himself.

He stared at Cass, reeling, stunned by how she had made him feel with only a smile.

He watched her go inside, too shaken to follow as his mind whirled.

He wasn't looking for a woman. Penelope was the only woman he would ever love.

But as he stared after Cass, drawn to following her, he couldn't shake the feeling that he was lying to himself.

That he had been lying to himself for years and that was why he constantly felt as if he was drowning.

Cassandra was forcing him to face the truth—that he was lonely and to protect himself from the pain of that loneliness, he had convinced himself that he was being noble, that he still loved Penelope and that being loyal to her was vital to him.

The real reason he was always on edge around Cass, always quick to anger and fast to lash out at her verbally to drive her away, hit him like a thunderbolt.

He wasn't angry with her because he felt she was trying to destroy his loyalty to Penelope, attempting to steal him from her.

He was angry because he wanted Cass.

He looked down at his gloved hands, lifted them palm up before him and watched the frost flowers blooming across the black leather.

And he couldn't have her.

CHAPTER 4

Daimon cringed as Valen hollered an obscenity across the main living room of the house, launching it like a missile at Cal as he flipped him off. He had been pleased when his brothers had regained consciousness, but now he was beginning to wish they had stayed asleep. At least the mansion had been quiet then.

Keras had mistakenly ordered the two of them to rest, and they had spent the last two days on the cream couches in the TV area, dressed in sweatpants and worn T-shirts, lounging and playing video games, and fighting whenever one of them won.

"You sure you can't go home yet?" Daimon aimed it at Valen, who shifted his hand to flash his extended middle finger at him too.

"Captain's orders." Valen grinned and waggled his finger. "You're stuck with me."

"You seem well enough to go home," he grumbled as he picked up several empty discarded packets of potato chips and shook his head at the number of juice glasses occupying the coffee table.

He swore Valen and Cal used a fresh glass every time they wanted a drink.

Valen fake-swooned, pressing the back of his right hand against his forehead as he sagged back against the couch cushions, still hammering buttons on the black controller with his left hand. "I'm sick, man. Have a heart."

The television announced a winner.

"Shit, kid, I can beat you one-handed." Valen pressed his bare left foot against Cal's shoulder where he was sitting on the floor, surrounded by popcorn and broken chips.

"Fuck off." Cal grabbed Valen's ankle and shoved his foot away. "Your stinky feet are putting me off my game."

Daimon pretended to check an invisible watch on his wrist. "You guys have around a minute before Eva and Marinda get back from the store."

He cast a pointed look at the mess surrounding his brothers.

"Is this the impression you want to make on them?" He shook his head. "Reckon they'll think you're both losers and dump your arses."

Valen and Cal were on their feet in a heartbeat, Cal rushing to the kitchen for a dustpan and brush while Valen bundled the glasses and bowls into his arms, spilling more food onto the table and floor. Daimon made a mental note to threaten them with their women thinking they were losers in the future, whenever the two of them were being annoying. It was a great motivator.

Cal paused halfway through sweeping the floor, his shoulders going rigid beneath his khaki T-shirt. "They're here."

He raised his hand and the air in the room shifted, swirling into a miniature tempest that gathered all the mess into the pan for him.

"Cheater," Valen muttered as he rushed to the kitchen with another load of dishes. "If I used my powers—"

"Esher would kill you." Daimon didn't let him finish that sentence, because Valen could command lightning and had come close to incinerating the mansion enough times already. He didn't want his brother getting ideas about using his power to any degree within the vicinity of it.

Valen sobered. Shrugged stiffly. "Wasn't going to do anything."

If his brother had tacked 'spoilsport' onto that sentence, it wouldn't have made him sound any sulkier.

Daimon dragged a hand down his face and sighed as he prayed for strength. He wasn't cut out for this. Esher was meant to be the one in charge at the mansion, not him. He definitely wasn't cut out to stand in for Keras or even Ares. The two of them should have been here taking care of things, but Ares had gone to pack some things for Megan so they could move into the mansion, and Keras was busy doing something.

The gods only knew what.

His brother was becoming more and more secretive.

Daimon had a feeling that was not a good thing.

The front door opened and Cass's scent of magic and sin hit him hard, had his gaze straying towards her despite his effort to keep his focus fixed on what he was doing.

Eva stared at the stack of empty wrappers in his hand and then her blue eyes shot to Valen, her black eyebrows lowering above them. Her Italian accent was sharp as she said, "Did you eat all of that when you knew we were getting food?"

Valen pointed at Daimon. "He ate it. I told him not to, but you should see him carb load. It's impressive. These gods, huh, thinking they can eat what they want and not put on a single pound. Well, when he gets fat, I'll have to say that I told him so."

Eva didn't look as if she was buying it.

For a split-second, Cass did.

Daimon scowled at her and stomped towards the kitchen. "Like I'd eat this crap."

He shoved the wrappers into the bin, turned back towards the living room and froze.

Cass stood in the doorway, clutching a dark glass bottle that had silver scrollwork and bands overlaid onto it.

She gave him a painfully slow once-over. "Your body is a temple."

He narrowed his eyes, daring her to say anything more than that.

With a wicked, saucy smile she murmured, "What I wouldn't give to worship it."

He huffed, glaring at her. "You worship the god, not the temple."

"Oh, I could worship you. You just have to stop fighting me." She set the bottle down on the counter.

"Not going to happen." He stepped towards her, but she stood her ground, blocking the exit. If he wanted to get past her, he would have to move her, and the victorious glimmer in her eyes said she knew he wouldn't do it. He wouldn't risk touching her.

He stepped up to her, raised his hands and planted them against the doorframe on either side of her head as she leaned back to avoid contact with him.

"Can't worship what you can't touch." He lowered his hands and stepped, appearing on the other side of the doorway.

"That's what you think," Cass whispered.

He frowned over his shoulder at her. Wanted to ask what she meant by that. The look in her eyes as she casually flicked her long fall of wavy black hair over her bare shoulders challenged him to do it, so he let it roll off his back instead.

Or at least tried to.

It plagued him as Marek appeared with Caterina and then Ares appeared holding Megan to him a split-second later, as if they had all sensed the bounty the women had brought into the house and wanted their share of it.

Aiko busied herself with setting the cartons in the white plastic bags out in a line down the middle of the long mahogany dining table, passing comments with Megan and Eva as they set some plates out. He was glad Eva and Marinda had proposed getting takeout, giving Aiko something to do with them. She needed a moment of normal, a brief reprieve from the pain.

They all did.

Ares fussed over Megan, helping her down onto some cushions, and Megan swatted at him, trying to stop him. Daimon fixed his focus elsewhere, helping Aiko open the containers and using a spoon to smack Valen on the back of his hand when he tried to steal a piece of chicken.

Valen glared at him, noticed Eva was watching and clutched his hand to his chest. "Did you see what the mean god did to me, baby?"

"The mean god will do more than that if you try to steal more food." Daimon gathered the lids of the containers.

"I might help him." Eva smiled when Valen scowled at her.

He raised his hand and clawed at his black T-shirt over his heart. "She wounds me when I'm sick."

"Sick is your default setting," Ares muttered.

Valen huffed. "Whatever. No one loves me. I get it."

He rolled his shoulders and pouted. Eva sidled over to him, planted her hands to his chest and leaned in close, so their black clothes blended together. She gazed up into his golden eyes.

"I love you," she whispered.

Valen clammed up. Averted his gaze. Might have even blushed.

Everyone noticed the shift in the air around him, how it went from playful to awkward in the blink of an eye, but it was Ares who had the balls to jump on it.

"Don't tell me you haven't told her you love her yet?" Ares straightened, shook his head and issued Valen one hell of an unimpressed look as he sighed.

"He hasn't." Eva shrugged, a playful edge to it.

"I have," Valen bit out, and tiny arcs of electricity sparked around his fingers. He glared at each of them in turn as everyone stared at him, none of them looking as if they believed that. "I fucking have."

"When?" Eva turned a curious look on Valen.

He looked at his feet and grumbled, "First time you told me."

She frowned, her lips flattening, and was silent for a few seconds before she said, "When you covered my ears and spoke—"

"You told her in the language of the Underworld?" Marek cuffed Valen around the back of his head, causing the long lengths of his violet hair to shoot forwards and fall over his face.

Valen swept them back. "So what? I still said it."

"Say it so she can hear it." Cal shoved Valen at Eva.

Valen growled, his golden eyes rapidly brightening, and looked as if he wanted to attack them all.

But then he sighed, shifted foot to foot, and muttered, "I love you too."

Eva bit back a smile. Ares and Marek groaned. Cal sighed.

"What?" Valen looked at them all in turn, shrugging his shoulders as he raised his hands at his sides. "Not good enough?"

Valen huffed.

"Fine." He grabbed Eva's wrist, pulled her into his arms and brought his lips to her ear as he closed his eyes. He whispered, "I fucking love you. You know that, right?"

Eva wrapped her arms around him and ploughed her fingers into the choppy sides of his hair. "I do. Fucking love you too."

Valen kissed her hard and disappeared in a swirl of black smoke.

Cal waved his hand through the vapour trail of the teleport and grinned. "That's him gone for two minutes. I say we eat it all before he gets back."

Daimon sank into his seat that almost resembled a western dining chair with the legs cut off, the wooden seat sitting directly on the tatami mats with a cushion on top of it, and the low back offering him some comfort. It had taken months to convince Esher to switch from just cushions to this more modern type of Japanese dining chair, but every one of his brothers had thanked him when Daimon had succeeded.

He crossed his legs and tried to shut out the crazy that was his family as he ate.

Valen actually took close to seven minutes to reappear, his cheeks flushed and eyes glowing gold. He settled Eva onto his lap, ran his tongue up her neck which had her murmuring something about the stud that pierced it, and then fed her, all of which Daimon also chose to ignore.

Keras arrived just as the meal was finishing, a distant edge to his emerald eyes.

"What's up?" Ares came out of the kitchen with a fresh glass of water and set it down in front of Megan.

"I want to test something." Keras idly spun the silver ring on his thumb with his index finger.

Not a good sign. Keras had a bad habit of doing that when he was troubled by something. Was that why he had disappeared on them, going AWOL again? Ares had told them all not to worry, but it was hard not to when the enemy could attack at any moment, targeting the gates.

Or one of them.

Keras was powerful, but he was vulnerable when alone.

It was about time his brother realised that.

Before something bad happened to him.

"What do you want to test?" Ares said.

Not a single ounce of emotion touched Keras's eyes as he lowered them to Marinda. "Her."

Marinda didn't hesitate. She stood, neatened her mulberry woollen sweater, nervously smoothing it over her blue jeans, and met Keras's gaze. "What do you want me to do?"

"We'll take you to the Tokyo gate and see if you can open it. If you can, then we'll come back here and wait another few days before trying again." Keras finally stopped playing with his ring, drew the two sides of his long black coat back and slipped his hands into the pockets of his pressed black slacks.

"I'll go with you." Cal stood and his blond eyebrows knitted hard above stormy blue eyes when Keras shook his head.

"No. Both you and Valen will stay here. Eva too." Keras didn't budge an inch when Valen growled at him.

"You're benching me?" Valen barked.

"You're still recovering," Ares said, a sharp edge to his voice. "And someone has to stay here to protect Megan and Aiko."

Valen's golden eyes lost their spark as he leaned back in his seat, folded his arms across his chest and grunted, "Fine."

His older brother could pretend he was in a mood about being told to stay put, but Daimon could see straight through it to the truth—Valen was honoured that Ares wanted him to protect Megan and Aiko.

"I need to go too." Air swirled around Cal, teasing the tips of his blond ponytail.

"You need to stay here." Keras placed a hand on his shoulder and gently gripped it as he looked down into Cal's eyes. "We are only going to do a little testing. We shall not be long."

That didn't allay the fear building in Cal, shining in his stormy irises.

Daimon nodded towards Marinda. "I'll keep an eye on her."

Cass stood, brushed down her dress and tipped her shoulders back. "Nothing will happen to Mari on my watch. You have my word on that, Calistos."

It grated that Cal hadn't looked relieved when Daimon had sworn to keep an eye on the woman he loved, but he had when Cass had made her promise.

Cass was powerful, but she had her vulnerabilities. He couldn't be the only one of them who had noticed that her magic tapped her out, draining her of strength, leaving her as weak as a mortal if she used too much of it.

Ares helped Megan onto her feet and his eyebrows furrowed as he gazed lovingly down at her.

"Oh, stop coddling. Even when you're not coddling... you're coddling." Megan huffed and pushed at Ares's broad chest, but he stood firm, not moving an inch. Her hand lingered, her touch softening to a caress as she looked up into his dark eyes. "I'll be peachy."

She didn't look as if she believed that.

"You'll be peachy too, right?"

So that was the reason behind her worry. She was afraid something would happen to Ares.

Ares lowered his hand to her swollen belly and pressed his palm against it, splaying his fingers out. She dropped hers to cover his and a smile wobbled on her lips.

"I'll just be a few minutes, and I'll be careful." He dropped a kiss on her forehead, one she leaned into as she closed her eyes. "I'll be back before you know it."

He smoothed the fingers of his other hand over her brown hair, skimming it down to the tips at her shoulders, and then tangled his hand in it and pulled her to him for a kiss.

Daimon looked away.

His eyes landed on Cass.

She frowned at him, and he had the terrible feeling she was trying to pick apart his feelings.

He wanted to tell her not to do it.

"And then we can all have a glass of ambrosia," Cass said.

Everyone stared at her.

"Well, everyone except Megan, since she's pregnant." Cass looked at her. "Sorry, no ambrosia for you."

Ambrosia? That was what she had in that bottle with the silver filigree on it?

"Ooh, ambrosia." Valen rubbed his hands together, causing tiny sparks to leap from them.

"Where did you get ambrosia?" Daimon put in, holding her gaze.

Her right shoulder lifted slightly, a coy edge to her smile as she said, "I have my sources."

Meaning, she had a dealer.

He jerked his chin towards the others in the room with them. "Ambrosia isn't for mortals."

"Good thing that I'm not mortal." Her blue eyes flashed fire at him, warning him he wasn't going to dissuade her.

At least not easily.

"Just a sip. You could have one now for courage if you need it." She pretended she was going to turn to get the bottle and then looked back at him.

Why was she pushing this?

He rolled his eyes when it hit him.

She was trying to get him drunk.

This was her new method of attempting to break down his walls.

He shook his head. "Not going to happen."

"Keras will have a drink, won't you, Keras?" She smiled sweetly at his older brother, and for some reason, Daimon felt a powerful need to flash fangs and snarl at him.

Keras just arched a black eyebrow at her and stepped, leaving ribbons of black swirling in the air behind him.

Valen raised his hand. "I'll drink with you."

Ares loosed a deep sigh. "Why doesn't that surprise me? Getting drunk, Valen? I thought you were sick?"

"I'm feeling a little better." Valen shrugged. "I could handle a shot or two."

Cass pouted. "I don't feel like drinking anymore. You're no fun."

She aimed that at Daimon, but Valen answered.

"I'm more fun than you can handle." That earned him a smack around the back of his head from Eva. He looked at her as she wriggled off his lap, caught her around the waist as she twisted away from him and pulled her back onto it. "I don't want to play with the bitch-witch, baby. Let's wait till she's gone and then sneak some ambrosia from the bottle and get wicked."

"The bottle is sealed with a spell." Cass tipped her chin up, and Valen reacted like she had announced the end of the world was coming.

Daimon looked out at the garden.

Which it probably was.

The otherworld flashed over the present, the future of this world should he and his brothers fail in their mission. The Moirai had made sure they knew what fate awaited the realms if the enemy won, taunted them with visions of it. Beyond the crumbling walls of the mansion, buildings burned, the sky blazed orange, and harrowing screams cut through the thick smoky air.

Many in this world believed the Underworld was hell.

Hell was what awaited both this world and his one if he and his brothers failed.

"It doesn't look great, does it?" Valen sobered, his deep voice turning serious as he stared in the direction Daimon was.

"It got better a little while ago, but now it's worse. I figured we were winning. Now I'm not sure." Cal sounded worried.

Marek gripped his shoulder. "We're winning. It's in a state of limbo right now. We just need to score another victory and it will get better again. You'll see."

Cal looked up at him and nodded.

Daimon found it hard to believe that, even when he wanted to.

"Are you sure you don't need a sip of ambrosia?" Cass drew his focus to her and he frowned as she waggled the bottle she now held in her hand.

He sighed, muttered, "Not going to happen."

And stepped.

CHAPTER 5

Cass set down the bottle of ambrosia she had taken great pains to get her hands on, one that had cost her a small fortune. It had seemed like a good plan at the time, but Daimon was determined to resist her.

She had to admit it was getting annoying now.

The more he fought her, the more she wanted to tear down that wall he had built around him, and the more it became about something other than using him as a nice diversion.

Or at least, she was beginning to realise this infatuation of hers was becoming dangerous.

It had all the hallmarks of something else, something she couldn't afford to indulge in.

Marek took hold of Caterina and Marinda, and Cass didn't wait for him to teleport with them. She summoned a spell that was draining to say the least and cast it, disappearing in a wink of crimson light.

Cool air buffeted her as she appeared on the rooftop of a skyscraper in the middle of the Ginza district of Tokyo, carrying the scent of the city and Daimon. Snow and spice. He smelled of it, roused memories of the desolate lands that had been her home for the first sixty years of her life, before she had found the courage to strike out on her own and leave the coven to live in warmer climes.

Only rather than chilling her as those memories did, Daimon's scent stirred heat in her veins.

"Since when can you teleport?" Daimon glowered at her from his position near Keras, his arms folded over his chest as he leaned against a block-shaped construction that had vents on all sides of it.

"Since always." She looked at the blue sky and pursed her lips. "Well, since I learned the spell. I don't remember how long ago that was, but I don't think you were asking for specifics."

Marek appeared with Caterina and Marinda, and Ares quickly followed them, curls of black drifting from the shoulders of his black T-shirt as he stepped forwards, towards Keras.

"How come you complained so much about being left behind the other day then?" Daimon's white eyebrows lowered over icy eyes, narrowing them. "Why not just use the spell then?"

Partly because she had wanted to be picked for the team. Partly because when she hadn't been picked, she had decided to sulk about it and take it out on him when he returned.

"Perhaps I was waiting for you to see my value and do the gentlemanly thing of teleporting me with you?" It seemed like a safe answer, one that would get a reaction from him.

He huffed.

Before he could speak, Ares said, "Are you two a thing?"

"No," Daimon snapped and pushed away from the wall. He cast her a black look and stomped away from her, towards the other end of the roof. "Never."

"Never is a long time," she murmured, hearing another's voice in her mind as she uttered those words. "Just like forever."

Daimon looked over his shoulder at her, frowned, and then carried on walking.

Eric had said them to her, before Marinda had been born, when Cass had told him it was foolish to fall in love with someone who would only end up dying. He had turned to her and asked her if she had ever been in love.

She had responded with never.

He had told her that never was a long time and things would change, and one day she would fall in love and realise what he had—that true love was forever.

Cass had countered that forever was a long time too—a long time to be stuck with the same person.

Eric had shaken his head, his look one of despair, and had given up trying to convince her that love was worth the risk and that forever was better than never.

Cass smiled as she looked at Mari, crossed the expanse of roof between them and looped her arm around hers. "That one is a might prickly with me."

She glanced at Daimon's back. His shoulders stiffened.

36

"Because you prod and poke him," Mari said, her French accent adding a lightness to her words that wasn't really there.

Eric might not have been Marinda's biological father, but the two had ended up with similar personalities. Mari was one of those sweet, forever kind of hearts too.

Cass preferred things to be more for now than forever.

Keras, Marek, Ares and Daimon stopped in a line and Keras looked back at her and Mari.

"The gate is over there. We can't get any closer without influencing it. The rest is down to you." Keras's cold green eyes settled on Mari.

She nodded and drew down a deep breath that had Cass squeezing her arm, unable to hold back the need to reassure her.

Cass led her past the brothers, deciding to pick the route furthest from Daimon, just to irritate him. She hadn't missed how he had looked when she had spoken of drinking ambrosia with Keras. She sidled close to the black-haired man who was a clone of his father, held a fathomless darkness in him that always warned her away from him.

And as predicted, Daimon's gaze instantly seared her.

He didn't like her near his only single brother.

She noted that and continued walking, the power that emanated from the hidden gate luring her towards it. When it buffeted her as strongly as the autumnal breeze did, she halted and looked at Mari.

"You're up." She released Mari's arm and took two steps back, but refused to go any further, just in case Mari needed her.

The wind caught ribbons of Mari's golden hair as she stood in the middle of the rooftop, her back to Cass. Tokyo stretched around her, a million buildings crammed together into one sprawling claustrophobic space bathed in fading evening light. She swore she could see all of the city from up this high, and it stretched for miles. Endless in all directions. A sea of rooftops with sparse patches of green.

She missed home.

Not the coven in Siberia, but her home in the Aegean.

It was quiet there, filled with long sunny days and few people to bother her.

Plus, everyone there adored and respected her.

Mari moved, pulling Cass back to the present as she raised her hands before her and her head lowered slightly. Cass waited, staring at the point where the power of the gate felt strongest and on high alert, just in case something bad happened.

She lined up a series of spells.

It always paid to be prepared.

Violet light flickered just beyond Mari, and Mari stretched her arms out towards it, her entire body tensing and then beginning to shake as she grunted. The pinprick of light glittered as it hovered a few feet above the flat roof of the towering building, but didn't expand into the central disc of the gate.

Mari's shoulders shook as she strained.

Cass focused on her and swore under her breath. This was taking too much out of her. She broke towards her, ignoring the muttered comments coming from their audience, and took hold of her.

"That's enough." Cass gripped her arm and lowered it for her, wrapped her other one around Mari's waist as she sagged, breathing hard. She looked back at Keras. "Satisfied?"

He nodded. "Hopefully the enemy has also lost their ability to command the gate. Do you feel you would be able to open it if there were two of you?"

Mari wearily lifted her head. "I'm not sure. I don't think so."

Cass's gaze drifted to Daimon.

His ice-blue eyes slowly widened, his eyebrows rising as his lips parted.

But he wasn't looking at her. He was looking beyond her.

Cass whipped around to face that direction. Violet-black clouds billowed outwards from a point near the edge of the rooftop, sparking with green and purple lightning that chased between them as they expanded to fill an area five feet wide by seven feet tall.

A portal.

She grabbed Mari's wrist and shoved her behind her, pushing her as she quickly backed away from the opening portal, heading towards the brothers and Caterina. Daimon appeared in front of her together with Ares.

"It can't be the wraith." Frost glittered on Daimon's gloves as he curled his hands into fists.

"Gates are shut to traffic." Ares didn't take his eyes off the portal. "No way for Eli to get out of the Underworld. It's them."

"That's worrying," Mari said from behind Cass, and Cass couldn't agree more. "I lost my ability to cast a portal and they still have it."

Meaning there was a chance they could still open the gate? Cass glanced at it, a brief look to check that it wasn't forming. The flicker of violet light had disappeared, leaving no trace of the gate behind, other than the power she could feel humming in the air and in her bones.

In the split-second she took her eyes off the ball, daemons poured from the portal. Ares and Daimon leaped into action, launching into the midst of them. Several of the human-looking males hissed and grunted as the waning light of day hit them, causing wisps of smoke to rise off their clothes. The rumours about daemons were true then. Most of them couldn't handle sunlight without getting burned.

They backed off towards the portal, their gazes seeking shadows. The rest surged forwards to meet the brothers.

Marek swept past her, rushing to join his brothers as they fought to hold back the daemons, stopping them from nearing the gate. Caterina followed hot on his heels. Cass watched as the hybrid cast a barrier in front of the brothers and the stronger daemons slammed into it. Blue hexagonal glyphs appeared in a wave and disappeared.

A curious power. Effective too.

But it cost Caterina.

She wobbled on her feet and Marek turned back to her, grabbed her wrist and spun her so her back was to his.

Together, they fought a wave of daemons as they piled around the edges of the barrier, breaking left and right. To the right, they ran right into Daimon and Ares, who were combining ice and fire with devastating effect, ravaging the enemy forces.

Cass cursed when something caught her eye and looked to her right, to the other side of the roof, beyond where the gate was located.

Violet-black smoke boiled there, writhing and spreading.

Another portal.

She wasn't surprised when the two other Erinyes stepped out of it, looking like twins, a perfect reflection of Marinda with their blue-green eyes and blonde hair twisted into a Greek plait across the tops of their heads. These two wore form-fitting black clothes though, leather pants and tanks that showed off their figure.

Cass had always tried to get Mari to dress a little more like her, a little more provocatively to make the most of her figure. Cal would have a heart attack if he saw Mari dressed like her half-sisters.

Shadows rushed across the rooftop, snapping at the black tar and each other, sapping the warmth from the air as they passed Cass. She shivered and watched, fascinated as they rose up from the ground and launched at the Erinyes in a malevolent wave. The two furies broke apart, leaping over the sharp spikes of the shadows and rolling under others, evading them all. The points of the shadows slammed into the rooftop, piercing it before they dissipated.

Another wave of shadows rocketed towards the two.

Cass lent them a hand, launching several spells, twisting spears of red and gold that shot through the air, aimed at points where she hoped the Erinyes would be foolish enough to leap into their paths.

One of the Erinyes managed to evade them all, but the other wasn't as fortunate. She cried out as a spear sliced through her left calf and hit the roof.

"Sister!" the second Erinyes shrieked and launched towards her, faster than Cass or Keras's shadows could track. She pulled her fallen sibling up just as a shadow reached them, and the injured one gasped as it stabbed into the roof where she had just been.

The two Erinyes turned as one towards the gate.

That violet light flickered brightly again.

Everything and everyone went still, all eyes shooting to the gate.

Time seemed to slow as Cass summoned more spells to her fingertips, her breath hitching as she waited for the gate to expand.

Only it didn't.

A thick earth wall shot up before her, a dome that swept over the point where the gate was located, obscuring her view of the Erinyes. The rich brown mud baked in an instant, small cracks forming across it.

"Tell me you all just saw that too?" Ares grunted as he backhanded a daemon and sent him flying across the roof into two more, knocking them over the edge. They screamed as they fell to the road far below and then silence.

"I saw it," Daimon offered.

"How can they cast a portal so well but their ability to command the gate has weakened just as mine has?" Mari kept her eyes on the dome covering the gate, her fingernails turning into short claws as she spread her feet shoulder-width apart.

A warrior's stance.

It was still unsettling seeing her sweet, kind-hearted Mari transforming into a vicious, battle-hungry furie.

Violet shone in Mari's eyes, edged with black.

Caterina muttered something in Catalan and turned with Marek, her back still plastered to his. He finished off the daemon she had been fighting, snapping the man's neck with nothing more than a well-aimed uppercut with the heel of his right hand.

"Blood," Caterina hollered as she lashed out at another daemon, driving the female back with her sword. "Eli gave me a cocktail of blood. It gave me powers."

She grabbed the daemon by her hair and shoved the female's head down fast as she brought her knee up hard. It cracked against the daemon's forehead and Caterina released her, letting her crumple to the ground.

"What if they have more of that blood?" Caterina looked at Keras, Ares and then Mari.

"I don't like the sound of that." Marek turned with her again and she shoved her right hand forwards, driving the sword through the eye of a male daemon.

Ares bit out a black curse.

"So now the enemy can siphon powers from blood?" Daimon raised his hand and five shards of ice shot up from the rooftop, impaled the daemons he had aimed them at and lifted them into the air.

The wretched humanoid things struggled, desperately clawing at the ice protruding from them, causing black blood to roll down the slick surface to the roof.

"We will find out later." Keras sent a wave of shadows racing over the dome and Cass's gaze followed them, because she wasn't sure what he was aiming at.

The Erinyes.

The two blondes were coming over the top of the dome, the one on the left falling behind as she limped.

"Complete the mission. Grab her," she bit out from between clenched teeth.

The furie on the right nodded.

They were talking about Mari.

Cass grabbed hold of her and pulled her back when she went to launch forwards, held on to her and refused to let go, weathering a hiss as Mari turned on her, her violet eyes flashing dangerously.

Daemons surged towards them from her left, driving Ares and Daimon back towards her, and more poured through the portal, into the falling night.

Two daemons made it past Ares, snarling and snapping sharp teeth as they lunged in her direction.

Daimon appeared between her and the vicious creatures, threw his left hand forwards and sent two spiralling daggers of ice at them. The one on the left went down shrieking. The one on the right nimbly dodged the attack.

"Stay close," Daimon growled.

"I have this," Cass countered and unleashed her own attack, a spell designed to freeze blood. "I don't need protecting."

The twin bolts of blue shot past Daimon as he turned icy eyes on her. "I'll decide that."

He swept his right arm up and before her spell could connect and prove that she didn't need him watching out for her, three spires of ice shot up from the rooftop, impaling the daemon in his thigh, stomach and shoulder.

Cass glared at Daimon as black blood oozed down the jagged clear ice.

"I had that." She pulled Mari closer to her. "Snegovik."

He scowled at her but said nothing, because he was a snowman. Cold as ice. Standing alone in this world. Bringer of brief joy followed by despair and misery.

Perhaps that was a little too harsh, but he had ruined her fun. She had been about to prove she could handle herself, maybe even make him see that she could fight on the frontlines if she chose to, and he had spoiled it.

Keras hurled another wave of shadows at the Erinyes, and a portal formed behind them. The one on the right backed towards her sister, took hold of her arm and helped her into the portal. She stopped and glared down at Keras, her violet eyes glowing in the fading light, and then stepped into the portal.

The shadows tore through it, twisted around and attacked it again, decimating it.

Keras turned to her. "Get Marinda away from here."

She nodded and summoned a spell, but it was chilling darkness that took her and Marinda from the rooftop, cold that seeped into her from a spot on her wrist, spreading outwards along her arm. Her feet touched solid ground again and the cold released her, warmth seeping back in to chase it away.

She looked at Daimon where he stood beside her, his glacial eyes on her arm.

"You all right?" he grumbled, his gaze not leaving the point where he had touched her.

She released Mari and rubbed at it, deeply aware of his eyes on it and what he was thinking.

Feeling.

He was worried he had hurt her. He didn't need to worry. She was tougher than she looked. Far tougher than he believed. She skimmed her hand down her arm, revealing where he had touched, and his eyes widened slightly.

Leaped to meet hers.

Cass lowered hers.

To her perfect, unmarked skin.

CHAPTER 6

Daimon backed away from Cassandra, needing some distance between them. It was a trick. It had to be. She had used magic to heal her injuries when she had held her arm, undoing the damage he had done by foolishly grabbing her and teleporting with her. It had been reckless of him, but in the heat of the moment, he hadn't been able to stop himself. The need to get her away from the enemy had been too great.

When they had all rushed towards her, something dark inside him had howled for freedom, for him to unleash it on the daemons.

To protect her.

Keras and Ares appeared, shortly followed by Marek and Caterina. Keras gave him a look, one that had Daimon averting his gaze, hoping that his older brother wouldn't mention what he had done. Whatever wound he had dealt Cass by touching her, she had healed it.

No harm, no foul, right?

So why did he feel terrible?

Cass busied herself with checking Marinda over from head to toe. Daimon stared at her arm, at the smooth, unblemished skin. He stared at it so hard he began to get the feeling he was willing a mark to show, some evidence that he had hurt her as he suspected and that she had covered it up.

Why?

His foolish heart answered that.

Because she didn't want him to hurt, to feel bad because he had injured her.

Her earlier words came back to haunt him, the ones she had murmured when he had told her that she couldn't worship what she couldn't touch.

That's what you think.

43

Was he wrong about her? Could he touch her without harming her? He had teleported her to the pond and dropped her in it, had stepped with her in Paris too, when they had been tossed over the side of a steep hill. She hadn't shown any pain. Anger, yes. But not pain.

He shook those thoughts away, before they could take hold and spread roots. He couldn't touch her. He couldn't touch anyone. Even Megan hurt if their skin was in contact for more than a minute, and even though he didn't give her frostbite, he still chilled her flesh as badly as a frigid snowy winter's day might.

He distanced himself from Cass while she was distracted, heading for the TV area on the right side of the long open-plan room and leaving her near the dining table at the other end of it.

"We need to test to see if it's possible for a furie to siphon powers from blood." Keras neatened the cuffs of his black dress shirt, his eyes on Marinda.

She looked up at him, her eyes blue-green again now, and nodded.

"We have to what now?" Cal came from the corridor beyond the wall that separated the TV area from the north wing of the house.

"We suspect the Erinyes can gain abilities by having contact with blood." Marek finished giving Caterina a thorough once-over. "Caterina suggested it as a possibility when the Erinyes appeared through a portal, using a power that has faded in Marinda."

"Your girl-fiend makes a good point. I mean, blood is power, right?" Valen looked over the back of the couch, his golden eyes fixing on Marek and an expectant look on his face.

Marek's jaw flexed. He gritted, "I told you about calling her my girl-fiend."

Caterina petted Marek's arm and pressed close to him, her black T-shirt blending with his linen shirt. "I don't mind it. I actually sort of like it."

Marek looked as unimpressed with her as he was with Valen.

It was still strange having a human-daemon hybrid among their ranks. According to Marek, Caterina was still developing powers courtesy of the blood Eli had injected her with, a cocktail donated by several members of the enemy ranks. So far, she could teleport, cast barriers, and was faster and stronger than before. She could also see emotional auras.

And could release a pheromone that messed with every male in the vicinity.

Thankfully, she was learning to control that one, had been focusing on taming it because sometimes it slipped the leash. The first time it had happened, and Daimon and his brothers had been hit with an uncontrollable hunger for pleasure, Keras had banished Caterina from the meeting and the mansion. Marek had come up with a plan—satisfy that succubus side of Caterina before any meeting.

Since then, there had only been a few mishaps.

Daimon still hated it whenever it happened.

He kept a wary eye on the hybrid as Keras filled the others in on what had happened at the gate. The last thing he needed was Caterina feeling frisky when Cass was around. He would be fine, wouldn't act on anything he felt and would resist the urges it stirred.

Cass wouldn't.

He could easily see the witch using it as an excuse to throw herself at him again, attempting to break him.

"Cal, it's probably safest if we use some of your blood." Keras looked their youngest brother over. "If you are up to it?"

Cal swept rogue strands of his blond hair back into his ponytail and nodded stiffly. "Sure."

He didn't look sure.

"It shouldn't take much. Just a drop or two." Ares gave Cal a concerned look. Keras might be the oldest, but Ares was the real big brother of the group, the one who showed how much he was worried about his siblings rather than hiding it all behind a calm façade and empty eyes.

Sometimes, Keras was too much like their father.

Cal nodded again.

Keras went to the kitchen and returned with a shallow bowl and the biggest knife Daimon had ever seen.

"You expecting him to chop his hand off?" Daimon jerked his chin towards the blade. "Little excessive."

Keras arched an eyebrow at the knife. "A blade is a blade."

And yet, Keras had picked the biggest of the bunch.

Cal swallowed hard at the sight of it, but still crossed the tatami mats to their oldest brother and held his wrist out.

"Not inside," Daimon snapped.

Keras stilled with the knife poised close to Cal's wrist.

"Esher would flip." He strode over to Keras, took the blade from him and walked into the kitchen. "He'd flip if he knew you'd used his sushi knife for slicing a vein open too."

He set the prized knife back in position on the counter, smoothed his fingers over the handle and lingered. Esher had waxed lyrical about the knife for close to three months after he had bought it, braving entering a store filled with mortals to pick one out. It had been a win for his brother, and a serious test of his strength and courage. Esher despised mortals, had done since they had captured and tortured him centuries ago, driving him close to death several times before he had managed to escape.

Daimon picked a smaller paring knife from the block on the counter, walked back into the living room and straight through it to the front door.

He stepped out onto the porch and didn't stop until he was in the middle of the front garden, standing on the largest of the steppingstones. At least if Cal bled here, he could wash it away and Esher might not notice.

Keras and Cal appeared in the doorway, took the step down to the broad flat stones set among pale gravel, and crossed the short distance to him. Marinda followed, tucked close to Cass, who rubbed her arms as she guided her towards them.

"Just relax, sweetie. It's only blood," Cass murmured and Marinda nodded and blew out her breath.

Had it been anyone but Cal's blood, Marinda probably wouldn't have minded as much. Daimon could see it as she looked at Cal, concern shining in her eyes.

Cal held his wrist out the moment he reached Daimon. "Get it over with."

Instead of slicing his vein open as he clearly expected, Daimon ran the knife over his palm, making the cut just deep enough to draw a sufficient amount of blood.

Cal looked down at the thin dark line on his palm and shrugged. "That works too."

Keras offered the shallow white bowl and Cal held his hand over it, turned it sideways and curled his fingers into a fist. He squeezed and droplets of blood formed on the edge of his hand, trembled and fell into the bowl, stark against the white.

When a small pool had formed in the bottom of it, covering it in a layer, Cal withdrew his hand and Keras pulled a handkerchief from his pocket and offered it to him. Cal wrapped the black material around his hand and then took the bowl from him and turned to Marinda.

Marinda swallowed hard. Pulled down another breath. Blew it out.

She hesitated and Cass rubbed her shoulders as she murmured gentle words of encouragement.

Marinda raised her hand and edged her fingers towards the bowl, and hesitated again. She clenched her hands into fists, closed her eyes and then opened her hand and quickly dipped her fingers into the blood. Her mouth twisted.

"That should do it." Cass gently took hold of Marinda's wrist and drew her hand away from the bowl, produced a cloth out of thin air and used it to wipe Marinda's fingers clean. "Now, do you feel anything?"

Marinda opened her eyes and shook her head.

"Try anyway." Cass offered an encouraging smile.

It was strange seeing this side of her—the warm, caring side that she worked so hard to hide from him and his brothers. Normally, he only caught glimpses of it, when she thought no one was looking and she was alone with Marinda.

Marinda closed her eyes again, breathed in slowly and tipped her head up, going still.

Cal inched back a step. Keras remained where he was. Daimon stood his ground too. At worst, Marinda would send him flying.

A thought hit him.

Or she could accidentally suffocate him.

He was about to ease back a step too when Cass's gaze landed on him. He planted his boots to the floor, refusing to let her see that he was afraid of Marinda and what she might do.

Which was apparently nothing.

Marinda opened her eyes and muttered a curse in French. "I don't feel anything. I can't do anything."

When she huffed and threw her hands up in the air, her frustration getting the better of her, Cal's lime-green and black motorbike slammed into the other one and knocked it over and one of the stone lanterns wobbled and then settled again.

"The hell," Cal muttered and stepped, appearing near his fallen bikes. He grabbed the racing bike and had it back upright just as Marinda reached him, speaking to him in rapid French, apologising over and over again. He huffed, sighed and gathered her into his arms. "It's okay."

Daimon exchanged a worried look with his brothers.

They were going to have to be more careful now. If the enemy got hold of their blood, they could use it to open the gates.

Everyone on the porch turned away and headed back inside, and Keras followed, leaving Daimon alone with Cass, Cal and Marinda.

Cal looked Marinda over and slung his arm around her shoulder. "Let's get you cleaned up."

Cass trailed after them as they headed inside, paused on the porch and looked back at him.

Daimon turned away from her, heading towards the bikes and past them, following the path of steppingstones around the north wing of the house. He needed a moment to process everything, and not just the fact the Erinyes, and therefore the enemy, could use blood to gain powers.

He needed to process how he had reacted at the gate when Cass had come under attack.

Anger simmered in his blood, burned in his heart. Not aimed at her. He aimed it at himself. He tried to reason that he had only reacted like that, leaping in to protect her, because she was part of their team and they couldn't afford to lose another one of them. They needed all the warriors they could get, and he was man enough to admit Cass was useful in battle, was powerful and capable, kept her head no matter how bad the situation got and did all she could to help and ensure they won.

But it wasn't the truth.

There was something about her, something that tied him in knots and had him hating himself. He shouldn't be thinking about her. He slipped his hand into the pocket of his black jeans and touched the pendant on his phone, tempted to focus so he could see Penelope.

Needing to see her.

He had to do something, because the iron-will he had forged over the centuries was beginning to buckle.

He shouldn't be thinking about another woman, shouldn't be wanting another woman. He was loyal to Penelope, and that loyalty had stayed strong in the past, when other females had approached him.

So why was it failing him now?

His heart answered that question.

Things were different with Cass.

She tempted him like no other had before her.

He reached the rear garden and skirted the edge of the koi pond, his gaze drifting to the end of the north wing, where the covered walkway extended over the water. He could almost see Esher sitting there with his legs dangling over the edge, his feet almost touching the water, all the colourful carp gathering beneath him as he fed them.

Gods, he missed his brother.

Needed him now more than ever.

He needed to speak with someone, just as he always had whenever he had a problem.

But Esher wasn't here and he didn't know where he was.

His blood slowly chilled, his steps faltering as he stared at that spot Esher had loved so much, unable to hold back the fear that rose to grip him, to sink icy claws into him and tear open his heart.

Was Esher in danger? Was he fighting for his life even now? While Daimon stood in the garden doing nothing, waiting for him to come back?

He shuddered as a chill swept through him and huddled down into his roll-neck top.

What was he doing? Esher needed him and he should be looking for him, doing something to bring him back. He should be in the Underworld, leading his father's legions in their search. He should be there for Esher, doing all in his power to keep him safe from harm.

He clenched his fists at his sides and frowned at the walkway.

He was letting his brother down, leaving him to fend for himself, leaving him alone.

Just as Esher had left him alone.

"Daimon?"

Anger swelled like a fierce tide within him as that female voice pierced his thoughts, shattering his solitude. Never giving him a moment's peace.

He narrowed his eyes on Cass's feet where she stood on Esher's spot, and rage curled through him, had ice forming over his hands as he lifted his gaze to her face and glared at her.

Pain pulsed through him with every beat of his heart, a constant agony that was slowly ripping him apart, fuelling the frustration that mounted inside him each day Esher was missing.

Frustration he couldn't hold back as he stared at Cassandra.

"How many times do I have to tell you to leave me alone!" He stepped up onto the decking and strode towards her, the part of him that said to rein in his temper easily crushed under the weight of his pain and fear. "You dare come here. Standing on this spot. *His* spot."

He was being unreasonable, he knew that as he advanced on her and rather than standing her ground, she backed away.

"I didn't know," she bit out, defensive. "I was only worried about you."

"Well stop," he barked. "Stop worrying about me. I'm sick of it. I'm sick of everything. I'm sick of this place. I'm sick of—"

He reared away and turned his back on her, breathed hard and tried to rein in his emotions, before he did something he would regret.

Or at least something worse.

"Very well," Cass muttered, none of her usual strength or bite in those two words.

She stormed away from him, the distance between them yawning like a chasm that flooded him with cold.

Because it dawned on him that she had finished his sentence for him and that was the reason she was getting away from him as quickly as she could manage without using magic.

She thought he had been on the verge of saying that he was sick of her.

He hadn't been.

He had stopped himself from confessing something, something that would have given her a glimpse of what was in the heart he protected behind a wall of ice.

He was sick of being alone.

He walked to the corner of the wooden deck and looked left, towards the main room of the house. As his anger and frustration faded, the fear lingered, had his gaze seeking her as regret flared inside him.

He scrubbed his right hand over his white hair and sighed when he couldn't spot her. He focused his senses and regret turned to relief when he located her on the other side of the topiary garden that filled the space between the three sides of the mansion.

He really needed to learn to keep his temper in check around her. The last thing he wanted was to drive her away. She was liable to do something foolish, like thinking she didn't need him or his brothers and striking out on her own. She would be vulnerable alone.

The thought of her coming under attack, targeted by the enemy, had his gut churning with acid, scouring his insides and filling him with a need to find her.

Rather than surrendering to that need, he kept his senses locked on her, satisfying his need to know she was safe.

He looked to his right at the garden, and then heaved another sigh. He needed to cool off.

He looked down at himself.

And wash off.

Black blood streaked his clothes, thick lines of it that were glossy against his jeans and navy long-sleeve. It had dried on his gloves too.

Rather than seeking solitude in the garden, he followed the raised walkway back to the main room of the house and banked right, heading for the panels that had been pushed aside to join the house to the garden.

And almost ran straight into Cal.

His younger brother stopped dead, narrowly avoiding the collision. "You good?"

Daimon nodded. "Yeah. You?"

He looked down at Cal's hand and stilled as his gaze caught on the blue script that tracked along the inside of his brother's right forearm.

His favour mark.

Before he could stop himself, he said, "It can take me to the Underworld, right?"

His heart missed a beat and thudded hard against his chest, his breath stuttering from his lips as he waited, the need to find Esher blazing back to life inside him, stronger than it had been in the garden before Cass had come to him.

Cal placed a hand over the ink. "It can, but I don't really have the strength to use it right now… and if I did, I'd be the one going."

Daimon lifted his gaze to lock with Cal's.

For once, his brother looked serious.

Cal's fingers tightened over his arm, pressing into his flesh. "It's my fault he went. I should have stopped him."

"I can bring him back, Cal." Daimon reached for his brother's hand, filled with a need to rip it from his arm and read the words written on his skin, a gift from Hermes. He stopped just short of touching his brother, labouring for breath as he saw how close he had come to grabbing him. He flexed his fingers and eased them back, swallowed and looked into Cal's eyes. "I need to bring him back."

"I know." Ares's deep voice rolled over him like a soothing wave, chasing the cold from his veins.

Daimon looked across at him, his brow furrowing.

"I know," Ares repeated and raised his hand, ghosted it over Daimon's shoulder, the closest they could come to touching each other without risking injury. "But you know he wouldn't want you there."

He did, and it was hard to swallow that bitter pill.

Esher had turned on him when he had tried to stop him from entering the gate, his other side firmly in control. That side of Esher would fight him if he tried to reach him, would believe he was trying to interfere with his hunt and would lash out. His brother would hate himself if he hurt anyone in his family, especially Daimon. He knew that, but it didn't make it any easier on him. He needed to find his brother and bring him back.

To the only home they had right now.

Ares sighed, his broad shoulders lifting with it. "Father has legions scouring the Underworld for the wraith, thankfully to assist Esher rather than capture him and bring him in for breaking into the Underworld again. All we can do is wait for someone to find Eli and therefore Esher and for Dad to send word, or for Esher to capture his prey and come home."

Daimon forced himself to nod.

It wasn't enough for him, and it pained him to pretend that it was. He kept his eyes off the mark on Cal's arm, deeply aware of it and the power it held, that it could take him to the Underworld.

To his real home.

The place where he belonged, where his power would no longer be a problem.

"You need to take five?" Ares canted his head, concern warming his dark eyes as he stared into Daimon's.

Daimon blew out his breath and nodded, grateful for the fact his brother could see that he was struggling, that this was all becoming too much for him and he needed to get away for a while. He wanted to be here for Esher, keeping Aiko company and keeping the place in order, waiting for him to return, but being here was a constant reminder that Esher was missing and he couldn't do anything about it.

"No more than an hour or two, okay?" Ares's eyes gained a hard edge that quickly faded back to concern. "You'll be careful?"

Daimon nodded again. "Anything feels off, I'll step back here."

Ares still looked reluctant to let him go.

So Daimon stepped without saying another word, landing on the broad white terrace of his home on the steep side of Victoria Peak, Hong Kong spread in all its towering neon glory below him.

Rather than feeling relieved to get away from the mansion and finally have the space he needed, all he felt was concern.

Worry about a witch.

He tipped his head back and closed his eyes.

A single thought flowing through him.

No good could come from that.

CHAPTER 7

Cass remained with her back to the wall at the end of the corridor near the kitchen, lingering long after Daimon had stepped, his power disappearing from the tangle that filled the air.

She inwardly cursed.

She should have known better than to approach Daimon when he had been seeking solitude, but some ridiculous part of her had needed to be near him.

Had needed him to know he wasn't alone, even when he felt he was.

The same ridiculous part that had hoped he would show her that the same was true for her.

She wasn't afraid, not of anything.

She wasn't.

She didn't feel this pressing need to be close to him because she wanted him to protect her, to save her from the fate that loomed on the horizon ahead of her, casting her future in a black shadow.

She could protect herself. She always had. She didn't need anyone.

She didn't.

Yet she couldn't stop herself from hurrying through the main room of the mansion to Calistos's room, poking her head inside, looking at Mari and saying, "I'm going to rest for a while if you don't mind."

Mari shook her head. "No. Of course. I'm a little tired myself."

Mari was absolutely that, if tired was a synonym for horny. Her friend was restless, fidgeting with folding clothes and idly cleaning the sparsely furnished room. When Cass lingered, Mari gave her a look that screamed that she wanted her to go away so Cal would come to her.

Cass had far too much dignity to be a cockblocker. It was beneath her. Mari was her ward but she was a grown woman, and Cass accepted that grown women had needs.

Especially when a handsome god was in the vicinity.

Where had her handsome god gone?

She dipped her head to Mari, turned and rounded the corner, and strode past Calistos, murmuring, "Don't do anything I wouldn't do."

For some reason, he shuddered.

She supposed she had been on his case since meeting him. He wasn't used to this side of her—the one that didn't want to string his entrails around the mansion like bunting.

The moment she reached her temporary quarters in Keras's room, she slid the panel that acted as a door closed and focused, checking her surroundings. All the brothers were far away enough.

She muttered an incantation, one that would give the illusion she was in the room, and then followed it with another spell.

One that transported her to Hong Kong.

The moment she touched down on the winding road that cut up the side of the steep hill of Victoria Peak, she paused. What was she doing? Hadn't she already disturbed Daimon's solitude? She stood there on the narrow road, the only sound the trees rustling in the gentle breeze and her heart beating in her ears.

Why couldn't she leave him alone?

She stared straight ahead of her, up the slope that would lead to his impressive modern home perched on the side of the hill, one she had visited more than once during her study of him before she had met Calistos.

Before she had really met Daimon.

Back then, everything had been so uncomplicated. He had been nothing but a target, someone to study and catalogue so she could be sure he was worthy of being one of Mari's protectors as Eric had wanted.

Now?

Now she wasn't sure what he was to her, but she knew what he couldn't be.

Now everything was too complicated.

She told herself to leave, to give him the peace he needed, but her feet carried her forwards against her will.

She needed to see him.

Just needed to see he was all right and then she would go.

She would keep her distance so he wouldn't sense her, would watch over him to make sure nothing happened while he was lost in his thoughts. Ares wasn't the only one who had noticed that the disappearance of Esher weighed heavily on Daimon and despite his best efforts to do what he felt was right, taking care of the family home that Esher cherished and Aiko, sometimes it became too much for him.

During her study of the brothers, she had watched Daimon taking care of Esher, always there for the beast, always watching over him, always ready to bring him back from the edge. She had mused that the fates had gotten their entrance into this world the wrong way around, and that Daimon should have been the older brother.

Now she could see how wrong she had been.

Daimon needed his older brother as deeply as Esher needed him, possibly even more so. He was falling apart without him, gradually succumbing to whatever dark things plagued him and stole pieces of his strength each day.

Each hour that Esher was missing.

She reached a fork in the road and stopped, her eyes fixed on the illuminated white concrete, glass and steel building at the end of the route in front of her. The city lights reflected off the thick glass that acted as a railing around the terrace.

And shone on the man standing at those railings, his profile to her, wind tousling his white hair.

She slowly lifted her hand and lightly pressed her fist to her chest, fighting the need to go to him, to show him that he wasn't alone and lift that sombre look from his face, shattering the hopelessness that she could see in his eyes.

He would hate her for it.

He was hurting, and he would lash out at her.

And then he would hate himself.

She had been caught up in that cycle with him several times since Esher had disappeared, seemed as bound by some cruel master of their fates as he was, feeling as if someone behind the scenes was pulling strings to make her do these reckless and foolish things.

Things she knew would only end in the same way.

With him lashing out.

With her hating herself.

With him hating himself.

And then a brief truce, a point where they were calm around each other, able to enjoy the others company without inflicting pain.

Daimon stepped.

As she stared at the black vapour trail of his teleport, her heart whispered at her to follow.

She knew where he was going.

She summoned the spell, even though it taxed her to do it, had her legs wobbly beneath her when she landed near the water.

She stared across the narrow stretch of it to the Star Ferry dock, watched him boarding one as he often did, making the journey from the island to the Kowloon district. She couldn't understand why he did this ritual. He avoided contact with others, especially with humans, yet he always chose to cross the water in this manner—on a rickety green and white double-decker boat that was always packed with humans.

And he always took the same route when he reached the other side, walking the Avenue of the Stars for a short distance before he stopped to stare back across the water at the Hong Kong island skyline, taking it in.

Or did he see something else?

She had done her research and knew that if the brothers focused they could see the future of this world in all its morbid fiery horror, and sometimes even when they weren't trying.

She muttered the spell again, risking it, and transported herself to the other side of the water, landing near a group of tourists. They would provide her cover.

As predicted, Daimon walked to the same spot he always did and stopped, gazing across the water that rippled with colour from the neon on the buildings on the opposite bank.

His handsome face hardened.

She suspected he wasn't viewing the here and now, but rather what was to come.

She fell into studying him, as she always did whenever he wasn't aware of her, whenever he came to this spot, trying to piece together a clearer picture of him.

He idly touched the roll-neck of the top he wore beneath his long black coat, stroking his gloved fingers along it, his eyes still locked on the skyline. His shoulders trembled, a brief shudder she would have missed if she hadn't been watching him so closely. His power was acting up.

Did it hurt him when it did that? Did he hate the cold that wracked him? Was it the reason he kept his distance from everyone?

She couldn't imagine what it was like to live as he did, unable to touch anyone, fearing he might kill them by mistake if he let them get too close to him.

Hades was an unsympathetic bastard to force Daimon to remain in this world when he was suffering because of it.

Daimon masked it well, but she could see it, especially when his brothers and their women were around. He often singled out Ares, secretly watching him interact with Megan. She wanted to know why he watched Ares more than the others. Because Ares shared his problem? Because Megan was immune to the heat that constantly shimmered over his skin?

She wanted to reveal herself and ask Daimon about it, but more than that, she wanted to watch him, drinking in this side of him, this quiet thoughtfulness, and how handsome he was when he wasn't snapping at her.

If she revealed herself to him, he would push her away.

He frowned and lowered his head, pulled a phone from his jeans pocket and stared at it, the screen illuminating his face. He pocketed it again and turned away from the view, his long legs swiftly carrying him back the way he had come.

Where was he going in such a hurry?

She trailed after him, curiosity gripping her. That curiosity only increased when he stopped where the pedestrian pathway met the road and hailed a cab. She hurried to catch up with him, hailing a taxi for herself when she reached the road and slipping into the back of it.

Felt like a cliché as she said, "Follow that cab."

It was strangely thrilling as the vehicle pulled away, tailing the one Daimon was in as it moved deeper into the heart of the city, beyond the business districts and high rises to smaller buildings and a more suburban setting.

"Stop," she hissed as the cab Daimon was in pulled up outside a long stone building that had a colonial air about it.

Daimon stepped out of the taxi and jogged up the steps, pushed one of the large double doors open and disappeared inside.

Cass paid her driver and slipped out onto the pavement. She eased towards the three-storey building, her heart hammering in her throat and that curiosity tugging her forwards, even as part of her screamed to leave and not snoop into things for once.

Her gaze drifted over the building, with its columns and tall sash windows. It looked like a bank or the head office of some grand company in Europe, was out of place among the tattered buildings that surrounded it. Someone had taken great care of this one building while the others of its age had fallen into ruin around it.

She came to an abrupt halt as she reached the five steps that led up to the door, her gaze snagging on the brass sign mounted on the wall beside it.

An orphanage?

Why had Daimon come to an orphanage?

She was so busy staring at the sign trying to find an answer to that question that she missed the door opening.

"It's no problem. If anything happens again, call me. Little guy needs some extra attention to help him settle in, that's all." Daimon turned away from the middle-aged Chinese woman and froze. "What are you doing here?"

Cass tensed, her eyes leaping to him, instinct pushing that same question to the tip of her tongue.

He huffed and for a moment, she thought he would lash out at her, but then he calmly turned to the woman behind him and offered her a warm smile. "Anything, really. Just call."

She nodded and disappeared inside.

Daimon closed the door, the sound of it slamming cranking up the tension Cass felt.

She braced herself.

Rather than turning on her, he casually walked down the steps and up to her.

"This goes no further. Got it?" he said, and she wanted to argue with him, because she hadn't meant to snoop, and she knew he was angry with her but she didn't want him kicking her out of the Tokyo mansion or banishing her or whatever he had in mind. She would stop irritating him, would pretend she didn't give a damn about him, if he would relent and let her stay. He scrubbed a hand over his hair. "None of my brothers know about this place."

Her eyes widened.

Oh.

He meant, knowledge of this place went no further than the two of them, not things between them went no further and she was out on her backside.

"I've never seen you come here before." Her shoulders went rigid when he frowned at her and she realised she had just confessed to following him before tonight. "I had to study all of you. I had to be sure Mari was in safe hands."

Daimon looked back over his shoulder at the building.

"Is that what you do here?" She glanced at the sign and then back at him. "You keep children safe?"

He sighed, raked fingers through his hair again and looked as if he wouldn't answer those questions.

But then he nodded.

"There's a lot of less fortunate children in this city. Kids who have no parents… Kids who have parents who hurt them. I opened this place for them. Everyone gets an education, food and the choice of finding new parents. My brothers don't know about it and I don't want them to know. Do you understand that, Cass?"

She shivered at the delicious sound of her name on his tongue. She couldn't remember him saying it, and if he had, he had never said it like that—softly, almost tenderly.

She nodded. "Why is it a secret though?"

"Esher."

That one-word answer was enough. His brother wouldn't understand why Daimon was taking care of humans.

"Why did you do this for the children?" She couldn't stop that question from leaving her lips as she gazed up at the building and thought about what he was doing, and realised that the reason the building appeared as it might have back when it was built was because Daimon had been the one to pay for it then.

He had been running this home for children for two centuries.

His expression turned guarded.

"Why, Daimon?" She risked a step towards him, her tone softening as she stared deep into his ice-blue eyes, seeking the answer there.

"Go back to the mansion." He stared down at her, a cold edge entering his eyes.

"No." She took another step, closing the distance between them down to only a few inches.

Daimon made a lunge for her and she was quick to evade him, aware that if he got his hand on her he would teleport her back to the mansion and she wouldn't have the strength to teleport herself after him again when he came back to Hong Kong.

"Why are you so difficult all the time? Why do you never do as you're told?" he barked as he made another attempt to seize hold of her.

Cass froze a short distance from him, beyond arm's reach, and stared at him as shock rolled through her, a chilling sort of cold that irritated the hell out of her.

"As I'm told?" she bit out, her eyebrows lowering as her lips flattened, the thought that he believed she should do as he bid raising her hackles. "I'm a powerful sorceress, Daimon. I can take care of myself. I don't need a man to take care of me. I'm not some weak, delicate little female you can order around."

She hurled the last few words at him, fury getting the better of her, tinged with disappointment. When had she ever given him the impression that she couldn't handle things, that she needed some white-knight figure to protect her?

His face darkened, his jaw ticking as he glared at her. The pain that surfaced in his eyes was phenomenal.

Pain that went deep.

She had struck a nerve, but she wasn't sure how.

Or why.

"Make your own way home then." He backed off a step, still glowering at her. "It's not my fucking business, and this here…" He pointed to the building to his right. "This isn't your business so stay the hell out of it."

He disappeared, leaving a trail of black smoke in his wake that was thicker than normal, swirled eerily in the disturbed air.

Cass's shoulders sagged as all her tension rushed out of her.

She bit out a curse.

How did things between them always end in an argument? She didn't mean for it to happen, and part of her felt it wasn't entirely her fault. Daimon was a minefield, and even the slightest misstep on her part had him exploding at her.

She tipped her head back, closed her eyes and loosed a long sigh.

Time for another apology.

This time, she would make it good enough to heal whatever wound she had inflicted on him, even though she wasn't sure what she had done to hurt him.

She tried to summon the spell to transport herself. Weakness rolled through her before she managed to finish the first part of the incantation.

Great.

She walked to the main road and hailed a cab.

It was going to take longer than she wanted to reach Daimon. A cab. A ferry. Another cab. She only hoped he had gone back to his home in the hills, because if he had gone back to Tokyo, she was even more screwed.

She chuckled mirthlessly at that.

It turned out she needed him after all.

She sighed as she sagged into the back of a taxi.

In more ways than she wanted to admit.

She stared out at the city as the vehicle moved, her mind filled with one thought.

If she'd had a different life, another life…

Would Daimon have been hers?

CHAPTER 8

Daimon cut through the water, focused on his breathing, on each stroke of his arms and pump of his legs.

Trying to shut everything out and relax.

Something which seemed impossible these days.

He pivoted at the wall, pressed his feet to the white tiles and kicked off, propelling himself back down the length of his pool. The heated water cooled around him, but not enough that he caused any icebergs to run into as he reached the end of the pool, twisted under the water and kicked off again. He wasn't sure how many lengths he had done.

Or how many more he would need before he was too tired to think.

He wanted to forget the things Cass had thrown at him, but they echoed in his mind, filling it with thoughts of her. Her words troubled him, and so had the thought that had hit him in that moment.

No. She wasn't a weak female he could order around, one who would do as she was told.

She wasn't meek. Obedient.

She wasn't Penelope.

He gritted his teeth and slammed his hands against the wall of the pool as he reached it, stopping dead.

He shouldn't have thought those things about her. He shouldn't have compared Cass to her.

It had been wrong of him.

He growled at himself and pushed off, floated backwards and stretched out on the surface, staring at the faint stars.

He couldn't take that thought back though. No matter how much he wanted to. It had been wrong of him, but it was the truth.

Penelope had been the sort of woman to do as a man bid, but times had been different. Obedience in a female had been expected back then.

He squeezed his eyes shut.

That wasn't true either.

His mother had never been obedient to his father, not really.

Calindria, his sister, had never been obedient to their parents or any of her brothers, not even her twin, Cal.

He hated himself for thinking badly of Penelope, finding fault in her when he should have loved everything about her, but all these centuries on, the fact that she had been that way, had been meek and accepting, rather than confident and challenging, still didn't sit well with him.

He bumped against the edge of the pool. He lowered his legs and stretched his arms along the curved lip of the wall, stared towards the road beyond the gates of his garden. Was it wrong of him to find faults in Penelope? Was it wrong of him to find the things that she had lacked appealing in Cassandra?

Was it wrong of him to find Cassandra appealing at all?

Was it wrong of him to want her with a ferocity that shook him at times?

He flinched as a sharp pain stabbed his right arm just above his elbow and looked there, the city beyond the glass barrier a blur as his eyes focused on the mosquito. It was fat, sucking greedily on his blood. He raised his arm before him and frowned at the bug, cursing the fact he had been given such a warm place to protect. The damned things would eat him alive if they had the opportunity.

He didn't swat it away.

He waited.

Watched.

Smiled as it slowly froze and dropped off him.

Sometimes, being ice-cold was a blessing not a curse.

Daimon tipped his head back and rested it on the smooth edge of the pool as he stretched his right arm out again. Small chunks of ice knocked against him, but they didn't bother him. It was par for the course when he stopped moving, and tonight he wanted the cold.

Insect song filled the silence as he stared at the stars glittering above him.

Peaceful.

What he needed.

What he had been trying to find since Cass had come crashing into his life.

So why couldn't he stop thinking about her?

Why did he feel bad that he had left her in the city, in a part of it that could be rough at times—dangerous?

Why did he want to step back to the orphanage and try to find her?

She didn't need his protection. She had made that clear several times now, grew angry with him whenever he tried to look out for her.

A shiver ran through him.

Not cold.

Heat. *Incredible* heat.

He slowly opened his eyes and lowered his head.

Cass stood at the other end of the long pool, her back to the black iron gate and her eyes on his body.

He frowned at her. "How did you get through the wards without me feeling it?"

He subtly braced himself for a fight when she lifted her pale blue eyes from his body, a frown marring her pretty face. He hadn't sensed her breaching the wards, and he should have. He stretched his senses out around him, checking them. They were all still intact.

Cass drew down a long breath, raised her right hand so her palm was facing him, and her expression went slack. "I beseech you to listen to me, Son of Hades, Guardian of the Sixth Gate, Ruler of Ice, King of Hong Kong, Tamer of—"

Daimon raised his hand too. "I know the long and boring version of my name. What I don't know is why you're using it. I'm trying to relax. I told you to go back to Tokyo."

Her right eyebrow arched. "And I told you, you have zero authority over me."

"Leave." He didn't want her to do that, was relieved to see she was safe, but he couldn't stop himself from pushing her to see what she would do.

She scowled at him, a mulish twist to her soft lips. "I don't want to leave."

"You need to get out," he countered.

She responded by stepping forwards, her black dress slinking around her long legs with each step, flashing a lot of creamy skin as the slit up the left side opened.

Gods, she was beautiful.

Her fall of onyx hair shimmered in the light from the pool and the house to his left. Her pale blue eyes were bright as she locked them on him, ringed by black make-up that only made the colour of them even more striking.

And she smelled of sin and magic, that scent teasing his senses as wickedly as her smile did as she slowly bent and grazed her fingers across the water of the pool, as if testing the temperature.

Blocks of ice formed, clunking together and breaking apart, spreading towards him.

The water temperature dropped to a dangerous level, where it was liable to freeze completely.

"You need to cool down." She held his gaze, her smile drawing his to her lips, his thoughts to things he shouldn't be contemplating. "And listen."

She drew her hand away from the water and it began to warm again.

Daimon stared at her. She was singing a song to his heart. The icy water was a delight, exactly what he needed tonight. Sheer pleasure rippled through him and her smile turned more wicked.

She gave him a coy look, one that said she knew what she had done, how she had pleased him, and that she took pleasure from it too.

"Will you hear me out? Perhaps you will be more inclined to listen if I joined you in there?" She stroked her fingers across her cleavage and his gaze tracked her black nails.

He wanted to touch her like that.

She reached beneath her arm and he shivered as she lowered a zipper, the sound of it sending a hot wave of need bolting through him.

His breaths came faster as she eased the front of her dress forwards, flashing the side of her breast. Her bare breast.

If she got naked, if she came into the pool, he would want to touch her and he wouldn't be able to stop himself.

He shook his head. "You shouldn't get too close to me, Cass."

She smiled knowingly and held her dress up with one hand as she stroked the fingertips of the other one across her chest. "You can't freeze this heart. It's been frozen for a century… but I could thaw yours."

She dipped and touched the water again. The ice melted in an instant and steam rose from the water.

Daimon stepped, appearing on the broad white tiles of the terrace. He stared at the steaming water and then sneered at her, need tangling with anger, pain with fury. It all collided inside him, tearing at him, filling his head with ridiculous impossible things.

She was tormenting him.

"What do you want from me, koldun'ya?" He stalked towards her, determined to get an answer, because he was tired of her toying with him when she knew all about him.

When she knew he couldn't touch anyone without hurting them.

She disappeared when he reached her and reappeared behind him. He turned on a growl and lunged for her, but she was too quick, nothing more than a blur as she sped around behind him again, evading him. She laughed, high and infuriating, pushing him right to the edge.

Darkness poured through his veins, roused by the thought she was taunting him, toying with him.

Out to hurt him for some reason.

He let it get the better of him as he tried to grab her again, as she evaded him and moved to the other end of the pool. Her smile ripped a growl from him and he stepped, appeared and stepped again when she went to move. He snagged her arm but she disappeared in blue-black smoke, and he realised it had been a decoy, a false impression of her.

His senses sparked.

He turned on a pinhead to face her, raising his hand at the same time.

Her fingers locked around his wrist, stopping him from grabbing her.

Her gaze ran over him, heat rolling in the wake of it as she stared at his bare chest and stomach, and then ventured lower, to his black swimming trunks.

"Such a chilly reception." She smiled dazedly, her eyes glittering with sparks of silver and blue. "Here I thought you would have warmed to me by now."

He glared at her and then realised something.

His eyes leaped to her hand where it gripped his wrist. It was warm. Soft.

And his touch wasn't harming her.

He couldn't believe it.

Cass released his wrist and trailed her fingers along it, sending a thousand lightning strikes chasing up his arm. She stroked her nails over his hand and all he could do was watch her, lost in sensation, swept up in the feel of being intimately touched by a female for the first time in centuries.

"I only wanted to apologise," she murmured, that pout back in her voice.

He kept staring at her hand, shivering and on the verge of groaning as she teased his palm.

"What for?" he muttered, struggling to convince himself to stop her.

This was wrong of him.

Wasn't it?

Was it so wrong that he wanted this?

Penelope flashed across his mind.

It was.

He pulled his hand away from Cass.

Her eyes lifted to collide with his. "For everything."

Those words were sincere, as if she actually meant them. He tried to convince himself that she didn't, that this was all some cruel game to her, a way of amusing herself.

But he got stuck on the fact she had touched him without being hurt.

That he could touch her.

Was this rush of sensation, this overload of need, how Ares had felt when he had met Megan? If it was, then he couldn't blame his brother for succumbing to it.

But it wasn't real.

Or at least what was happening between him and Cass wasn't real.

Wasn't what he needed deep in his heart.

She proved that by sidling closer to him, a seductive sway to her hips, and letting her dress droop a little lower, flashing the curves of her breasts at him as she smiled and gazed up into his eyes.

"I told you I could worship you if you let me," she husked, her voice a throaty whisper. "Now all you have to do is let me, Daimon. Just drop that guard and take what you want. Whatever you need… it's yours."

Tempting, but a lie.

What he wanted, what he needed, would never be his.

She lifted her hand and brought it towards his chest.

Daimon seized her wrist and stopped her.

"Spare yourself the trouble and disappointment, Cassandra, and give up now. Nothing can melt my heart." He tightened his grip on her wrist, driving his point home, and pain flared in her eyes as his power finally managed to make contact with her, breaking past whatever spell she was using to protect herself from him. "Nothing."

He cast her hand away from him and didn't look at her as he moved past her, heading for his house. His feet dragged, his steps slowing as the distance between them grew, filling him with a need to stop and look back at her, to forget everything and take her up on her offer.

No strings attached.

That's what she wanted.

It had been right there in her eyes.

For some reason, that irritated the hell out of him. Why had she targeted him? Because he was single? Because she believed he would be easy to sway because of his problem?

It definitely wasn't because she viewed him as anything more than a brief fling, a nice conquest to add to what was probably a long line of them. Was this how she operated? Seeking men out to satisfy her needs? How many had she been with? How many more would she be with once she was done with him?

He curled his fingers into fists and clenched them, his arms shaking as the darkness rose within him again, fuelled by the thought she wanted to use him.

That she was determined to break him.

He looked back at her, and not a single ounce of regret or guilt shone in her eyes. Maybe her heart was as cold as his was and she didn't know how to be warm, only knew how to take what she wanted, regardless of the consequences or devastation she might leave in her wake.

Well, he wasn't going to give her what she wanted.

He wasn't going to break.

He needed to remain faithful to Penelope.

But gods, Cass made it hard. He stared at her, drawn to her even as he wanted to push her away, aching with a need to feel her skin against his and know her taste.

He silently cursed her, hated how easily she stole his focus and how readily his body responded to her, even before he had known he could touch her. Now, her presence was a torment.

No, it was a test of his strength.

And he wouldn't falter.

The feelings he had for Cassandra were just lust, fuelled by how long he had gone without a woman's touch. It was infatuation. Nothing more. In time, it would pass. She would move on and he would return home.

"I can see the battle in you, Daimon," she whispered and canted her head to her left. "Why fight this? Why fight me? This attraction between us isn't going anywhere. Just surrender to it."

He stood his ground.

"I told you before, Cassandra. I'm not interested. You're attractive, I'll admit that, but this... between us... this isn't going to happen."

He turned his back on her.

"I meant what I said. My heart belongs to another."

"I don't want your heart," she whispered.

And it hit him.

That was the problem.

She didn't really want *him*. She wanted his body. He was just convenient. Attractive. Feelings didn't come into it for her.

She just wanted something fast and fun to pass the time.

He wanted something else.

Something more.

Something he had no right desiring.

A cold hollow feeling opened in his chest.

He wanted her.

All of her. Nothing held back.

Not just for now.

The darker side of his blood snarled at the thought of giving her up.

He shoved his fingers through his wet hair.

What was she doing to him? He had been fine before she had come along, his heart constant and his mind clear, his focus on his mission and on returning to the Underworld.

He closed his eyes, shutting the world out.

He hadn't been fine.

He could see it now that Cass had opened his eyes. He had been lying to himself for centuries, slowly falling apart and trying to hold himself together by pretending being loyal to Penelope was everything to him, telling himself that he was noble for remaining faithful to her, and it was what he wanted.

When it wasn't.

He wanted more than this hollow existence, more than drifting through the years alone, lying to himself to stop him from crashing and burning. He wanted to feel again, wanted what others had, yearned for it with a ferocity that shook him and had him wavering on the edge, on the verge of doing something foolish.

Like surrendering to Cass even when he knew it would only end badly for him.

He wanted her.

She wanted him.

It didn't have to be complicated.

All he had to do was turn and she would see his fight was over, that he couldn't go on resisting her. All he had to do was let her take the reins.

He turned to do just that, his pulse hammering in his throat.

And cursed.

She was gone.

CHAPTER 9

Cass stomped around her room in a very unladylike manner, uncaring of whether anyone saw her. Her skin felt too tight, flushed hotly whenever she thought about Daimon and how delectable he had looked in that pool, almost naked. Heat rolled through her veins, stoking her temperature as she ran her fingers over her wrist, recalling how firm his skin had felt against hers, how cool he had been to the touch.

She shivered as she let that moment play out again, loving the way his eyes had changed, the flare of passion she had ignited in him warming them as they had tracked her fingers.

For a moment, she had felt as if she had been getting somewhere with him, and then he had shut her down with his ridiculous talk of hearts.

But she had seen the interest in his eyes, the need that she had stirred when she had touched him and he hadn't hurt her. She had felt the hunger in him.

The desire.

Gods, she wanted to unleash that side of him. She wanted to know the man he was holding back. She wanted to break down his barriers again and this time not relent until he had surrendered to her.

Why couldn't he just give her what she wanted from him?

He just had to keep resisting her.

It was frustrating to say the least.

She was used to getting what she wanted, at least where her coven wasn't concerned. She couldn't recall the last time she'd had to fight this hard for something, but fight she would. Daimon didn't stand a chance against her. The more he resisted her, the stronger her determination to crack the wall of ice surrounding him became.

She reminded herself that she didn't want his heart.

This thing between her and Daimon was purely physical.

She kept telling herself that as she rifled through her things, trying to find something to wear, something that would fit her mood.

She paused and stared at the mound of black clothes on top of the dresser before her as a feeling crept up on her, sneaking in while she struggled to convince herself that Daimon was nothing more than a fling to her, a nice way to pass the time.

Cass struggled to shake it off. There was no room in her life for the sort of thing part of her clearly foolishly desired. It was impossible. Ridiculous. Dangerous.

She balled her hands into fists in her clothes and stared hard at them, trying to shut down the rebellious feeling.

She really didn't want his heart.

She couldn't afford to fall for anyone.

Yet there was something about the stoic, silent Daimon that drew her to him, had her finding it difficult to keep her distance from him. His eyes shimmered with pain at times, fathomless and dreadful, and she wanted to know the source of it.

He wasn't helping her keep her distance either.

He was making himself a challenge, and Cass had always risen to a challenge.

So far, all she had learned was his heart apparently belonged to another, something Cal had shrugged off and said he knew nothing about when Cass had subtly dropped it into a conversation, and that the cold aura Daimon projected was about more than the manifestation of his power.

Her hand stopped on a dress in the middle of the pile, and she lifted it before her. It was sexy, sheer down the sides, perfect for drawing the eye of an eligible male.

Especially if she wore it with no underwear.

A hot flush tripped through her when she recalled how Daimon had reacted a few weeks ago in the garden here, when she had been chasing after him and had lifted her dress because it had been slowing her down.

How his eyes had burned with hunger when he had stared at the exposed curve of her hip and realised she hadn't been wearing any panties.

Cass closed her eyes and pictured that moment, let it build in her mind again as she feathered her fingers down her neck. She tweaked the scene a little, had him take a step towards her and close the distance, gasped as she imagined him reaching out and fisting her dress in his hands.

Tugging her towards him.

She lowered her hand to her breast, licked her lips and tilted her head back as he kissed down her throat, as he pulled her dress up and planted his strong hands against her bare backside.

Pulled her against him.

A moan threatened to slip from her lips.

She held it back, her breath coming faster as imaginary Daimon behaved far more nicely than his real-life counterpart, surrendering to the attraction that burned between them.

Her fingers slipped from her breast, palm skimming over her stomach, that liquid fire Daimon had ignited in her veins in Hong Kong roaring back into an inferno as she pictured him in those tiny shorts, delectable body spotted with water, light shimmering across hard muscles made for fingers to explore.

To tease.

Cass rolled her hips forwards as her hand reached them, screwed her face up when pleasure arced through her and the fantasy built in her mind.

Daimon squeezed her backside, dropped his lips to her breasts to tease them with a skilled cool tongue before falling to his knees before her.

She arched forwards, her head falling back as his mouth covered her, that wicked tongue sending her out of her mind as it stroked between her thighs.

Oh gods.

She sank her teeth into her lower lip and surrendered to the fantasy, her heart pounding and blood rushing as pleasure built inside her.

Close. She was close.

Gods she needed this, had to take the edge off somehow.

Release eluded her though and frustration began to replace pleasure as she sought it.

She clung to the fantasy, desperate now, her breaths coming faster as she stretched for that one flick of her fingers that would send her over the edge.

It refused to come.

Damn it.

A shiver bolted through her when she sensed Daimon return, smelled snow and spice in the cool morning air.

Release hit her like a wrecking ball, had her legs wobbling beneath her and her hand flying to cover her mouth as she cried into it.

Oh sweet gods.

She fumbled for the dresser with her other hand, clutched it and leaned into it for support as wave after wave of bliss swept through her.

Cass sagged forwards, her hand dropping from her mouth.

Unsure she would ever recover.

"You look like shit," Cal said.

Cass tensed and turned, her heart shooting into her mouth as panic gripped her and her cheeks burned, the thought she had just been caught pleasuring herself wreaking havoc on her and causing a whirlwind of lame excuses to fill her mind.

Only the sliding white door of the room was closed. He wasn't talking to her.

She crept to the panels that formed the wall of the room near the covered walkway, eased the one that acted as a door back a little and peered out through the gap.

Daimon stood on the wooden walkway of the wing opposite her, bathed in early morning light. She shivered, achy again as she studied him. She cursed him. What was it about him that had her on fire with just a glance at him?

Cal approached him from her right, the direction of the main room of the house. Daimon shrugged, rolling toned shoulders beneath his tight long-sleeve turtleneck sweater. She wanted to peel that off him. She shook that rogue thought away.

"Tired," he muttered and stifled a yawn.

"Still can't sleep?" Concern filled Cal's blue eyes.

Daimon was having trouble sleeping? She could help him with that if he let her, and she wasn't even talking about wearing him out with sex.

Although, that was far more appealing than using a spell on him.

Daimon shook his head and ran a hand down his mouth. "I need to unwind or something."

Cass could help him with that too.

He had certainly helped her unwind just now.

She couldn't imagine how he would react if she told him he had starred in a wicked fantasy that had given her one hell of a memorable release.

Her cheeks heated again.

She huffed, irritated by the reaction. She was a grown woman and there was absolutely zero reason for her to feel ashamed of what she had done.

"Where is everyone?" His icy blue eyes scanned the garden and she ducked back behind the panel as they neared her, not wanting him to see her.

She swore his gaze lingered in her direction, that she could feel him staring straight through the panels of the room at her.

She looked down at herself.

Just how good was their sense of smell?

Her face heated again.

Could he smell her, what she had done?

The thought he might be aware of it had a hot achy shiver rolling through her and her nipples beaded, her breasts yearning for his touch. She huffed and ignored her rebellious body, trying to regain control of herself. She was damned if she was going to let Daimon see how flustered he had gotten her.

"Ares took Megan back to get some rest. Keras just left. Marek took Caterina to see her brother." Cal hesitated. "Aiko is… she went out with some friends for the day. I think she needed the pick me up today. Valen and Eva are keeping an eye on her from a distance."

"I thought the place seemed quiet."

"Me and Mari just got done with the bath," Cal said and Cass peered at them again, tempted to scowl at him.

She reminded herself that Mari was a grown woman. It was still hard to accept that at times. Mari would always be the little girl she adored, had watched growing up and had been sad when she had been forced to keep her distance so she wouldn't notice that Cass didn't age.

Although, Mari had had a wonderful idea.

A bath did sound good.

"You should have one. Might help you relax and sleep." Cal shrugged, his shoulders hiking beneath his black T-shirt. "Just an idea."

"It's a good one. Long baths are always nice." Daimon smiled at his younger brother.

A genuine one.

He was right. Long baths were always nice.

But long baths with another were even better.

She huffed as she looked back at her clothes and hit a snag.

She didn't have a bathing suit with her.

Cass shrugged that off. Cal would be occupied with Mari for some time, and Aiko was out of the house for the morning at the very least. The only one liable to see her was the only one she wanted to see her.

She had some decency though.

She plucked a black lace bra and matching panties from her pile of clothing and slipped them on, following it with an onyx satin robe. She hurried from the room. Not a sprint. Sprinting wasn't very ladylike.

But she did make it to the bathing area in record time, beating Daimon there.

She stopped on the damp tiles that separated the showers on her left from the stone pool on her right. It was large, almost a small swimming pool, and the view from it was breathtaking. Her gaze traversed the sweeping lines that had been raked into the pale gravel of the zen garden to swirl around rocks and pockets of greenery, danced over the delicately clipped topiary, to the large maple tree that was turning red, and then the crisp blue sky beyond.

Steam curled from the surface of the water, tempting her to slip into it to chase away the chill of the autumn morning.

She shed her robe, placing it on one of the dry stools at the side of the bathing area, and then twisted her black hair into a knot at the back of her head, securing it with a pin she formed with a spell. She washed off, hurrying through the process, and then stepped into the water.

It was hot, reminded her of the spring bath the older witches had been allowed to enjoy at the coven. Only here, she wasn't expected to get all warmed up in the bath and then do something ridiculous like jumping into the snow or icy water.

Here, all she had to do was relax.

She stepped down from the submerged step that ran along the width of the pool, acting as a seat, and sank into the water. She ended up kneeling near the showers and staring out at the zen garden as the sun rose higher. It touched the maple first, chasing the shadow down it and brightening the vivid colour of its leaves.

Had reached the stone lantern at the far end of the zen garden when she realised she wasn't alone.

She looked over her shoulder at Daimon where he stood at the end of the corridor that led to the main room, clutching a white towel in front of him.

Banked heat burned in his ice-blue eyes, had another achy shiver tripping through her.

"What are you doing?" he growled.

"Bathing." She swished her hands through the water as she turned to face him. "I thought that was obvious?"

Heat chased over her skin, sending waves of tingles down her arms and spine, as she soaked in the glorious sight of him in his tiny shorts.

And decided the sight of Daimon nearly naked should be illegal.

All that immaculate bare flesh stretched taut over honed muscles. It was just too much.

She ignored the way he growled at her like a rabid animal and took her time, drinking her fill of him, tracing her gaze over the flat slabs of his pectorals and down the valley between them, to the start of his stomach muscles. They flexed as her eyes landed on them, and she bit back a moan. Wicked god. He was doing it on purpose, taunting her with what she wanted to touch. Looking at him wasn't enough. She wanted to explore him with her fingers.

Wanted to trace the valley between his eight pack and circle his navel.

Just as that ink did.

She frowned. *Ink.*

How had she missed that last night?

The tribal sun was all sharp spikes a few shades darker than his skin, but as she stared at it, she swore it shifted, darkening a shade more towards black and those straight lines gaining a subtle wave.

Maybe it had been too dark at the pool for her to see it.

Or maybe she had been too swept up in the glorious sight of him to notice the small things.

Now, she couldn't take her eyes off it.

It was definitely changing. Softening.

Like his mood?

She dragged her eyes away from the ink, wanting to see if that was the case.

His blue eyes were darker than she had ever seen them, flecked with diamonds, fixed not on her face but on her body.

"Is that your favour mark?" She waggled a finger towards his stomach.

His eyes shot up to lock with hers and his white eyebrows knitted hard above them as his irises went from blue to white.

And the lines of his favour mark went from subtle waves to jagged spikes.

It definitely reflected his mood.

"Get out. It's my turn to bathe." His fingers tightened in the towel, causing a ripple effect. Muscles tensed in a wave, a symphony that delighted her.

Cass swept her arm out above the water. "The bath is big enough for the both of us."

His eyes narrowed in a way that said he didn't believe it was.

She murmured softly, "Unless you're scared of bathing with a woman? I could get out."

She slowly stood, the water sluicing down her body, dragging his eyes down from her face.

He stared at her.

Really stared.

Passion flared in his eyes again, lighting them with sparks of white and silver.

Cass trembled as goosebumps erupted across her skin, savouring the feel of his gaze on her as he took her in.

All of her.

His lips parted, his gaze distant as he muttered, "Get moving. Out or under the water... I don't care which. Just cover up."

Cass rolled her shoulders and waded deeper, heading towards the end of the stone pool nearest the zen garden, giving her back to him to flash the fact her black lace panties didn't cover the curves of her backside.

A sharp thrill chased through her as his gaze fell there, scalding her, and she swore he growled under his breath.

Water splashed behind her, adding to that thrill, quickening her breath and heating her blood. Part of her had expected him to leave. To run as far as he could from her. Was she making progress with him?

Cass reached the far end of the stone bath and shyly turned to face him, sinking under the water at the same time so he barely caught a glimpse of her front.

She stretched her arms out along the edge of the pool, tipped her head back and loosed a long sigh as heat suffused every inch of her and her breasts crested the surface.

"This is bliss," she moaned.

"Knock it off," Daimon grunted. "I'm meant to be relaxing."

She lowered her eyes to him. Almost chuckled. He had his head tipped back and a small damp towel draped over his eyes.

She snuck closer, slipping silently through the water, her pulse accelerating as anticipation rolled through her and she waited for him to catch her.

"How come you don't freeze the water?" A little light conversation would keep him distracted from her closing the distance between them.

He muttered, "I don't want to talk about it."

"Well, I do."

"Do you always get what you want?" he bit out and dragged the towel from his face as he lowered his head. His white eyebrows knitted hard as he noticed her and the fact she was closer now.

"Most of the time." All the time.

Well, at least until Daimon had walked into her life.

Perhaps not all the time even then. The coven was another exception. What they wanted, they got, whether she liked it or not. She pushed that out of her mind, refusing to let it sour her mood when she had Daimon in the water with her, deliciously close to naked and not looking as if he was going to bolt.

He huffed and tipped his head back again. Progress. He wasn't pushing her away or forcing her back to the other end of the bath.

His bare chest heaved on a sigh, muscles stretching and flexing in a way that lured her gaze down to it and mesmerised her. "The water is cooler around me, but the constant heat from the thermal spring below the house that supplies it is enough to stop it from turning to ice."

"Is it cooler around you?" She moved before he could protest, using a swiftness spell to have her pressed against him in the blink of an eye.

He jerked away.

Scowled at her.

"I only wanted to see if you were telling the truth." She pouted.

He stared at her, looking as if he wanted to lash out at her.

But then he grabbed her nape and dragged her to him, their bodies colliding and mouths dangerously close as he gazed down into her eyes.

He husked, "Does this satisfy your curiosity?"

A shiver tripped along her spine as he palmed the back of her head, his hand cool against it, addling her mind.

She retained enough sense to give the spell she had used to prevent his ice from hurting her another top-up.

Her breath trembled, the strangest feeling running through her as she stared into his eyes, able to pick out all the flecks of blue and white, and silver this close to him.

Nerves.

She couldn't remember the last time she had been nervous about anything, and definitely couldn't remember the last time a man had made her feel this way, as if she was coming and going at the same time, spinning in circles and being turned inside out.

Afraid of what might happen, but desperate for it at the same time.

His cool breath fanned across her lips, his chest shifting against hers as his breaths quickened.

Did he feel the same sense of anticipation?

She mustered her courage and settled her palm on his left pectoral, stroked her fingers downwards to graze his nipple and the start of his stomach. His breath hitched, his body tensing beneath her questing fingers, and his gaze turned distant and hazy again.

"Does this satisfy yours?" she whispered, her mouth drying out as she dared herself to inch her lips towards him.

He ruined the chance by turning his profile to her, his gaze falling to her hand as he murmured, "How do you do that?"

Cass smiled softly. "It's magic."

He turned his head towards her again, their lips almost touching, and an ache bloomed inside her, a powerful need consuming her.

She needed him to kiss her.

She wanted to know what it would feel like.

He leaned closer and she swore her heart stopped.

Water slammed over her, her senses reeled, and she gasped. It poured into her throat, triggering dark images, memories she wanted to forget. They flashed across her mind in rapid succession as she desperately clawed her way to the surface, as she coughed and struggled to get air into her lungs and purge the water.

When she could breathe again and the fear that had gripped her subsided, she narrowed her eyes on Daimon where he lounged at the other end of the pool. Looking for all the world as if he had done nothing wrong, as if he had felt nothing as he'd watched her struggling to surface and fighting for air. Her hoarse breaths raked in her ears as fury poured through her veins to obliterate the softer things she had been feeling.

"That's twice you've tried to drown me," she snapped and stood, and the water around her trembled as her magic rose within her, filling her with a need to give as good as she had gotten and show him what it was like to be drowned.

Not a flicker of regret crossed his handsome features as he stood and stepped from the water, as he scowled at her as if she were to blame for everything.

She didn't bother holding back this time. "You were the one who tried to kiss me!"

He flashed short fangs and stormed away from her.

But in the brief moment before he had turned away, she had caught the pain in his eyes.

Fathomless. Dreadful.

Cass sank back into the water, all her fight draining from her.

He had said his heart belonged to another, but that wasn't the truth. Someone had broken it and for some reason he was holding on to the tattered remains rather than trying to heal it.

She stared in the direction he had gone.

Whispered.

"Who hurt you?"

CHAPTER 10

Daimon sat on the edge of the king-size bed in his home in Hong Kong, staring at the pendant resting on the palm of his hand.

It had been wrong of him to want Cass like that.

Unfaithful.

He closed his fingers over the pendant and shut his eyes.

Penelope appeared before him, a smile budding on her lips as she worked in the small garden of her home, tending foxgloves and gladioli. A dirty white pinafore covered part of her dull blue-grey dress, but the scooped neckline was low enough to reveal the pendant. It swayed and twinkled in the summer sunshine as she leaned over, her knees pressing into the grass.

Beyond her, the old cottage had seen better days, needed repairing again.

Would forever need repairing.

She sat back and brushed her hand across her forehead, clearing damp strands of sun-kissed auburn hair from it.

He held the pendant more tightly, watching her as she worked, tending to the garden she had loved so much.

Waiting for him.

The pendant could show him any moment when she had been wearing it, allowing him to see how happy she had been when he had given it to her, among other things.

Rather than soothing him as it usually did, today the sight of her only made him question his feelings about her.

He waited, hoping, needing to feel that calm he did whenever he watched her like this, that sense that remaining loyal to her was what he wanted more than anything, that his love for her was eternal.

It didn't come.

She wasn't the woman he wanted to see.

She wasn't the one he needed to see.

He opened his fingers and stared at the pendant, cursed himself as another memory played out before him.

One of Cass going under the water, of her breaching the surface and fighting for air, of her looking at him with hurt in her eyes, and a hell of a lot of anger.

Anger he deserved.

Hiding here in his home in Hong Kong wasn't going to get him anywhere. He wouldn't feel better until he had apologised to her.

It had been a knee-jerk reaction, one he should have been strong enough to contain. She was right. He had been the one who had tried to kiss her, and he had blamed her for it, and for how guilty he felt because he had wanted to taste her lips, and so much more.

He sighed and stood, slipped the pendant back onto the clasp on his phone and shoved the device into the pocket of his black jeans. He grabbed the navy turtleneck sweater he had discarded on top of the white dresser and tugged it on before he stepped.

Darkness whirled around him and then he was standing in the front garden of the Tokyo mansion. He strode to the house and unlaced his boots.

Froze when Cass's voice rang in the late afternoon air.

"I need to take care of Milos. I've left him alone too long already." Cass sighed, a light sound that teased his ears but did nothing to calm his mood as it took a sharp nosedive.

Who the hell was Milos?

Acid burned through his veins, settled in his stomach and scoured it.

Cass had been giving him the cold shoulder since Hong Kong and the moment in the bath, had avoided him for two days straight. It had been what he wanted, so why had he hated every moment of it?

Why had he hated the fact she had been keeping her distance?

Was this why she had avoided him? She felt bad that she had wanted him in that moment, when she had another man. Whoever the bastard was, he was Greek. For some reason, that only made him angrier.

"Are you strong enough to do this?" Marinda sounded concerned.

"All charged up again. I have enough strength to transport myself to Karavostasis, take care of Milos's needs for a day or two, and then I'll be able to transport myself back here."

Take care of Milos's needs?

Daimon wanted to growl at that.

"Give him my love and a hug from me." Marinda's warm words only increased Daimon's urge to growl.

Cass's signature disappeared and Daimon kicked off his boots, dumped them on the rack and opened the front door, trying to ignore the black urge to follow her. He made a beeline for his room in the north wing, striding past Marinda, needing a moment to rein in his needs before they got out of control and got him into trouble.

The darkness seething in his veins refused to abate, had him shoving the white panel door of his room open and pacing in a circle on the golden straw mats. Who was Milos? Her lover? Husband?

He tunnelled his fingers through his hair and clutched it, clawed it back until his scalp stung.

What did it matter to him?

A growl pealed from his lips.

A lot.

It mattered a lot.

He pivoted and stepped before he could consider what he was doing, and the cold dark of the teleport gave way to warmth as sunshine bathed him. The dry air smelled of earth, and to his right waves gently rolled over a stony shore, tugging at the pebbles and shifting them around.

Daimon blew out his breath and opened his eyes, stared at the white blocky two-storey buildings that hugged the curving bay of Karavostasis and the brown hills spotted with pale boulders that rose above them.

The small ramshackle village was quiet in the morning sunshine, only a few older mortals coming and going along the seafront beneath the trees that followed the sweeping line of the beach, clutching bread and exchanging greetings as they passed each other.

This was where Cass lived?

Did she live here with Milos, playing the doting wife?

He tried to shut out the image of her with another man as he picked his way down the bluff, the ochre soil already warm beneath his bare feet.

He should have at least put some shoes on. What did it matter though? He didn't intend for anyone to see him. When he reached the bottom of the small rocky promontory, he eased down onto his backside and waited. He had no idea where Cass lived, but if she had been gone a while, there was a chance she might need to visit the small store.

Unless her lover had already stocked the cupboards for her.

He squeezed his eyes shut, not wanting to picture her in one of the small villas, doing mundane things like cooking lunch or baking bread. Homely things.

It wasn't a problem.

He found it impossible to imagine Cass in that role. She didn't dress like a woman who did such things, and she hadn't once shown any inclination to cook. She struck him as the sort of woman who preferred to have someone wait on them.

He opened his eyes and scanned the area.

None of the houses were big or grand enough to warrant hiring staff.

He growled when his mind supplied that Milos probably took care of the domestic things.

Worshipping Cass in every way possible.

That growl cut short as the blue door of the store opened and Cass walked out.

Wearing the same slinky and sexy black dress she always did.

No one batted an eye as she greeted them. In fact, they all bowed their heads and one of the older women even stopped her for a brief conversation. When the woman walked away, it was with a smile.

And a look of relief on her face.

It struck him that no one viewed Cass as out of place because they knew she was a witch, and that she helped them.

Which seemed impossible.

Cass didn't have a kind bone in her body.

He instantly took that back. She did. He had seen it more than once, especially when she was around Marinda, and she had done all she could to heal his brothers whenever they had been injured.

He just didn't want to soften towards her, and admitting she had good traits as well as bad ones, was a path that would lead to him doing just that.

He wanted to be angry with her.

His eyes slowly widened.

Because he was jealous.

He tried to discount that, to laugh at the impossible notion that he was envious of the bastard Cass had come to see, who lived on this beautiful island with her.

But he couldn't.

He eased onto his feet and tailed Cass, keeping his distance from her, nodding as he passed the old woman who Cass had comforted. He was tempted to ask what Cass had said to her and about the things she did for the community, but the thought of losing sight of Cass kept him moving forwards.

She followed the road as she reached the other side of the bay and he kept the distance between them steady. Stones that had fallen into the road from the hill that gently sloped up to his right bit into the soles of his feet, but he ignored the pain as he followed Cass. She turned left, following a trail downwards, towards the shore.

Daimon hurried after her and stopped at the start of the path.

Below him, crystal clear blue water lapped at the rocky coast and a small stony beach.

Set just back from that on a stretch of flat pale rock was a single-storey flat-roofed white villa, surrounded by a white painted stone wall that needed repairing. It had fallen down in some places, the stones tumbling into the small patch of dry dirt that had been turned into what appeared to be a herb garden.

Or it had been.

The plants were all dead now, shrivelled and brown.

From the front of the villa, a terrace with a low wall extended outwards towards the sea and looked as if someone had painted it white more recently than the rest of the house. Stripped tree trunks as thick as his arms supported a dark wooden flat roof over the terrace, giving it some shade.

He ducked down as one set of blue wooden shutters opened, revealing a dark interior.

"Come now, Milos… don't be moody with me." Cass's voice held a playful note.

Daimon growled low, the darkness surging through him with renewed ferocity. He stood and shoved the rickety gate open, and stormed down the path, determined to see who this Milos was.

What did this bastard have that Daimon didn't?

There had to be some reason she had given her heart to this male. He had to be the reason she had declared she wasn't interested in Daimon's heart.

Because she already loved another.

A vicious hiss greeted him as he neared the terrace, a low growl following it.

Daimon stopped dead and looked down at the mangey white and ginger cat on the terracotta tiles. Ragged scar tissue ran over its nose and part of its left ear was missing, and it looked as if it either needed a good brush or a heavy dose of flea killer.

From inside the house, Cass made a kissy noise.

Daimon took a hard step forwards, determined to stop whatever was going on in the house.

The cat growled louder.

The kissing noise grew louder too.

Daimon froze as Cass stepped out onto the terrace, her blue eyes on the cat. And then him.

She huffed. "I had wondered why Mister Milos was grumpy. I can't blame him. I'm not exactly pleased to see you either."

Daimon's mouth flapped open.

Milos was the cat?

He looked down at the ancient thing that was still blocking his route. The cat hissed, baring three yellowing fangs. The bottom left one was missing.

Gods, he was an idiot.

All the fight that had been building inside him suddenly bled out of him.

"I could mention how you're stalking me. I shan't… but I could." Cass smiled when he frowned at her and her shoulders lifted in a slight shrug. "I just wanted that out there."

Fine, so she wasn't the only one with a bad habit of stalking, but how was he to have known Milos was a damned cat?

Cass looked down at the beast, her voice like a sigh as she said, "It's a cliché, but it's true. All good witches need a cat."

Daimon hunkered down and held his hand out to the animal. It snubbed him, standing and turning away, flicking its tail.

"Milos is normally so sociable." Cass looked at him. "Maybe he's picking up on the fact I don't want you here."

He sighed and stood again, and jerked his chin towards the feral tom. "Cats don't tend to be very impressed by gods. That's all this is."

She shrugged again and turned away from him too. "I can't imagine why."

He clenched his jaw, bit back the words he wanted to say, and focused on the reason he had come back from Hong Kong to see her.

"I'm sorry."

She stopped in the doorway and looked across at him, her eyebrows pinned high on her forehead. "Did you say something?"

Daimon huffed. "I said I'm sorry."

"For what? Another attempt to drown me? Being as frigid as your power? Upsetting Mister Milos? Or perhaps you're sorry for stalking me?" She turned back towards him, her black eyebrows lowering into a frown. "I'm not even going to point out how angry you would have been if our positions had been reversed. I'm bigger than that."

She hit him with a sly smile that said she was enjoying this—having him at her mercy.

"I'm only here because I pulled the short straw when we were deciding which of us was going to protect you and get your arse back to Tokyo." He folded his arms across his chest.

She chuckled, swept the black nails of her right hand across her chest and smiled again. "You're a terrible liar."

She turned back towards the door.

"I'm flattered you felt the need to stalk me."

And disappeared inside.

Daimon glared down at Milos, who glared right back at him and moved to block his path again.

"You have something against me. I get that. All your kind do." He kept his voice low as he crouched in front of the cat. His gaze flicked to the door and then back, meeting Milos's green eyes. "Small god, I ask you that if… when… the time comes that you'll do your duty as a guardian deity and protect the one you clearly treasure and love."

The cat stared at him for a moment, and then stood and rubbed against his knee, purring deeply.

Daimon took that as a yes.

Milos moved aside and hopped up onto the white wall, his tail flicking back and forth as he stared out at the sea.

Did Cass know that Milos wasn't just a cat? He wasn't sure what things about his world she did or didn't know, but maybe it was time he found out.

He stepped up onto the terrace, the tiles cool beneath his feet, and into the small house. It was cramped on the inside, with an open kitchen and living room, and a corridor leading deeper into the house.

It was far from the glamourous home he had imagined Cass living in. This was as rustic as it came, with furniture that looked hand-made and a tiny kitchen consisting of an old white stove, a sink and two cupboards. The only light in the room was a naked bulb hanging in the middle of the ceiling and an oil lamp on the desk to his left.

Maybe the coven didn't pay their witches well. He knew a thing or two about covens, and most of them operated like mercenaries, taking on contracts across the world. He glanced around at the small home again. Either the coven only paid Cass a small wage for her work and kept the bulk of the money for themselves, or Cass liked being off grid for some reason.

"I'm just grabbing some things." Cass's voice drifted from the shadowy corridor. "Make yourself at home."

Outside, Milos growled. The deity wasn't happy about being left behind again.

"Cass…" Daimon started, shoved his hand up his forehead and over his white hair, and blew out his breath. "I *am* sorry."

He wasn't sure why he needed her to accept his apology so badly, but he did. He needed to know things were all right between them, that he hadn't messed everything up, and he needed her to know that he was aware he hadn't been the easiest man to put up with. He knew he had done a lot of things wrong.

"About trying to drown me?" She poked her head out of a room, an expectant look on her beautiful face.

"About that… About a lot of things…" He clenched his fists at his sides, fighting for the right words.

"I could list them for you if it makes it easier." She stepped back into the corridor. "But I won't."

He waited for her to go back to packing, but she lingered, and her aquamarine eyes gained a sombre edge he didn't like.

"Do you know why I moved here?" She glanced around the small house, her fine black eyebrows furrowing slightly. "I came here because it was quiet… a world away from persecution… a world away from everything."

Everything?

The way she had said that word made him feel that her coming to this remote and sparsely populated island had been about more than just avoiding humans who had wanted to drown her for being a witch.

She had been trying to escape something else too.

"Was there another reason you moved here?" He wanted to take a step towards her to regain her attention, but forced himself to keep still, giving her space he could feel she needed.

"No. None. It was warm, quiet. The people respect me." She was quick to duck out of sight, back into the other room.

He wasn't the only terrible liar in the building.

He mulled over what she had said, and how she had looked.

She had picked somewhere warm where people respected her.

She didn't feel respected in chilly Russia?

He took in his surroundings. This island home in the Aegean had to be the complete opposite of where she had grown up. All the covens he had come across had lived together in a building big enough to accommodate them all. The last coven he had crossed paths with had owned an enormous estate in

England with acres of land and several large buildings on the land, including a palatial main house.

He imagined Cass's coven lived in a large compound complete with a mansion too.

So why had she traded a life there for a life of quiet?

And respect.

His gut squirmed in response to that word, one he could hardly apply to his actions around her. Neither he nor his brothers had shown her respect. They had all treated her with distrust and tried to keep her out of their business.

Maybe he needed to be the one to change that.

Because deep down, he did respect her. He saw her value, what an asset she was for his side, and that in the battle ahead, she could be the key to them winning.

He would make her see that he believed in her.

He blew out his breath.

He just wasn't sure where the hell to begin.

He looked out of the door, struck by the beauty of the place Cass called home. Endless blue water. Dusty hills. White houses that seemed to reflect what light there was, making the place seem even brighter. The warm air was dry, not moist as it was in Hong Kong, and the fresh breeze carried the scent of the sea.

Everything about this place felt so tranquil.

He could picture himself here, whiling away his days, eating well and living off the small patch of land Cass owned. He imagined her garden had been lush before, well-tended.

He drifted towards the other window to his right, wanting to see the view in that direction. When he'd had his fill of the beautiful coastline and the itch to check on Cass had grown too fierce to ignore, he turned back towards the main door and his gaze caught on a letter on her desk.

On a word that leaped out at him and had him frowning as he leaned closer for a better look.

Offspring?

He scanned the letter and then read it again, a weight settling in his gut as he tried to make sense of it. His thoughts spun as he kept reading it over and over, only a few things sticking in his mind.

It was from her coven. It was the last time they would ask her to return home. There was a man awaiting her arrival.

She would bear a child as expected of her.

It was dated four days ago.

He swallowed the lump in his throat and braced one hand against the desk, supporting his weight. He reached for the letter and stopped, his hand hovering barely an inch from it as he battled the urge to screw it up and toss it away, as if that would make a difference.

Cass was promised to another.

He had come here fearing she had a man, and she did, one who was waiting for her, expecting her to bear him a child for her coven.

"Ready." Cass's voice had him jerking upright and spinning away from the desk, his heart rushing in his ears as his gaze settled on her.

She sauntered towards him, her hips swaying enticingly, a slight smile curling her rosy lips.

Flirting with him again.

All his feelings, his frustration and anger, must have been painted across his face because she drew up short and her ice-blue eyes warmed with what looked a hell of a lot like concern.

"What's wrong?" She lowered the black bag she had packed to her side and canted her head, leaning towards him.

"Nothing," he snapped. "I'm bored of waiting for you. I'm leaving now… with or without you."

She frowned at him. Stared into his eyes for so long that he feared she would be able to read why he was upset with her, even when he wasn't really sure himself. He had told her that he didn't have a heart to give her, and she had told him that she didn't want it anyway. Everything that had happened between them had been nothing more than harmless flirting.

So why the hell did he feel as if she had just ripped out his heart and squeezed it until it shattered?

"I'm leaving." He turned away from her and came face-to-face with the cat.

The ginger and white tom glared at him and then sauntered past him with his head and tail held high, heading for Cass.

"Oh, Milos. I'll have to come back to feed him now the nearby summer residents have gone home to the mainland." She began to bend to pet the cat.

"Not going to happen." Daimon bit those words out from between clenched teeth, wrestling with his feelings, fighting to find some balance again. "You'll have to ask a neighbour."

She straightened and scowled at him. "I just said they've all gone away. This cat is my responsibility and he's been with me a long time. I won't leave him behind like that. I won't abandon him."

Abandon.

That word stuck in his mind.

He could see in her eyes that she meant what she had said. If she wouldn't abandon an animal, she definitely wouldn't abandon the man who was waiting for her.

She had only been flirting with him.

He hammered that into his head, over and over again when it refused to stick. None of it had been real. She had been teasing him, tempting him, probably finding it amusing. She knew about his problem. Had it given her pleasure when she had found a way to circumvent his ice and she had touched him, making him believe something impossible?

That he didn't have to be alone anymore.

"I'm leaving." He closed his eyes and turned away from her.

"Daimon." She grabbed his arm, sending a hot shiver rolling up it. "What's wrong? Don't tell me nothing. Something is wrong."

He opened his eyes and looked across at her, thought of a thousand things he wanted to say.

He had foolishly thought she had really liked him.

He had foolishly allowed himself to feel something for the first time in centuries.

He had foolishly admitted the truth to himself—that while he had loved Penelope, it hadn't been true love, the sort that would have lasted forever.

He had grown to love her and then he had lost her, and he had mourned her but part of him knew he had mourned what had been taken from him more than he had grieved her.

He had foolishly admitted that the loyalty he felt towards Penelope had been forged as a shield to protect him from the loneliness he had endured for centuries, giving him a reason to not look at other females, a reason not to feel cold and forsaken whenever he was around his brothers and their women.

In the end, only one word rose to the tip of his tongue, the rest of them held back by fear, by pain that had grown since meeting Cassandra, agony that ripped at him every moment he was near her.

"Nothing."

She bit out a curse in Russian, picked up her cat and cuddled the wretched thing. All the while, Milos glared at him. Daimon glared right back. He knew he was being a dick. He didn't need the small god pointing it out to him. He was sure Milos had been a dick himself more than once in his life, had probably been a bastard to Cass countless times since she had found him.

"He's coming with us then." She tipped her chin up, her sparkling blue eyes daring him to say a word against it.

"Fine. Whatever." Daimon took hold of her bare arm and stilled as that heat rolled through him again, marvelling over the fact he could touch her and she wasn't in pain, wasn't in any danger.

He brushed his thumb over her skin, wanting to feel it without his gloves, flesh-to-flesh, as he had in the bath.

He shut down that need. She couldn't be his. She already had someone waiting for her.

"Daimon," she whispered, pressing closer to him, until the heat of her body soaked into his clothes and ignited a need to tug her closer still, so they were pressed together, not a molecule of air between them.

He stepped instead, embracing the cold darkness, letting it wash over him to give him strength.

Milos hissed and growled throughout the teleport, and continued as they landed in the middle of the main room of the mansion.

Cass struggled with the cat, gently chastising it.

Increasing that feeling Daimon had, the one that said she didn't know the truth about cats.

"Neko!" Aiko leaped onto her feet from the couches in front of him and hurried over to Cass, her dark eyes bright for the first time since Esher had disappeared. "Kawaii!"

She drew that word out as she melted over the raggedy cat who was in no way worthy of being called cute. Milos went still in Cass's arms, purring now and evidently enjoying the sudden attention.

"What is its name?" Aiko didn't take her eyes off the animal.

"Mister Milos," Cass offered.

"Ah, Milos-chan. You are so cute." Aiko went to touch him and then hesitated, her dark eyes lifting to Cass. "Can I?"

"Of course." Cass smiled, the first one she had given to Aiko, and it was strange but nice to see her more relaxed around her.

Daimon wanted to warn Aiko that Milos was one cranky son of a bitch, but she touched the beast before he could. The cat was all sweetness with her, rubbing her hand and purring deeply.

Aiko smiled properly for the first time in too long, her eyes lighting up as she petted the cat, who greedily devoured the love she poured onto him.

He watched her as Cass let her take Milos into her arms, as she carried him like a baby to the couches and petted him, a smile constantly etched on her face. He hadn't been able to make her feel better, no matter how hard he had tried, and gods, that made him feel like a complete failure. He had wanted to make her smile like this, lifting her spirits.

Cass's gaze lingered on his face.

"Don't feel bad. You're a bit too frosty for Aiko to pet and petting cats makes a lot of people feel better about things." She walked away before he could glare at her and whispered words trailed in her wake. "But I'd rather pet you."

Daimon turned slightly, looking over his shoulder at her back as she walked away from him, an ache building inside him, a consuming need to go after her so she could do just that. He fought it, waging war against the urges she stirred in him, the attraction that blazed between them, but he wasn't strong enough to deny those things, even when they only caused him pain worse than anything he had felt before.

He wanted her.

He could touch her.

Yet he still couldn't have her.

The ground shook and the air trembled.

Daimon's senses lit up.

Daemons.

CHAPTER 11

Cass had barely had a chance to set her bag down in her quarters when the ground shook and the air trembled, and then went eerily still.

Voices broke the dreadful silence, Daimon and Cal.

Had something happened?

Her eyes widened as she sensed it.

Power. Familiar power.

The Erinyes.

She rushed from her room, bare feet loud on the wooden slats of the covered walkway, and didn't stop until she had reached the main room of the house.

"What was that?" She did her best not to sound as out of breath as she was, the combination of running and adrenaline enough to have her panting for air.

Daimon didn't take his eyes off the front door of the mansion. "They can't breach the wards. They'll keep bouncing them back."

"I'll believe that when I see it." She stretched her arms out for balance as another miniature earthquake hit and was gone in a flash.

She hurried to Aiko and Marinda. Megan got up from the couch, her hands lowering to cover her baby bump, rubbing it through her loose mulberry jumper. Her chocolate eyes sparkled with worry as she looked at Cass, her brow furrowed. Cass presumed Ares had dropped her off for some time with the girls, something he often did.

As gruff as the god of fire could be, Cass shared Megan's wish that he was here.

Three gods protecting the mansion seemed better than two.

"Someone care to send a message?" she said and Cal gave her a black look. She shrugged it off. "I'm not saying you two strapping gods can't handle this alone, but I would rather have six strapping gods standing between us and whatever is on the other side of this barrier. You have a pregnant woman here."

Daimon looked back at her, a scowl darkening his features, darkness reigning in his eyes.

Darkness that had nothing to do with the fact she had questioned their strength and prowess, or the mention of Megan.

It looked a lot like jealousy.

Because she would rather have six gods fighting at her side?

Her eyes widened slightly, enough that he noticed and turned away from her.

Because she had referred to his brothers as strapping.

It was all right for her to call him strapping, but gods forbid she speak well of his brothers.

Cass checked on the ladies when another tremor rocked the building and the power she could sense in the air grew stronger. Aiko frantically petted Mister Milos, who was still purring happily, as if nothing out of the ordinary was happening. Mari had closed ranks with Megan, her eyes verging on violet as she stared ahead of her at the door. Megan was rubbing her belly with one hand, worry scored on her face, and in her other was a mobile phone.

Her thumb shook as she tapped the on-screen keyboard.

A relieved breath escaped her as she sent the message.

"It'll be fine," Cal said, far too much confidence in his tone. He wasn't sure either. "They're just trying to frighten us."

"Might I remind everyone that frightening a pregnant woman is a bad thing?" Cass checked on Megan again.

She was breathing faster now, holding her stomach.

When she noticed Cass looking at her, she forced a wobbly smile. "I'm peachy."

She wasn't. She was as far from peachy as she could get. She was petrified.

Something big hit the barrier and everyone fought for balance, Mari clutching Megan and keeping her upright. Cass refused to be rattled by it.

She gathered her strength.

Just in case.

These daemons and goddesses didn't frighten her.

Daimon muttered a black curse, drawing her gaze to him. She knew the look on his face, could read it like a book as he glanced at Cal. Things didn't look good.

"Stay inside." He turned to her and the other women as he motioned for Cal to move forwards.

Cass snorted at that.

"Stay inside? I don't think so. I'm not some cowering, weak female." She looked over at Mari. "Stay inside with the others."

Mari levelled a glare on her. "I don't think so. I'm not some cowering—"

"Someone has to protect the others." Cass cut her off, because she didn't have time for this.

The sensation of power in the air was growing stronger.

Or the barrier around the building was growing weaker.

Which didn't bear thinking about.

Daimon stopped at the door and looked over his shoulder, his expression warning her that he was going to argue against her.

His gaze caught on Megan and he paled, phenomenal pain darkening his eyes, deeper than anything she had seen in them before.

"Cass," he said, her name like ambrosia as it rolled off his tongue, flooding her with strength and heat. "Muster the best protective spell you can manage… because one of the wards just went down."

Ice cascaded down her spine.

She began an incantation in her mind, one that would drain her, but might be their best shot at keeping everyone safe, and followed Daimon as he opened the front door and stepped out onto the porch, Cal trailing behind him.

Cass built the spell, weaving together several different ones, a slave to her need to protect not only the women sheltering behind her.

She wanted to protect the god striding ahead of her too, his shoulders back and head tipped up, ice glittering on his black gloves as he curled his fingers into fists.

Cass closed her eyes, centred herself and raised her hands as she uttered the words to cast the spell, the strongest barrier she had ever created. She felt it as it launched into the air, as it hit a point forty feet above her and swept downwards in all directions to form a dome over the house and the grounds, expelling anyone she viewed as a threat, knocking them backwards.

Her legs turned to jelly beneath her, but she kept her focus on the barrier, poured more strength into it until she was on the verge of collapse.

The daemons battered it, pressing against it and slashing at the invisible wall, rolling up on it in waves.

She opened her eyes and pressed her hands forwards, weathering the blows and shoring up the barrier where it began to weaken. Another wave came at it. Followed by another.

Each of them a coordinated attack.

As if they were testing it.

Testing her.

That feeling only grew when violet-black smoke billowed above the white rendered wall of the mansion grounds, as dark as the ribbed tiles that topped it, and the daemons suddenly disappeared.

Two female voices trailed into nothing.

"She is stronger than the others."

"She will give us what we need."

A shiver tripped down Cass's back and arms, spreading over her thighs as words whispered in the wind.

"She will be pleased to hear that."

CHAPTER 12

Marinda helped Cass into the house, bearing her weight as the witch fumbled each step, her eyes fixed on the ground in a distant stare.

Daimon trailed after her, obeying the deep need to be close to her, still shaken by the fact she had collapsed and what he had heard.

She was too pale as Marinda helped her down onto one of the couches, close to Megan.

Ares appeared, the haste of his teleport and how swiftly he turned disturbing the black ribbons of smoke that tried to cling to him. His fiery gaze scanned the room and the moment he spotted Megan, he was moving, closing the distance between them and sinking to his knees beside her.

"You okay, sweetheart?" He stroked her cheek as he gazed up at her, his hand trembling, worry written across every line of his face.

She nodded. "Cass kept us safe."

Ares looked at her, gratitude shining in his eyes before he even said, "Thank you."

Cass managed a nod and then went back to struggling for air. Daimon stood near the door of the house as the rest of his brothers appeared, staring at her and unsure what to do, torn between going to her and remaining where he was. He wasn't sure she would appreciate him coddling her in the way Ares fussed over Megan. She was strong, and had reacted badly when he had questioned that strength before.

Voices filled the tense silence as Cal filled Marek, Valen and Keras, and Caterina and Eva in on what had happened.

Daimon was glad his brothers had all brought their women to the mansion. He had the feeling it was better they remained here, where they had a better shot at protecting them all. In fact, he was going to propose that everyone move back into the mansion, something that probably wouldn't go down well with some of his brothers.

Cass finally lifted her head and her weary eyes settled on him.

He lifted his hand, stopped himself and lowered it again. Whatever look was on his face, whatever feelings she was reading in him, ones he couldn't hold back right now or cover up, it drew a shaky smile from her.

He stared into her eyes, the foolish part of him hoping that she could see that he would do all in his power to protect her, even though she couldn't be his, was destined for another.

"I don't think I'm the first witch they've targeted." She sounded as tired as she looked, her voice weak, tearing at him, increasing the need to go to her and tend to her, even when he wasn't sure what he could do.

"I don't think so either." He hated the way she looked down at her knees as he said that, how worry creased her brow and she picked at her dress, looking small and vulnerable.

Darkness rose within him, a snarling and twisted thing that demanded he protect her.

Roared at him to hunt those who were a threat to her before they could get near her again.

Ares slowly stood. "How the hell did they breach a ward on the mansion?"

His older brother stroked Megan's hair, a constant motion, as if he needed to feel her beneath his fingers to make himself believe that she was safe, there with him.

Daimon could understand why Ares was shaken. The mansion was the one place that should be safe, impenetrable.

Valen and Cal shrugged at the same time. Sometimes, the similarities between them were frightening. Same athletic build. Same moody personality. Same recklessness. The only thing that had made them stand apart once was the colour of their eyes. Even their hair had been the same golden colour until Eva had decided to dye Valen's a neon shade of violet.

Marek was too quiet, and Daimon wasn't the only one who noticed it.

Keras twisted the silver band on his thumb around it as his green gaze settled on their brother.

Marek must have felt the weight of expectation on his shoulders, because he looked at Daimon and then Keras, and said, "The wraith."

"What about that bastard?" Daimon snarled, the darkness getting the better of him as it conjured images of Esher in the Underworld, hunting that daemon.

"Eli stabbed me with his blade. He must have taken my memories as he did with Esher." Marek looked at Keras, his dark eyebrows furrowing slightly above his earthy eyes as he shoved his hand through the wavy lengths of his short hair, pushing it back. "It was after we changed the wards after Eli penetrated them to save Lisabeta... When we all picked a ward and kept it secret."

"Where did you place your ward?" Keras's deep voice was calm, but held a note of concern that echoed in his eyes.

"The maple in the south-east corner."

Keras looked to Daimon.

Daimon nodded. "That was the one that went down."

"I can pick another ward," Marek said.

Keras shook his head and worried his lower lip with the pad of his thumb as his black eyebrows drew down, his green eyes falling to rest on the golden mats beneath his feet. Something was troubling his brother, and he wasn't the only one who could see it. Ares watched Keras closely, the concern that filled his eyes growing.

"I will send a Messenger to Father to ask for a new one." Keras spoke those words slowly, and something dawned on Daimon.

He was worried about admitting to their father that they had messed something else up, and Daimon couldn't blame him. As the oldest brother, Keras had taken on the role of leader of their small force, and with that role came the responsibility for everything that went wrong as well as right.

Hades didn't look favourably upon failure.

He had drummed that into all of them from an early age.

Marek looked at everyone in turn, and Daimon couldn't recall the last time his older brother had looked as if he felt he had fucked up.

"Don't sweat it." Ares's deep voice rolled over the room like a calming tide and seemed to set Marek at ease. "Nothing bad happened and it wasn't your fault. There's nothing you could have done about it."

Keras continued to stare at the mats.

"We could have changed the ward sooner," Marek put in.

Keras finally lifted his head, settling his gaze on Marek. "We could have, but none of us thought to do it. This is on all of us."

But Keras would be the one to take the full force of their father's disappointment and anger.

Marek looked as if he wanted to say something, but Ares shook his head, and Marek's face crumpled. Ares was right. Offering to be the one to tell their father about this wouldn't change the outcome. As far as their father was concerned, Keras was responsible for what happened, and he would lay the blame squarely on his shoulders and his shoulders alone.

The air in the room turned gloomy, oppressively silent.

Daimon looked at Cass and Megan, and then back at his brothers. "I think everyone should move into the mansion."

That didn't meet with the resistance he had expected.

Everyone nodded.

Well, everyone except Keras.

"We can layer in new wards, enough to keep the daemons out." Cal glanced at Keras, who dipped his head this time.

"I will ask for several." Keras's green gaze slid to his left to land on Cass, who was still too pale for Daimon's liking. "You cast a barrier around this place?"

She shifted to face him and nodded, plastered on a façade that couldn't hide her true feelings from Daimon. She was worried. He was worried too. He didn't want the enemy near her, and the thought that they were after her had him on the verge of losing himself to the darker side of his blood, the protective and possessive side that had come from his father.

"What other magic can you do?" Keras said.

Cass stood, waving away Marinda when she tried to help her, and walked on what she probably thought were steady legs towards his brother. In Daimon's eyes, she looked ready to collapse again, stoking that need to go to her, to make her take his support and not let her push him away as she had with Marinda.

Now wasn't the time to be prideful.

She had taken a hit, was shaken by it, and that was fine. It was okay to be weak sometimes. It didn't mean she wasn't strong. No one here would question her strength or think less of her if she let her true feelings show, revealing how badly this had shaken her.

"Offensive magic, defensive too, like the barrier." She sounded distant, as if she wasn't quite there in the room with them.

Daimon took a step towards her, driven by a need to be close to her, and she looked across at him. "Is there any other magic you can do, anything not classified as offensive or defensive?"

Her black eyebrows rose, her gaze unfocused as she looked right through him, a thoughtful edge to her expression.

"You healed Mari." Cal rubbed Marinda's arm through her dark orange sweater. "Maybe they want you for that."

Cass tensed.

It was the smallest tightening of her shoulders, but Daimon noticed it.

"Whatever you just thought, spit it out," Daimon said as he took a step towards her.

Her blue eyes shifted to his and she looked as if she wanted to tell him 'no', but then she sighed and her shoulders relaxed. "There is magic I researched, but I've never performed it before. It's forbidden. No witch has used such spells in centuries."

"What spells?" He didn't like the feeling of dread that settled in his chest.

She cast a glance around them all, gauging their reactions. "Necromancy."

Shock crossed his brothers' faces in a wave.

Cass quickly raised her hands, her palms facing him. "I never attempted it. I only know the theory. What others have done. I've only read notes and reports from other witches, centuries-old accounts that are probably more fiction than fact."

Cal took a hard step towards her, a storm building in his eyes, the tips of his blond ponytail catching a breeze as he stared at Cass. "Do you think you could restore a soul into a body?"

Cass's gaze shifted to Cal and her black eyebrows furrowed, the flicker of emotion in her eyes revealing that she knew the path of Cal's thoughts just as Daimon did. "Maybe... but I wouldn't do it. I'm sorry, Calistos. It's too risky. The chances of that soul coming back... wrong... are too high."

Keras reached out and laid a hand on Cal's shoulder. "We will find Calindria's soul and find a way to guide it to the Elysian Fields. That will be enough for her. She will be happy."

Cal turned on him, his face darkening as the breeze that swirled through the room gained strength. "But if we could bring her back—"

"No." Ares cut him off, his voice a deep growl, harder than Daimon had heard it in a long time. "Tampering with her like that... Cass is right. What if something went wrong, Cal?"

Their youngest brother blanched as the wind suddenly dropped, swallowed hard and looked at them all, his eyebrows furrowed, desperation written in every line of his face. "But..."

He didn't seem able to finish that sentence.

He just stood there, looking between them all, a storm raging in his eyes that slowly abated, leaving his irises blue again.

He lowered his head and looked down at his feet. "I'm sorry."

"There's nothing to apologise for." Keras touched his shoulder again, gripping it gently as he closed the distance between them. "We all want to see her again."

Cal nodded. So did everyone else.

Daimon looked at Cass, studying her, trying to piece together what the enemy wanted with her magic. "So the enemy wants a new necromancer. It's a good enough theory. The gates are closed to all traffic. The only ones who could perform such a role for our enemy now is a necromancer who happened to be in this world, which would be extremely rare and hard to find, or a witch. But what do they want with one? They want someone to raise the dead?"

Cass's eyes slowly widened, a horrified edge filling them as she shook her head, causing her long wavy black hair to brush her bare shoulders. "Not raise the dead. Raise *their* dead. Necromancy... The magical form of it could hypothetically place the souls the enemy holds in their possession into new physical bodies. It could restore them completely. The necromancer used the souls he held as puppets, but with magic... they might be able to restore them to how they had been... independent beings under their own control."

Marek folded his arms across his chest, his dark linen shirt tightening over his muscles. "That would be bad."

Everyone murmured in agreement.

They had been dealing blows to the enemy, weakening them. The last thing they needed was the enemy raising their dead, strengthening their side again.

"We'll keep Cass out of the enemy's hands." Daimon schooled his features, hiding the dark need to protect her that filled him, but knew he had failed to conceal it when Cass's beautiful face softened, her eyes warming as she stared into his.

Keras turned to Cass. "Will you be all right?"

She looked at his brother and wearily nodded.

Daimon barely bit back the growl that rolled up his throat, his darker side pushing to the fore as he levelled a glare on his brother. He should have been the one to ask her that question. Instead, he had hidden his worry for her behind a veil, giving another male a chance to be the one who showed concern for her well-being.

He thought about the letter, about what he had read in it. She was promised to another. What point was there in showing her that he cared about her? He couldn't afford to grow closer to her if she was only going to end up leaving him for another man. He wasn't sure he would survive such a blow.

"I'm concerned about the enemy. What they said." She sighed. "They've been testing other witches and it felt as if they were testing me. Those daemons hit the barrier in waves, as if they had wanted to see how much damage it could take before it would fall."

"I think it was just a test to see how powerful your magic was, not how much damage a barrier cast by you could take before it failed." Daimon shoved his hands into his pockets and took hold of his phone, found the pendant attached to it and held it.

It was better he kept his distance from Cass, endeavoured to keep things between them as they were, not letting his feelings grow into anything more. He would remain loyal to Penelope. He owed her that much, didn't he?

Or was he just using her memory to keep his heart closed, to protect himself from more pain?

Ares cast a worried glance down at Megan. "I think I should take you to the Underworld."

Megan turned on him, planting her hands on her hips at the same time. "No. You need me here. I'm not going to the Underworld. I won't be separated from you. Not right now. Not ever."

Her hands shifted to her baby bump and she clutched it through her jumper, shaking her head.

"I won't go." Her voice hitched. "I need to be here."

"It's okay, sweetheart. It's okay." Ares stretched his hands out to her and she backed off a step, shaking her head more frantically.

"Maybe we shouldn't have gone through with it." Her voice tightened with each word and Daimon could sense her mounting panic.

Ares's face crumpled and he took hold of her arm, gently pulled her to him and settled his left arm around her trembling shoulders as he placed his right hand on her belly. He rubbed it gently between her hands.

"Don't talk like that, baby. This is a blessing. Nothing will happen to the baby. Nothing will happen to you. I swear it. I love you both." He dropped a kiss on her forehead.

"I'm fat," Megan muttered, the panic Daimon could feel in her washing away as she sagged against Ares.

Ares smiled softly, his eyes warmed by love. "You've never been so sexy. You're beautiful."

Daimon looked away, unable to bear it. He felt Cass's eyes on him, but refused to look at her, kept his head down so he didn't have to see anyone. He couldn't bring himself to look at them, not when the rage he had been holding on to for centuries still wanted an outlet.

Not when it hurt so much he couldn't breathe.

A single fear consumed him, tearing down his walls, ripping him to pieces and stoking the rage.

That his brother was going to suffer the same painful fate as he had.

CHAPTER 13

Enyo didn't take her eyes off the sun-kissed terracotta roofs of the white city that sprawled below her on the side of Mount Olympus as her brother swept into the room, the gentle patter of feet that accompanied the heavier thuds of his boots telling her that his usual entourage was with him. Ares didn't go anywhere without at least four attendants, all of them female.

They prattled on as they hurried after him, taking two strides for each one of his as he briskly walked across the colourful mosaic floor of the main room of their house.

She frowned at the world beyond the window.

His house.

The fact the mosaic featured only him amidst the glory of an ancient battle, a war in which she had fought beside him together with Eris and her siblings, would have made it clear he viewed the palatial white marble building where she lived as *his* home even if he hadn't told her that a million times to her face.

Women and men dressed in fine clothing drifted along the cobbled street far below the promontory of pale rock upon which Ares's grand temple and home stood. A trio of females dressed in elegant pale blue, soft pink and lilac dresses halted beneath one of the towering cypress trees that lined the broad road and glanced up, their gazes lingering as they bent their heads towards each other.

No doubt speaking about the man of the house.

The scent of ambrosia permeated the air as she heard the slosh of liquid behind her. Ares grunted and slammed a hand against the furniture, most likely the finely crafted wooden sideboard that acted as his bar.

"This batch is good." He refilled his goblet as she turned her side to the window, adjusting her position on the elegant blue velvet chaise longue that was her favourite perch.

He strode into view.

Sunlight streamed in through the window where she sat, bathing his tanned skin as he came to a halt in front of her. The warm rays glinted off the gold plates of his greaves and vambraces, and the pointed slats that hung from his thick gold belt. The white leather those slats were mounted on and the pale blue cloth that hung beneath them to hide his upper thighs and give him a modicum of dignity were both splattered with crimson.

Her brother had been brawling again.

She idly toyed with the three braids on the left side of her long black hair, pretending she hadn't noticed that he had been off getting into fights and whoring himself while she had been left to do the work at the temple.

Greeting and tending to pilgrims who had come to see him, and who were inevitably disappointed to be seen by her instead.

The twittering group of 'aides' that constantly followed him lingered just beyond him, watching him closely. She didn't recognise some of their faces. Her brother had an appetite for war and for sex, and the whole of Olympus knew that securing a position within his circle of attendants was a sure-fire way of getting bedded by him. She swore he went through a new set of aides every week, discarding and replacing them when he grew bored of what they had to offer.

Sometimes, she was sure her brother didn't have a heart to give, or perhaps he had already given it to himself.

The golden-haired male grinned at her, his blue eyes brightening with it.

She waited, because he obviously had something he wanted to tell her and he wanted her to ask him about it—playing the doting sister—and she wasn't really in the mood today.

When she said nothing, he shoved his gold goblet at one of the females and unlatched his rich blue cloak. It dropped to the mosaic floor and another attendant was swift to stoop and gather it into her arms before backing away from him.

Ares grumbled as he unfastened the leather straps of his golden chest piece, removed it and inspected a dent in the moulded metal that had been crafted to mimic his body. A body he now proudly displayed as he turned to his aides, causing a wave of blushing and heated glances at his muscular torso.

"Take this to the blacksmith. I want it repaired immediately." His deep voice rolled through the room with authority as he held his breastplate out with one hand and snatched his goblet back with the other. "Leave us."

All four females immediately obeyed.

Ares lapped it up, his twisted smirk telling her how much he enjoyed having the females do his bidding without question, leaping to execute whatever order he gave them.

When his blue gaze shifted back to her, that satisfied edge melted into something akin to disappointment.

Because as the centuries they had lived together progressed, his dominating nature had begun to chafe and she had begun to defy him?

"You do not ask me for news from Olympus. It is not like you to not want to know the rumours spreading through the city." Ares quaffed his ambrosia, a twinkle entering his eyes as he studied her over the rim of the goblet. "You seem out of spirits since that last war in the mortal realm ended."

"Not at all." Enyo smoothed her black skirt down as she shifted her legs over the side of her seat and sat up. "It is a little too warm for my tastes today and I am tired."

Unlike her brother, she didn't feel the need to wear her full armour when in Olympus. Her black leather and silver breastplate and matching boots were enough protection for her.

She glanced back over her shoulder.

It wasn't as if anyone would dare attack her in Ares's home after all.

She couldn't remember the last time he had allowed her to venture into the city without him plastered to her side, there to take whatever gratitude was offered to them for their assistance in wars and disputes, stealing every drop of it for himself.

"Hermes has been getting into trouble again." Ares sank into a throne-like armchair on the other side of the low wooden table to her and swirled his ambrosia, a thoughtful look on his handsome face as he pursed his lips. "Morpheus has been off causing trouble in dreams again. Predatory bastard. Apparently this time, he targeted many Nereids."

Enyo wanted to snort at that. Her brother had the gall to call Morpheus predatory because he had been inserting himself into the dreams of the sea nymphs? Ares had tried to insert himself into their lives countless times, had stalked the most beautiful of them and had managed to convince many of them to open their thighs to him.

"And the Underworld is in an uproar of course."

Enyo jerked to attention, her jade eyes fixing on her brother.

The glint in his blue eyes told her that he had known she would react to the mention of that realm, and that he was going to torment her by drawing out this news because she wanted to hear it.

"Ares," she whispered, imploring him, not above begging him now. Her heart drummed a sickening rhythm against her breast and she fought to calm it, aware that if Ares noticed the urgent tick of her pulse that he would only make this more agonising for her. "What news comes from the Underworld?"

Ares hiked his bare shoulders and crossed his legs as he eased back in his chair.

Her lips compressed, anger spiking in her blood and igniting a hunger to leap at him and force him to answer her.

His wicked smile said he had sensed that in her too.

Before she could warn him not to torment her, he spoke.

"The third-born of Hades has re-entered the realm, apparently in pursuit of a daemon. Hades has his legions hunting for the male."

Esher.

Esher had once again ignored the terms of his banishment, but this time to hunt down a daemon. One of their enemy?

It worried her.

She knew Hades.

She knew the weight of what Esher had done, along with everything else, rested firmly upon Keras's shoulders. She couldn't imagine the pressure he was under now.

Her dark eyebrows furrowed as she thought about him, about how Hades would expect him to take full responsibility for whatever mayhem Esher caused in the Underworld, and for any harm the daemon caused in that realm too.

The pressing need she had been fighting for the last few months returned, stronger than ever, pushing her to do something.

To help Keras.

"A daemon has breached the gates. That is war, brother, and—" She cut herself off when Ares narrowed bright blue eyes on her.

"Our hands are bound, I'm afraid." He twirled the goblet in his right hand, his face a calm mask, not a single trace of concern touching it. "Hades made it very clear that we are not to interfere. This war has nothing to do with Olympians like us."

She bit her tongue, hating the way he drew that line between her and Keras. He had never liked her friendship with the firstborn of Hades and Persephone, and he had done everything in his power to force them apart.

And she hated him for it.

Just as she despised herself for letting him succeed.

She should have been stronger. She should have stood up for herself and what she wanted.

She twisted away from him and stared out of the window, desperate to occupy her mind with something else, anything else to stop her from saying something to her brother. Speaking her mind when she was pushed to her limit like this was never wise.

She had done it once, and only once.

Because Ares had locked her in the pitch-black basement of the house for a full lunar cycle and forbidden anyone to go to her, not even to give her food or water.

He had gone to war and when he had returned, she had been starving, out of her mind and weak with hunger. Even immortals like her could starve given enough time. She had been so desperate for food when Ares had unlocked the door that she had promised she would never speak out of turn to him again.

He had patted her head and told her that he would hold her to it, and if she broke her promise, he would destroy what she held most dear.

His cold smile had told her that he knew what that was.

Keras.

"You are quiet," Ares said and pushed onto his feet, the metal of his boots clunking against the tiles as he crossed the room. More ambrosia flowed into his goblet.

Gods, she would kill for a cup to quieten her nerves.

She was trying to wean herself off it again though.

"We are gods of war, brother," she murmured, watching two red birds as they flitted over the terracotta rooftops of the sprawl of buildings below her, moving from one tree-shaded courtyard to the next. They joined a flock in one garden and danced in the hot still air, some of them landing on the white statues that stood at the marble edges of many of the rooftops. Lucky carefree birds, able to come and go as they pleased. Free to do as they wished. She watched them from her gilded cage, a pang of envy lancing her heart. "Should we not be a part of this battle?"

He huffed, but his voice was level and calm, as close to tender as he ever got, when he replied, "We are gathering information to give to Hades, and therefore his sons. That is enough."

It wasn't enough for her.

She twisted onto her feet and swept her onyx hair back from her face, battling a fierce wave of nerves.

"You seem restless, sister." Ares planted his backside against the wooden sideboard and crossed his legs at his ankles, his gaze narrowing on her as he studied her closely.

"I think I have stayed inside too long today. I need some air." She smiled and crushed her nerves, aware he would sense them if she allowed them to keep running rampant. He would know what she was going to do.

As it was, his eyes narrowed further, drilling into her. "I hope you do not intend to leave Olympus."

She was quick to shake her head, keeping her features schooled as she said, "Not at all. I was going to take a turn in the garden. The lilacs are blooming and you know how much I love them."

Suspicion glimmered in his blue irises.

She canted her head. "Besides, I believe I hear your aides returning, and I am sure you have many other tasks you wish to discuss with them."

The twist of his lips and the banked heat that shimmered in his gaze said that he did.

He waved her away. "No further than the garden."

She dipped her head and swept away from him, past the four females as they bustled into the room, not drawing a single breath until she cleared the tall white columns that supported the roof and broke out onto the grand terrace that overlooked the southern slope of the mountain, a view that stretched all the way to the glittering azure sea.

She paused and focused behind her on Ares, reassuring herself that he was suitably occupied before she hurried to her right. She crossed the patio, dipping her head to the two guards who stood to attention, and reached the olive trees that formed a lush wall between the terrace and the garden.

Enyo followed her favourite path deep into the garden, to a smaller terrace with a pergola covered in lilac blooms. She stopped at the ornate marble balustrade and pressed her palms against it as she stared into the distance, west towards the point near the shore where the gate between Olympus and the Underworld stood.

A gate she had used countless times over the centuries.

A gate she hadn't passed through for two hundred years.

She ached for those halcyon days, wished with all her heart that she could bring them back again, even when she knew that was impossible. Everything had changed two hundred years ago, and there was no way to put things back to how they had been.

But she could patch them up, and hopefully it would be enough to set her back on the path she had wanted to take in her life.

She focused and teleported, disappearing in a swirl of white-blue smoke.

Slammed into something solid as she reappeared and sent it toppling forwards.

"Godsdammit," Marek snarled and jerked his left shoulder backwards, dislodging her. He pivoted to face her, his handsome face etched with darkness that reigned in his earthy eyes too. When he saw it was her, he huffed and shoved his unruly brown hair out of his face. "I really don't need this."

Enyo scowled at him. She hadn't failed to notice that over the last few months, Marek had become increasingly less respectful towards her.

She opened her mouth to pick him up on it and warn him to show her more respect, as she normally did, but snapped it closed when Marek turned his back on her again and bent over.

And she noticed he was packing.

He carefully layered clothes into a suitcase on his double bed, along with some other personal items.

She backed up a step and looked around the spacious main living area of the Spanish villa. His books were gone from the coffee table and there was no sign of his female.

"You are leaving?" she said with a glance at him.

He shut the lid on the suitcase and zipped it closed. "Moving into Tokyo. It was Daimon's idea. Things are getting… It's better we're all in one place together."

Enyo didn't like the sound of that. "Esher has returned?"

Marek looked over his shoulder at her and slowly straightened, coming to face her. "No. You know about him?"

She nodded. "Brother told me."

Before he could ask her something else, such as requesting she leave him alone as he normally did, she continued.

"Ares tells me that we will not be allowed to participate in the coming war. Hades forbids it."

Marek's face darkened and he grunted, "Sounds like Father."

Enyo lifted her hand, stopped herself from reaching for Marek's arm and flexed her fingers.

"Is there nothing you can do…" She swallowed and steeled her nerves. "Keras can do… to change Hades's mind?"

Marek's rich brown eyes warmed. Because she had dared to speak of Keras for once rather than dancing around things? She was tired of trying to suppress her feelings, tired of letting her fear control her. She needed to know he was going to be all right.

Marek shrugged, shoved the suitcase aside and dragged an empty one across the bed to him. "I doubt it. You know our father. Hades is set in his ways and his word is absolute."

That worried her. If Keras couldn't convince Hades to allow Olympians to participate in the war, he would be at a disadvantage, and her brother would force her to remain on the sidelines, stopping her from helping him.

"How is… How does Keras fare?" She curled her fingers into fists at her sides, battling another bout of nerves as she stared at Marek's broad back, waiting for him to tell her to ask his brother herself.

"I think he's feeling the pressure now." Marek paused halfway through folding a shirt and set it down, concern shining in his eyes as he looked over his shoulder at her. "He's more distant than usual and he's decided to remain in Paris rather than come to Tokyo with the rest of us."

Fear arrowed through her.

He would be vulnerable alone.

"Ares—my brother Ares—he messaged to say he's trying to change Keras's mind but you know Keras." Marek smiled solemnly. "He's as stubborn as our father."

She knew that all too well. "Speak to him. Try to convince him that moving to Tokyo is the wise thing to do. He will listen to you if you all work together. I know it."

He sighed, a weary edge to it and his eyes as he scrubbed a hand over his hair. "I'll try. We'll try."

He frowned and looked down, reached into his trouser pocket and pulled out a device. The screen illuminated his face and then darkened, and he lifted his gaze to lock with hers.

"I have to go. Keras wants a meeting."

Enyo tensed, stopping herself as an urge to ask to go with him whipped through her.

"I'll speak to him," Marek said.

She dipped her head and forced herself to leave, before she did something foolish like teleporting to Tokyo. She landed back on the small terrace, the scent of lilac swirling around her in the warm breeze. Her heart remained heavy as she stared at the distant shimmering gate, and she told herself she was doing the right thing. Her brother would be furious with her if he found her missing.

Her brother was right too—this wasn't her fight. Joining the battle now would only result in her brother and Hades being furious with her.

She plucked a bloom from the ones that hung to her left, running down the column of the pergola to the wall. She lifted it to her nose as she thought about Keras, about how she had stood with him in this very spot once, seemingly a lifetime ago now.

It had been night, and the full moon had kissed the sea and the city, revealing all to her. The streets and houses had been dotted with the golden glow of torchlight, and the cool breeze had been heavy with the scent of flowers. Laughter had rung in the air, coming from all around her, loudest at her back where her brother had been hosting a grand party to celebrate Anthesteria, a festival focused on wine, and one which most of Olympus used as an excuse to get drunk for three days.

She had been taking a break from the merriment and had come to the secluded terrace, and Keras had joined her. She had lingered, enjoying his company, and he had spotted the first bloom of the lilac and plucked it for her. When he had tucked it behind her ear and told her the flower suited her, it had become her favourite.

They had spent the whole night talking, until the sun had broken the horizon and the sound of merriment had been replaced with snoring, among other wicked things, and she had grown tired.

She turned her back to the city and looked at the marble bench set in a leafy alcove opposite her.

The very same seat where she had fallen asleep with her head on Keras's shoulder, his rich masculine scent overshadowing the subtler fragrance of the flowers, sending her into dreams of him.

Dreams she had hoped would become reality.

Enyo closed her eyes and shut out the past, switching her focus back to the future because if she didn't do something, that dream she'd had would never become real.

Marek's words troubled her.

Was Keras trying to lure the enemy out by remaining in Paris, or perhaps goad them? He was strong, but he wasn't invulnerable. She had witnessed that plenty of times when they had sparred, or when he had fought in the festivities that often took place in the Underworld or Olympus, tests of strength in grand arenas.

It wasn't like him to be so reckless.

She opened her eyes and stared at the bench.

She had to do something. Her heart screamed that at her.

For the second time in her life, she was truly afraid.

Last time, she had feared she would never see Keras again.

Now she was afraid of facing him.

CHAPTER 14

Cass walked to the couch, waving away Mari as she hurried to help her. She wasn't an invalid. Her strength was already returning, steadily flowing back into her. She just needed a few moments off her feet.

Three of the brothers left, leaving Eva and Caterina, and Ares behind. Ares guided Megan to the couch and settled her beside Cass, a wealth of worry in his dark eyes as he looked her over.

Eva and Caterina fell into conversation in the middle of the room, drifting towards the dining table as they discussed the pros and cons of living in the Tokyo mansion with everyone else. The cons list was far longer than the pros.

Daimon remained where he was as Cal came to Mari, and they slumped onto the other couch together, facing the wall that separated the TV area from the corridor outside Cal's room.

Cass looked down at Megan's baby bump.

Tried to imagine herself pregnant.

She just couldn't picture it, even when she knew it would happen sooner rather than later. She wasn't really getting a choice about that. She had put things off for long enough and the coven was getting annoyed with her now. Her time was up.

Tradition was about to take the reins in her life and there wasn't anything she could do about it.

She still wasn't sure how she felt about it all—putting her life on hold for a year or more, bearing a child for the coven, leaving it there to be raised by them.

"What's it like?" Cass had avoided learning about pregnancy, had buried her head in the sand, some part of her believing it would never happen to her.

Her maternal instincts weren't exactly strong. Milos was her baby and she doted on him, and she loved Mari with all her heart and would do anything for her. Did that mean she would feel some degree of hurt when she gave up her child?

Megan settled her hands on her stomach as Ares kneeled before her, rubbing her thighs through her jeans. "I'm sick more than I'm not. I'm tired all the time. I get awful sleep. I have the weirdest cravings."

Ares grinned at Cass. "She really does."

Doting idiot.

He looked as if the entire world revolved around the woman before him.

"Can I… I mean… I know some women don't like it… but could I touch it?" Cass glanced at Daimon as she asked that. A mistake.

A thought pinged into her head.

Would he ever look at her the way Ares looked at Megan?

Did she want him to?

Her heart whispered the answer.

She did.

"Sure." Megan shifted her hands aside.

Cass gingerly placed her palm against the top of Megan's belly. Power curled through her, emanating not from Megan but from the baby growing inside her. She focused on it and a smile teased her lips against her will.

"She's strong," she whispered, glancing at Megan.

Who went awfully still.

Megan's chocolate eyes slowly widened and edged towards Ares. "She?"

Ares teared up like a fool. "A little girl."

Megan choked on what Cass hoped was a happy sob, covering her mouth with her hand.

"Oh gods, you didn't know," Cass blurted. Was it too late to backpedal and say she always referred to babies with the female pronoun?

Ares grinned.

Megan laughed, a little hysterically. "I told you there was more than one sex."

Ares ran a shaky hand over his overlong tawny hair, his smile fading. "Shit. A little girl."

He looked as if he didn't know whether to be deliriously happy or absolutely terrified.

Megan's face fell. "We'll keep her safe."

And it dawned on Cass.

Ares feared his daughter would suffer the same horrible fate that his sister had.

"She is strong." Cass palmed Megan's belly. "Very strong. Forged by flame like her father, but she will be kind-hearted like her mother."

Caterina and Eva joined the group, all smiles. Calistos moved in to crowd Megan with Mari, and Cass turned to look at Ares.

Her gaze caught on Daimon.

He still stood in the same place, his eyes holding that pain she hated seeing in them as he stared at Megan and Ares.

Why?

It wasn't because he couldn't touch someone the way Ares was touching Megan, because he could touch her if he would only allow himself that pleasure.

So what was holding him back? Why did he look so hurt as he watched her touching Megan's belly, when everyone else looked so ridiculously happy about the situation?

He turned his cheek to her and walked into the garden without a word.

Cass watched him go, the joy of the moment fading into concern that ate away at her, had her filling with a need to rise and follow him.

She pushed onto her feet and trailed after Daimon, following the steppingstones that wound between the manicured pine topiary in the central courtyard. Moonlight bathed the garden beyond, shining on Daimon where he sat on a boulder on the far side of the koi pond.

Cass stilled and watched him.

He stared at his bare upturned palm, his gaze distant. Miniature ice sculptures formed on his hand. Was he aware of the shapes he was making with his power? He looked as if he was staring straight through them, lost in thought and unaware of the world around him.

She edged closer, proving that to herself when he didn't stir, not even when she reached the arched wooden bridge that spanned the pond.

The air was colder here, had her breath fogging in front of her face, and she looked at Daimon's feet, unsurprised to see frost flowers blooming across the boulder. Whatever he was thinking about, it was upsetting him.

The ice melted and then reformed, taking on the shape of a woman.

Her?

The belly of the curvy figure swelled.

Megan?

No emotion touched his face as he ran a lone finger over the belly of the woman, but Cass could feel the turmoil beating in his heart.

A sorrowful edge crossed his features as he continued to touch the ice sculpture, as he lifted his hand and stroked her face. There was affection in that caress.

His mouth moved, his whisper so low she couldn't hear what he was saying to the woman. In response, the ice sculpture shifted, touching her stomach first and then extending her arms towards Daimon.

His shoulders tensed beneath his turtleneck and he drew a shaky breath and then released it, shuddering as he did so.

He whispered something else.

The statue shattered, raining shards of ice like diamonds onto the rocks at his feet.

She should go.

She knew that deep in her heart, but that same heart needed to know the things Daimon wouldn't tell her, the things he had buried deep—the cause of the barrier he kept lifting between them.

The source of the pain that often shone in his eyes.

Cass told herself again to go, not to intrude when he clearly needed some time alone.

But she couldn't bring herself to move.

Couldn't ignore the burning need to know why he was sitting alone with an ice sculpture of a pregnant woman.

"You're a very talented artist," she whispered, afraid of disturbing him, unsure how he would react.

He didn't look at her.

Didn't say anything.

"Is it someone you know?" She braved a step closer and rubbed her arms to keep the chill off them as the temperature dropped another few degrees.

He barely dipped his head in response, his ice-blue eyes fixed on the melting ice fragments around his feet. She had never seen someone look so alone. So lonely. So in need of someone to hold them together.

Cass wanted to be the one to reach out and hold him, to wrap her arms around his strong shoulders and ask him to tell her about the pain he was holding caged in his heart.

All this time around her, he had looked strong, almost invincible, even when pain had shone in his eyes. Now, he looked so vulnerable, and she couldn't bear it.

"Is she waiting for you back home?" she murmured.

"No." A shaky inward breath. "Yes."

Which was it?

She looked at the ice littered around his feet and it dawned on her. His home was the Underworld. The woman was dead. That was why she was there, waiting for him still.

Her experience of consoling people boiled down to taking care of Mari when they had lost Eric, and Eric when Mari's mother had died during childbirth. She wasn't sure she had done a good job on either of those occasions. She wanted to console Daimon, but feared she would only make things worse.

That fear held her back, had her keeping her distance when all she really wanted to do was hold him.

She looked down at the melting ice. Had Daimon's woman died in childbirth?

"She was beautiful." Cass wasn't sure whether hearing that from her would make him feel better or worse.

He was silent for so long that she was on the verge of leaving him alone when he finally spoke.

"It wasn't a true representation of her."

Maybe the woman hadn't been so beautiful.

He lifted his head, his pale eyes hollow and cold, bleak and edged with darkness. "She wasn't showing when daemons killed her and our unborn child."

Before she could ask about it, before she could even think to reach for his hand to comfort him, he was gone, only swirling black smoke left behind.

Twin emotions filled her heart. Jealousy that he had loved this woman and still mourned her, clearly wished she was still alive and he'd had the family they had been building together.

Sorrow that he had gone through something so terrible, still lived with the pain it had caused, allowing it to fester inside him.

Gravel crunched off to her right and she looked there.

The lights from the mansion threw Marek's bulky figure into silhouette, stealing his features from her until he drew close enough that the slender moonlight revealed them to her.

"Keras wants to talk about potentially closing another gate." His dark eyes slid to the lingering ribbons of smoke. "Where's Daimon?"

"He left." She meant to leave it at that, but then she blurted, "What happened to Daimon's wife?"

Marek's dark eyebrows knitted hard. "Wife? Daimon has never been married. There was Penelope. She was killed before Father sent us here. Why?"

She told herself not to say anything more.

Her mouth moved anyway. "I found him making ice sculptures, one of them was of her, I think. She was pregnant, right?"

Shock danced across Marek's face. "Pregnant?"

She nodded and inwardly cursed. How many times tonight was she going to reveal things that were unknown or clearly a secret in this case? She needed to learn to watch her mouth.

"You never knew," she said.

Marek shook his head. "None of us did. Daimon never told us. He's never spoken about what happened. Penelope lived in the mortal world, and I knew he'd been seeing her, but nothing about his behaviour ever led me to believe things were serious between them. He would go and visit her from time to time, leaving weeks between each trip. Normally, it was when he grew bored of the females who regularly visited Father's estate. I always thought he had just been mixing things up."

Mixing things up? Was Marek right and Daimon hadn't been serious about Penelope? Maybe his brother was wrong. Daimon had clearly loved this woman, mourned her still, and Cass had figured out Penelope was the reason he kept guarding his heart, refusing her advances. He had said his heart belonged to another.

"He never seemed serious about her?" Cass couldn't stop that question from leaving her lips, need to know more about Daimon and this woman pushing her to discover all Marek knew about the two of them.

Marek shrugged. "Perhaps. Towards the end. Maybe in the month or so before her death."

After Penelope must have told Daimon she was pregnant.

Someone called to Marek.

"I'll make excuses for Daimon. Keep this between us?" Cass didn't want the others discovering the things Daimon wanted to keep secret. It was his place to tell his brothers, not hers.

Marek nodded and went back inside.

Cass lingered on the bridge, her gaze lowering to the boulder where Daimon had sat. She replayed what she had seen, how he had looked at her.

This was the reason he took care of the children in Hong Kong. Another secret he kept from his brothers.

A shiver chased through her.

Beneath his frosty exterior, there was a warm heart, and it was broken— shattered just like the ice sculpture.

And all this time she had been pushing him, hadn't taken his rejections seriously, had kept prodding and poking him and trying to tear down his defences, unable to believe there might be a reason other than the manifestation of his power behind why he didn't want to get involved with her.

A reason that had been festering inside him all this time.

She straightened as resolve filled her, the need to make amends a driving force behind it.

She was going to help him come to terms with what had happened to the woman he loved and his unborn child, so one day he would finally be able to love again, to live again, without remorse or guilt.

Not for her sake, but for his.

She would be long gone by the time he was finally ready to take the leap and be with another woman. She could only hope that he would be happy at last.

That one of them could be happy.

She looked down at herself, sorrow and sickness washing through her, stirred by a wish that she cast aside before it could fully form, because it was impossible. Allowing herself to feel something for Daimon would only cause her pain in the long run.

Believing Daimon could come to love her would only destroy her.

Happiness was far beyond her reach.

Fate had other plans for her.

CHAPTER 15

Daimon stepped back to the Tokyo mansion, landing near the porch. Sunlight bathed the building and the grounds, the air still and silent. Just as he had hoped. Everyone would be asleep and he could avoid them all, at least for a few more hours.

He toed his boots off, taking his time about it, his thoughts slowing him down. He wasn't sure what he was going to say to Cass when he saw her again. His guard had been down in that moment by the bridge, and things had slipped out, things he had always wanted to keep secret.

Or at least he had thought he wanted to keep them secret.

He would never admit it to her, but talking to her about Penelope, even for that brief moment, had lifted some of the weight from his shoulders. He had been in a foul mood when he had left, had returned to Hong Kong and cursed her a thousand times over, but once he had realised he wasn't really angry, that he was only acting out because he felt he should be furious, he had felt... good.

He had never realised that Penelope was a sword hanging over him, a weight that constantly pressed down on him. He had loved her, or at least he had grown to love her, and he truly believed that if she hadn't been killed, he could have been happy with her.

Guilt stirred but he pushed it away, unwilling to let it take hold. He had been loyal to Penelope from the moment she had announced she was pregnant, had made the decision to stand by her, and he had stood by her for decades after her death, believing doing so would make him happy.

But it hadn't.

And when he had been sent to this world and his power had manifested, he had driven deep into that desire to remain faithful to her, using it to shield himself from the pain of being unable to touch another without potentially killing them.

He had fooled himself.

Cass had opened his eyes.

Cass who had looked so wounded last night, as if her heart had been bleeding for him.

He wasn't the only one who had revealed something about themselves last night. Cass had too. Beneath her often cold exterior, she cared. She cared deeply. She only affected the air of someone who didn't form attachments, who expected everyone to do their bidding without question and who didn't care what others thought of her.

He set his boots on the rack, still mulling over how he was going to approach her once evening rolled around and everyone in the mansion woke up.

Daimon pushed the door open and a sweet, tempting aroma hit him.

He tracked it to the kitchen, paused when a muttered curse broke the silence, and then edged forwards.

He peered into the kitchen. It was a mess. Bowls and tools were scattered all over the surfaces, bags and tubs of ingredients filled the spaces between them, and there was flour on almost everything.

He froze again.

Cass hummed as she bent over and removed something from the oven, the cute cat paw gloves out of place with an outfit he could only describe as a real heart-stopper.

Black leather moulded to her long legs, the trousers riding low enough that it exposed a strip of creamy toned stomach between them and the fitted ribbed black corset she wore.

Heat rushed through Daimon, his blood raging at the sight of her, his mouth going dry as he drank his fill of her curves and kept on picturing her as she had been in the bath, clad in only revealing underwear.

"What are you doing?" He squeezed the words out, struggling to think let alone speak as he attempted to banish underwear-Cass from his mind.

She whirled to face him, straightening at the same time and almost dropping the black deep metal tray she clutched. "Are you in the habit of sneaking up on people?"

He shrugged that off. "You should have been able to sense I was back."

She averted her gaze, lowering it to the pan she held. "My powers are a bit... low... right now."

He frowned at that. How much of her powers had she had to put into that barrier to make it that effective? He took a good look at her, shutting out her tempting curves and wicked outfit, keeping his gaze trained on her face. She looked tired, dark circles around her eyes, her skin still a shade paler than before.

"You should be resting," he bit out, harder than he had meant, earning a frown from her.

He braced himself, waiting for her to mention again that she didn't like people ordering her around.

Instead of lashing out at him, she muttered, "I can't. There's too much going on in my head, so here I am... baking."

Baking. It seemed like such a homely thing to do, so domestic and old-world feminine, words he had never thought he would apply to her. There was a side to her she kept hidden from the world, a side that she evidently hadn't wanted anyone to witness judging by how awkward she looked as she glanced at him.

"Do you like to bake?" He leaned his hip and shoulder against the doorframe, gunning for casual to cover how eager he was to know more about her, about this side of her in particular.

She set the rectangular pan down on a rack on the counter to his left and wafted the dark brown contents with a baking sheet. "Only when I'm stressed."

He couldn't imagine her being stressed that often back home on the island. If he lived there, he would never be stressed. All that sunshine, sea and endless blue sky. He always had found the quiet life appealing.

Cass took a plate from the cupboard, picked up a slice of something from a tray beside the one she had been fanning, and offered it to him. "Brownie? It's a new recipe I'm trying. Guaranteed to make you feel good."

Daimon stared at the square of chocolate cake and held his hands up. "If by good you mean bouncing off the walls and probably causing an ice storm, then sure."

She frowned at him, a puzzled edge to her blue eyes.

"I can't have caffeine. There's caffeine in chocolate. Enough that I may or may not go off the rails. Personally, I don't want to risk finding out which it would be." When she just continued to stare at him, he added, "None of us can have caffeine. It's like alcohol and mortal drugs. All very bad things and strictly forbidden."

She looked disappointed to hear that as she lowered her gaze to the slice. "I thought I knew you all better, but all the information I gathered never revealed you and your brothers can't have caffeine."

Or maybe she was irritated with herself.

She huffed. "There's so much I didn't know about you."

He knew she was talking about him specifically now. Before he could overcome how strange it felt to want to talk about his past and say anything about what she had witnessed, she continued.

"What will I do with all these brownies?" She gazed longingly at them, revealing she had an idea what to do with them.

"Aiko and the others would probably love them. They need a pick me up right now."

The longing edge to her gaze only grew stronger as she muttered, "Everyone does. I'd eat them all, but a moment on the lips…"

She patted her hips.

Her very shapely hips.

Surprise claimed him when he was tempted to say she would only look better with a little more flesh on her curves. The words refused to leave his lips, dying quickly when he recalled the letter he had seen on her desk and the way she had touched Megan's belly and asked about pregnancy.

She was meant for someone else, destined to bear his child.

He twisted and eased his backside against the counter, watched her in silence as she leafed through a cookery book, muttering things to herself about recipes without chocolate.

The silence felt comfortable, even as it cut at him, filling his head with thoughts of Cass with some nameless, faceless man. Milos graced him with a hiss as he strolled past and glared at him as he wound around Cass's ankles.

She blew kisses at the raggedy tomcat, her voice light and airy, as if she was talking to a baby. "What kind of baked goods do gods like, Milos?"

The cat meowed sweetly, and then issued another glare at Daimon when Cass went back to the book.

Unwilling to have a cat of all things steal her attention away from him, Daimon said, "I have a sweet tooth."

She looked across at him, her eyebrows rising. "You do?"

He nodded. "I like rice cakes. I go to Asakusa sometimes to stroll along the stalls and buy some. The local gods don't like me treading on their turf, but they've never tried to kick me off. They have more of a problem with Esher."

The light that had been in his voice, that had been filling him, faded as he thought about his brother. Where was he? He stared at the cupboards opposite him, the temptation to force Cal to open a portal for him growing again.

Cass's voice broke into his thoughts. "What else do you like?"

He glanced at her, saw in her eyes that she had noticed the change in his mood and was trying to distract him.

"Moon cakes. Mochi," he offered, and tried to think of something she would be able to make with the ingredients scattered around the kitchen. "Victoria sponge cake."

"That was a little left field." She frowned at him.

"My brothers like it too… and you have all the ingredients right here."

"Oh, so you picked something I could make. Heaven forbid the women get all the sweet things and the gods don't get any offerings." She looked as if she wanted to tease him some more and then picked up a bag of flour. "Very well… but I warn you, I make the very best Victoria sponge cake. Every one you have after today will be pale in comparison."

Daimon shrugged, one that felt so easy that it surprised him, together with the smile that curled his lips. "Unless I get you to make another sometime."

She looked at him, suddenly serious, and his smile faded as the light that had been filling him again switched off.

Her blue gaze dropped to her work as she picked out a clean bowl and gathered ingredients. "I like sweet things too. I always got along well with Eric because of it. He made the best sweet treats. Chocolates to die for. The man was a genius. I really missed that once Mari grew up and was old enough to notice I don't age like others. Eric would send me boxes of chocolates from time to time, but it wasn't the same as sitting in his shop eating whatever I wanted as we talked."

It took Daimon a moment to remember who Eric was, and even when he did, it didn't stop him from feeling jealous. The sparkle in her eyes as she spoke of Eric told Daimon that she had loved him.

It was ridiculous of Daimon to be jealous of a dead man, but he couldn't help it. The possessive side of him wanted her all to himself, didn't want to share her with anyone, dead or alive.

He reminded himself that it didn't matter what he wanted. She wasn't destined to be his. He had come here ready to speak with her, to brave the next step and give in to his attraction to her, but now that he was near her again, he couldn't stop thinking about the letter.

How was he meant to give in to her when he knew another man was waiting for her? How could she want him when she already had someone?

Was she really only flirting with him, not expecting him to do anything about it, enjoying the rush of attempting to break down his walls, or was she serious about him?

If she was, did that mean she wasn't serious about the man waiting for her?

His thoughts spun in circles in his mind, gathering speed, becoming a dizzying blur that had him unsure which direction he was going but aware that danger lay ahead. Her coven had been serious about her returning and bearing a child. Daimon had grown up in a world where goddesses were often betrothed from birth, their family deciding who they would marry.

Had Cass's coven done the same with her, selecting the man she would be with and expecting her to follow through with it?

Would she follow through with it?

She glanced at him, the feel of her eyes on his face only strengthening the storm building inside him. He had come here wanting to give in to her, but now he wasn't sure he could do it.

He wasn't sure he could get over what he had learned about her or the thought she was destined for another man.

He needed to drive that home so he would stop forgetting it, before he did something stupid.

Like falling for her.

It was going to hurt like hell, but it was better to wound himself now than let her utterly destroy him when she left.

"You're good at this." He waited for her to look at him again, cursed her for smiling at him and looking happy that he had complimented her when he wasn't done. He felt like a bastard when he added in a casual tone that hid everything he was feeling, "You'll make a good mother."

Her head jerked up, her gaze colliding hard with his. "What do you mean by that?"

Her pulse was off the scale.

She knew exactly what he meant and the fact that she did turned his stomach, had cold sweeping through him as his mood darkened.

Daimon shoved his feelings down and forced himself to continue, driving the wedge between them deeper.

"I saw the letter on your desk."

CHAPTER 16

Cass cursed Daimon in Russian. A whole string of them. Every single one she could call to mind. He deserved all of them as he stood there, casual as anything, his expression flat and empty, concealing all of his feelings from her. She wished she could do the same, masking the anger and hurt that swamped her, the fierce need to explain things even when she knew that whatever she said it wasn't going to make things better.

He had already made up his mind about her and what he had read.

"You snooped at my private things?" she snapped once she could say something that wasn't a swear word.

"It was right there." He folded his arms across his chest, the navy roll-neck long-sleeve T-shirt he wore tightening over his muscles as they flexed. "It was pretty hard to miss."

A little like the bite in his tone.

He had read the letter the coven had sent to her. That was the reason he had turned so frosty with her back at her home, had announced he was leaving with or without her, and had been flip-flopping between pulling her closer and pushing her away more rapidly than before.

He was jealous.

Even when there was no need to feel that way.

He was angry too.

It flashed in his eyes as his irises brightened, turning as white as snow ringed with black, flecked with diamonds.

"Besides, you've done your share of snooping." He threw the words at her.

She planted her hands on her hips but couldn't deny that. Just because she might have poked her nose in here and there, didn't mean she didn't get to be angry when he did the same thing.

She wanted to lash out at him, slave to a powerful urge to slap him for looking at the letter she had discarded on her desk the moment she had opened it, tossing it aside without reading it when she had seen the coven letterhead.

It would only make things worse, and she ached for things to be better, back to how they had been before he had turned cold towards her. Only a minute ago, things had been good between them, better than they had ever been, and she had been enjoying it. For a moment, she had honestly believed he was close to giving in to her.

Now, he was so far away from her that she felt like a fool for thinking something was about to happen between them.

She nibbled the corner of the brownie she had cut for him, needing the sugar and the sweet fix, a dose of chocolate to keep her spirits up and maybe give her a little courage.

She should have kept the ambrosia on hand in the kitchen, regretted taking it to her quarters now.

"It's tradition." That word sounded cold, hollow, no doubt revealing how she felt about it. She was done hiding things from Daimon though. He might be happy switching emotions every minute, and keeping everything to himself, but she wasn't. He was the only one who knew what awaited her, and gods, she needed to talk to someone about it, even when there was a chance she was only going to do more damage to the fragile bond that had been developing between them. If she was lucky, it would both lift some of the weight from her shoulders and make him see that she wasn't really getting a choice. "When a witch in my coven reaches two hundred years old, they must return home to bear a child with what you and your brothers call a Hellspawn. The child will be female and a witch. It's the way of our coven."

It sounded so sterile when she put it like that, and she wanted it to be that way.

What she didn't tell him was that she had been putting it off. She was loyal to her coven and planned to obey the summons eventually, but first she needed to be sure Mari would be safe and she needed to keep her promise to Eric.

"You seem all right with this." Daimon sounded bitter, his deep voice colder than she had ever heard it, and the air around him chilled a few degrees.

"It's tradition." And she wasn't all right with it. Not anymore.

She wanted to tell him that, but her voice failed her. Her coven was her everything. Her family. Everyone did their part to keep it strong, and she wasn't going to be the one to break from tradition. She couldn't.

But it didn't mean she didn't have her reservations, her doubts.

Even fears.

She had never known her parents. Her loyalty to her coven and her belief in their system had been unwavering before she had met Eric and Mari had come into the world. Since then, she had often wondered if her life would have been different if she had known her parents, even just her mother.

When Mari had discovered Eric wasn't her biological father, the conflict inside Cass had only grown. She had started to wish she'd had parents, a father in her life, even one who had chosen to have her as his daughter as Eric had with Mari, had chosen to raise her and love her.

Seeing Mari's life from the moment she had been born, how being raised in a warm, beautiful part of France, and in a loving family, had shaped her into a good woman, one who was very balanced and kind, had made Cass question what she was doing even before she had been summoned by her coven on her two-hundredth birthday.

Before Eric and Mari, she had been happy to do her duty, viewing it as only a minor inconvenience in her life, a year sacrificed for the greater good of her coven.

Now, she couldn't imagine doing it, even when she was resolved to go through with it.

Even when being around everyone in this damned house was only making her more aware of how little she knew about being part of a family.

She didn't know how a family really functioned, and discovering the ups and downs of one, witnessing the love and the fighting, the reconciliations and the protectiveness of everyone in this one was only making things harder for her.

She closed her eyes and forced a confession, admitted something she had been denying, too afraid to allow herself to voice it, even to herself.

Too afraid of how much it would hurt her.

Cass opened her eyes and looked at Daimon, wishing she was brave enough to put a voice behind what she was about to admit to herself.

She didn't want to bring a child into a cold world like her coven, where it would never know her, where she would have to stand by and watch her daughter grow up never knowing who she was and not allowed to tell her either. Several witches would bear children along with her, and those babies would be given the same birth date regardless of when they had been born, and would be kept away in a nursery until they were all one year old.

Something the coven did to ensure none of the mothers knew which one was their child.

A battle raged inside her, fiercer than ever, a war between duty and desire. She owed her coven everything. They had raised her, taught her all she needed to know to succeed in the world, and had given her the freedom she had desired, passing contracts to her that had kept her in enough money to do as she wished and had given her the opportunity to see the world.

In return for all that, she could do this one thing, couldn't she?

She stared into Daimon's eyes as they slowly softened, concern surfacing in them, and cursed him.

Being around him had only made things harder for her.

The scent of snow and spice came from him, a smell that reminded her of home, but with him, it wasn't cold that she felt.

He made her feel warm.

He made her question everything.

He made her *feel* everything.

And that was bad.

She couldn't—wouldn't—fall for him.

He was meant to be a pleasant distraction, whatever they shared all about fulfilling lust and having fun while it lasted.

But she had the terrible feeling it was too late and he was already so much more than that to her.

That the frozen heart that was melting wasn't his.

It was hers.

CHAPTER 17

Daimon grunted as he ducked and rolled, came up onto his feet and reached beneath his left arm at the same time. He slipped his finger into the ring on the hilt of one of his throwing knives, funnelled his power into it and let it fly. It shot across the gently undulating grassy hill and nailed a daemon in his shoulder.

The male went down.

Two others jumped over his body and rushed Daimon. Lightning struck the one on the left. The daemon exploded, showering his comrade in black blood and bits of flesh and bone, and the ground rocked as a boom echoed across the hilly landscape of Lantau Island, rolling into the pitch darkness.

The second daemon reached him and Daimon threw his hand forwards, unleashing three spears of ice that pierced the male in his thigh, stomach and chest at a diagonal.

Daimon breathed hard as the male hit the dirt, sliding to a halt just a few feet from him.

There were too many of them.

He checked on his brothers, tracking Cal and Valen as they battled the daemons who were attempting to keep them away from the gate.

A gate which the two Erinyes were trying to open.

A wall of daemons stood between him and his brothers and the goddesses. So far, the two furies had only managed to make the gate appear, at which point Daimon had felt it and had ordered Cal and Valen to come with him while Ares remained with the women. He hadn't expected to find the Erinyes here, with at least four dozen daemons surrounding them. He had thought they would be long gone, teasing him and his brothers again, drawing them out before running away.

Gods, he was glad he had demanded Cass stay at the mansion with Marinda.

The sorceress had had a few choice things to say to him in response to that, and he knew her anger hadn't all been about him ordering her to remain where she was, sidelining her again in order to protect her from their enemy.

She was still angry with him for reading the letter, and he deserved it.

"I can get closer." Cal's voice broke into his thoughts and Daimon shook his head.

They couldn't risk approaching the gate, because it would open if they got any closer to it. They also couldn't risk attacking the Erinyes with any of their powers, just in case the gate was caught in the crossfire. The two goddesses were standing too close to it.

And on top of that, they couldn't risk spilling their blood, just in case that was the reason the Erinyes had remained this time, hoping to injure one of them so they could get their hands on some of their blood. It would give them the power to open the gates again.

The best thing they could do was leave, but it was their duty to protect the gates and they couldn't leave this one vulnerable. He wasn't sure whether the Erinyes would be able to coax it open given enough time, and he wasn't about to risk it by withdrawing.

One of the two blonde females looked over her shoulder at him, fury shining in her violet eyes.

He wasn't the only one who was pissed.

Were the furies angry because he and his brothers were evading more than they were attacking, keeping the daemons busy while they kept an eye on the gate to make sure nothing happened to it, or were they angry because they had expected more than just Daimon, Cal and Valen to show up to fight them?

The central purple disc of the gate flickered, weakly glowing, and he focused on it as Valen and Cal launched another attack on the wall of daemons, attempting to weaken their forces enough that the Erinyes would be forced to withdraw.

Daimon struggled to focus as his thoughts kept shifting course, veering back to the angry sorceress he had left in Tokyo.

One who had looked as wounded by his demand she remain there as she had by his announcement that he had seen the letter on her desk.

He scrubbed a hand down his face and fixed his mind on the gate, on closing it. He felt the hum of power running through him as he connected with it, a comforting touch that boosted his strength, enough that he felt he could force it closed. If he could make it disappear, they could attack the Erinyes.

He could get back to Tokyo.

To that damned sorceress who had him tied in knots, going in circles, hating himself each time he completed a cycle of drawing her closer and pushing her away. He needed to get his head straight and his heart back in line.

He couldn't shake how relaxed she had been with him in that cramped kitchen. She had been so open, offering smiles that had warmed the coldest parts of him, making him feel things he had no right feeling.

So he had ruined it all.

But gods, he had needed it out there, in the open between them.

He had needed her to know that he was aware she was meant to return to her coven, to the man waiting for her.

He was no longer sure whether he had been attempting to drive a wedge between them to save himself, attempting to force a confession from her or something else.

But as he stood focused on the gate, his mind emptying, his heart supplied a possible answer.

He had done it because he wanted her to pick him.

He wanted Cass to look at him the way Megan looked at Ares. He wanted everything his brother had, everything he had denied himself for centuries, everything he had never wanted but now craved to the point it made him crazy.

And it wasn't because he could touch Cass.

He had been craving her from the moment he had set eyes on her.

But he couldn't have her.

So he kept trying to force her away from him, even when he knew it wouldn't change how he felt.

But he couldn't give in to her.

This kind of feeling was going to last longer than the time he had with her. When she left, he was going to feel bad enough as it was, but if he let her get any closer, it would destroy him. He would never get over her.

"Daimon, are you fucking listening?" Valen's voice broke into his thoughts and he turned his head to his right, his gaze landing on his violet-haired brother where he stood right in front of him. "This is *not* the time to zone out. What the hell is wrong with you?"

Daimon had been asking himself that question since Cass had stormed into his life, throwing everything into disarray. He didn't have an answer to give his brother.

Lightning struck all around them, shaking the hills that stretched in all directions, slender moonlight casting silver highlights on their sides and sloping peaks. Half a dozen screams rent the night air, the vile scent of daemon blood thickening and choking him. Wind swept across the battlefield beyond Valen, sending another half dozen daemons crashing into each other.

"I'm listening," Daimon snapped, ignoring the look Valen gave him that blatantly said his brother didn't believe him.

"Get your head out of your pants," Valen barked and reached a hand towards him, looking as if he was going to seize Daimon and shake him. He stopped just inches from him and glared instead. "Because you're fucking this all up."

Valen's golden eyes dropped.

Daimon looked down as warmth suddenly seeped across his stomach and hip on his left side, stared at the slick patch that was already several inches wide.

He hadn't noticed someone had landed a blow on him.

He growled, anger at the daemon who had done this to him colliding with fury aimed at himself for letting his mind wander during a fight. He swiftly checked the Erinyes, relieved to find they were still at the gate, and were no longer focused on attempting to open it.

They were struggling to defend themselves.

Marek and Keras worked as a team, using earth and shadows to drive the daemons back, taking several down in the process as they fought to reach the Erinyes.

The two blonde goddesses had closed ranks and were holding hands now, their bright violet eyes glowing in the darkness as they slowly backed off.

Behind them, the gate shrank and winked out of existence with a violent burst of purple light that dampened Daimon's vision.

Not only had he failed to notice a daemon had landed a blow on him, but he had failed to notice the arrival of his brothers.

He cursed Cass, and then himself.

Black shadows raced from Keras, screams filling the air as they cut a path through the daemons, and then a keening feminine shriek.

"Sister." One of the Erinyes turned a growl on his oldest brother. "You will pay dearly for that."

But rather than attacking him, she cast a portal. The violet-black smoke rapidly billowed outwards and she backed into it, helping the other furie as she hobbled. Marek and Cal stepped and sprinted for it, and Daimon kicked off too, determined to get his hands on one or both of the goddesses.

Daemons crowded the path ahead of him and he snarled through short fangs as he threw his arms forwards. Jagged shards of ice shot up from the grass, impaling several of the daemons. The rest were swift to leap out of the way. His gaze shot to the portal and he bit out a curse.

It was gone.

On a black growl, he turned on the remaining daemons, hurling spears of ice in rapid succession, quickly taking down six of them as his brothers joined the fight again. The daemons didn't stand a chance. Several of them scrambled to escape but Valen didn't let them. Lightning crashed down around them, striking half of the daemons as shadows killed the rest.

Daimon pressed his hand to his side and breathed hard as the last daemon went down, needing a moment to gather his strength again.

Cal, Valen, Keras and Marek picked their way over the dead to reach him and he looked at the point where the gate was hidden.

A weight settled in his gut.

"I don't like what happened here," he muttered, his voice distant as his thoughts turned to Esher again. He glanced at Keras. "They attacked Hong Kong. This gate is bound to Esher, meaning it's the one gate we can't seal right now."

Keras's handsome face turned grave and he dipped his head, his green eyes revealing he'd had the same thought. "The enemy is aware of which gate each of us is bound to by blood."

"Well, that's a big fucking problem," Valen put in as he shoved the long lengths of his violet hair out of his face, his golden eyes glowing in the darkness. "So the enemy knows way more about us than we thought?"

Marek nodded. "It appears so."

"How the hell is that possible?" Cal looked between them all, the tips of his blond ponytail fluttering in the breeze that gently swept around him. "They took Esher and Marek's blood... maybe that—"

Marek shook his head this time. "No. This is... It's almost as if someone is feeding the enemy information."

Which was exactly what Daimon had been thinking.

"Or they're with the enemy." Daimon exchanged a troubled look with Marek.

"The woman they keep mentioning?" Cal said with a concerned glance at Keras.

Keras twisted the silver band on his thumb. "I am not sure, but I shall send another Messenger to Father to see if he can think of anyone who might be working with them."

"Last time you asked, he sent a list as long as my dick," Valen muttered.

"So a short list?" Cal grinned at Valen when he scowled at him.

Keras raised his right hand and that was all it took to have both of them falling back into line.

Valen was right though. The list of possible enemies Hades had sent back had been hundreds of names long, far too many for their father to investigate, especially when Esher was missing and the majority of his legions were searching for him in the Underworld.

Keras's green eyes shifted to Marek. "Are you feeling strong enough to close Rome?"

Marek was quick to nod. "Whatever it takes to turn the tide in our favour."

"I can close New York." Daimon lowered his hand from his side, aware that it wouldn't be dark in New York for hours yet. As it was, Rome would only be on the cusp of nightfall. They were going to have to wait in the city for at least an hour before it was dark enough to summon the gate and close it. "We could go there after Rome. Ares and Cal could assist me."

Keras looked down at Daimon's side, his gaze gaining a concerned shimmer as he shook his head.

"It is best we do one at a time."

Which was a nice way of saying he didn't think Daimon was strong enough right now to handle it. That grated a little, but he tamped down that feeling and crushed it out of existence. His brother was right, and it was better they didn't weaken their forces by too much. Marek being out of action for a few days would be bad enough.

He wasn't really sure why he had been so quick to offer anyway.

He looked at Marek.

Realised that he had wanted to be the one to sleep for a few days.

Between the nightmares of Esher in the Underworld that plagued him whenever he tried to sleep, and the nightmare that was Cass plaguing him whenever he was awake, he was bone-deep tired, on the verge of collapse.

Being in a coma-level sleep would give him back his strength, and if he was lucky, when he woke, either Cass would be long gone or she would have been so worried about him that she would have fallen madly in love with him while taking care of him.

A guy could dream.

He didn't have such luck though. He knew that. If he slept for a few days like he wanted, he would probably never see Cass again.

And gods that would kill him.

He tilted his head back and looked at the stars that covered the heavens, at the spine of the Milky Way that arched overhead, and sighed.

He couldn't go on like this.

He was drowning.

Darkness surged through him.

He let the wave roll over him and pull him under.

CHAPTER 18

Cass tried to listen to what Mari was saying as she talked to Caterina and Eva, but it was hard to focus when her mind was filled with Daimon. Anger clashed with worry, the spark he had ignited in her when he had *benched* her, as Valen had called it, still going strong despite the thousand troubling scenarios that were running through her head.

She nibbled the corner of a second brownie square and glanced at Ares. He was coddling Megan again, sitting with her on the cream couch to Cass's left, his arm slung around Megan's slight shoulders. His smile didn't hide the concern that shone in his dark eyes, flickering in the embers that lit them.

Those eyes slid to her and narrowed in the way they had done every time he had looked at her over the past hour.

When Daimon, Calistos and Valen had left to go to the Hong Kong gate, she might have taken out her frustration and anger on Ares. Just a little.

Mari had talked her down, convincing her to remain in the mansion when all she wanted to do was transport herself to the gate. She knew staying tucked within the wards was the safe thing to do to when the enemy was targeting her, but the thought of Daimon out there, fighting those goddesses and the gods only knew how many daemons, turned her stomach.

Had her burning with a need to go and help him.

Mari patted her knee. Cass looked down at her hand as it came to rest on her black leather trousers and then up into her friend's blue eyes, catching the worry she tried to hide with a soft smile. Calistos was out there too, and Mari had suffered the same *benching* as Cass had.

Only Mari hadn't taken out her frustration on the sole brother left in the mansion.

Tremendous power suddenly pressed down on her and she stiffened and twisted at the waist to look over the back of the couch, her eyes locking on the door.

It opened and Keras strode in, darkness rolling off him, fiercer than she had ever felt it. Had something happened? Calistos followed hot on his heels. Mari was on her feet in a heartbeat and rushing to him.

Cass rose more slowly, her heart fluttering in her throat, blood thundering in her ears. "Where are the others?"

Because she couldn't sense Marek and Valen.

Or Daimon.

Keras's green eyes fixed on Ares rather than her. "Marek is going to seal the Rome gate."

The anger that had been burning at a low simmer in her blood flared into an inferno.

Keras had sent Marek, Valen and Daimon to close a gate straight after they had defended one? She levelled a glare on him and then looked at Calistos, worry tangling inside her as she spotted all the bruises and cuts on him, and how tired he looked.

Was Keras trying to get three of his brothers killed?

She glanced over her shoulder at Ares, silently demanding he say something.

He glared at Keras too, the fires of the Underworld burning in his eyes. "It couldn't have waited?"

Keras shook his head. "We need another gate closed. Daimon offered to close New York too, but one gate at a time now. We shouldn't rush this."

Shouldn't rush it? He had rushed it by sending three of his brothers straight to a gate fresh from a battle, when they were probably tired and in need of rest.

Keras's cold green eyes slid to meet hers. "I would like a word with you."

Cass tipped her chin up and stared right back at him, not hiding any of the anger she felt as his words ran around her head, and as she thought about Daimon. Why had he offered to close a gate? Doing so would render him unconscious for days, if not weeks.

She recalled what he had said to Calistos about being unable to sleep. Was he so desperate to escape reality and snatch the sleep that eluded him that he would endanger himself to achieve it? She knew the disappearance of Esher weighed heavily upon him, but placing himself at risk to escape that was foolish. Reckless.

The anger that burned inside her only blazed hotter. She was going to be having words with him when he returned.

Just as she was going to have words with his brother.

She followed Keras out through the white wood-framed panels that had been pushed back to reveal the garden. He banked left, following the wooden walkway that ran around the courtyard. He moved like a shadow in the darkness, his steps unnervingly silent. The boards creaked beneath her weight from time to time, cutting through the tense silence, but he never made a sound.

When he reached the end of the walkway near her temporary quarters, he stopped and stepped down onto the wide stone slab that had been placed there. He slipped his feet into a pair of slippers and she did the same, and followed him into the garden, her anger giving way to nerves as the darkness encompassed them and the voices of the others drifted into the distance.

The moonlight cast faint silver highlights in Keras's black hair and over his shoulders.

When he reached the bridge that spanned the koi pond, he stopped and pivoted to face her. The moon cast his face in shadow, but green flecks glowed in his eyes. She moved around him, forcing him to turn his profile to the moon, because something about the way his eyes glowed unnerved her and had her pulse quickening.

When light bathed the side of his face, those nerves settled and her courage rose again.

She spoke before he could.

"Sending your brothers to seal a gate straight after a fight was reckless. Dangerous."

His features remained flat, unreadable, as he stared at her in silence.

As time trickled past, she struggled to keep her nerves at bay, to keep her chin tipped up and confidence shining through. He wasn't the first one to attempt to impose some sort of command over her by looking at her in such a way, and he probably wouldn't be the last.

It didn't bother her. She wouldn't be cowed by him. She wasn't afraid of him.

She really wasn't.

She was about to demand that he say something when he finally spoke.

"I have seen you with Daimon and I witnessed the effect you are having on him on the battlefield tonight." His voice turned colder, chilling her as she subtly curled her fingers into fists at her sides, steeling herself. Keras took a step towards her, and she barely resisted the urge to back off one. Darkness rolled off him in menacing waves, blackening his eyes, and the power he always emitted rose, wrapped like shadows around her that felt as if they were choking her. His eyes narrowed slightly, a cruel twist to his lips as he leaned towards her and whispered, "If you hurt my brother, I will see to it that not only you but your entire coven suffer for it."

Her spine stiffened.

"How dare you threaten my family." She slapped him hard, her hand flying before she could consider the consequences, her heart jacking up into her throat as her blood thundered and adrenaline surged.

He didn't even flinch.

Cass struck him again, the sound of her palm connecting hard with his cheek ringing in the still night air.

His pupils widened for a heartbeat before they shrank back to normal.

She hit him a third time, catching his mouth more than his cheek.

He exhaled hard, the sound breathy as his pupils dilated and contracted again, but she felt no anger in him, no sense that he would retaliate.

There was only the strange feeling that he wanted more.

She stared at him, scratched out the thought she'd had about him when he had moved like a shadow along the walkway.

This side of him unnerved her the most.

Something was seriously wrong with this god.

He lifted his right hand and brushed the pad of his thumb across his lower lip, catching the blood there. He sucked it from his thumb and stared at her, silent and still, an air of expectation surrounding him.

Because he wanted her to strike him again.

She stood her ground despite her nerves, despite the fact half of her wanted to leave and the rest wanted to slap him again.

"I would never hurt Daimon so there's no need to threaten my family," she bit out, emphasising each word as she stared into his green eyes.

She wasn't sure how long she stood there in the garden, her flesh chilling as the night dragged on, locked in a silent battle with Keras.

But it was growing light and she was cold to the bone when the scent of snow and spice hit her.

Warmed her.

Daimon.

Keras must have sensed his return too, because he blinked and when he opened his eyes again, it was as if nothing had happened. His perfect features lost all the darkness they had held and his eyes lost the twisted hungers that had filled them.

He turned away from her and strode towards the house, and when he reached it and stepped up onto the walkway, he said, "I will tend to him."

He took Marek from Valen and carried him towards his room, turning his profile to Cass.

She stared at him, studying his features and the feelings she could sense in him, and frowned. He was the calm and collected god she had always witnessed, not even a lingering trace remaining of the person who had been standing here with her, craving violence from her.

Taking pleasure from it.

Did his brothers know about that side of him, the one who had looked ready to provoke her just so she would strike him again?

She edged her eyes towards the main room of the house.

Cursed in Russian when she saw the state of Daimon.

Her heart lurched into her throat as he hobbled onto the walkway, his right arm banded around his stomach and blood covering the left side of his face.

The urge to strike Keras blasted through her, coupled with a desperate need to go to Daimon, and a foolish hope he would accept her help.

Because she needed to take care of him.

She sent a prayer to the gods that for once, Daimon wouldn't fight her.

Even when the darkness that shone in his eyes as they met hers said that he would.

Said more than that to her.

It whispered a terrible truth.

Keras wasn't the only one who courted pain.

Daimon had let the daemons hurt him.

CHAPTER 19

Darkness was a living, writhing thing inside him. It whispered, coaxed and seduced, and Daimon did his best not to listen to it, not to be swayed by its black magic.

To ignore the craving for violence that blazed inside him.

But it was strong.

Far stronger than he was in his current state, his mind fragmented, torn in two directions.

Images stuttered across the darkest corners of that mind, taunting him with flashes of Cass with another man, a faceless and nameless one who was her destiny.

Who she was apparently resolved to go to even though he had seen the doubts in her eyes.

Daimon stared at the daemons surrounding him, singling out all the males, his mind labelling them as Cass's intended. He cut through them, a whirlwind of ice and steel, taking some down with spears and shards of glittering crystal and others with a swift stroke of a blade over their throats.

Valen's lightning shook the ground, lashing down from the heavy black clouds like white-purple whips to light up the darkness. Each strike filled the air with the scent of daemon blood, rousing Daimon's darkness, keeping it at the fore.

It seeped deeper into him, snaked around his heart and murmured to him, whispering taunts about the males around him, about them and Cass.

About how she would never be his.

Daimon slid across the dry grass of the ancient Stadio Palatino and used one of his throwing knives to slice across the shins of a female daemon as her claws cut through the air above him. She shrieked and leaped backwards, into the path of a lightning strike. Blood and bone exploded outwards and Daimon was swift to step, avoiding being hit by it.

He landed in the middle of a group of six male daemons.

All of them turned on him, their eyes glowing with sick hunger in the darkness.

He was sure his looked the same.

From the ends of their fingers, long claws grew, four-inch talons that promised pain if they caught him.

Their dilated pupils narrowed into thin vertical slits as he faced them, rising to his full height, showing them that he wasn't afraid of them. Six or sixty, it didn't matter. They would never win against him.

Rain hit in a heavy downpour, turning the grass to mud beneath his boots, saturating him in a heartbeat. He casually ran a hand over his white hair, slicking it back.

His heart beat steadily, a hard drumming against his chest as he waited.

Beyond the six, in the middle of the long rectangular courtyard of the monument, Valen fought another half a dozen, keeping them away from Marek. Beyond Valen, Marek stood facing the gate that hovered a few feet above the floor of the Stadio Palatino. The colourful light it emitted shimmered over the broken columns that lined all sides of the grass and the crumbling walls of the ancient Roman buildings that enclosed it.

Two of the daemons nearest Daimon twitched, one shifting foot to foot as the other licked his lips, his forked tongue flickering over them.

Daimon had always hated the more lizard-like of the daemon breeds. None of these six had a scratch on them thanks to the tough scaly skin they could call in a heartbeat to cover their more delicate human-looking flesh.

One to his left hissed through razor-sharp teeth.

And suddenly all of them were on him.

He grinned and hunkered down, called on his power and savoured the rush as shards of ice shot up all around him, managing to catch at least one of the males and spill blood. He attacked the moment the daemons backed off a step, lashing out with the throwing knife he clutched in his left hand, pumping his power into it so the blade caused ice to ripple over the surface of every daemon it struck.

These daemons might be able to shield themselves with scales, but even that wouldn't protect them from his ice.

One daemon went down, hissing and snarling as he clutched as his arm. Ice cascaded over it, glittering in the light of the gate as it took hold, thickening and growing to encase the male's entire arm.

Daimon spun and brought his leg up, struck the male's arm with his boot. It shattered.

The daemon howled and backed off, desperately clutching at the stump left behind.

The remaining five daemons looked at their comrade and then at Daimon. He smiled slowly.

Waited.

A daemon behind him was the first to make a move, lunging for him rather than fleeing as Daimon had expected. He twisted to face the male, brought his arm up and blocked the daemon's attack. He grabbed the male's wrist with his other hand and went to throw him.

Daimon bellowed as claws raked down his back and he arched forwards, pain searing him like an inferno.

Bastards.

He spun on his heel and hurled his right hand forwards, unleashing the blade he clutched in it. It nailed the daemon in his shoulder, but the male didn't go down.

Daimon cursed.

In his haste to retaliate, he had forgotten to imbue it with his power.

Two daemons piled onto him, claws slicing through his roll-neck long-sleeve, the scent of his blood joining the vile coppery odour of daemon blood in the air.

The darkness he had been fighting to hold back surged forwards, the intoxicating rush of it consuming him in a heartbeat.

Daimon grinned and grappled with one of the daemons, grabbing his wrists and hurling his head forwards. His forehead cracked off the daemon's one and the male grunted and reared back. The second male attacked, slamming into Daimon's side and taking him down.

Pain erupted in a wave as he hit the slick grass.

And he relished it.

He grinned as the daemon pummelled him, not bothering to block his blows. He took every one of them as the darkness rose inside him, twisted tighter and devoured more of him. Daimon grabbed the daemon and rolled with him, pinned him beneath him on the wet grass and slammed his fists into his face, knocking his head left and right. Wherever Daimon's fists struck him, scales erupted and ice covered them.

He bore down on the male, his lips peeling back off his fangs in a wide smile as black blood flowed from the lacerations on the daemon's face, quick to freeze under Daimon's assault.

He didn't feel the pain in his side, didn't notice the heat spreading across it.

But he did notice the way the daemon laughed at him, his eyes lighting up with sick glee.

Daimon slammed his right fist into the male's head, bone cracking beneath the force of the blow.

Silence reigned.

He shoved onto his feet and stumbled, twisting to face the other wretches. Heat bloomed and spread down his left hip, fire pooling at the apex of it. It wasn't enough.

He bared his fangs at the daemons, goading them, needing more.

Two were quick to take him up, launching at him in tandem. He danced with them, his grin still in place as he pivoted and turned, ducked and dodged and landed blows.

And let them strike him.

Each kick, punch or slash of claws sent a ripple of satisfaction through him, had the darkness purring inside him, pushing him to seek more.

He did.

He surrendered to the dark wave, let it pull him under and savoured each blow they landed, every flare of fire and searing jolt of pain that struck him.

Leaving him only wanting more.

Daimon fought them, holding back his power as best he could, wanting this battle to last.

He gave up blocking them, closed quarters and took every blow.

He closed his hand around the front of one of the daemon's throats and frowned when the male withered before his eyes, skin turning blue and eyes rolling back in his head.

No.

He wanted more.

He shook the dead male, growled when he didn't respond and turned on his comrades, hurling the body at them. One took the bait, but another ran, leaving him with only two. He left himself open, inviting the pain, the darker side of his blood at the helm. Each slash of the male's claws only made him grin.

Impudent wretch.

As if this thing was strong enough to best him.

He shot a hand out and seized the second male, hurling him at the first, knocking them both down.

The urge to leap on them was strong.

Daimon fought it.

Staggered back a step and tried to rein the darkness in, to bring it back under control.

But he didn't want to. He wanted this pain. This oblivion. He needed it, because it was better than the other thing that awaited him if he regained control. Physical pain he could bear.

Emotional pain he couldn't.

The two daemons leaped on him.

He closed his eyes.

Welcomed the pain as they ripped at him, snarling and hissing.

No.

He growled and ice shot up all around him, the shards so close that they cut him as well as impaling the daemons.

He breathed hard and the ice shattered, freeing him of its cage. He stumbled backwards, shaking his head, driving back the darkness, clawing back control.

He didn't want this.

He didn't.

Darkness was a living, writhing thing inside him. It whispered, coaxed and seduced, and all Daimon could do was listen to it, to be swayed by its black magic, to crave more of the violence that had come before.

The pain.

Was this how Esher felt?

He stared at the gate, at the rings that were shrinking, winking out of existence, and reached for the other side of it.

For Esher.

Pain flooded him again, anger and desperation following it, together with despair.

Esher.

He stepped forwards, heading for the gate, picking his way over the remains of the daemons.

His brother needed him.

It gave him the strength to fight back, to resist the darkness and step towards the light. Esher needed him and he wouldn't fail his brother. He would be strong. He would do all in his power to conquer the darkness, the pain, and remain.

Ready for his return.

Esher needed him strong. He needed him to take care of Aiko. He needed him to be there for him when he came back.

So Daimon could bring him back.

Light flickered, the heavy pulsing weight of the power the gate emitted weakening, the connection between him and the Underworld fading with it as Marek finally finished sealing it.

His link to Esher faded too.

Physical pain gave way to emotional pain as the gate finally winked out of existence in the centre of the Stadio Palatino.

Marek collapsed on the muddy ground of the ancient monument, and Valen rushed to him, gathered him into his arms and looked at Daimon.

Daimon just stared at him, fatigue beating in every fibre of his being, mingled with the darkness that refused to release him now he had allowed it to take hold. Black thoughts whispered in his mind, terrible things that kept him skirting the edge of the abyss, kept him filled with agony and despair.

And rage the depth of which he had never felt before.

A twisted, dangerous need continued to consume him. He had been a fool to court the darker side of his blood, but he had been desperate for some release, for something he felt he needed even when he wasn't sure what it was.

"I'm taking him back." Valen weighed each word, eyeing him closely as his blond eyebrows slowly lowered over bright golden eyes. "You okay?"

Daimon managed a stiff nod.

He looked down at his left side, felt nothing as he watched blood trickling from the gash above his hip.

Darkness continued to writhe, to twist and snarl.

To murmur in his ear.

To taunt him with images of Cass with another man.

She was meant to be his.

He felt that deep in his soul, in the darkest corners of it where a possessive beast snarled and paced, tormented by the need to seize hold of her but fearing reaching out.

The fear always won.

It turned him in circles, always leading him back to the start, as if it enjoyed torturing him, making him feel he could win Cass only to throw a hundred moments at him when he had seen in her that she would never abandon her duty.

He wanted her, more than anything, but the thought he might come to know her taste, that he might find the courage to unleash his hunger and this desperate need for her only to lose her in the end, was unbearable. It would be torture far worse than having to endure centuries of loneliness because of his power.

Daimon stared down at the lacerations that covered his legs and chest, that littered his arms. What was she doing to him?

She was the wave. Washing over him to pull him under, letting him break for air only to suck him under again. She was killing him.

Another image of her with a faceless man flashed across his mind.

The darkness within him roared in response, flooding him with a need for violence, to lash out and strike at everything around him. The daemons were dead. There was no one to give him the pain and destruction he craved.

He shoved his hands through his hair and clutched the sides of his head, squeezed it hard as he gritted his teeth.

Tried to purge the darkness he had foolishly allowed to take hold of him.

"Daimon?" Valen's soft voice reminded him he wasn't alone.

The darkness turned its sights on his brother.

"Give me a minute," Daimon growled, hoping Valen would get the hint and leave him, because he didn't want to hurt his brother.

"Sure." Valen disappeared with Marek.

Daimon exhaled hard and sucked down another breath, wrestling with the black rage, the hunger and the hurt. He shut out its insidious whispers, refused to obey it and hunt the daemons who lived in Rome, seeking another fix.

Seeking more pain.

He squeezed his eyes shut as the fight at the Rome gate replayed, trying to stop it from happening even when he knew it wasn't possible. Everything fast-forwarded, rushing past his eyes in a bloody blur, culminating in the dreadful moment he had let the darkness overcome him.

In that moment, he hadn't cared what the daemons did to him.

He had welcomed it.

He clawed and tugged his white hair back, his scalp stinging as he gritted his teeth and growled through emerging fangs.

This wasn't him.

He just needed to rest, to recover from his injuries, to find some peace for a moment, and then he could pull himself back together and continue, without surrendering to the need burning inside him.

The need to take hold of Cass and never let her go.

He stepped and didn't bother to remove his boots, because he was going to leave an unholy mess in the mansion no matter what he did.

Rather than appearing inside, he landed on the walkway that ran around the courtyard.

A mistake.

Cass stood before him by the arched wooden bridge, facing Keras.

The darker side of his blood that had been slowly fading roared back to life at the sight of his brother so close to her.

Keras moved before the need to rip his brother away from her could manifest, distancing himself from the sorceress. His brother glanced at him as he reached the walkway. Daimon glared at him.

And then at Cass.

What had they been doing alone in the garden?

Why did Cass look flushed, her pale blue eyes bright?

Those eyes gained a horrified edge as they landed on him, swiftly followed by concern.

That concern wounded him more deeply than any blade could, cleaving him open, tearing at him. He didn't want to see such soft emotions in her eyes. Not directed towards him. It hurt too much.

Cass hurried over to him.

Daimon stalked past her, his head turning, vision blurring for a second before the dizziness passed. He held his side, stemming the flow of blood, unsure what to do as gravel crunched beneath his boots. He couldn't go to his room, even when he craved sleep. The covers of his bed would act as a wick, drawing more blood out of him. He needed to fix his wounds before he could rest, but he was so godsdamned tired.

His thoughts blurred together as he mindlessly walked forwards.

Going somewhere.

He just didn't know where.

Anywhere was better than here, near Cass.

Only he couldn't escape her.

She followed hot on his heels, her presence a pain he couldn't endure, rousing the softer emotions he had tried to banish tonight.

Tried to kill.

"Let me take care of you." Her voice was soft, sweet, a balm to his aching heart.

Gods, he wanted to give in to her.

He wanted to place himself in her hands and trust it would all work out exactly the way he wanted it to.

But he wasn't a fool.

"Go away," he grunted.

She huffed and stepped around him, blocking his path, her eyes glittering with silver stars as they narrowed on him. "I've seen you fight and you're stronger than any daemon. None of them should have been able to deal this much damage to you… unless you let them."

The last four words leaked from her lips as desperation filled her eyes. They danced between his, seeking an answer, one she wasn't going to like.

Her brow furrowed and she whispered, "Why would you do that?"

The softness, the concern and the hurt gave way to something far darker when he didn't answer, just stepped around her and kept trudging forwards.

She appeared in his path again, her face a mask of darkness, accusation in her eyes and anger in her tone.

"Why, Daimon?" She cupped his cheeks with both hands, her touch too warm and soft for him to bear.

It destroyed him.

He took one last look at her and stepped.

Cold wind whipped around him, cutting him to the bone, driving ice into his marrow.

He let it buffet and chill him as he stared at the endless, frigid white that surrounded him.

Let it numb him.

He wanted to laugh at that.

He had been numb for centuries.

Now, he wanted to feel, and he was too afraid to do it.

He was too afraid of where it might lead.

He was too afraid that if he dared to love again, he might lose Cass too.

CHAPTER 20

Darkness surrounded him, black lands as far as the eye could see. A valley rimmed with mountains stretched below him, spotted with clusters of golden lights that shone like dull stars in the night.

Esher grinned, felt the thick mixture of daemon blood and dirt of the Underworld on the left side of his face crack.

It was old now, dried and flaking.

Blood from the wretch he was hunting.

Taken the first time Esher had caught up with him shortly after he had dared to enter the Underworld.

He absently lifted his hand and touched the war paint, pleasure humming in his veins as his fingers traversed the rough spine of it that streaked over his left eye, covering that side of his face from his hair to his jaw.

The odour of foul daemon blood filled his nostrils, rousing the hunger, keeping it as sharp as a blade.

Fresh blood.

The darkness bayed for more.

And he howled with that need too.

He shuddered as he stared down into the valley, cold winds cutting through his torn shirt and jeans, unaware of the world around him, his focus fixed on one thing and one thing alone.

The hunt.

Pleasure rippled through him again, stronger now, a drugging sensation that had his lips curling further to flash his fangs as his eyelids grew heavy. He breathed deep of the daemon blood on his hand, anticipation rolling through him, bringing forth images of the last two times he had clashed with the wretch.

A wraith.

Frustration rolled in on the heels of the satisfaction he took from replaying his battles against the fiend, mounted inside him to pull a growl from his lips.

Twice he had clashed with the daemon.

Twice the male had escaped.

But Esher had his scent now.

He trudged forwards, boots skidding on the loose shale as he descended the mountain, pulled to the valley, a slave to the black need to hunt.

To kill.

He shook that thought away, the small part of him that was clinging to consciousness, refusing to fully succumb to the darkness, unleashing a distant scream in his ears.

Not kill.

He needed the male alive.

To torture. To torment. To plunge into a living nightmare, a hell he wouldn't be able to escape.

To make him pay.

His grin stretched wider.

Yes. Make him pay.

The male would suffer as his sister had, as his brothers had. Esher would see to it personally, drawing out his punishment so it lasted a lifetime and then another. It was what the bastard deserved.

His left boot hit a snag and he stumbled forwards a few steps, struggling to find his footing on the steep slope. A snarl tore from him as he found it and halted, as his feet throbbed, pain pulsing in a powerful wave up his legs to steal the strength from them.

How long had he been walking?

Always moving forwards.

Never stopping.

Never resting.

He had to keep going.

His stomach cramped near-constantly now, hunger stealing strength from him, thirst blurring his thoughts.

But he couldn't stop.

He was close now.

He could feel it.

He brought his hand back to his lips and flicked his tongue over his bloodstained fingers.

Tasted it.

He trudged forwards, unaware of the world, uncaring of it. A legion tracked him, but they wouldn't reach him in time. He was close now. He stalked the uneven terrain, his fatigue falling away as he neared the valley bottom, strength flowing back into him as he thought about what was to come.

The scent of blood curled around him and his gaze dropped, crimson eyes unerringly locking onto the spot of it that blended with the black rock.

His grin stretched wider still.

Fresh daemon blood.

Eli's blood.

Esher stalked forwards, his steps surer as adrenaline surged, as pleasing images of capturing the wraith and beginning his torment filled his mind, driving him onwards. No time to rest. No time to delay.

His crimson eyes scanned the valley ahead of him, leaping over everything, singling out each cluster of buildings, assessing them all.

The valley was filled with places to hide.

But not a single place where the wraith could hide from him.

The distant screams came again as thoughts of drenching his hands in daemon blood flooded his mind, coaxing a low moan from his lips and sending a shiver down his spine. He tried to quieten the voice, and when that didn't work, he growled at the other side of himself, the pathetic side that wanted to save this wretch.

It continued, battering his mind and his will with words about capturing the daemon, about questioning it, about the importance of keeping it alive.

Esher bared fangs at the thing inside him.

He wanted blood.

The daemon had taken his sister from him, had nearly destroyed his family, and had harmed not only his youngest brother but others that he loved.

The daemon deserved death.

The voice whispered.

And he would receive it.

Esher stilled, canted his head and listened to the other side of him, curious now. It wasn't like the weak thing to want to kill. He couldn't recall the last time they had been in accord with each other.

The distant voice promised blood, promised retribution, promised the chance to torture, to torment.

All things it kept promising.

But this time, it promised death to the wretch too.

Only if he had patience.

Patience?

Esher spat on the black ground, despising that word for some reason.

He had been patient. Hadn't he? He frowned, a thread of confusion knitting a jumble of thoughts together in his weary mind. He shook his head, trying to get his thoughts into order, trying to remember. Someone had told him to be patient.

Someone he loved.

An image began to build before him, a figure of a male, but it crumbled before it fully formed.

Esher rubbed his temples, closed his eyes and lowered his head, attempting to coax the memory. It refused to come.

So he clawed at his hair, raking black talons over it, drawing his own blood as frustration got the better of him.

He didn't want to wait.

He growled and turned, looked at his surroundings and frowned as a thought struck him. What was he doing? Who was he looking for? The owner of that voice was inside him. He clawed at his chest, ripping through the front of his shirt, tearing new gashes in it. If he could get the wretch out of his body, he could kill the daemon, just as he wanted.

No, he couldn't.

He stilled, claws buried deep in his own flesh.

He needed the wraith alive.

Eli was the key.

Killing him would only avenge his sister.

Capturing him and bringing him to his brothers might save her.

But he wanted to kill him.

He absently raked his nails over his pectorals as he considered every angle. There was a way he could both avenge his sister and save her.

Patience.

He had no love for that word, but he would do his best to be patient, even when he didn't want to play any sort of long game. He wanted blood on his hands. He wanted to see that glorious moment when hope turned to despair in the wretch he was hunting. He wanted to watch the light in the wraith's eyes fade.

The voice coaxed, whispering sweet words about torturing him, tormenting him, how he could draw out the pain and see that moment of hope giving way to despair over and over again.

If he had patience.

He huffed and stalked forwards. Fine. If patience was the price to pay for being able to draw out the wretch's suffering, then he would pay it.

Although he made no promises that he would be able to control himself when he had the wraith within his reach again.

The irritating other side murmured to him, things about the Blessed Isles, about getting his sister there.

He focused on them as he tracked the wraith.

Let them flood his head with pleasing images, ones that leashed the black need to kill, harnessed and honed it into something else.

A terrible need to make the bastard suffer at his hands for centuries.

He wouldn't kill him. Not even when the wraith had given up every drop of information. He would keep the fiend alive. To torture. To torment.

To keep locked in a cage for his pleasure.

He would do to the male what the wretches had wanted to do to him.

His gaze fixed on one black building, a small single-storey abode nestled among many others.

His grin stretched wider as he sensed the wraith inside.

He would make Eli his pet.

CHAPTER 21

Cass pressed her hand to her stomach, clutching it through her black corset as she stared at the onyx ribbons of smoke dissipating before her. Sickness brewed, the knowledge that Daimon had allowed daemons to hurt him rousing a thousand questions in her mind.

None of which she liked.

Was it her fault?

Gods, she felt as if it was.

That haunted and pained look he had given her before he had teleported was seared on her mind, together with the state of him. What he had done to himself scared her. The sight of him drenched in black daemon blood, crimson seeping from the deep lacerations on his stomach and arms and legs, scared her.

The thought that he had teleported when his stumbling steps had made it blindingly clear he was weakened by the battle, could be out there somewhere now, collapsed and vulnerable, terrified her.

She needed to see him.

She focused, lining up the incantation in her mind, piecing it together as she fixed her thoughts on a destination.

Transported herself there.

She appeared beside the pool set into the white terrace of Daimon's hillside modern home, fatigue washing through her as the spell stole her strength. She gave herself a moment as she peered through the huge panes of tinted glass that were set between white concrete and steel pillars.

As soon as her legs felt stable enough, she moved towards the building, her limited senses scouring the area for Daimon. She couldn't feel his power.

But he had to be here.

She approached the glass door and didn't hesitate when she reached it. She pushed it open, not surprised to find it was unlocked, and eased inside, her pulse picking up as she listened hard.

She wasn't sure whether Daimon would appreciate her coming after him, but he could be mad at her all he wanted. He needed someone to take care of him and she was determined to be that person.

Just as she was determined to find out why he had allowed daemons to harm him.

"Daimon?" she called, softly at first, nerves getting the better of her. When he didn't answer, she put more force behind her voice. "Daimon?"

She waited.

Still no answer.

She moved between the long couch and the immaculate kitchen area, heading deeper into the building, towards white doors she presumed led to bedrooms.

The first one she tried was empty.

"Daimon?" She backed out of the room and turned towards the other, the sickness growing stronger as she crossed the marble floor. She pushed the door open and looked around the huge bedroom, at the untouched dark blue covers on the king-size bed. "Daimon?"

That last attempt to get him to answer felt pointless, but she hadn't been able to stop herself from calling to him again.

He wasn't here.

She racked her brain, trying to figure out where he might have gone. He was hurt. He wouldn't have gone to the orphanage in that state, and she didn't know of any other homes that he owned. She doubted he had gone to one owned by his brothers, since they were all in Tokyo.

Cass pulled together the incantation again, her heart drumming at a sickening pace as fear got the better of her. Someone would know where he had gone. Someone would tell her, even if she had to beat it out of them.

She closed her eyes and finished the spell, opened them again as she landed back where she had been in the garden of the Tokyo mansion.

She reached out with a tracking spell to pinpoint the brothers. Most of them were in Marek's room, but there was one in the kitchen. Her legs wobbled as she headed in that direction, her steps unsteady. She breathed through the drain on her strength, refusing to give herself time to recover.

Daimon was out there, injured and vulnerable. She needed to find him.

Someone had to know where he had gone.

They just had to.

She entered the kitchen and drew up short as she spotted Calistos. He stood at the counter of the galley kitchen, clothed in a fresh T-shirt and jeans, his damp golden hair pulled back into a ponytail. He was already healing too, something she found curious since she hadn't attended to him and none of the brothers could heal that quickly.

She doubted he had allowed Megan to use her healing talent on him, not when he had refused her before. She also doubted that Ares would have allowed it.

Calistos was quick to look at her, easing back from preparing vegetables and wiping his hands on a towel. "Something up?"

His blond eyebrows knitted low over stormy eyes, ones that demanded an answer to that question as he stared at her.

She pushed down her nerves, pulled up her courage, and refused to let him see that she was shaken.

Because he would use it as ammunition against her for months.

She could see it in his eyes as they slowly narrowed, suspicion and curiosity forming in them. He wanted to find a weakness in her, something he could use against her, a fault he could point out to Mari as retribution for all the times she had brought up his failings in front of her ward.

That ward came up behind her, briefly wrapped her in a hug from behind and then released her and stepped around her.

She forced a tight smile as Mari looked at her. One that clearly failed to cover her worry because Mari's beautiful face fell, concern replacing the smile that had been brightening her blue-green eyes.

"Something's wrong. What is it?" Mari's blonde eyebrows furrowed as she took a step towards Cass.

All of Cass's strength drained from her as she looked into Mari's eyes, as her soft words curled around her and sank deep into her, stripping away the stubborn part of her and pulling forth an urge to let it all rush out of her.

"Daimon left. He was injured. Perhaps a little angry with me. I only wanted to help him. I don't know where he's gone." She looked at Cal. "I was hoping you might."

Calistos pursed his lips, a thoughtful edge to his expression that didn't mask the fact he was going to make her pay for the information he could give her.

"What's the deal with you and Daimon?" he said, his blue eyes gaining a victorious glimmer, because he thought he had her on the ropes, that she would surrender something he could use against her in some way.

"There is no deal." She tipped her chin up.

Cal folded his arms across his chest, his black T-shirt tightening over his honed muscles. "I'm not telling you where he might have gone until you fess up to things. You're crushing on Daimon."

Cass glared at him. "I am not."

She was.

But she feared this was more than a crush.

She had feelings for Daimon.

And they ran deep.

"It is pretty obvious—" Mari cut off when Cass turned her glare on her.

"It's complicated." Cass didn't want to say any more than that, not even when Calistos and Marinda both looked as if they were expecting her to do just that. She cursed herself when she couldn't stop her nerves, her fears, from getting the better of her and ended up adding, "I'm not sure Daimon really likes me."

Gods, she felt like an idiot schoolgirl with a crush as those words leaked from her.

Desperately hoping one of his friends would reveal his true feelings to her to allay her fears.

Cal shrugged. "He must... since he can't touch you. It can't be lust."

"He can touch me," she admitted, unable to hold that back too, and realised it was the crux of her fears.

Did Daimon only like her because he could touch her? Before she had revealed that she could use magic to negate his ice, he had been attracted to her, hadn't he?

But he had changed after she had revealed that to him. She couldn't deny that, and she had no way of knowing whether the knowledge that he could touch her had only unleashed him, freeing him and allowing him to act on the attraction he felt towards her.

"Shit," Cal muttered and looked at Mari, and then back at her. "I mean... I'd say it explains a lot because you're hardly girlfriend material, but—"

"What is that supposed to mean?" Cass snapped, her hackles rising as she glared at Cal, daring him to admit he had been insinuating that his brother only wanted her because he could touch her, and that Daimon would never consider her as a possible girlfriend.

Not that she wanted to be his girlfriend or anything like it for that matter.

Cal hiked his shoulders. "I'm just saying it as I see it. You, Cassandra, don't strike me as the girlfriend, long-term commitment, type."

"You are hardly in a position to judge me, or must I remind you of the numerous times I have seen you seducing your way through a bar, targeting a whole slew of women?" She gave him a black look, one that she knew conveyed every ounce of her anger because he stiffened.

Turned awkward.

"Yeah, well... shit, uh, changes. I'm just saying, is all," he grumbled and rubbed the back of his neck. His blue eyes filled with worry. "But this thing with Daimon... don't make him think it's more than it is, yeah? I don't want to see my brother get hurt."

Cass threw her hands up, frustration getting the better of her. "That's the second threat I've received tonight."

Cal's right eyebrow jacked up. "Second? Who else threatened you?"

She clamped her lips shut.

He looked as if he was going to push the subject, and then sighed. "Fine. Truth is, Daimon is probably in Hong Kong."

"He's not there." She didn't hide the worry that tinged her voice. "I already checked. There has to be somewhere else he might go."

Aiko appeared at the other end of the kitchen, rubbing her black hair with a pink towel. "Where who might go?"

Her brown eyes were ringed with dark circles, fatigue lacing them. Or perhaps depression. Cass had no experience of that herself, but she could see that Esher's continuing absence was weighing heavily on the young Japanese woman.

"Daimon." Cass's shoulders slumped as hope bled from her. "He was in a... mood. He left and I don't know where he went, and I'm... worried about him."

Cal gave her a look. Not one of his usual smirking glances that said he was going to enjoy pouncing on whatever she had just said or done to use it as payback. He looked worried, and perhaps a little relieved. Because she had just admitted without so many words that she cared about his brother?

"She checked Hong Kong." Cal twisted and eased his backside against the counter, so he could see Aiko.

Aiko's nose wrinkled slightly as she frowned, her eyes dropping to the floor as the towel paused against her hair. When she lifted her gaze and fixed it on Cass, hope dared to bloom again.

"I know where he might have gone." Each word that left Aiko's lips was carefully weighed, her gaze turning scrutinising as she looked across the room at Cass. "I heard them talking about it once... Daimon and... Esher."

Tears laced Aiko's dark eyes, the pain that beat in them sounding in his name.

"Where might he have gone?" Cass felt like a bitch for pushing, but she had the dreadful feeling that time was of the essence.

Aiko's lips parted and then closed, and she stared at Cass, studying her in silence for a long minute before she finally spoke. "He likes to go there when he wants to be alone."

Cass didn't miss the emphasis Aiko placed on the last four words, the warning to give Daimon space.

She couldn't heed it, no matter how much she wanted to do that. Something was wrong with him, and he needed help with his injuries. She couldn't let him be out there, alone, vulnerable, in a bad place. She feared he would do something reckless.

More reckless than allowing daemons to hurt him.

"Please, Aiko," Cass whispered, her voice heavy with the fear that flowed through her.

Cal and Mari exchanged a worried look. Aiko slowly nodded.

"Try heading to Antarctica, to Halley Bay. They talked about it once." Aiko's words offered both a solution, and a problem.

Cass looked down at herself, at her strapless corset and leather trousers.

Hardly the clothing for Antarctica, even in summer.

But she had been raised in the frigid remote reaches of Siberia. She had endured freezing winters. She was tough.

She could handle a little cold.

"Thank you." She bowed her head to Aiko and hurried to her room, dug out the mundane black woollen sweater she had brought with her and pulled it on.

She pulled open the drawers on the dresser, seeking more layers, anything that would keep the chill off her long enough that she could find Daimon.

Nothing in them was of any use to her, so she went to the wall to her right and slid the panel open, revealing a cupboard. It contained a lot of shirts and some trousers. She hurried through them, pushing them down the bar, and breathed a sigh of relief when she reached the end and spotted something tucked in the far corner of the cupboard.

A coat.

She pulled it off the hanger and brushed it down, sent up a prayer that nothing was living in it because the black woollen jacket looked as if it had been sitting there collecting dust for at least a decade.

Cass slipped her arms into it, pulled it closed and formed the incantation, hoping it would work. It was always hit and miss when she didn't know the location she wanted to transport herself to. Sometimes, the magical pathways that connected every place in the world had a different name for the location, and she ended up somewhere she didn't want to be.

Sometimes, there were far too many places named the same thing and she ended up going nowhere.

She focused on Antarctica, on Halley Bay, not knowing what to expect if the spell did work and transported her there.

Magic hummed inside her, pulsed in her bones and flowed in her veins, wrapping her in a layer of warmth that quickly dissipated as she touched down.

Frigid cold blasted her, the icy wind slicing straight through the layers she had donned, numbing her flesh and freezing her blood. She huddled down into the coat as she squinted against the bright vast white that encompassed her, shuddering as the wind felt as if it was cutting her to the bone, flaying the flesh from them.

Snow battered her, saturating her hair in an instant, turning it to tangled black ribbons that sapped even more warmth from her skin. She turned and winced as the wind drove the icy flakes into her eyes, twisted away again and looked around her. Her legs shook beneath her, her feet so cold that she couldn't feel them.

Cass scoured the area, expending valuable energy using a spell to seek out Daimon, a small voice at the back of her mind telling her this was reckless, dangerous, and that she had to go back. She couldn't see more than a few feet through the blizzard and she was already dangerously low on energy. If she lingered, the cold might steal enough of her strength that she would be stranded.

But she had to find Daimon.

A stronger blast of wind hit her in the back, sending her stumbling forwards. She trudged in the direction the wind was pushing her, eyes darting as she tried to make things out. Fear rolled up on her, making her doubt each step she took as her heart pounded, thoughts that she might walk right into a crevasse or off a cliff ricocheting around her mind.

This was foolish.

She had to leave.

She couldn't withstand such harsh elements for much longer. If she tried, she would lose her ability to teleport.

She would die out here.

Alone.

She pulled the jacket closed even tighter, burrowed down into it as a thought struck her, rising from her heart.

She didn't want to die without seeing Daimon's face one last time.

She wanted to see his heart through his eyes again, see him open to her, needed it and refused to give in until she had it. She ached for the feel of his arms around her, his skin heating her.

Cass pulled her right hand away from her coat and coaxed fire into her palm. It warmed her a little, but the flame was small, kept stuttering out in the wind.

She shuffled forwards.

Was it growing darker?

She looked around her, flinching as ice battered the side of her face. It was definitely growing darker. Her steps slowed. Her feet grew heavy.

The flame hovering above her palm died.

Cass's knees gave out and she sank into the snow, teeth chattering as her heart clenched. Mother earth. Sweet gods. She curled over, hugging herself, desperate to get some heat back into her body. She just wanted to see Daimon again.

Would give her last breath to see that he was alive and safe.

The darkness closed in and she tried to fight it, panic lancing her as she realised it wasn't night falling, but her body failing.

The cold that gripped her worsened, sapping the last of her strength.

But then warmth touched her face.

Something lifted her, cradled her gently against a hard chest. A heart beat steady and strong against her ear, loud in spite of the roaring icy wind. Wind that no longer touched her.

The sound died, spun away with the cold and the pain.

Leaving her dizzy and sleepy.

"Don't sleep, baby. Stay with me." Those words roused her, gave her the strength to open her eyes and catch the glimpse of Daimon she had prayed to mother earth to receive.

He leaned over her, his white hair slicked back, his cheeks pink, not concern in his beautiful intense eyes but fear—cold, stark fear that did nothing to warm her.

He bobbed up and down in time with her, kept glancing towards her lap. To her hands. Why? She tried to lift her head to see but it felt too heavy and she collapsed back against him.

Sleep beckoned again.

"Stay awake." He jostled her, jerking her left and then right, moving her arms.

The chilling cold of her coat and sweater disappeared and she tried to look at herself to see what he was doing.

Her eyes slid down to her hands as they felt different. Warmer. He was rubbing them. Her eyes widened, horror flashing through her. Her fingers were mottled, black and red, blue in places. Fear seized her, sank claws deep into her to steal her breath.

Daimon leaned over her and blew on her hands, hot and moist, chasing some of the numbing cold from them, and then he was lifting her again.

The sound of bubbling water filled the deafening silence and she looked down as he eased her into it, her fuzzy mind struggling to comprehend what was happening. The water felt cold, but there was steam rising from it. The fog in her mind gradually cleared as heat began to seep into her.

She looked at Daimon where he leaned against the edge of the hot tub to her left, his face stricken, fear lighting his eyes.

Fear that turned to relief and then to something darker as he sank forwards.

"Why did you do something as stupid as following me?" he bit out, his voice dripping with the anger that flared in his eyes.

Sleep washed over her again, threatening to pull her under as the warmth of the water suffused her. Her eyes slipped shut.

Gods, she wanted to sleep for days.

Maybe forever.

"Stay awake! I won't lose you." Daimon shook her.

She slowly opened her eyes and frowned at him. "I'm here. No need to shout."

"Sorry," he murmured, his white eyebrows furrowing as the anger that had been in his eyes abated, shifting to concern again.

He lifted his left hand and touched her burning cheeks, and she wanted to close her eyes again to savour the blissful coolness of his skin.

Cass struggled to keep her eyes open, stared at his face as he worked to warm her, rubbing her hands and her shoulders, scooping the water over her skin. She had never seen him look so afraid. It was strange to see such a strong warrior looking so weak, ruled by fear.

Fear she had caused.

"I was looking for you," she murmured, her voice hoarse, as if she had been screaming. She wanted to lift her hand and rub her throat, but she didn't have the strength. His pale blue eyes shifted to meet hers. She looked deep into them, drinking her fill of the concern that shimmered in them, the feelings he tried so hard to hide from her, ones that filled her too. "I wanted to make sure you were okay."

His white eyebrows met hard.

"I'm not. Not now. I don't think I ever will be. I feel sick." He lowered his eyes to the bubbling water and her heart clenched, the fear she had managed to banish rising again to consume her as it whispered in her ear, taunting her with the fact she had driven him to this, that she was responsible for him wanting pain. His eyes lifted again, colliding with hers. "I need to hear you'll be all right."

It hit her that he hadn't been talking about his state of mind, but about the state of her.

That touched her, deeper than he would ever know. It warmed her too, gave her back some strength, enough that she managed to lift her hand from the water and place it over his where it gripped the edge of the tub.

"I'll be fine, Daimon. Will you?" Her eyes searched his.

Surprise claimed her as he briefly tangled his fingers with hers, and then cold blasted through her as he released her hand and pulled away.

He busied himself with punching some buttons on a panel, doing it with a vengeance, with such force she expected him to poke a hole straight through it.

The water warmed, deliciously hot.

He settled back beside her again and slipped his left hand into the water, took hold of hers and inspected it.

Cass sucked down a breath, and then looked down at her hands, afraid of what she would see. Relief washed through her. They looked better—flushed pink and not blue or black.

Daimon gently submerged her hands and chunks of ice formed on the surface. "Sorry."

He went to take his hand away and she tried to stop him but wasn't fast enough.

She rubbed her hands together, sneaking a glance at him as he frowned at the panel again. The blood that had been covering him was gone, but the lacerations in his roll-neck remained, and the long gashes that were visible on his chest, shoulders and arms were angry red and still seeping blood in places.

"Will you be all right?" she whispered. "The cuts—"

"Already healing," he interjected, sending another wave of relief through her, this one so strong that she spoke before considering the consequences.

"Why did you let them cut you?"

Guilt danced across his noble features and he turned his cheek to her, and her stomach fell as he all but confirmed she had been right. He had let the daemons hurt him.

She gathered her courage and lifted her hand. Water sluiced down her bare arm and dripped from her elbow, the sound mingling with the gentle bubbling to fill the thick silence.

Daimon tensed when she touched his cheek, and then he closed his eyes, frowned and exhaled through his nose as he leaned into her palm.

"Tell me, please?" she murmured.

This time, he turned his face the other way, away from her, placing himself beyond her reach. He stood and backed off a step, and fear seized her again.

"Stay," she commanded. Her heart lurched into her throat. "Don't leave me. I need you here. I need to know."

"You don't... and I don't want to talk about it. Let it go." He turned and stalked into the house.

Like hell she would.

Cass gritted her teeth, gripped the edge of the tub and pushed herself up. The water weighed her down, making her legs tremble beneath her, but it quickly drained noisily into the tub. Her entire body shook as she lifted her left leg, clutching the tub as she laboured for breath. Her muscles cramped and protested, bones burned but she pushed onwards.

She managed to get her leg over the side of the tub.

Her foot pressed against the broad white tiles of the terrace.

Her leg gave out the moment she put all her weight onto it and she shrieked as the flagstones came at her.

Strong arms banded around her waist and stopped her from hitting it face-first.

Daimon pulled her onto her feet and set her down, muttering, "Foolish woman."

She felt as though she was. She was pursuing a man who wanted nothing to do with her, a man who electrified her and made her feel alive for the first time in her long life. A man she didn't want to leave.

She hadn't been prepared for this—for him.

Cass looked up at him, her brow furrowed as her eyes locked with his.

His beauty, the melancholy he wore, the heat that shimmered just beneath his frosty surface, all of it had entranced her.

Bewitched her.

Now, she didn't want to leave him even when he made her feel as if there was no point in her staying.

More of her strength returned, enough that she could probably cast smaller spells if she dared, maybe even transport herself if she pushed herself hard enough.

A gasp tore from her lips as he slid the zipper on the side of her corset down and her heart jerked, her hand flying to the front of the garment to keep it against her breasts.

"Just trying to get you warm. Getting you out of these wet things is a good place to start." He averted his eyes. "If I didn't think you'd fall on your arse, I'd let you do it yourself."

Cass hesitated, told herself not to read into things and failed dismally.

"I know how you can warm me." She looked up into his eyes when he glanced at her. "Kiss me."

He glowered at her. "No."

"Why not?" She sidled closer, pressing her body to his, and some of the ice in his eyes melted, giving way to heat.

"I can't," he croaked.

"Sure you can. Just purse your lips." She tilted her head up and leaned towards him. "Press them to mine."

"No." It was firmer this time and he gripped her shoulders and pushed her back.

She frowned at him. "Why not?"

"Because," he whispered, the sound tortured, distant, carrying so much pain that her temper shifted course, the spike of frustration and anger she had felt giving way to softer feelings. His eyes leaped between hers. "You are... You... can never be mine."

Cass blinked.

That was why he had changed, going from warming towards her to cold and seeking pain? Because he thought she could never be his?

His hands trembled against her bare shoulders and his breath shook as he stared at her.

Waiting for an answer.

"What made you think that?" It wasn't an answer, but she had to put it out there.

He turned his cheek to her. "You're promised to another."

His eyes brightened, dangerous white ringed with black, and he growled. His hands tightened against her shoulders, pain pricking her there in several places. She angled her head and looked at his left hand, at the icy claws that pierced her.

"Daimon?" She flinched when he snarled and pushed away from her, stalking into the house again. Cass slowly walked after him, not trusting her legs. They were stronger now, but pushing herself would only end with her hitting the ground and she needed to reach Daimon before he did something annoying like teleporting away from her. She breathed a sigh of relief when she made it to the door of the house and found him still inside. "Who am I promised to?"

She winced as she remembered he had seen the letter. For a wonderful moment, she had forgotten about that.

He growled over his shoulder at her. "I don't want to talk about it."

Well, she did. He had snooped at her things and now he was presuming things about her, things that weren't true.

Things that were on the verge of ruining everything.

She crossed the room, caught his wrist and pulled him to face her, almost falling on her backside in the process. "I'm not promised to anyone."

He wrenched free of her. "You are. Someone... I don't know. The letter said it. You must return to bear a child."

A child she didn't want.

With a man she didn't want.

Words bubbled up her throat, things she had only just realised but still hadn't thought she would confess to anyone.

"Daimon." She reached for him.

He smacked her hand away. "Don't!"

He stormed towards the room with the king-size bed in it.

Cass transported herself there and regretted it when she landed in front of him, blocking his path as intended.

And collapsed.

Daimon was there again, catching her, cradling her to him as he looked her over and softly muttered, "We need to get you out of these wet things."

Changeable, beautiful man.

She couldn't keep up with him when he was like this, flitting between polar emotions. She wanted him to stay like this, soft with her, taking care of her.

Letting her be close to him.

She didn't want him to remind her of the letter, or the fact her coven were waiting, expecting her to return.

To do the unthinkable.

She wanted to stay here, lost in Daimon, caught up in a life that felt like an impossible, but beautiful, dream.

"Warm me with a kiss," she whispered.

He stilled, his eyes hardening again. "No. I couldn't bear it."

If he wouldn't kiss her...

She looped her arms around his neck and kissed him.

He responded in an instant, his cool tongue pushing past the barrier of her lips to brush the length of hers. She melted in his arms as they tightened around her, pinning her to him, leaned back and lured him down with her. Her back hit the mattress and she moaned as his weight settled on top of her and he deepened the kiss, branding his name on her soul.

Daimon eased back and looked down at her, something shining in his pale blue eyes.

What was he thinking?

He swept his right hand through her wet hair, smoothing the tangles, his look softening.

"You're beautiful," he husked, sorrow lacing his voice. "I wish you were mine."

So did she.

She thought it, but she couldn't bring herself to say it.

She raised both hands and cupped his cheeks, stared deep into his eyes and lost herself in them, drowning in the emotions they contained. There was pain there, locked deep inside.

What did he want to say but couldn't?

Was it the same words she wanted to voice but refused to come?

"This is pointless," he muttered instead and pressed his hands to the mattress, pushing himself up.

Cass tried to pull him back down to her so she could kiss him again.

He went rigid, his arms locking tight, and she glared at him when she realised she couldn't move him.

"Daimon." She stroked his cheeks. "I don't want to think about all the tomorrows that await me. Please... just have this moment with me?"

Pain flickered in his eyes. "I can't."

"Why not?" Her throat closed up, but she refused to give in to the despair that trickled through her, refused to give up.

"I need more than this moment." He lowered his head and pressed his forehead to hers, his breath washing across her lips.

Familiar fear ran through her, tried to steal her voice, but this time she didn't let it, because her heart screamed that she wasn't the only one who was afraid.

Daimon was too.

Cass palmed his cheeks, drew down a steadying breath and closed her eyes as she whispered.

"So do I, Daimon... So do I. I need you."

CHAPTER 22

Daimon knew he should find the strength to walk away, that it was the best thing to do.

But it wasn't what he wanted.

It wasn't what he needed.

He needed this beautiful, irritating, sorceress who lay beneath him, her pale blue eyes glittering with desire that drummed in his veins too. Fear still had him in its hold, born of a combination of sensing Cass had followed him to Antarctica and discovering her collapsed in a heap, on the verge of death, and the thought of finally giving in to her.

To himself.

He wanted Cass, and he was tired of fighting it, was tired of letting thoughts of tomorrow hold him back when he should have been fighting for her instead. He would make her see that he was the one she really needed. He would give her the piece of himself he had been holding back.

He would make her fall in love with him just as he was falling deeply in love with her.

He pulled down a steadying breath, lowered his head and captured her lips. They were warm against his, incredibly soft, and tasted sweet. He couldn't recall the last time he had kissed someone, wasn't prepared for the way it hit him, rousing fierce hungers inside him and a deep, dark possessiveness.

Cass was his.

He angled his head and breached her lips, kissed her deeper and shivered as she moaned and arched up off the mattress to press against him. A groan slipped from his lips as she wrapped her arms around his neck, pulling him down into contact with her.

The damp from her clothes soaked into his, had him pulling back even when he didn't want to and breaking the kiss.

"Need to get you out of these wet things," he muttered, his breathing rough as he thought about stripping her.

Couldn't remember the last time he had undressed a woman either.

Nerves rose, trying to get the better of him, but he pushed them back down. This wasn't his first time, even if it felt like it.

He reached for the zipper on her corset and paused, glanced into her eyes. "This spell you use to stop me from hurting you, how long will it last?"

Cass's nose wrinkled and she shrugged.

"Maybe thirty minutes more. It's hard to tell." She stroked her palms over his shoulders and down his chest, a wicked edge to her smile. "But if you last longer than that, I can renew it after I give you a gold medal."

He groaned, his face crumpling at the thought of what was to come as heat washed through him, fire lighting up his veins and stirring his cock. It stiffened painfully in his damp jeans.

"If you feel even the slightest chill…" He stared deep into her eyes, making sure she understood, that she would do what he was asking.

"I'll let you know before it happens." She skimmed her fingers over his nipples, sending another shiver through him.

And then warmth.

He looked down, frowned as the cuts he could see through the slashes in his top began to heal before his eyes, and lifted his gaze to lock with hers again.

She hiked her shoulders. "Can't have you not at your physical peak."

He groaned again, wished she would stop reminding him where this was going, because he really wanted to last long enough to at least make it to the silver medal. The way she kept teasing him, making his mind leap forwards to imagine being inside her, was going to have him coming in at bronze if she kept it up.

Daimon focused on small things, starting with unzipping her black corset the rest of the way. When the two sides of the zipper parted, his heart hitched and his breath trembled, all of his focus shifting to his hands as he eased the front open.

"Sweet gods," he muttered, voice scraping low as he stared down at her breasts, transfixed by her dusky nipples as they stiffened, begging for his lips.

Cass looked down at her breasts and then up at his face. "What are you waiting for?"

He wasn't sure.

He swooped on them, telling himself that he had kissed her without hurting her, had touched her without hurting her. He could do this and so much more without hurting her too.

His lips closed around her left nipple and he groaned as she moaned and arched her back up, pressing her breast to his face. Her fingers tangled in his hair, twisting it hard as she clutched him to her.

"Daimon," she whispered, his name a breathless delicious plea that had his cock kicking against his jeans.

He sucked and licked her nipple, lavishing it with the attention it deserved, and lowered his hand to his jeans, palmed his length and shifted it into a less painful position.

Cass only made it harder when she dropped one hand to her other breast and played with her nipple, rolling and tweaking the bud.

Good gods, he felt sure he had never been with a woman who actively pleasured herself right in front of him. The sight of her teasing her own flesh, stoking her own arousal, had him as hard as steel.

He wanted to see what she would do if she had access to other parts of herself.

His hand drifted to her leathers, fumbled with the button and then the zip. They were too damp to push down with one hand so he reluctantly released her and eased back onto his knees.

He gripped both sides of her trousers and shimmied them down, Cass tormenting him the entire time he wrestled with them. She circled her nipples with her fingers, her gaze hooded and fixed on him.

"Really making this hard," he gritted as a thousand hot shivers raced through him, cranking his need up, pushing him to the edge before he had even gotten her naked.

She smiled saucily, lifted her left foot and ran it down his crotch. "Already seems pretty hard to me."

Daimon caught her foot to stop her, glanced at it and stilled. When he had removed her boots, her toes had been black, but now they were a delicate pink again. He dropped his head and kissed each toe.

"Didn't know you had a fetish." Cass's sultry voice teased his senses, keeping his need at a boil.

He lowered her foot and finished removing her leathers, and paused as he tossed them over his shoulder, drinking in the sight of her stretched out on his bed wearing nothing but a flimsy pair of black lace shorts.

Daimon reached for them.

Cass planted her feet against his chest. "Ah-ah... I think it's your turn to lose some clothing."

He was quick to stand and obey that order, tugged his top off and dropped it by his feet, swiftly following it with his jeans. He kicked them off and stood before her, battling another wave of nerves.

Her eyes drifted over him, her pupils dilating as her gaze traversed his chest and then his stomach, and finally settled on his trunks.

"And the rest." She waggled her right foot at his underwear, her eyes remaining locked on it.

He swallowed, ran his fingers along the waistband and then shoved them down and stepped out of them.

Cass moaned as he straightened, her teeth teasing her lower lip as she frowned at him. "Exquisite."

He definitely hadn't been called that before.

She crooked a finger at him before slipping it between her lips to suck it. He groaned as she popped it free of her lips and trailed it between her breasts, over the flat plane of her stomach to her navel and then lower. She traced the waist of her panties, her eyes dark and beckoning him.

Gods, there was a thousand things he wanted to do with her.

But he knew where he wanted to start.

He caught her ankles and spread her legs, leaned over her and pressed his mouth to her flesh through the lace of her panties. She gasped and bucked up, her hand flying to his head, fingers twining in his hair as her breaths came faster.

Daimon groaned and laved her, tasting her sweetness, aching with need that rode him hard, had him wanting to rush.

He tore another gasp from her as he ripped her flimsy underwear away, as his mouth met bare flesh and he stroked his tongue hard over her pert bead.

"Gods," she muttered and clutched him, hips rocking in a sensual way.

And he discovered he loved that about her, loved the fact she participated in everything, didn't just lay there and let him do the work. She rode his tongue, moaning things in Russian that cranked the heat in his veins up another ten degrees.

Daimon stroked his fingers over her soft slick flesh as he suckled her bead, groaned against her as he felt how wet she was, how ready for him. His cock kicked against the blue covers and he lowered his hips and rubbed against them, needing some relief.

Cass cried out when he eased two fingers into her, her heat gripping them tightly as she clenched, ripping another low moan from him. He pumped her as he rubbed his length against the mattress, his breaths coming faster in time with hers.

She suddenly stilled and wriggled, shifting up the bed and pulling away from him.

Had he done something wrong?

He lifted his head to look at her, sure that he had.

She did look angry.

But then her face softened.

"You keep doing that, and I won't get you inside me and I need you inside me, Daimon." She jerked her chin towards him and heat scalded his cheeks when he realised she was talking about him rubbing the covers.

"Been a while," he muttered. "Got a bit carried away."

She smiled softly. "Been a while for me too."

But probably nowhere near as long as it had been for him.

She patted the covers beside her.

He crawled up the bed to her but rather than going where she wanted, he prowled towards her instead. Her smile gained a wicked edge again as he forced her backwards, as she hit the bedclothes beneath him and he covered her again.

She skimmed her hand down his arm as he kissed her, savouring the way her tongue tangled with his, how their breath mingled. A groan leaked from him when she took hold of his hand and placed it between her thighs, stroked herself with him before her fingers trailed away.

He kept stroking her, lost in how slick she was.

So lost he didn't notice her hand moving until it suddenly wrapped around his cock.

He barked out a moan and gritted his teeth, shuddered as bliss rolled through him. Her hand was hot on his flesh, gliding up and down it, sending lightning striking along his nerves with every stroke.

"Gods," he uttered and pressed his forehead to hers, unable to focus on kissing her as she stroked him, as her fingers closed around his shaft to squeeze it.

He was about to tell her to stop when she flipped him and rose over him, her hands pinning his shoulders to the mattress and her lips descending on his. She moaned in time with him as she brought her hips down, as her slick heat pressed against his hard shaft.

Daimon swallowed hard.

Fought the urge to roll her over and bury himself in her.

Because he had the feeling his little sorceress wanted to be in charge.

And gods, he was fine with that.

She stroked her right hand down his chest. His heart drummed hard against it, and he tensed as she reached his stomach.

"Relax," she murmured against his lips.

Easy for her to say.

He breathed through the panic, through the spike in arousal, and focused on kissing her. It worked until she gripped his cock.

He reached for it too, needing to rush this part, before he lost his nerve.

He closed his hand around hers and positioned the blunt tip, groaned with her as it brushed through her soft flesh and nudged inside. The moment he began to inch inside her, he released his length and seized her hips, pushed her down onto it. A sweet cry left her lips, the sound drugging, his new addiction.

Together with the way she rotated her hips on him, swirling them in a maddening way.

He tipped his head back into the mattress, clutched her hips and pumped into her, lost in a thousand colliding sensations. She planted her hands to his chest, scalding him with her touch and kissed him again as she began to move on him, bouncing in time with his thrusts. Her breath stuttered against his lips, breasts brushing his chest each time he plunged into her, her soft cries guiding him.

Daimon pressed his heels into the bed and bent his knees, pumping her harder, losing himself as need built inside him, pushing him to the edge. He reached for release with every thrust, each downward plunge Cass made to take him back into her, every gasping moan that she breathed against his lips between kisses.

She murmured things in Russian again.

Demanding things.

Things that had him smiling as he gripped her hips, as he gave her exactly what she wanted, stroking her with the entire length of his cock on each long fast thrust.

She tensed, her moans growing more desperate, and his balls drew up as she gripped him, as she tightened around him and had stars winking across his vision. Good gods.

Cass broke away from his lips, feverishly kissed and nipped at his shoulder, and then pushed back. She threw her head back as she planted her hands against his chest, her black hair spilling like a waterfall down her back as she rode him harder. Her face twisted, bliss painted across it, and he groaned as he watched her.

As he watched his length entering her over and over again.

The dark possessive side of him snarled that she was his now.

He wouldn't let anyone take her from him.

He grasped her hips and thrust harder into her, possessing her, losing himself to that darker side of his blood. She moaned louder, her face screwing up, lips parting as she tilted her head back.

"Oh gods," she whispered.

And then screamed.

Her entire body tensed and then pulsed around him, her thighs quivering against his hips as she struggled for breath.

Daimon roared as he followed her, as seed boiled up his shaft and he sank it deep into her, spilling himself so hard his vision tunnelled. He held her on him as his length pulsed and throbbed, clutched her there long after he was done and couldn't convince himself to release her.

He stared at her, keeping her on him, feeling himself inside her—connected to her.

Mine.

The darker side of his blood snarled that word and he felt it in every inch of him.

She was his.

And he was never letting her go.

Eventually, Cass sagged against his chest, her warm breaths skating across his skin, and he wrapped his arms around her, heart thundering, body tingling as he struggled to come down.

He felt her smile against his chest.

Smiled too when she patted it and whispered.

"Gold medal."

CHAPTER 23

Cass lazed at Daimon's side, sheltered in his arms, her legs tangled with his and her fingers maddening him as they traced circles on his chest, teasing his bare skin with her warmth. A little smile curled her lips as her hand drifted lower, the satisfied edge to her pale blue eyes hitting him hard.

But not as hard as the fact he was holding her like this, sharing a quiet moment that felt intimate.

Life-altering for them both.

He lifted his hand and brushed two fingers through her wavy raven hair, clearing a lock from her face so he could see it better. Gods, she was beautiful. More so now her make-up had been washed away, revealing her natural beauty. Stunning ice-blue eyes that glittered with faint silver stars. Long black lashes framing them. A subtly sloping nose he wanted to drop a kiss on. Full rosy lips that begged him to kiss her there instead.

He had never seen a woman as beautiful, as bewitching as her.

He smiled slightly.

Maybe that was his feelings doing the talking, placing her on that high pedestal for him to worship. He was sure all his brothers would say the same about their women.

She leaned back and he didn't stop her, not when her fingers kept gliding downwards and arousal tightened his body, had his muscles tensing in a way that was sure to keep her eyes on his body and her mind on another round of lovemaking.

Her tempting lips pursed as her eyes dropped, following her hand. Her fingers encircled his navel. Her gaze flicked up to meet his.

"Is this your favour mark?" She traced one of the wavy beams of ink that arced towards his left hip.

The last time she had asked him that, he hadn't answered her.

He nodded and glanced down, bit back a groan as he watched her slip her hand lower, to follow the beam that reached down towards his groin.

"Who is it from?" She teased the pointed tip of the beam, far too close to his stirring cock for him to focus on delivering an answer to that question. She seemed to sense it, because she dragged her hand back up and circled his navel, a lazy swirl that kept his blood at a low boil. "Who?"

He swallowed, shunned the hungers that rode him, and looked back into her eyes. "Apollo."

"Apollo," she repeated, her voice low and thoughtful. "Odd that a god of the sun would favour a god of something aligned with winter."

It wasn't the first time someone had said such a thing to him, and he shut it out, refusing to allow Penelope into this moment. He had loved her, but now that he was looking back, that love had been slow to come, had only manifested after he had discovered she had fallen pregnant.

And gods, that made him feel like a dick.

He had wanted to stand by her, and he would have spent the rest of his life devoted to her and their family if she hadn't been taken from him, but the love he had felt for her was nothing like the feelings he had for Cass.

Those feelings made him see that what he had thought was love had been something born of obligation and a need to take responsibility rather than born of his heart.

If she hadn't fallen pregnant, he would have drifted apart from her soon enough, moving on to another woman.

He hated thinking about her in that way, but it was the truth.

He had loved her, but he hadn't been in love with her.

He stared at Cass, balancing on a precipice that felt dangerous, a fall in all directions.

Before a question could arise from his heart, he focused on what they had been talking about, using it to keep thoughts about his feelings at bay.

"According to my parents, Apollo saw the creativity in me, the ability to love art and music, and to create art too, and that was the reason he chose to give me his favour." He looked down at his navel, at the sun that was a shade darker than his skin right now, all calm wavy beams. When his mood faltered, it darkened to black and the beams grew pointed and jagged.

"You are good at sculpture." She pushed herself up on her left elbow and looked towards the door of the bedroom. "I noticed the marble statues in the garden."

All his work.

"You got me." He didn't miss the look that flitted across her face, one that said she did have him, and in more than the way he had meant it.

He also didn't miss the troubled edge that her eyes gained following it.

She had promised no talking about tomorrow, and he was trying not to think about it. It wasn't going to happen. Not if he had any say in it. Cass was his and he was going to fight to keep her. He was going to do all in his power to convince her that this was where she wanted to be.

In his arms.

He tightened those arms around her and kissed her, savouring the softness of her lips against his, how she opened for him and teased his tongue with hers as she leaned into his kiss, seeking more.

Daimon groaned as she pressed her body against his, her warmth seeping into him, her softness enticing him. He lowered his hands, one claiming the small of her back as the other cupped her bare backside beneath the covers. He eased her closer, relished her sweet moan as her hips rocked forwards to meet his.

He broke away from her lips and kissed along her jaw, trailed his mouth down her throat and peppered it with kisses as he held her, kept her pinned against him, filled with a need to clutch her tighter and never let her go.

"This is nice," she whispered and arched her head back, giving him better access to her throat. "I could get used to this... Waking in your arms. Being worshipped by you... Worshipping you."

He groaned again and nuzzled her neck. "I could get used to this too... and it's more than nice."

She sighed and skimmed her hands up his shoulders and neck and claimed his cheeks. She pulled him away from her throat and kissed him again, soft ones that roused feelings in him, sensations of warmth and lightness he hadn't experienced in a long time.

They were too much.

He pulled back and pressed his forehead to hers, needing a moment to get his unruly emotions back under control, before he did something that made him look like a fool.

Like tearing up.

Cass stroked his cheeks, her eyes fixed on his, the soft look in them saying it was too late and she already knew he was fighting emotions that were too powerful for him to handle.

He stared at her.

This had to last more than today, more than tomorrow. It had to last forever. He didn't want to give her up, never wanted to be apart from her.

He had to convince her that duty wasn't everything. Sometimes, it didn't make you happy. Sometimes, it was a torment, one that it was better to turn your back on. He was testament to that. He had hated every moment he had been in this world, trapped here within his ice, separated from everyone he loved by fear of hurting them.

He stared deeper into her eyes, trying to see her true feelings about what her coven wanted her to do, hoping to catch a glimpse of them. She had ignored their summons on repeated occasions if the letter was to be believed. That had to mean she had her reservations about going through with this tradition, fulfilling her duty to the coven.

It had to.

He needed to get her to admit the real reason she had been avoiding returning to the coven.

Something vibrated.

His phone.

He frowned as he drew back from Cass, torn between saying what was on his mind, trying to get that confession from her, and answering it.

It could only be one of his brothers, and the last thing he needed was whoever was on the other end of the line stepping to his house and finding him tangled in the sheets with Cass.

Maybe he could wait for the call to end and then fire off a message to them.

He rolled and leaned over the edge of the bed, fished his jeans from the floor and pulled his phone from the pocket. He grimaced as a glowering picture of Ares filled the screen and he saw the notification at the top telling him he had nine missed calls and a lot of text messages.

Daimon twisted onto his back and sighed as his head hit the pillows.

"Ares," he said as Cass gave him a curious look.

"Answer it." She nudged his shoulder and he reached for her, but she evaded him, scooting to the edge of the bed to stand and tease him with her nakedness. "I'll shower while you speak to him."

Daimon groaned. "That's not helping."

He wanted to be in the shower with her, washing her, worshipping her.

She cast a pointed look at his hips beneath the covers. "It isn't?"

He ignored the hard-on he was sporting and thoughts of forgetting his brother's call and showering with Cass instead, and answered his phone.

"What's up?" He gunned for casual and instantly regretted it when Ares's voice boomed down the line.

"What's up? What's up! I'll tell you what's up, little brother," Ares barked and Daimon flinched. "You go AWOL, Cass goes AWOL too, and then Cal tells me she went off to Antarctica, so I'm guessing she went after you, and then we don't hear from either of you for hours. *Hours*."

Daimon knew better than to take the pause as an invitation to speak. Ares was probably just wrestling his temper back under control, trying not to set his phone on fire.

Megan's voice broke the tense silence, too distant for him to make out what she said.

A noisy scratching sound hit him and then Ares responded, muffled by his hand. "I'm dealing with it."

A pause.

"No, I won't play nice," Ares grumbled. "Daimon knows better than to disappear like that."

His brother huffed, whatever Megan said to him cooling some of his fire, because when he next spoke, he sounded around three hundred percent calmer.

"Fine."

The scratching sound came again and then Ares's voice, louder and clearer now.

"Cal told me something else too. Apparently, Cass can touch you. So, do we need to mount a rescue or is this a do not disturb situation like Cal thinks it is?"

Daimon wasn't going to answer that question.

Apparently, his silence was answer enough for Ares.

"I'll call off the search party then. Valen was looking ready to step to Hong Kong. You're lucky you answered this time or you would have had unwelcome company." Ares's voice brightened, losing the hard edge, and he chuckled as Valen muttered something in the background, probably about stepping to Hong Kong to disturb them anyway. "Just be back before dark… and… be careful, okay?"

Now his brother sounded like a strict parent and it grated a little, but he let it slide because he had felt protective of Ares too when he had lost his power and found Megan.

Daimon had worried that Megan would end up hurting his brother. It was understandable that his brothers would feel the same concern about Cass.

"Sure," he mumbled into the phone, shutting out the sound of the water running in the adjoining bathroom. "Tell Marinda that Cass is fine… but next time she wants to do something as reckless as following me to Antarctica without the appropriate protective gear, someone better stop her."

"Got it." Ares paused, as if he wanted to say something more, and then added, "Laters."

Daimon ended the call and sank back against the mattress, his breath leaving him on a long sigh as he dropped the phone on the bed beside him and stared at the ceiling.

He wasn't looking forward to returning to Tokyo.

He could only imagine how badly his brothers were going to tease him, and Cass.

Daimon tossed the navy covers aside and rolled from the bed, and huffed when the shower switched off, his opportunity to join Cass there slipping through his fingers.

It was probably for the best. While she could use a spell to protect her from his ice when he touched her, he wasn't sure that magic would protect her if he froze the water around her, and that was bound to happen if he showered with her. He doubted she would find the alternative arousing. Normally when he showered, he cranked the water up to the point where it would scald a normal person, and even then he would end up with the parts of him that weren't directly under the spray of water covered in a fine layer of frost.

Cass emerged from the bathroom, tucking a black towel in around her breasts, and stopped. Her pale blue eyes lifted to meet his across the room, a small smile curling her lips, drawing him to her. He crossed the room and feathered his fingers down her jaw, eased her head back and dropped a kiss on her lips.

She made a small noise of appreciation. "I could definitely get used to this."

When he went to kiss her again, she pressed her palms to his bare chest, her touch light but commanding. He looked down into her eyes and sighed as he caught the question in them.

"Ares offered to send a rescue team. He thought maybe you were holding me against my will." He meant it to sound teasing, but her beautiful face blackened and sparks lit her eyes.

"All of your brothers think so ill of me." She twisted away from him and her shoulders lifted in a soft sigh.

"Not true." He shook his head when she cast him a glance that said it was. "They're just being protective. It's what brothers do."

The light faded from her eyes and she looked down at her feet. "I wouldn't know."

"You don't have any siblings?" When she hesitated to answer that question, a crinkle forming between her fine black eyebrows, he added, "Do you have any family?"

A tiny shake of her head.

She tried to smile, but it faltered, and gods, it broke his heart to see it and feel the shift in her mood. He hadn't meant to hurt her with that question, with talking about his brothers so casually. If he had known it was a sore subject for her, he would have kept his big mouth shut.

"Eric felt like family," she whispered, attempting another smile.

Her eyes glittered with emotions as she finally looked at him, with tears that tore at him, had him closing the gap between them again and wrapping his arms around her. He had been jealous of Eric before, too wrapped up in his own feelings to notice how badly hers had been hurt by his death.

"Sorry," he muttered and stroked his fingers down her damp hair.

He pressed a kiss to it and cursed when he left frost blooming on the wet strands. He tried to pull back, but she wrapped her arms around his waist, pinning him to her.

"Don't," she murmured, clutching him so tightly that the ache in his heart worsened. "The spell will kick in. Don't let me go."

He didn't intend to. Not now. Not ever.

He stroked her hair, caressed her shoulders, felt strangely vulnerable as he held her like this, as if he was the one who was hurting. Maybe it was seeing Cass, his indomitable sorceress, brought so low and desperate for someone to hold her together, for him to hold her together, that made him feel that way. He couldn't remember ever being needed like this.

Daimon stood there, holding her, giving her the moment she needed and wishing there was something more he could do for her.

He pressed another kiss to her hair and murmured against it, "I don't know anything about your situation, but you have family, Cass."

She dipped her head, released him and brought her right hand up to her face, her actions hidden by her fall of black hair. When she straightened, her eyes were red, but she had erased all trace of her tears.

Almost all of them anyway.

He lifted his hand and caught one glistening teardrop on his index finger, stared at it as it froze into a perfectly clear crystal of ice that glittered like a diamond.

"The coven—" she started.

He shook his head. "I meant Marinda. Marinda is your family. I didn't get to choose my family, but if I had been able to choose it, like you were able to choose Eric and Marinda, I probably would have chosen my brothers. Or maybe subbed a few out. They can drive me crazy at times. I'm not saying this well. I just wanted to say that you got to pick your family and I think you chose pretty damn good. I can see Marinda means a lot to you."

Cass nodded. Smiled. "She's like a sister, and a daughter. I've known her from before she was born and I watched her grow up. I learned so much about what it was like to be a real family from her, or at least I thought I did. Coming here... meeting you and your brothers... it's made me realise I didn't really know what a family was."

"Your coven isn't like a family?"

She shook her head, frowned and then nodded. "It is. It is my family, and it's dear to me, but it's just... different."

Warmth shone in her eyes, backing up her words, making him see that she meant them and that her coven was dear to her, important and necessary. He wanted to probe more so he could understand what was different about her coven that made her feel she had never really known what a family was like, but she drew down a breath, sighed it out and tilted her head up.

"I had an idea when I was in the shower."

He smiled. "Did it involve me being in the shower too?"

A pretty blush stained her cheeks and she pushed his chest with her right hand. "No. Yes... but this idea came after that."

He slipped his arm around her waist and tugged her closer to him again, glad to see the storm clouds lifting from her eyes.

His gaze dropped to her lips, hunger to taste them rising inside him again. "So let's hear it."

"I can't when you're looking at me like that. I just want to kiss you." She leaned towards him, pressing her chest to his.

"So kiss me," he husked.

She tiptoed and captured his lips, her kiss brief but passionate, rousing fire in his veins that lingered when she pulled back again, a sigh escaping her.

He wanted more.

Wasn't sure he would ever get enough of kissing her.

"I want to help you and your brothers." She raised her hands and framed his face with them, looked deep into his eyes, hers revealing how much she wanted that. "I have some books at home, ones about forbidden magic. They might be helpful. If nothing else, they speak of necromancy. I'd like to get them and some other things."

He nodded. "I'll take you."

Mostly because he didn't want to let her out of his sight. He wasn't sure how much the Erinyes knew about her, and he wasn't going to risk them knowing about her island home, letting her go off alone. He wouldn't be able to live with himself if she ended up hurt or worse because he hadn't gone with her.

"I was hoping you'd say that." She pressed closer, the smile that tugged at her lips sending a hot thrill through him as her gaze turned hooded. "Maybe we could hide from your brothers a little longer there."

That sounded more than good. He didn't want to face his brothers, and he had the impression she didn't want to face them yet either. Both of them were going to get a grilling when they returned.

He forced himself to release her, and rifled through his dresser for some underwear and a fresh roll-neck long-sleeve T-shirt. As he tugged on his trunks, Cass sighed, drawing his gaze to her.

She stared longingly at his backside.

And then her blue eyes lifted to lock with his. "It's such a shame to cover up all that perfection."

He stifled the blush that wanted to climb his cheeks by jerking his chin towards her bare curves. "I'd say the same about you, but I'm damned if I want you parading around like that in front of anyone but me."

Her smile turned wicked. Teasing. "Someone sounds a little possessive."

"A little?" He shook his head at that. "Try a lot. I'm doing my best not to lock you in this room to keep you away from my brothers and…"

He trailed off, the words he had been about to say echoing around his mind.

And any other male.

"Daimon," she whispered.

He shook his head. "Let's not. Not right now."

Because he wanted to keep living in this dream, fooling himself for as long as he could.

He pulled his top on and followed it with a pair of black jeans, found some socks and then hunted for his boots, leaving Cass in the bedroom.

Needing a moment to breathe.

Daimon stopped in front of his boots where he had discarded them near the couch, stared at them as he tried to piece himself back together, rebuilding the illusion that everything was going to go the way he wanted it to.

Things never did.

He tugged his socks on and jammed his feet into his boots, had just finished lacing them when Cass emerged, her sinful curves clad in black leather trousers and her corset.

The look on her face said they were going to have to talk about things eventually.

Eventually was a damned long way off as far as he was concerned.

He was going to fight for her and he was going to win.

He crossed the room, his boots loud on the pale marble floor, and took hold of her hand.

Stepped with her to Karavostasis, to the small walled garden that hugged her island home.

Power immediately pressed down on him from all directions, had his gaze whipping to the terrace of the white building.

To the five women who stood there, all dressed in black.

Witches.

Cass tensed, her fingers clenching his so tightly it hurt, and her fear washed over him.

Daimon stared down the five witches.

It seemed he was going to be fighting for Cass much sooner than he had anticipated.

Because he was damned if they were going to take her from him.

CHAPTER 24

Daimon guided Cass behind him and faced the witches. One with sleek golden hair stepped down from the terrace and moved towards him, the other four following her.

"What is the meaning of this?" The blonde sorceress looked from him to Cass as she emerged from behind him.

"I'm helping this god and his brothers with an important mission." Cass's voice hitched, wobbled a little as she tilted her chin up and he wanted to check on her but kept his eyes on the witches.

She was afraid of these women.

He could sense it in her as she braved a step forwards, drawing level with him.

"Cassandra, we have given you time. More than enough. We have accepted your delays… your excuses."

"They weren't excuses. I have important—" Cass slammed her mouth shut as the blonde cast her a withering look, silver-violet flecks sparking like lightning in her dark eyes.

"You will come with us. You will return to your family and fulfil your duty. No more delays."

Over his dead body.

He had only just found Cass and he wasn't going to lose her. He wasn't going to let these witches take her from him when she clearly didn't want to go with them. While he had been trying to fool himself into believing she didn't want to give herself to another male, to bear his child, he felt sure of it now.

He focused, silently mustering his strength, calling forth his power, stoking it so it was ready for him to unleash it at a moment's notice.

The lead witch's dark eyes slid to him. "It dares to threaten us?"

Damn. She had sensed the rising power within him.

Nothing else for it then.

He shrugged and ice shot up from the earth beneath her. His grin faded before it could fully manifest as she disappeared, gone in the blink of an eye, together with the other witches.

Had they teleported away?

Had he won?

That was easy.

He almost grinned.

"Daimon." Cass lunged for him, panic lacing her voice.

Before she could reach him, one of two brunette witches appeared between them and shoved her back while launching an orb of twisting blue and violet light at him.

Daimon stepped and reappeared on the flat roof of the small white house, exhaled hard when the spell tore up the garden, leaving a huge crater in the dirt where he had been.

Maybe this wasn't going to be so easy after all.

He growled and threw his hand forwards, launching shards of ice at the witch as she made a grab for Cass. The brunette gasped and shot backwards, snatching her hands to her chest as the ice shards slammed into the earth between her and Cass, creating a wall between them.

"Please, I am only helping this god. It's a contract—" Cass's voice cut off as she threw a panicked glance at him, her gaze colliding with his.

He tensed as he sensed power behind him, stepped and snarled as fire raked down his back, flames licking around him in the darkness of the teleport.

"Daimon!" Cass shrieked, her fearful scream following him into the black abyss.

When he landed behind Cass, he grabbed her arm in one hand and swept his other one upwards. Great spears of ice shot up from beneath the witch on the roof. She nimbly dodged them but he kept them coming. They rolled in a wave towards her wherever she ran, the ice shattering a few feet behind the tip of the wave.

A tip that caught her in the calf and ripped an agonised cry from her as she went down.

Daimon grinned and focused his power on the witch, on dealing a killing blow.

"No!" Cass seized his arm and pulled him backwards, and he faltered, looked at her and caught the fear in her eyes.

Fear for her fellow witch now.

He hesitated and the witch was swift to make her escape, disappearing into the ether.

"Shit," he muttered as he sensed the conflict in Cass, saw it shining in her eyes as she glanced between him and the remaining witches where they were regrouping, forming a wall between him and Cass's home.

As much as he wanted to do it, he couldn't kill these witches. If he did, it would only upset her. He could see how torn she was as she turned to the witches, her dark eyebrows furrowing as she stepped in front of him. They were Cass's family, and he would hate it if someone killed one of his family.

"Please, this is just a contract." Cass cast him a pained look when the lead witch looked as if she didn't believe that, as if she knew that Daimon was something more to her.

He hated that look in her eyes, because he had the terrible feeling she was considering going with them to stop the fight.

He couldn't let that happen.

He couldn't let them take her.

Darkness surged through him, had his nails transforming into short claws and his canines aching as they elongated into fangs. Ice rippled over his fingers, hardened and transformed them into long talons as the air chilled around him. He flexed them and snarled at the witches as colourful light glowed from their palms, magic that laced the air with a tremendous feeling of power.

Cass didn't want them to fight, but neither he nor the witches were willing to back down.

He didn't want to hurt Cass, but he was going to have to in order to keep her with him, because he couldn't let these witches take her. He wouldn't. She belonged with him.

She was his.

Mine.

The darkness within him snarled that word, it drummed in his blood with every hard beat of his heart as he prepared himself.

He would do his best not to kill any of the witches, but he was going to fight.

For her.

The witches hurled the spells at him as one and he stepped, appeared behind one. He grabbed her by the back of her neck. She shuddered and cried out, the sound harrowing as it echoed across the sea before them. Ice rapidly spread over her shoulders and back and he released her as she went down.

Out of action but not dead.

He wasn't sure if these witches knew the same spells as Cass did, or how long his ice would be effective against them when he was using it to drain them of their strength and knock them out rather than kill them. All he knew was that he needed to protect Cass.

That need blazed inside him, controlling his actions, commanding him to deal with the witches in the only way he could without hurting his sorceress.

He stepped again and landed near the next witch, roared as pain ripped up his side and he staggered backwards. Violet smoke poured from a wound above his hip, the same place he had taken a nasty hit from the daemons last night.

He bared his fangs at the blonde witch who had her arm outstretched towards him and cast his right hand at her before he could consider what he was doing, rage getting the better of him. Five spears of ice formed and shot towards her.

The witch didn't move.

She casually raised her hand, her palm facing him, and the ice spears shattered as they struck an invisible barrier.

"Deal with him." The witch turned imperiously away from him, as if he was nothing more than a gnat, insignificant and unworthy of her time.

He was a son of Hades. A god. He would teach her to show him more respect.

The darkness pouring through his veins surged stronger, claiming more of him, and he was swift to give in to it.

He leaped at the lead witch on a vicious snarl.

One of the other witches shot into his path and he grabbed her by her throat, didn't even look at her as he tossed her aside. In the distance, water splashed as she hit it. He lunged for the blonde witch, growled when the woman evaded him, too fast for him to grab.

The same spell Cass had used to taunt him in Hong Kong.

He focused his senses, grinned as he felt her, and twisted and launched his hand out. His hand clamped down on her forehead as she appeared, icy talons curling around to pierce her flesh and draw blood that stained her blonde locks.

"Belle!" another witch shrieked and fire slammed into his back, shoving him forwards and heating his skin to an unbearable degree for a moment before his ice kicked in again.

He stared into Belle's dark eyes and grinned at her to flash fangs as he tightened his grip.

But still couldn't bring himself to kill.

He glanced at Cass, caught the pain and fear in her eyes as she stood as still as a statue, saw the conflict that ran through him as it ran through her too.

Belle's irises brightened to silver-lilac and she grabbed his arm in both hands.

He bellowed, entire body juddering as pain lit him up, fire that felt as if it was searing his insides, melting them.

His icy talons shattered.

"Daimon!" Cass's voice rang in his ears as he struggled against the next wave of fire as it wrapped around him and consumed him. Her voice gained pitch. "Please don't hurt him."

She said something else, something muffled by the sound of his own agonised roar as it tore from his lips.

And then the fire ceased.

The witch released him.

Daimon sagged to his knees, breathing hard, entire body still aflame as he called on his ice, desperate for the cold to soothe him and steal away his pain.

"Stop and I'll go with you," Cass said.

For a sweet moment, he thought she was speaking to him.

"Very well." Belle's voice cut through him, had him surging to his feet as he heard the victory in it.

She hadn't won this battle.

He mustered his ice, fought the lingering effects of her spell to reform the crystal talons over his fingers, and locked his knees, refusing to let the weakness invading him send him back onto them.

He had to stop the witches.

This time he wouldn't hold back. He wouldn't. Cass would hate him if he hurt her family, but he would bear it, because he couldn't bear the thought of losing her.

Or the thought of what would happen if she returned to her coven.

Cass stepped between him and Belle.

"Move aside, Cass," he said, his eyes remaining locked on the witch she was protecting. "You don't need to go with them. I can handle this."

"Daimon," Cass murmured and he glanced at her, meant only to check on her but lingered as he saw the hurt in her eyes, the pain she tried to mask with a smile.

She didn't want to go. It was right there in her eyes for him to read, all of her feelings about her coven and what was going to happen to her laid bare.

"Just come to me, Cass. We can leave. Never come back." He extended his hand to her, let the ice melt from it as he turned it palm up, reaching for her, silently begging her to take it.

Sorrow flitted across her face, and he wasn't sure whether it was because she was going to do as he asked and was sad that she was turning her back on her family, or because she was going to leave him.

"Cass," he whispered and stretched for her, needing her to take his hand. Needing her to choose him.

She drew down a breath, tipped her shoulders back and came to him.

Relief swept through him as she stroked her fingers over his palm.

His smile faltered, a frown flickering on his brow as his head grew foggy, thoughts spinning and colliding, and his body felt heavy.

He looked at her, his eyebrows furrowing as disbelief swept through him.

"I'm sorry," she whispered, voice so low he barely heard her, her eyes shimmering with hurt and regret, and fear.

He tried to shake his head, growled through his teeth when it felt too heavy to move, and struggled to find his voice as the fog grew thicker, clouding his mind.

"Don't..." He couldn't manage any more than that, could only stare into her eyes and see she had heard the rest of what he had wanted to say.

Don't do this.

Don't leave him.

A smile wobbled on her lips and he silently cursed her for putting on a brave face, for hiding her true feelings from him and her coven. She didn't want this. He was right about that. He had to be. So why was she doing this to him?

"Go do your duty," she murmured softly, a hint of sorrow in it, "And I'll be back as soon as I've done mine."

Daimon cursed her again in his head and struggled against the effects of the spell, desperation mounting inside him, driving him to do something because doing her duty meant getting pregnant. He couldn't bear the thought of her with another man, doing something she didn't want, letting that male and her coven use her in that way.

"You... don't... want... this," he croaked, each word a labour that stole his strength.

Each word seeming to cleave a wound in Cass, pulling the pain she was trying to conceal to the surface of her eyes.

"I have to do it," she said, nothing more than a throaty, pained whisper.

Her black eyebrows furrowed and she reached her hands up towards his face, stopped herself and flexed her fingers.

Before he could say another word, Belle seized hold of her and they all disappeared.

Pain tore through him, chased by fury so deep that the darker side of his blood howled for violence, for revenge, hurt by the thought she would betray him like this.

He wrestled against the spell she had hit him with, refusing to let it disable him any longer. She didn't want this. He couldn't let her do it. He had to stop her.

She would hate herself if she let someone do this to her.

A feeling hit him, rocked him so hard he was surprised he remained standing as the entire world seemed to tilt on its axis around him.

He more than cared about her.

He was in love with her.

He stared at her small home, feeling her in it and the garden, smelling her in the warm air, replaying over and over how she had looked at him when she had been in his arms.

Recalling how he had felt then.

Happy. Afraid. Excited.

It dawned on him that he had never really taken a risk in a relationship, even when he thought he had. He had always gone with the flow, never feeling anything he could label as true love, never willing to let anyone in too deep.

But gods, he wanted that with Cass. She was under his skin already, had burrowed her way deep into his heart, had done it without him noticing. Or maybe he had been in denial because he had thought a relationship with her was impossible.

Maybe he had been falling for her from the moment he had first set eyes on her.

It had been more than a craving he had felt then.

It had been the first stirrings of love.

And now his beautiful, enthralling, brave sorceress had left him.

But he wouldn't let her go that easily.

He knew she needed to do her duty, that it was important to her, just like her family were, but he couldn't stand the thought of her bearing another man's child. There had to be a way to keep her with him. She was his and he needed her, more than he could ever make her see even if he had thousands of years with her.

An image popped into his head.

Cass pregnant, her gaze downcast at her swollen belly as she ran her hands over it, heavy with child.

His eyes stretched wide.

With *his* child.

He shook at the thought of that, wanted it but feared it so much at the same time. It would keep her with him, but it would also place her in even more danger. The daemons would target her, seeking to weaken him by taking her and their unborn child from his life.

He couldn't survive that again. Not this time.

Losing Cass would kill him.

His love for her was soul deep, burning inside him, fierce and consuming. Absolute. He *loved* her.

The sort of love that made a god crazy.

He didn't want to risk her, but he didn't want to lose her either.

He wasn't sure what to do. He wasn't sure what he wanted.

Did he want a child with Cass?

The image of her pregnant with his child was wondrous and addictive, warming him despite the cold that numbed him. He wanted to see her like that.

But it was too dangerous.

He cursed and fought to inch his foot forwards, shock rippling through him when he found he could move. His feet were heavy, muscles liquid beneath his skin, but he managed a few steps, reaching the terrace of her home.

Daimon clutched the wooden pole that supported the slatted roof and pulled himself up onto the terrace. He pressed his hand to the white wall to his right and supported himself as he trudged forwards, breathing hard with each step he managed.

A god on a mission.

He had to find Cass.

He wasn't sure what he would do when he located her and he wasn't going to worry about it. Finding her came first. He would tackle whatever came after that when it came.

Right now, he just needed to see her.

He just needed to speak with her.

Before it was too late.

Daimon made it inside and turned left, gripped her desk and pulled the drawers open. He grabbed all the papers she had stacked inside them and tossed them onto her desk. He ignored the ones that weren't from her coven and read the ones that were, and something struck him.

They were all summons.

And they dated back years.

He pressed his hands to the top of the wooden desk and leaned forwards, over one letter in particular. The first one she had received and ignored.

She had been avoiding this for so long, and it boosted the feeling he had.

She didn't want this.

What had made her change her mind now?

Him.

He squeezed his eyes shut and dug his claws into the desk. She had gone with the witches to protect him, to stop them from killing him.

Daimon cursed her again.

And stepped.

CHAPTER 25

Black blood sprayed from the puncture wound in the male's neck, splattered across the front of Keras's shirt as he tightened his grip on the daemon, pressing claws into his flesh as he lifted him into the air. The thing writhed, legs thrashing as he desperately grappled with Keras's arm, short claws tearing through his black shirtsleeves.

Keras grinned as his grip tightened further, as the wretch's face reddened and his eyes rolled back, gasping breaths leaving his lips as his struggles slowed.

Pleasure rolled through Keras, sweet and intense as he watched the thing slowly die.

As he sensed the others in the shadows around him, twitching in the darkness, closing in on him where he stood in the middle of the broad swath of green in the heart of Paris.

When the daemon had gasped his last desperate breath and stared at him with sightless eyes, Keras casually discarded him.

Slowly turned and scanned the darkness, his heightened vision picking out all the daemons that hid in the bushes and behind the trunks of the trees that surrounded the edge of the park.

Keras canted his head.

Waited.

Anticipation hummed in the air around him, the night thick with it.

Buzzed inside him.

He rolled his shoulders and twisted his neck, loosening and warming up his muscles.

Waited.

A breath.

A shift in the air.

Keras pivoted, lips stretching in a grin as he slammed his palm into the throat of a female and grasped it, as shadows wrapped around her legs and she screamed, rending the silence with her desperate, pathetic shriek.

She died too quickly.

He tossed her aside and flexed his claws.

Waited.

Two broke cover and rushed him. Another two following hot on their heels.

Keras let them reach him, let them land a blow.

Because it was nice to let them feel they stood a chance against the darkness.

Against him.

The last of the four reached him and he began to fight back, raked claws over the thigh of one as he dropped and spun his leg out, catching the ankles of another. The two collided and grappled with each other as they went down. He spun up onto his heels and grinned as he backhanded the only female, sent her flying across the grass to slam into a tree. Wood cracked. Black blood gushed from the point where a branch impaled her.

Five more daemons charged him.

Keras ducked beneath the blow of a large male and twisted, slammed his fist into the daemon's gut and lifted him off his feet with the force of his blow. He pulled back and before the wretch's feet could touch the earth again, he smashed his other fist into the fiend's face in an arcing blow that drove him into the dirt on his back.

He kicked his right foot forward, the heel of his black leather shoe hitting its target—the wretch's cheek. A wet crunch broke the silence and the male went limp.

Keras's green eyes flicked to his next victim.

The one he had clawed, who was spilling foul smelling blood all over the place as he tried to limp away, heading for the treeline.

Keras tilted his head back. Looked down his nose at the thing. Grinned.

Shadows shot up around the male, twisted and branched into a hundred vicious barbs that pierced the male all at once.

He didn't even get the chance to scream.

The hideous mash of feelings inside Keras still refused to dissipate.

He glared at the five daemons and took them all down in one exhilarating blast of shadows.

He needed stronger opponents.

Worthy opponents.

He needed this tangled, twisted web of feelings out of him.

Needed to purge.

A thousand thoughts raced through his mind, too many to handle. A hundred unwanted emotions followed them.

Calistos. Valen. Marek.

All harmed because of his decision to seal the gates.

Esher.

Missing because he had failed to close the gate here in this very city—a gate he was meant to be in total control of and should have been able to shut down before his brother had recklessly chased a daemon into it.

Eli.

A bastard daemon now roaming the Underworld because of that failure to control the gate.

Keras sucked down a breath, and then another, but the weight remained pressing heavily upon his shoulders. A weight that refused to lift. A weight he knew he should bear.

The welfare of his brothers rested on his shoulders.

What happened to the gates was his sole responsibility.

His father had made that painfully clear.

Together with something else.

Failure was not an option.

And he was failing.

A grin stretched his lips as he punched a hole through the chest of a daemon, as he pulled his fist free and the male fell.

But he felt nothing.

So he did it again. Cutting down another daemon. And again. Devouring one with his shadows.

And again.

And again.

And again.

Until twenty dead daemons formed a circle around him, another dozen scattered across the grass at a distance.

And it still wasn't enough.

It was never enough to purge the pain.

The one that festered deep inside him.

Eternal.

More daemons broke from the shadows.

Keras didn't pay them any heed as he looked down at his bloodstained hands, as the plain silver band on his thumb caught the slender light and glinted at him. He rubbed his other thumb over it, clearing the blood away, feeling the warmth of the metal.

Metal of the gods.

Forged on Olympus.

Where she was.

Images flashed across his eyes. Images that had haunted him for weeks now, a constant presence whether he was asleep or awake. They tormented him.

He saw *her*.

Sleek black hair twisted in braids knotted at the back of her head. Curves clad in black and silver armour. Pale green eyes soft and warm, and rose lips curling with a smile.

As she looked at another male.

As she took his hand and clutched it to her.

As she drove a blade through Keras's heart over and over again.

Just as she had that day.

He jerked to his left, and then his right, pain stinging his body as the daemons tore at him. He kept his eyes on the ring she had given him. A token of their friendship. She had called it that, and he had foolishly believed it to be so much more.

He growled when something obscured his view of it, ripped them away and shoved them. As soon as he could see it again, he continued to stare at it, aware of the daemons tearing at him but uncaring.

If they tore him apart and he died here, would she mourn him?

He stroked the ring he couldn't bring himself to discard. The warmth of it was comforting, easing some of the noise in his head, the feelings tangled inside him.

A tie to Enyo that he couldn't bear to sever.

Did she ever think of him?

She had never shared the feelings he had for her. He was certain of that.

She couldn't even bring herself to look at him.

Couldn't bring herself to speak with him.

She always chose Marek when she had information to relay.

Never him.

She would never choose him.

Because she belonged to another.

She belonged to that man he kept seeing her with, the one the daemon Lisabeta had revealed to him in one of her illusions.

Her husband.

The darkest part of him snarled at that and shadows exploded around him, instantly killing the daemons nearest him. He felt nothing as he slaughtered those who remained, ripping through them with his claws and his shadows, drenching his hands in their black blood.

Until only silence remained.

No daemons on his senses.

No matter how fiercely he wished there were.

He spun the ring around his thumb with his index finger, staring at it as he reached into his pocket with his other hand.

As he withdrew the small black stone box.

He slid the lid open with his thumb and plucked a single black pill from it, snapped the box closed and stared at the tiny oval balanced between his thumb and index finger.

At the ring that encircled his thumb just below it.

A ring that caused him pain.

A pill that took it away.

Keras closed his eyes, shutting out the sight of that ring, and placed the pill on his tongue.

Swallowed it.

Fell onto his back in the middle of the carnage he had wrought and flicked his eyes open.

Stared at the stars as the chilling cold slowly crept through him.

As that tangle of unwanted emotions unravelled and dissipated.

Leaving nothing behind.

Leaving him empty.

Just the way he liked it.

CHAPTER 26

Cass walked in silence, numbed not only by the frigid cold of the white world around her but by the thought of what she had done, and what she was about to do. She kept her chin up and shoulders back, refusing to let the witches who were marching her towards the grim grey building ahead of her see her fear. Her guilt. Her despair.

Her destiny loomed in that featureless block-shaped building that had never resembled a factory as much as it did now as she approached it, a soulless place built for churning out witches, keeping her coven strong. One of the most powerful in the world.

Her thoughts and her heart were back in the Aegean with Daimon.

She was falling for him, and there was nothing she could do about it, and gods it was frightening. He wouldn't understand why she was doing this, and he wouldn't forgive her for hurting him as she had.

She was sorry for both of those things, but this was the only way.

It hurt though.

Had tears threatening to line her lashes as she marched forwards, the pain in her heart in danger of rending it in two.

For a moment, she had been swept up in a glorious dream, one where she was able to love someone and have a future of her own choosing.

"Come now, Cassandra," Belle said beside her, that motherly tone grating and making Cass want to glare at her. "This is your home. It is time you remembered that."

Cass looked at the building again. It wasn't her home. That feeling beat deep in her aching heart.

Her home was back on that island, with Mister Milos.

She looked at the witches around her.

This wasn't her family. Her family was in Tokyo, probably worrying about her. She wished she could have spoken to Mari before coming here, could have had the chance to explain things to her and to tell her that she would be home soon, back with her.

Back with Daimon.

The ache in her heart worsened to a deep throbbing pain and she lowered her eyes to the path someone had shovelled. Would he ever forgive her? Would he ever understand?

Belle's hand clamped softly around her wrist, pulling her focus away from him. "Cassandra, this is your duty."

She nodded. "I know."

"You must fulfil it, as everyone does. There are no exceptions. What we do, we do for the greater good of the coven." Belle's eyes remained cold as she smiled, one Cass assumed was meant to be reassuring.

At close to eight hundred years old, Belle was one of the most powerful witches in the coven and one who ran it with only two other witches. The blonde had been in charge of Cass since the moment she had been born, had overseen her upbringing and education. Belle was the closest thing to a mother that Cass had.

But she still wanted to rebel, to flee into the endless white and hope they never caught her.

It was pointless.

If they didn't catch her, they would target those who were dear to her to draw her out of hiding.

Mari and Daimon would be at the top of that list.

"I know," she repeated hollowly, sickness brewing inside her as she thought about what she was going to do.

Warmth washed over her as two of the witches opened the doors to the coven and she stepped inside with Belle still gripping her wrist. Wise witch. If Belle didn't keep hold of her, she was liable to run, wasn't sure she could stop herself even when she knew it would be a terrible mistake.

Cass forced herself to look at the blonde, at the other witches who escorted her into the enormous foyer of the coven as the doors closed behind them, and at the groups of young witches who were silently moving across it, dressed in the same drab grey colour as the building.

She had been one of those children once, a little over two centuries ago, obeying the rigid rules of the coven and remaining silent, afraid of smiling in case she was reprimanded.

Terrified of laughing.

But there had been better times too, when she had been in the dorms with the other witches of her age, away from the scrutinising and firm gazes of the teachers. There had been laughter then, potions gone hilariously wrong, incantations that had gone awry with amusing consequences, and a hell of a lot of bonding over a mutual dislike of the teachers and the adults.

She had made friends here, ones she remained in contact with despite the fact many of them were now spread across the globe.

So as much as she hated it at times, this was her family.

She told herself that on repeat, hammering it home.

She had sworn to do this duty when she had been on the verge of embarking on her life in the wider world, reciting a promise in a ritual that took place for every witch who chose to leave the coven, and she would, for the sake of her family.

"We shall give you a moment to prepare in your old quarters." Belle finally released her.

Cold swept through Cass. She swallowed hard.

They expected her to go to the man right now?

She had thought she would have some time to settle in at least, to gather her courage. She pressed a hand to her stomach, unable to stop herself from reacting, and Belle's dark eyes narrowed.

"This isn't going to be a problem, is it?" Belle looked ready to seize hold of her hand again and drag her to the man if Cass said that it was.

She forced herself to shake her head.

Breathed through the panic that gripped her and tried to calm her mind. She had been prepared to do this for centuries, had known this time would come. She could do it.

She blew out her breath.

It fogged in the air.

She frowned and looked at the other witches, at the way their breath did the same, and then down at her arms as her skin turned to gooseflesh.

The doors behind her burst open and frigid wind blasted into the room, had her teeth chattering as she whirled to face that direction at the same time as Belle. She struggled to maintain her balance as ice rapidly spread across the floor and climbed the walls, chilling the soles of her feet and tearing shocked gasps from several witches.

Snow swirled into the building, as thick as a blizzard, obscuring her view of the outside world.

She peered into the storm as it battered her, tiny flakes stinging her eyes.

A shape formed.

Tall.

Lean.

Formidable.

The snow fell to form a thick layer on the floor, swirled around her ankles and piled up in the corners of the room and against the furniture.

The temperature dropped so rapidly that many of the younger witches collapsed and older ones rushed to help them, gathering them into their arms and transporting them away.

Out of the reaches of the god who strode towards her through the storm, his handsome face set in dark lines, his eyes as white as snow ringed with darkness and spikes of clear ice rising like a crown from his silver-white hair. Icy talons glittered over his fingers as he flexed them and fangs flashed between his lips as he sneered at Belle.

A god on a warpath.

A god who had never looked so damned hot.

Around Cass, the other four witches began muttering incantations and colourful light flared from their palms as the spells built.

Relief to see him gave way to dread.

Cass cursed him for coming after her and making this all so much harder on her. Just the sight of him had her wanting to run into his arms, but she had to go through with her duty. She couldn't turn her back on her family. She couldn't.

He raised his hands and ice shot up around her, numbing her skin, and the four witches spat foul words about him as it encased them.

Leaving just Cass and Belle for him to deal with.

She glanced at the blonde witch, a plea bubbling up her throat.

But Daimon held up his hands and spoke.

"I'll give Cass the child you want."

Cass rocked back on her heels, her gaze whipping to him as a single word burst from her lips. "No."

Shock danced across his face, followed by darkness that invaded his irises, tainting them with more black.

"I'm not good enough for you?" His eyes searched hers and she cursed herself again as she caught the pain in them. "You're rejecting me?"

No, she wasn't. She shook her head, hoping he would see that in her eyes, afraid of putting voice to those words as her heart ached, throbbing painfully in her breast.

When he looked as if he might attack the coven to stop her, or do something worse like leaving without another word, she dragged her courage up. He deserved to know the reason she didn't want him to be the one to impregnate her and provide the coven with the child they demanded.

She took a step towards him, regaining his focus, pulling his eyes away from Belle and the others and narrowing the world down to only him at the same time.

"It'll kill you," she whispered, her eyes leaping between his as her eyebrows furrowed. "Surrendering a child to this place… Sacrificing all ties to it."

His eyes rapidly darkened and shifted to beyond her, to the place where the children had been when he had entered, and something built in them. Something dark and terrible.

"Is that what happened to you?" he said, his voice a low growl as his gaze edged back to her. "You said you didn't have a family. Is this what you meant? You never knew your parents. You don't know if you have siblings here."

She closed her eyes, drew down a slow breath, and fixed them on him as she opened them again. "It's the way of all covens."

He stared deep into her eyes, the pain that built in his a reflection of what she felt inside. She watched as it all dawned on him, as he realised that she was right and that he hated it.

He couldn't let the coven take a child of his and strip everything from it—the love of its parents, its family—to mould it into a witch loyal to the coven and the coven alone.

"Go," she whispered, pain expanding inside her, spreading through her until it filled all of her and she had to fight back the tears.

"I can't." Two words, spoken with an edge that said he meant them. "Not without you. I can't leave you here, Cass… knowing that you don't want this."

She swallowed hard.

He held his hand out to her, his eyes softening, the darkness in them fading to reveal ice-blue.

"Fuck this place. Fuck this duty." The ice talons that covered his fingers shattered and he flexed them, tempting her to take his hand. "Do you really want to bring a child into this world only to abandon it?"

War erupted inside her, a battle between two sides of her heart, one that needed her family, her coven, and was afraid of losing it, and one that feared losing him and Marinda.

He was asking her to choose between them.

If she went with him, she would be turning her back on her coven. They had been there for her for two centuries, had raised her and supported her. While she didn't agree with their methods, they were her blood.

Her family.

If she didn't go with him, she would have to do something abhorrent, something that might end up destroying her. Giving herself to another man. Sacrificing a child. Losing Daimon.

"She wouldn't be abandoning it," Belle snapped and closed her hand over Cass's left shoulder. "This coven would be its family, just as it is Cassandra's family."

Cass looked at her, at the children now gathered on the landing at the top of the stairs beyond her as the snow finally settled, at the faces of her friends who had remained at the coven to work there with the children.

Hurt rolled through her, because whatever path she chose, she would be losing something dear to her. If she went with Daimon, she would be ostracised, exiled from the coven. She would no longer have their protection, and they would order everyone to break all ties with her.

She would no longer have her family.

Her life would completely change.

"This is her family," Belle said.

Daimon snorted. "A family? This isn't a family. Look at it."

The power in the room grew, buffeting her as the older witches with the children began to ready spells and the four who flanked her and Belle broke free of the ice Daimon had used to cage them.

Belle's grip on Cass's shoulder tightened, pinning her in place.

Cass looked at Daimon, the fear rising inside her filling her head with images of him bloodied and broken, killed in the battle that would break out if he didn't leave now.

"Go." This time, that word lacked conviction as it left Cass's lips, as she struggled with the polar desires that warred inside her, no longer sure whether she really wanted him to leave her here.

Fearing he might.

He folded his arms across his chest. "I can't. Not without you. If you can honestly, hand on heart, swear to the gods, say that you want this, that you're fine with it... then I'll go."

She felt the weight of everyone's gazes on her.

Daimon stared at her.

She looked into his eyes, knowing what he could see as his softened further, warming this time, and a hint of concern surfaced in them. He could see her wavering. He could see that the confidence and courage she had always worn was missing now, stripped from her.

She swallowed hard again and opened her mouth, only to snap it shut.

Daimon didn't take his eyes off her, didn't say a word as she fought with herself, shutting out Belle as she tried to convince her to do her duty and the other witches as they all demanded permission to attack him.

"I can't," she whispered and shook her head. "I can't."

Her shoulders suddenly dropped, all the tension rushing from her.

"You're right." She smiled slightly, gave a mirthless chuckle that seemed so out of place in the thick silence, but she felt as if she had lost her mind, because she was on the verge of doing something crazy. "I don't want this. I don't want to abandon a child. I don't want to inflict the upbringing I had on another. I don't want any of this."

She looked deep into his eyes, the numbing coldness she had felt upon letting Belle take her away from him giving way to warmth as it filled her, as hope buoyed her and chased the darkness from her heart.

"I want you."

He held his hand out to her. "You got me."

"Cassandra," Belle barked and when Cass shirked free of her grip, the witch snarled, "Stop him."

Daimon stepped, appearing barely an inch from Cass, and banded his arm around her waist.

Kissed her as darkness embraced them.

Stole her away from her old life.

To a new one where she could have the future she wanted with all her heart.

A future with Daimon.

CHAPTER 27

The heat of Hong Kong embraced her as Cass's feet touched solid ground again and she kept hold of Daimon, kept kissing him as she tried to quieten the voices at the back of her mind, the ones that ran over what she had done. She didn't want to listen to them. Her heart already felt heavy, the thought of never seeing her coven and her friends again a weight that pressed upon it.

Would any of her friends visit her, risking punishment from the coven if they were discovered?

The coven was strict about such things, liable to exile whoever was caught visiting her.

"Hey," Daimon murmured as he pulled back and brushed his palm across her cheek.

His eyes were soft as she looked up into them, filled with understanding that made her feel as if there was an invisible ribbon that linked them, allowing him to see into her mind and her heart.

She stared into them, her sombre thoughts weighing too heavily upon her for her to conceal how she was feeling. She had just turned her back on the only family she had ever known and the only place where she had ever belonged, and she needed to believe it had been worth it.

She needed to know she had made the right decision and that what she had with Daimon was going to last, that she wasn't going to find herself alone in a few years or even months because he had grown bored with her.

Or had failed to fall in love with her.

Like she was in love with him.

His white eyebrows knitted hard above eyes that revealed so many feelings to her as they softened further, as they warmed and held hers.

She felt loved when he looked at her like that, as if she was his entire world and the sight of her in pain was killing him, filling him with a need to do something about it even when he no doubt knew he couldn't.

He brought his other hand up and framed her face, his gaze earnest as he looked down into her eyes. His palms were cool against her cheeks, but she felt warm from head to toe.

"I couldn't lose you," he husked, his voice a sultry whisper that teased her ears, his words and the feelings she could read in his eyes lifting some of the weight from her heart. "I didn't think about the consequences… I only thought about how much I needed you… and now…"

He trailed off into a sigh.

Brushed his left thumb across her cheek.

Smeared cool dampness into her skin.

She blinked away her tears, ashamed of them and not wanting to hurt him. She had done enough of that for a lifetime.

"Tell me what's wrong. Talk to me." His eyebrows furrowed as his eyes darted between hers, the look that filled them drawing the words up from her heart because he honestly looked as if he wanted to know. "Whatever is on your mind… you can talk to me."

She couldn't remember anyone other than Eric bothering to take the time to just listen to her woes and her worries.

It felt so nice to have someone who would do that for her.

Someone who looked as if he would move heaven and earth to make her feel better.

"They're my family… Were my family. This is going to take a little getting used to and I'm…" She glanced at his chest as her courage faltered, and then blew out her breath and lifted her gaze to lock with his again, because she needed it out there. If she held it inside, it would fester and rot, eating away at her. "I'm… afraid… I'll find I made a mistake in turning my back on them."

His face darkened slightly, a brief hardening of his features that lifted a moment later as his eyes softened again, like a storm cloud passing over the sun.

He sighed. "You think I'm going to leave you."

Before she could say a word to defend herself, he shook his head and sighed again, drew his hands towards him and lured her closer with them.

He stared down into her eyes, his swirling with white flakes that looked like the blizzard he had caused at the coven, tempestuous and wild.

"I'm not going to leave you, Cass. What I'm feeling..." He swallowed hard. Hesitated. "What I'm feeling isn't going to change. Never. This feeling... This is forever."

Another's words echoed in her mind as she stared up into Daimon's eyes.

Eric.

Asking her if she had ever been in love. She had told him never.

Eric had said that never was a long time and one day she would fall in love and realise what he had—that true love was forever.

Cass had countered that forever was a long time too—a long time to be stuck with the same person.

But as she looked at Daimon, as she realised that she was already in love with him, she finally understood Eric.

"Forever with you doesn't seem long enough," she whispered, feeling on edge as those words slipped from her lips, anxious as she waited for him to say something, fearing he would ridicule her.

Daimon tilted her head back, brushed his thumbs over her cheeks and smiled down into her eyes, one filled with love. "Doesn't seem long enough for me either. So we'll make it forever and a day."

He dipped his head and kissed her, a tender exploration of her lips that had warmth rushing through her, had her insides lightening as she leaned into him and wrapped her arms around his neck. He bent at the knee, banded his arms around her backside and lifted her.

Her legs fell open, his hips nestling between them as he walked with her, carrying her inside his home.

She kept kissing him, her lips dancing over his, feelings bubbling to the surface, ones she no longer wanted to fight.

Ones she no longer feared.

Cass sighed as he laid her down on the bed and covered her, stroked her fingers through his hair and clung to him, a different sort of fear washing through her. She had been so afraid she would never see him again.

The way he held her to him, the desperate edge the kiss gained, said she wasn't alone in that feeling either.

She kissed him deeper, her tongue tangling with his, losing herself in it and the feel of him holding her, in the emotions that rippled through her, ones she had thought she would never experience.

Gods, she loved this man.

He broke away from her lips and kissed down her neck, nipped at it and sent a shiver tripping along her nerves. She leaned her head back into the mattress and relaxed into it, sighed as he stripped her corset away and worshipped her breasts.

Cass lifted her arms above her head and closed her eyes, a smile working its way onto her lips as Daimon drifted lower, as he eased her leather trousers off. She shivered as he pressed kisses to her bare thighs, as his skin brushed hers and she realised he was naked. An electric thrill chased through her as he covered her again, skin-to-skin, and kissed her.

She wrapped her arms around his neck and sighed into his mouth as he eased into her, as he withdrew and filled her again, his pace unhurried, stirring a deep sense of connection inside her. She had never felt anything like it.

Was sure she never would experience anything like it with anyone other than Daimon.

He kept saying that she had him, but gods, he had her too.

All of her.

Right down to her soul.

She stroked his shoulders as she kissed him, as his breaths mingled with hers and he thrust into her, feeling as if every part of them was connected.

Becoming one.

Release built achingly slowly and she savoured it, lost in the moment with him, feeling as if they were the only two people in the world.

When it swept over her, the depth of it rocked her, had her floating in his arms and never wanting to come down. She moaned into his mouth, each meeting of their bodies sending a fresh wave of pleasure through her, warmth that rolled over her again and again.

She swallowed his groan as he joined her, as he pulsed and throbbed in time with her.

His breath skated across her lips as he stilled inside her. He brushed his fingers through her hair, gazed down into her eyes with so much love in his that she melted a little.

She wanted to say something, but the words wouldn't come.

All she could do was stare into his eyes, drowning in the love they held, warmed right down to her soul.

He skimmed the backs of his fingers across her cheek.

"I love you, Cass."

Words she had never thought she would hear, and words she had never realised how badly she needed to hear from him.

"I love you too." She choked a little on those four words, ones she had never thought she would say to anyone.

Ones that felt so right.

She never wanted to be without Daimon, and the love she had for him would last forever.

And a day.

His phone vibrated and she cursed it as he pulled out of her, as the peacefulness of the moment ebbed. He gave her a fine view of his backside as he went for his phone though. Delicious.

She smiled wickedly as she imagined smacking it.

He straightened and the screen lit up, illuminating his face.

He went deathly still.

"What is it?" She bolted upright, fearing her coven had somehow managed to find him and were already seeking retribution.

Daimon swallowed hard.

"Esher is back."

CHAPTER 28

Daimon stepped the moment Cass was dressed and in his arms, his mind whirling as Ares's message ran around it. It had only been four words.

Esher back. Code red.

Code red meant everyone had cleared out of the Tokyo mansion because Esher was liable to kill anyone who set foot in it.

Daimon landed in the front garden of the single-storey building and looked at Cass, painfully aware of the danger he was placing her in by bringing her with him. He hadn't been able to stop himself. He couldn't leave her in Hong Kong, where she was vulnerable to not only the Erinyes who wanted to get their hands on her, but her coven too. He was under no illusion that the witches weren't going to try to take her back from him.

Their fight wasn't over.

He drew down a deep breath and looked at the closed wooden door of the mansion.

This fight was just beginning.

He could feel Esher inside, sense the rage that beat within his brother, darkness that pulsed like a wave over him.

Daimon took hold of Cass's hand and led her towards the door, nerves rushing through him as he closed the distance between him and it. He wasn't sure what to expect. Chances were, Ares had ordered everyone to leave the moment Esher had returned, and that was the reason the message had been so short.

Ares didn't know what state Esher was in.

The scent of foul daemon blood hit Daimon.

His eyes widened as he realised he couldn't only sense his brother.

He could sense the wraith too.

"I need a barrier, some sort of containment spell." He looked at Cass.

She nodded. "Coming right up."

It was handy having a witch for a partner.

"I don't know what we're walking into, but if there's any distance between my brother and the daemon, use the spell on it."

"And if there isn't?" Light glowed from the palm of her free hand, casting a green hue across it.

He wanted to say to do it anyway, to encase both the wraith and his brother within the barrier, fear that Esher might attack Cass getting the better of him.

"Give me a moment to get Esher away from him. If I can't..." He didn't want to finish that sentence.

She nodded. "I got it."

He stopped, turned and gripped her shoulders, holding them tightly as he stared into her eyes. "As soon as the wraith is caged, you go to my room and you don't come out until I come for you... no matter what you hear."

"But—"

He pressed his finger to her lips to silence her. "I know you can handle yourself... but Esher... You. I can't bear the thought he might hurt you."

The soft light that entered her aquamarine eyes told him that she understood. He didn't want Esher to attack her. He didn't want to have to fight his own brother, not when Esher wouldn't be aware he was doing something wrong and would be acting on instinct.

Wanting to protect Daimon from someone he viewed as a threat.

Daimon stepped up onto the wooden porch and removed his boots, and waited for Cass to remove hers before he opened the door.

His heart pounded in his throat as the main room came into view.

Esher stood in the middle of it, clutching the right ankle of the unconscious black-haired male sprawled on the tatami mats behind him.

Relief hit Daimon hard, but it was short-lived as he took in the state of his older brother.

Dried blood and dirt caked every inch of him, streaked across his bare chest and arms, and matted his black hair and thick scraggly beard.

Cass tensed, the barest twitch of her hand in his as rain lashed down outside and thunder pealed overhead, the typhoon hitting out of nowhere.

He glanced through the open panels that revealed the garden.

Not a drop of rain touched it or the house.

It gave Daimon hope.

Hope that Esher was aware on some level that Aiko was liable to be here in the mansion and he didn't want to hurt her. Hope that he could get through to his brother.

Daimon's gaze briefly darted to Cass. She shook her head, silently telling him that she couldn't cast the barrier while Esher was holding the wraith. He nodded and released her hand, held his palm up to her to silently tell her to give him a moment and to stay where she was.

He stepped into the room, drawing slow deep breaths to keep his nerves in check, closely watching Esher. He doubted his brother would broadcast his intent to attack, but it didn't hurt to watch for the slightest twitch. There was a chance he could reach Cass and step with her before his brother managed to strike him down.

Esher continued to stare straight ahead, his face placid as he breathed hard, bare chest straining with each one. Daimon checked his wrists. Both of the braided black bands that limited his power were still in place. That was good. He lifted his gaze, fixing it on the trident inked on the inside of his brother's wrist—his favour mark from Poseidon.

It was as black as night.

Not so good.

Daimon's eyes leaped to the arrowhead pendant that hung from the black thong around Esher's neck. The stone was tranquil blue. Daimon breathed a little easier with the knowledge that the moon was on his side at least and not affecting his brother. When the moon was full, Esher's pendant turned black, a sign that it was messing with his power and his mood, pulling on him as strongly as it did on the tides.

When that happened, Esher had to be locked in the cage.

Daimon hated placing him in it, but it was the only way to suppress his powers and keep the mortal world safe from harm.

He rounded Esher, keeping his distance. When he could see Esher's face more clearly, relief bloomed even more sweetly inside him.

His brother's eyes were blue.

Not red.

His other side wasn't fully in control.

But shit was still liable to go south at a moment's notice.

It had been a long time since he had seen his brother this bad.

He glanced at the unconscious daemon. He needed to get his brother to release the male so Cass could cage him, but he wasn't sure how to make that happen. The wraith was Esher's trophy, the reward of a hunt that must have been intense judging by the state of his brother. If he tried to take that prize away from Esher, his brother would attack him.

He needed to convince Esher to release him.

Easier said than done.

Esher's blue gaze didn't shift from the wall at the other end of the room. Blood dripped down into his left eye, turning the white red and his iris a strange shade of purple. He didn't blink it away. He just kept staring.

Locked in a battle with himself.

Daimon had seen it enough times to recognise it.

His brother was still under the influence of his other side, was waging war with it.

There was a sharpness in his eyes, cold calculation and darkness. Exactly how he looked when his other side was in control.

Daimon motioned at Cass to stay where she was and to keep quiet.

And then risked it.

He stepped into the path of his brother's gaze, his nerve barely holding as he did his best to look unthreatening.

Esher still didn't look at him.

"You've been gone a while. I was worried about you." Daimon knew better than to mention *we* and *everyone* when Esher was so far gone.

He needed to just talk about him and Esher. In the singular. Man-to-man.

Bringing up his family was liable to send his brother into a tailspin that would end with him attacking anyone he viewed as a threat to it.

Daimon was deeply aware of Cass as he braved a step closer to Esher.

Esher's gaze tracked him this time. His brother eyed him closely, that calculating edge to his gaze sharpening further. Daimon felt as if he was looking at another person—a cold predator weighing up its potential prey.

Was his brother really in there?

He kept his steps slow as he rounded his brother, hoping to draw his focus away from Cass's direction, aware that if he moved too fast he could provoke a reaction from Esher.

Priority one was convincing Esher to release his prize and to secure the wraith before he woke up. His gaze flickered to the daemon, a glance he had hoped would be quick enough that Esher wouldn't notice.

Esher growled and bared fangs at him.

His grip tightened on the wraith's ankle.

The daemon moaned.

The male was alive, which was good. He could use that. Esher had clearly managed to retain enough control to convince himself to spare the wraith so they could use him for information on their enemy.

"You've done well. I have the daemon. W—I'm safe now." Daimon hid his grimace as he subtly braced himself, hoping Esher hadn't caught the fact he had almost said *we're*. "I was worried about you. You have to rest now. Take care of yourself. Let me take care of you. Remember how I used to?"

He searched Esher's eyes, hoping to see that he did.

Emptiness stared back at him.

"You're my big brother and I was always the one who took care of you when you got into trouble." Daimon slowly reached a hand out to Esher as his cold eyes began to brighten, losing their intensity. "Come on. Let me take care of you now, Esher."

His brother's expression darkened at the sound of his name, a frown knitting his black eyebrows together and causing the onyx crust that ran down one side of his face, from his hairline to the scruffy beard that coated his jaw, to crack further.

"You remember me. You know you do." Daimon kept pressing, feeling he was getting somewhere. "That's why you came to me. We've always been close, always had each other's backs. That's why you came. You're safe here. I'll take care of you."

He reached a hand towards the one Esher gripped the daemon's ankle in.

Big mistake.

Esher snarled and twisted, dropping the wraith's ankle to step between Daimon and his prey.

Daimon backed off as his brother advanced, flexing black claws as scarlet ringed his irises.

Cass was swift to act on the opening she had been given.

Green light burst from her palms and wrapped around the wraith, forming a circle of shimmering light around him.

Esher turned on her with a roar.

"Go!" Daimon grabbed Esher's arm and pulled him back, cursing himself as ice spread across his brother's skin.

He grunted as Esher elbowed him in the face.

Cass disappeared in a flash of crimson light.

He grappled with Esher, struggling to keep hold of him as he snarled and elbowed him again. Stars winked across Daimon's vision as he took a hit to the nose, as blood streamed over his lips and heat spread across his face.

Outside, the rain pelted the garden, filling the air with the smell of earth, and lightning struck nearby.

Esher twisted free of his grip and dread washed through Daimon as he lunged for him, fear that his brother would leave and destroy anything that stood in his path. Wind howled through the house as he managed to grab hold of Esher again and his brother turned and slammed his palm against Daimon's throat, grabbed him and hauled him into the air.

Daimon locked his hand around Esher's wrist.

And hesitated.

His brief reluctance to use his ice against his brother cost him.

Esher slammed him into the nearest wooden pillar and the air burst from Daimon's lungs as fire rolled across his back.

His vision tunnelled as he fought to breathe, struggling to get air into his burning lungs, and fear swamped him as his heart began to slow.

No.

Esher sneered at him, red invading the blue of his stormy eyes.

Daimon's thoughts blurred and he tried to prise Esher's hand from his throat, his actions sluggish and body slow to respond as his blood crawled through his veins and his heart stuttered.

Esher was using his power over water to control Daimon's blood.

His brother was going to kill him.

Cass would be next.

That thought had icy talons forming over his fingers and he growled, the sound half-pain and half-rage, as he clawed at Esher's arms, spilling blood that instantly froze in jagged red icicles.

Esher released him and he crashed to his knees, gasped in a breath. He stumbled onto his feet and staggered left, determined to reach Cass before Esher could and get her and himself away from his brother. He glanced back at him.

Esher roared and lunged for him.

Their mother appeared between them in a swirl of black smoke that spiralled downwards to blend into the layers of her dress.

She seized hold of Esher, gripping his shoulders in both hands.

Esher growled and lashed out at her, a vicious and savage beast as he clawed at her, drawing blood as vibrantly scarlet as her hair.

His nostrils flared as he drew in a deep breath.

He suddenly stilled.

Stared at her.

Through crimson eyes.

Daimon sank to his knees, unable to believe what he was seeing.

He had never seen Esher's other side calmed by anything. He had never seen it so docile.

Persephone was soft and gentle as she lifted her hands to Esher's face and framed it with her palms. "Let go. You have the wraith now, my love. You can rest."

Esher drew down a breath, was still for a tense moment where Daimon didn't dare move, and then he nodded and passed out. Persephone caught him as he fell, bringing him down gently to rest with his head on her knees. Outside, the weather instantly calmed.

"I do not have much time," their mother said, her voice as soft and light as a summer's breeze as her green eyes came to rest on Daimon, the flecks of gold in them sparkling. "The Underworld has been in an uproar. We have been trying to catch up with Esher from the moment he entered it, but whoever we sent to stop him ended up dead. In the end, our only hope was that he would find the one he was hunting so I might have an opportunity to reach him."

She gently stroked Esher's matted black hair and looked down at him, her gaze overflowing with the love she held for him and with relief.

"I wish I could stay longer," she whispered.

Daimon glanced at the garden. The seasons were at war with his mother present, flowers attempting to grow as if it was spring and birds singing mating calls even as the autumnal colours remained.

She looked at him. "Take care of him. He has been through so much."

Daimon nodded.

Persephone lingered.

He dropped his gaze, aware of the reason she was hesitating to return to the Underworld. Long gashes cut across her shoulders and her chest, seeping blood. His father was going to be furious with Esher when she returned and he saw the state of her, and she didn't want to get Esher into more trouble.

She stroked Esher's cheek, bent over and pressed a kiss to his dirty forehead. "Rest. Get better."

And then she was gone.

The ground shook violently, the tremor rocking Esher where he lay on his back on the golden straw mats.

When the quake stopped, Daimon pulled his phone from his pocket and fired off a message. In less than a heartbeat, his brothers surrounded him, together with Caterina, Megan, Eva and Marinda.

And Aiko.

Tears spilled down her cheeks and she sobbed as she darted forwards.

Keras grabbed her arm and held her back.

She looked back at his brother and then at Daimon.

Daimon nodded. "Mother was here. He won't wake for a while. It's safe."

Keras released her.

Aiko sank to her knees beside Esher, caressed his cheek and murmured things to him in Japanese.

She lifted her head, her dark eyes bleak and tears glistening on her cheeks. "We should clean him."

Daimon wanted to do that too, but he shook his head. "Esher needs to rest right now."

He didn't want to risk disturbing his sleep.

"I'll take him to his room." Keras moved around Esher, stooped and carefully lifted him, and when he looked at Daimon, Daimon nodded at him, silently thanking his brother for doing it for him.

Aiko followed Keras, and Daimon trailed after them, leaving his brothers to guard the wraith.

When he reached the door of his room, he slid the panel open.

Cass immediately turned to face him, relief filling her blue eyes chased by anger as they narrowed on his nose. "Oh, that beast."

She hurried to him and he didn't chastise her about the term she insisted on using for Esher as she fussed over him, was too relieved to see she was safe too. His nose ached as she brushed her fingers down it and then the pain was gone, the stuffiness clearing and allowing him to breathe through it again.

"I could get used to having you around," he murmured and stroked his knuckles lightly across her cheek. "Thanks for that, and for leaving when I asked."

"If I had known he was going to make mincemeat of your nose, I would have stayed." She petted it with a slight pout to her lips. "Your beautiful nose."

"It'll be fine. Not the first time it's been broken and it won't be the last." He dragged his gaze away from her as Keras emerged from Esher's room to his left. He nodded. Looked back at Cass and caught the question in her eyes. "Mother made Esher sleep. He needs rest now. I'm not sure how long the gift Mother used will last."

"I can do a spell that will keep him asleep for a few days."

Gods, could his sorceress get any more wonderful?

He dropped a kiss on her lips. "Thank you."

She wrinkled her nose when he pulled back. "You taste like blood."

He followed her as she swept from the room, her head held high and shoulders back, not missing the nerves she was doing her best to mask as she strode with purpose towards Esher's room.

A flicker of relief danced across her delicate features as she reached the doorway and saw it was only Keras and Aiko in the room with Esher.

Although he also didn't miss how she kept firmly to the right, as far from Keras as she could get.

He gave his oldest brother a questioning look as he entered the room and came to stand next to Aiko, but Keras refused to look at him, kept his green eyes locked on Esher where he lay on the bedding in the middle of the room.

Cass kneeled by his head and swirls of blue, purple and black emanated from her palms, drifted over Esher's head and disappeared into his mouth and nose as he inhaled.

She lifted her gaze to Daimon, and then settled it on Aiko. "He should sleep for at least seventy-two hours. I can renew the spell then if necessary."

"Thank you," Aiko said.

When she went to kneel beside his brother, Daimon stopped her, stepping into her path.

"How much do you know about my brother?" He searched her eyes.

They were open, clear, not a hint of malice or fear in them as she said, "I know about his past. Esher told me everything."

Good. That was good. But he needed to be sure she knew what she was in for, because when Esher came around, he was going to be delicate. The slightest thing was liable to set him off again.

"When Esher... flips... he's a different person. He might not remember what he's done when he comes around." Daimon held her gaze, needing to know she was listening to him. "He might not want to remember. Esher was never big on killing. Not really. His other side... it doesn't care. It's happiest when it's killing. Esher won't be strong enough to handle remembering that. Mother said he killed everyone they sent after him. If he remembers that..."

She nodded. "I won't probe. I promise."

She tried to pass him, but he didn't let her.

He looked back at his brother, darkness coursing through him, howling at him to keep everyone away from him and keep him safe. He needed to protect Esher.

A hand came to rest on his shoulder.

Drawing his focus to Cass where she now stood beside him.

Her blue eyes were soft as she murmured, "Let Aiko look after him too."

It was hard, but somehow Daimon managed to nod and step aside.

Keras remained silent, a sceptical edge to his eyes that Aiko noticed. It was enough to halt her in her tracks.

"I won't disturb his sleep," she said, a pleading edge to her expression as she faced his brother. "I promise."

Keras stared at her for a tense minute.

Finally nodded.

Aiko was quick to move to Esher, to kneel beside him and brush her fingers across his brow.

Daimon looked at Keras.

"We have a wraith to question."

CHAPTER 29

Sixty-seven hours, fourteen minutes and twenty-two seconds had passed since Keras had placed a veil on the wraith using his shadows.

Sixty-seven hours, fourteen minutes and twenty-three seconds in which he hadn't slept.

Sixty-seven hours, fourteen minutes and twenty-four seconds in which Eli hadn't uttered a damned word.

Keras loomed over the daemon they had locked in Esher's cage in a separate building on the mansion grounds, staring down at him where he dared to sleep.

Sleep.

His head canted to his left, green gaze assessing, hunger igniting.

Hunger to reach between the heavy enchanted bars of the cage and drag the fiend kicking and screaming up from his slumber.

Fatigue blurred his thoughts together into a pleasing stream of bloodshed, a thousand outcomes that flickered before his eyes.

"Keras?" The soft voice belonging to the sorceress invaded his thoughts, purging them from his mind, leaving it blank by the time he looked across at her where she stood in the doorway.

Daimon right behind her.

His brother kept a close eye on him, a wary edge to his gaze and his posture. He was contemplating whisking Cassandra away from him.

Had she told Daimon that he had threatened her?

He doubted it.

He looked into her eyes, seeking the answer there, and she tensed, the briefest tightening of her shoulders that drew a reaction from his brother. Daimon wrapped an arm around her and ushered her into the room. Her confidence returned in a heartbeat, silver stars sparking in her eyes as she narrowed them on Keras.

"We came to relieve you. Ares's orders. You need to eat." Daimon kept his distance from Keras.

Kept Cass firmly away from him.

But she hadn't told him.

It was there in his eyes.

She had kept their conversation to herself.

Most probably a good thing.

If Daimon knew he had threatened her, his brother would want his head. It was right there in his pale blue eyes as they glittered with ice, on the verge of turning white. That dangerous, possessive side of their blood rearing its ugly head.

He scoffed.

That side of his blood was poison.

It caused him nothing but agony.

If he could cut it out of him, he would.

His right hand twitched with the urge to lift to his chest, to sink claws into his flesh to remove the thing responsible for pumping that poison around his system.

Something he was better off without.

He didn't need a heart.

Cassandra and Daimon stared at him. Waiting.

"Get some rest," Daimon said, his words carefully weighed, his gaze cautious.

Keras inclined his head and walked to the door, paused there to look back at the sorceress. "Keep him cloaked."

She must have heard the thinly veiled threat in his voice because her spine stiffened and fire lit her eyes. "I know how to do this spell, thank you. It will not fail."

When she looked as if she might strike him, he found himself lingering. His cheekbone heated with the memory of the blows she had delivered to it, dealing pain that had surprised him and caught him completely off guard. He knew she had seen one of his deepest, darkest secrets in that moment.

His gaze flickered to Daimon.

Another thing she hadn't told his brother.

Perhaps the sorceress wasn't so bad after all. She was strong, capable, and as much as it sickened him to say it, it was clear she felt something for Daimon.

All six of his brothers mated.

He pondered that as he walked away, heading for the main house across the moonlit garden.

If oblivion claimed him now, he could rest easy knowing they weren't alone.

No, he couldn't.

He still had a duty to fulfil.

Once it was done, so was he.

He couldn't go on like this.

Shadows wrapped around him, cloaking him from the world just long enough that he could slide a pill from the box in his pocket and place it on his tongue. The effect was instantaneous, cold washing through him, spreading to erase the poison that coursed in his veins, and stealing some of his fatigue with it.

The shadows dissipated as he stepped up onto the wooden walkway that led to the bathhouse.

Ares leaned with his back against the stone wall of the showers, his long legs crossed at the ankle, his black jeans and T-shirt making him blend in with the night. The sparks of fire that danced in his dark eyes gave him away.

"There you are." Ares's deep growl rolled over him. "Thought for a moment I was going to have to come and get you myself."

Keras stopped level with him and looked across at him. "The wraith will not speak."

Ares shook his head, his wild tawny hair brushing his broad shoulders. "Doesn't mean I'm going to let you go poking around in his head. It's too dangerous, Keras. You're too tired from having to cloak the bastard. If you tried to read his memories—"

Keras held his right hand up and Ares fell silent.

He knew the risks.

Eli was a strong daemon, an old daemon. He would be able to resist Keras's mind probe and there was a chance it would drain Keras further, leaving him vulnerable.

But they were getting nowhere.

He had spent the last three days torturing the daemon, doing everything short of looking into his mind to get the answers he wanted. Aiko had even tried to read the daemon, but the male's mind had blocks in place. Whatever Keras tried, Eli withstood it all, refusing to break.

Unlike his body.

Keras had broken bones, must have fractured every one in the daemon's body at some point, and had stood by as Cassandra had used spells to put him back together, tearing agonised screams from him that Keras's shadows had greedily absorbed.

Cal had even taken a shot at the daemon, intent on making him pay for what had happened to their sister. His youngest brother had revealed a dark streak as black as Keras's own one, had revelled in using his power over air to choke the daemon, suffocating him and pushing him close to dying more than once.

Cal was hungry for another go at the daemon. All of his brothers were.

But Keras was determined to be the one to make him speak.

The only path left open to him was cracking the daemon's mind open.

Ares remained hot on his heels as he strode into the main room of the mansion. Aiko was coming out of the kitchen to his right as he entered, a tray of food clutched in her hands.

The petite raven-haired woman paused and nodded at him. "Esher is looking brighter today. Cass helped me clean him."

He could see the relief that gave her, even felt a glimmer of it himself, the barest hint of comfort that was there and gone in the blink of an eye as the pill erased it.

"That's good." He managed to layer relief into those two words, knowing she would want to hear it.

She smiled and bobbed her head again before continuing across the long living room, passing the low wooden dining table where the others sat and then the couches that formed the TV area at the other end of it. She disappeared around the corner and he caught a glimpse of her through the open panels to his left as she hurried along the covered wooden walkway, heading for Esher's room.

He felt Ares's gaze on the back of his head, was deeply aware of the others as they stared at him. Was he meant to say something? About Aiko? About Esher? About the daemon?

He was too tired.

Keras sank to his backside in an open spot at the long table and stared at the empty plate and bowl set before him. Ares was kind enough to fill them for him.

Although load them up might have been a more appropriate choice of words.

When his plate was overflowing with meat and vegetables, and his bowl held a mound of rice so high that it was in danger of toppling over, he looked at his brother.

Ares eased into the seat opposite him and hefted his broad shoulders in a shrug. "You need to eat."

Keras stared at the food. None of it appealed to him. He was hungry for answers, not sustenance.

He picked at the food though, eating small mouthfuls to appease Ares and get his brother off his back. If he didn't eat, Ares would dog him until he gave up. The others would make a fuss.

He wanted them all gone, busy with other things, their eyes no longer on him.

Megan swayed to her right and leaned against Ares's shoulder, a sigh escaping her as she rubbed her belly. "I'm so full but she wants more."

Ares chuckled and covered her hand with his. "She has my appetite."

They had recently discovered the baby was a female, not a male as they had been expecting.

That news had been enough to place several of his brothers on edge.

It had placed him on edge too.

None of them wanted what had happened to Calindria to happen to another female in their family.

He cursed the Moirai for making the child female.

Females were vulnerable, weaker than males.

An image of Enyo flashed across his mind, sword a silver arc as she gracefully cut through a horde of enemies, her moves more like a well-choreographed dance than a fight. She spun and dropped, the black leather pieces of her skirt lifting upwards as she hit the ground and rolled. Her onyx hair flowed behind her as she came onto her feet in a lightning fast move, the silver plates on her armour flashing as they caught the bright sunlight.

She decapitated the warrior she faced and twisted, soft green eyes bright with the high of battle.

Perhaps not all females were weaker and more vulnerable than males.

Keras dropped his head and rubbed his temples, harder and harder, trying to purge thoughts of her. Emotions tangled inside him, had him shaking with a need to reach into his pocket and seek the calm oblivion of another pill.

It was getting harder to stop the feelings from coming.

"Keras," Megan murmured, concern in her tone.

He shook his head, hoping to stop her before she could ask him what was wrong, before she could show more feelings for him that would only stir emotions in response.

"I am just tired." He pushed to his feet and didn't miss the way Ares looked at the food he had barely touched. Hoping to fend off his brother before he could make a fuss, he smiled tightly. "I will eat more later once I have slept and am feeling better."

Ares continued to stare at him, a calculating edge to his sharp gaze, and then he gave a slight nod. "Fine. But I'm holding you to that."

Keras drifted away from them, the sound of the conversation that surged to life the moment he was out of sight drifting into the background as he trod the well-worn boards of the walkway.

Thankfully, Cassandra had vacated his room, moving into Daimon's one instead.

He eased the panel that acted as a door open and then slid it closed behind him.

Turned towards it.

Kneeled.

He rested his palms on his thighs, closed his eyes and waited.

It wasn't long before the house fell silent and still.

He focused his senses, sharpening his internal radar until he could pinpoint everyone. They were all in their rooms.

All except Daimon and Cassandra.

Keras pushed to his feet, shook it off when he wobbled a little, fatigue rolling over him, and opened the door of his room. Cool air kissed his skin as he stepped out onto the walkway and cloaked himself in shadows, moving stealthily past the other bedrooms in the south wing of the house.

When he reached the separate building that contained Esher's cage and the daemon, he let the shadows dissipate and pushed the wooden door open.

"You look like shit," Daimon muttered as he glanced at him, lifting his gaze away from Cassandra.

"I am fine. Fed and rested. You two should do the same." He looked at the daemon who was still sleeping curled up on the bottom of the square cage. "Anything?"

Daimon shook his head. "It's like he's hibernating."

"Conserving his strength." Keras ran an assessing gaze over the wraith, from his black hair, over his tattered long black robes, to his bare feet. "Go. I will watch him. I doubt he will wake any time soon."

He was going to wake.

Keras was going to wake him.

He schooled his features as Daimon studied him, not allowing his younger brother to see his intent.

"You sure? You don't want company?" Daimon looked reluctant to leave.

His brother was suspicious and he wasn't the only one. The sorceress looked as if she didn't believe him either.

"Do not make me issue an order, Daimon." Keras eased down onto one of the benches that lined the walls of the square building.

For a moment, Daimon looked as if he might, but then he jerked his chin towards the door. "Come on, Cass. Let's see if anyone left us some food."

Daimon issued him a black look as Cass swept past him, pausing for a second before following her out into the fading night.

Leaving him alone with Eli.

Keras's green gaze slid to the sleeping daemon.

Shadows rose from the ground and snapped at the cage, rattling it as they tried to pierce the barrier that surrounded the enchanted metal.

Eli shot to his knees in the centre of the cage, violet eyes darting to the shadows. He jerked left and right as those shadows lashed at the cage, rocking away from whichever side of the bars had been hit.

Keras leaned forwards and rested his elbows on his knees as he folded his hands together.

The daemon looked at him and hissed, flashing fangs.

Keras slowly smiled to reveal a hint of his own emerging fangs.

The wraith stiffened, realisation dawning in his eyes a split-second before he tried to back away from Keras. His spine met the cold metal bars of the cage and he tossed a fearful look at them and then Keras.

Keras's smile widened as their eyes locked.

The world dropped away, everything familiar to him blurring into nothingness.

Something pushed back against him.

Keras gritted his teeth and resisted it, drew down a breath and focused all of his will on breaching that barrier that stood between him and what he wanted. Pain splintered across his skull in agonising waves that seemed to steal more of his strength with each one that washed over him.

His breaths shortened as he leaned forwards, as he peered harder into the darkness, determined to shatter it. He was a master of shadows and they would obey him.

He flinched and grunted as heat speared his mind, as his teeth ached and darkness writhed within him, snarled and gnashed its fangs at the threat before him.

Keras pushed it all back down inside him, shoved aside the fear and the pain, and tried again, pressing forwards into the darkness.

Eli whimpered. A pathetic sound.

From the darkness, a new place constructed itself, greenery rising to tower over him as blue and white tiles fell into position around a fountain, and golden dirt rolled across the ground beneath his feet.

Seville.

A female lay before him, eyes fixed on him in a sightless stare.

Lisabeta.

Anger rolled through Keras, fury that stole his breath and had him wanting to lash out.

He lifted his head and glared at the ones responsible for her death.

His brothers.

Keras growled and pushed past the memory, seeking another. When it was one of Lisabeta again, he sought another. This one had the female daemon on her knees before him, naked and smiling. Keras tore it down and cast it aside. Sought another. Cold trickled down his spine and his hands shook as he flipped through the memories of the female daemon, following them deeper, sifting through layers and layers of them.

Eli was using them to hide the information Keras wanted. He was sure of it.

The wraith was resisting him.

Keras dropped to his knees and gripped the bars of the cage, rattled it as he snarled at the daemon it contained.

Muscles clamped down on his bones, his limbs trembling as he leaned hard against the cage, pushed deeper into Eli's mind.

Pain wracked him, fire that devoured every inch of him as shadows twined around his limbs and dragged him deeper still, under the next wave.

He pushed through it, dived deeper and deeper, tearing down the memories of Lisabeta, racing back through time.

Jagged black lines spread across his eyes, forming fault lines like lightning that forked in all directions.

He caught a glimpse of a mansion. European.

Then another memory.

This one a building that looked more American. He tried to focus on it, but the black lines were spreading too rapidly, obscuring too much of it and it was gone before he could seize hold of it and watch the memory play out.

He spun into the next one, bile rising up his throat as his entire body ached and his muscles turned to water.

Darkness surrounded him.

Not darkness caused by the fault lines.

Keras stood on a bluff, cold air buffeting him, his eyes fixed on the valley below him and a small village.

Fixed on two golden-haired children where they hid behind a boulder.

His targets.

Pain lanced him, straight through his heart as he recognised them. Calistos and Calindria.

He tried to stay with the memory, but it fractured and shattered, crumbling around him as another one replaced it.

A beautiful blonde female.

She was slow to come into focus.

He pushed through the pain that seared him to piece together the memory.

A cage shimmered into being around her, suspended by a thick chain from the roof of a cavern.

Black rock blended with the darkness in all directions, making it impossible to pick out any details.

Other than her blonde hair.

And tattered scraps of sky-blue material that hugged her curves, looked as if she had pieced them together from a garment that had been too small for her womanly frame.

He stilled as a huge male dressed only in leather pants trudged towards her, as she noticed him and backed into the corner of her cage that was furthest from him, causing it to sway.

Couldn't breathe as she shook her head, her blue eyes pleading the meaty warrior.

The male flexed fingers around a spear tipped with a black blade.

Crusted with blood.

Keras fought to move, snarled and struggled when his feet refused to cooperate. He looked down at them, at the jagged black shadows snaring his legs, creeping up them. Devouring him.

He had pushed too far.

He lifted his head and looked at the woman.

Swore she looked right at him as the male drove the spear towards her.

As she screamed.

Keras screamed with her.

The shadows engulfed him.

CHAPTER 30

Daimon stepped the moment the harrowing scream cut through the night air, landing in the building where he had left Keras.

Keras gripped the bars of the cage, his eyes locked with the daemon's, his fangs long and irises black as he unleashed another pained bellow.

Daimon grabbed him by his shoulders and tore him away from the cage, shattering the connection between him and the daemon. His brother hit the floor in a sprawl and Daimon's heart hammered in his throat as he crouched to check on him, fearing the worst.

Ares and Calistos appeared in the doorway.

Cal was quick to reach Keras and feather his fingers over his neck, his sigh saying it all as it escaped his lips and he sank back onto his haunches.

Relief washed through Daimon, and through Ares too judging by the way his shoulders sagged, the tension draining from him.

Ares raked his hands over his tawny hair and stared at Keras, his dark eyes lit with gold and red sparks. "What the fuck did he think he was doing? I told him not to fucking do this."

Ares hadn't been the only one to lay down the law with Keras either. Daimon had told him the same thing, and so had the rest of his brothers. Keras had agreed he wouldn't probe the daemon's mind and then he had gone ahead and done it anyway.

It wasn't like Keras to be reckless.

Valen and Marek appeared beyond Ares and Cal, Caterina and Eva in tow.

"What the hell happened?" Valen looked at Keras, his golden eyes bright. He stooped, his violet hair falling forwards to obscure his face as he grabbed hold of Keras and helped Cal get him onto the nearest bench.

Keras remained deathly still.

Valen cast a worried look at Marek and Ares. "He's gonna be all right... yeah?"

Ares didn't look sure, but he nodded anyway.

Esher charged into the room, knocking Ares and Marek aside, Aiko hanging off his left arm. The petite female gave up trying to hold him back as Daimon stepped into his path, quickly obscuring his view of Keras.

"Good to see you up and about," Daimon said, keeping his voice calm and letting none of his fear show in it.

Esher glanced at him and then turned his glare back on the wraith. "What happened to him?"

That growled question had everyone looking at the cage.

At the daemon who sat in the middle of it, hugging his knees and rocking, babbling incoherent things to himself.

Gods, he wasn't sure what he would do if Keras had suffered the same fate. "His mind fractured."

The tension suddenly washed from the air as Keras's deep voice rolled over it.

Daimon stepped back and twisted to face his brother.

Keras curled over, dug his fingers into his black hair, and clutched the sides of his head as he slowly breathed.

"And you?" Ares snapped. "You break your own fucking mind too?"

Keras lifted bleak green eyes to Ares, but didn't say a word.

Which wasn't reassuring.

Ares took a hard step towards Keras, heat shimmering over his body as fire raged in his eyes. "I fucking told you not to do it."

Keras dropped his gaze back to the floor and closed his eyes, his voice thick with fatigue as he said, "We were getting nowhere."

Daimon glanced at Esher, checking on him as his brother began to breathe harder and faster. "Esher?"

Esher's dark blue eyes snapped to him and he blinked, his breaths coming more slowly again. "I want answers. I wanted..."

Daimon knew what his brother had wanted. He had wanted to be the one to break the wraith. He had needed to be the one to get them answers.

But Keras had beaten him to it and he wasn't happy about it.

Daimon looked at the daemon. Although he wasn't sure what answers Keras had managed to get from him.

One thing he did know—they wouldn't be getting any more.

Eli was a mess, babbling strange things as he rocked, his violet gaze unfocused.

Esher went to take a step forwards, darkness emerging in his eyes, and Daimon stood his ground. When Esher dragged his gaze away from the daemon and narrowed it on him, Daimon lifted his right hand and hovered it over his bare shoulder, offering comfort in the only way he could and hoping it would be enough to calm his brother.

Crimson ringed his brother's sapphire irises as he snarled, "I wanted answers. I was patient, Daimon… *Patient.* I wanted answers. I brought him here… I—"

Daimon inched closer to Esher. "You did good. You did what was right."

He didn't glance at Keras, but Keras's gaze landed on him, and Daimon knew his oldest brother had read between the lines and knew Daimon thought he had done wrong. Hell, it was obvious everyone thought he had been out of his mind to attempt to read the daemon's memories. There wasn't a single person in the room who thought Keras had been right to do it.

Esher breathed harder, his chest straining with each one as he stared straight through Daimon, as if he could see the daemon on the other side of him.

"Esher," he whispered. "We can still get answers."

He wasn't sure how though. Eli certainly wasn't going to be giving them any information. Esher hadn't needed this. Daimon could only imagine how difficult it had been for him to convince himself to capture the daemon rather than kill him, to bring him back here for them to question rather than torturing him for answers in the Underworld.

Now, that battle had been for nothing, and Esher was dangerously close to slipping back into the darkness of his other side.

The crimson invading his brother's eyes began to spread and Daimon motioned to Aiko. She hurried forwards and took hold of Esher's arm, slipped her hand into his right one and smiled when Esher looked down at her. His brother blinked as she stroked his arm and blue began to win against the scarlet in his irises.

"Maybe we should get some air?" Aiko breathed, her voice steady and no trace of nerves in her eyes even when Daimon knew she had to be afraid of losing Esher to his other side again.

Esher's brow furrowed, his gaze darting between her and the cage, and he made a pained sound, as if having to choose between obeying Aiko and pleasing her, and unleashing his rage on the daemon was killing him.

"Get some air," Daimon whispered. "I can come with you if you want."

Esher swallowed. Hesitated. Nodded.

"Did you get anything out of him?" Marek eased into the room, allowing Megan to reach Ares and blocking Esher's path.

Megan hesitated as she reached for Ares's hand.

His older brother noticed her at last and paced away from Keras, heading out into the night. Megan trailed after him. She would get his brother's mood back under control, but Daimon wasn't sure it would stop Ares from tearing Keras a new one.

"Calindria," Keras whispered just as Daimon had been about to escort Esher out for some air too. Everyone fell silent, an air of expectation settling over the room. Keras buried his face in his hands and his back shuddered as he inhaled. "I saw her. All grown up. Locked in a cage... Somewhere in the Underworld. A hellish domain."

"She's grown up?" Cal sank to his knees in front of Keras. "How is that possible? A soul doesn't grow up... does it?"

Cal looked at Marek.

Marek shrugged. "It shouldn't, but we don't know the particulars of what the wraith and the necromancer did to her soul."

"She can feel everything," Keras murmured and everyone looked at him. Cold slithered down Daimon's spine as Keras continued, "She can feel it as if she's flesh and blood. I saw it."

"That can't be right." Cal's voice hitched, breaking as he threw a panicked look at everyone before settling his stormy blue eyes back on Keras. "It has to be a lie. Something he showed you to hurt you. It has to be a lie. The daemon couldn't enter the Underworld until he went through the gate, and Esher was on his tail the whole time, so he couldn't have been there because Esher would have seen her too and she couldn't have been grown up like me..."

Marek placed a gentle hand on Cal's shoulder. "She's been dead a long time, Cal. It's possible the wraith saw her when she was grown, long before we were sent to the mortal world. He might have managed to slip into the Underworld before."

"No." Keras spoke that word in a calm tone but it seemed to crack like lightning, shaking the room. He lifted his head and looked at Cal. "I don't think it was a memory belonging to the wraith. I think it belonged to the necromancer."

"Eli took his blood?" Daimon didn't want to believe that.

"Maybe. It wasn't Eli. It was someone else's memory." Keras scrubbed a hand over his face, sat up and leaned back, sagging against the wall as his hands fell into his lap. "It was real though."

"You think it was recent?" Daimon flicked a glance at Cal, keeping an eye on him.

His youngest brother stared straight ahead and looked as if he was struggling, his eyes wide and unfocused. Daimon had his hands full with keeping Esher on the rails. He wasn't sure he could handle both Esher and Cal going off them.

"I'm not sure." Keras pushed forwards and took hold of Cal's shoulders and Cal looked at him. "We will find her."

Cal nodded, the movement jerky. When he didn't stop nodding, Keras kneaded his shoulders.

"Don't think about it for now," Keras murmured, fatigue laced with concern in his deep voice. "I shouldn't have told you."

Cal shook his head this time. "No. I want to know these things."

He might want to know them, but he was having trouble handling them without passing out. His brother's affliction had been slowly improving over the past few weeks, since they had dealt with the necromancer and Cal had discovered that Calindria's soul was still out there, giving him a chance to save it and guide it to the Elysian Fields where she could rest.

He had managed to remember some things about what had happened to him and Calindria all those centuries ago without passing out.

"That's not good." Marek's bass voice rolling over the room had everyone looking at him, and then in the direction of his gaze.

Black blood trickled from Eli's nose and ears.

The wraith stilled.

Rubbed his fingers over his lip and brought it away, staring at the blood.

He smiled and then coughed, spraying more blood across the floor. It rolled down his chin and coated his teeth as he looked at Keras.

"This isn't over," Eli calmly said and coughed again, sending more vile black blood oozing down his chin. His violet eyes brightened dangerously as he stared hard at Keras, his voice dropping to a hiss. "I am not the last."

The wraith lurched forwards, vomiting blood, his entire body shaking so hard he rattled the cage as he clawed at the bars on the floor of it, hands slipping around in the oily black liquid.

"Cass!" Daimon leaped over Cal and shoved past Marek, hitting the doorway of the building as quickly as he could. "Need a healing spell."

Cass twisted away from Mari, Megan and Ares. Her eyes widened and she hurried to him.

"Godsdammit, Keras!" Ares boomed and rushed after her.

Daimon looked back at Eli.

Too late.

The daemon lay in a pool of his own blood, his eyes fixed on nothing.

He was gone.

Esher roared and grabbed the cage, shaking it hard, as if that would revive the dead daemon. Aiko tried to calm him, clinging to his arm and speaking to him in Japanese, fear and panic written across her face as she kept her eyes locked on Esher's profile.

Ares levelled a black look on Keras, accusation in it that had Keras lifting his green gaze to him. Keras's eyes darkened, a warning in them to his second in command, one that was apparently enough to have Ares backing down. Ares huffed and scrubbed a hand over his tawny hair, mussing it as his fiery gaze shifted to the dead daemon.

"Damn it," he muttered, echoing the feeling Daimon had as he looked at the wraith.

Keras had pushed too far and now their shot at getting valuable information from the daemon was gone. It wasn't like Keras to be so impatient. He looked back at his brother, trying to figure out what was wrong with him recently. Keras refused to meet his gaze, pushed to his feet and strode out into the waning night.

The wraith's final words rang in Daimon's mind.

They knew there were others on the enemy's side, but it still felt like an ominous announcement.

The Erinyes were still alive, and if the two females had their way and got their hands on Cass, Esher would probably get his wish too—Eli would be alive again, reanimated by the enemy and Cass's dark magic.

Daimon fixed his senses on her as she came to stand beside him, needing to know that she was safe.

He would keep her that way.

He wouldn't let anything happen to her.

Esher stiffened, locking up tight.

"What's wrong?" Daimon went to him and hovered his hand over his brother's back.

Esher didn't take his eyes off the daemon. Didn't move a muscle.

"Penitence," Esher whispered.

Nemesis was summoning him for punishment. Daimon couldn't imagine what kind of torment he would receive as retribution for all the rules he had broken. Esher wouldn't be strong enough to survive it, not without losing himself to his other side again.

"I'll go," Daimon said.

And stepped before Esher could stop him.

CHAPTER 31

Daimon landed beneath a dim shaft of light, surrounded by infinite darkness. He peered through the weak light, hating the way it stole his vision, making it hard to see into the shadows.

He wasn't alone.

From those shadows, a haughty feminine voice echoed.

"You are not the one I summoned."

"But I am the one you'll punish." Daimon stood his ground when a delicate foot clad in a blood-red sandal emerged from the darkness, followed by the soft sway of layers of sheer black fabric.

Nemesis's scarlet eyes drilled into his face as she sashayed from the shadows, her face a placid mask that gave away none of her feelings.

Her eyes revealed them all.

She wasn't happy that he had taken Esher's place.

"So loyal to your brother," she murmured and banked right, skirting the edge of the light, her gaze assessing him as it raked over him, sending a cold shiver down his spine. "I always did love that about you, Daimon."

He shuddered at the sound of his name uttered on her vile lips.

He wanted to tell her to get on with things and announce the punishment he would receive for his brother's apparent crimes, but knew better than to rush her. Rushing her normally ended with her doubling the punishment.

He preferred to keep the number of lashes in the four-digits area not push them into five.

He tracked her with his senses as she moved behind him, aware that moving would be a mistake. He had to endure this leisurely perusal of him, even if the feel of her eyes on him sickened him. She had always enjoyed tormenting him like this, always pointed out how handsome she found him, had even gone so far as propositioning him once.

Because the bitch was aware that in this world—the Underworld—his ice was no longer a problem and he could touch without hurting someone. She played on that, thought to goad him into surrendering to his base needs and letting them get the better of him, slaking a thirst for physical contact that he was denied in the mortal realm.

It was just another form of punishment.

She appeared to his right and he slid his gaze that way, tracked her as she moved around him and concealed the shudder that wracked him as she licked crimson lips.

Beneath the sheer layers of her onyx robe, her nipples beaded.

When she raked her gaze down him this time, it remained at his feet.

Daimon looked down at the thick metal ring just a few inches in front of his boots.

Metal of the gods.

He cursed that infernal ring, recounting all the times he had been bound to it, how it never moved even when he thrashed and tried to break free of it.

He swallowed and dropped to his knees before it.

Sucked down a fortifying breath as he held his hands out to it.

"Let's not rush." Nemesis drifted into the beam of light and it reflected off the gold filigree that formed a corset over her stomach, cinching the black layers of her dress in to reveal her curves.

Cold skated over his flesh as she ran her hand over his shoulders and he closed his eyes as she crouched behind him, her fingers easing down his spine.

"We would not want to bloody this." She stroked the hem of his top and he dutifully lifted his arms above his head as she pulled it up. "There's a good boy."

He scowled at her over his shoulder when she finished removing his top.

She leaned towards him, her crimson hair brushing his bare skin, her breath cold against his ear as she whispered, "Now, now. Best keep that temper in check lest I decide a different sort of punishment for you."

She skimmed her palms across his shoulders and her hands shook as she sucked in a trembling breath.

He didn't want to imagine the vile things she was contemplating, tried to shut them and the sudden spike of fear that lanced him out of his mind. She wouldn't violate him like that. The terms of his punishment were hers to set, but it would overstep a line and his father would have her head.

She brushed her lips across his left shoulder.

Daimon clenched his fists. She wouldn't.

She chuckled into his ear. "So tense. I would have thought you would be more relaxed these days."

He wanted to look at her and demand what she meant by that, but he knew the answer in his heart.

She knew about him and Cassandra.

Which was strange.

She had never taken an interest in any of their lives before now. He had never realised she could see such things from her domain in the Underworld.

Rich brown leather snapped around his wrists and jerked him forwards as the straps attached themselves to the heavy metal ring.

Nemesis stroked two fingers down his spine and murmured, "How many lashes are adequate punishment for breaking an exile, entering the Underworld without permission, and murdering hundreds of people here in your father's domain?"

Daimon really didn't want to know the answer to that.

"I would have given Esher twenty-thousand at the very least."

Daimon closed his eyes and bowed his head, fighting the urge to ask her to give him less than that, to use the attraction she felt towards him to bargain with her.

Her lips feathered across his ear. "Perhaps… ten thousand?"

Gods, that was still too many. A few thousand with her barbed metal whip was bad enough, always had him close to blacking out. Part of the terms of penitence was that he had to remain awake for it all to utter an apology, one for each lash of her whip. She would be forced to wait for him to heal and wake again, and would no doubt increase the number of lashes.

Keeping him here in her realm for longer and longer.

She loosed a soft moan as she caressed his shoulders, as she lowered her hands down his back and then under his arms. Her breasts pressed against his back and he bit his tongue as she raked nails over his bare chest.

"It has been so long since I have been with a man," she whispered into the shell of his ear.

"No." Daimon jerked backwards as much as he could with his hands bound to the ring, attempting to dislodge her.

She chuckled and nipped at his earlobe. "Would you really get a say if I decided your punishment would be to service me?"

He wouldn't, but someone else would. "Father would have your head."

She sighed. "Unfortunately… that is true. Fifteen thousand lashes it is."

"Fifteen?" He twisted his head towards her, his cheek colliding with her lips. "You said ten."

"You were insolent." She pressed a kiss to his cheek and edged backwards, rose onto her feet and rounded him, standing so close that he had to tilt his head back and look up at her to keep his eyes on hers.

Just the way she liked it.

She liked having him and his brothers on their knees.

At her mercy.

"Kiss me, and I will halve that number."

He scowled at her. "No."

She inspected her nails, a dark edge to her crimson eyes. "So loyal to your little sorceress. She has you well under her spell."

He wanted to ask her what that was supposed to mean too, but held his tongue, because there was no mistaking the emotion that surfaced in her eyes as they shifted back to lock with his.

She was jealous.

He lowered his gaze to the metal ring and his bound hands, focused on it instead of her, hoping she would get the message that he was done talking. He could see where things would go if he let her have her way. She wanted to turn him against Cass, would probably say anything to get him to break up with her, spouting lies about her that were bound to involve his enemy and her being a member of them. Cass wasn't. She was loyal too—loyal to Mari, and to him.

The gritty black floor bit into his knees through his jeans as he waited. Seconds stretched into minutes.

Nemesis finally huffed.

A whirr cut the thick air and he gritted his teeth, adrenaline coursing through him as he braced himself. He grunted as the metal whip cut down his back, catching his spine.

Muttered his first apology.

She struck him again, forcing another from him, and then again, this one catching him from his left shoulder all the way down to his right hip. He arched forwards, barely stifling the cry that rose up his throat.

Apologised again.

Daimon tried to keep count of the lashes as she hit him over and over, focused on Cass to help him bear the pain of each strike, filling his mind with something pleasant to counter the torment.

But the pain began to win, blurring his thoughts as his entire body ached, heat throbbing across his back and his shoulders in sickening waves as blood rolled down his skin and drenched his jeans.

As sweat stung the lacerations.

Nemesis stopped.

They weren't done.

His head was a little foggy and it was near impossible to focus, but he swore she had only delivered two thousand lashes.

Was she giving him a breather? It wasn't like her. She had whipped him close to four thousand times once without giving him a break.

He grimaced and clenched his teeth as she drew her fingers across his shoulders, fire rolling in their wake as she caught each deep laceration.

She rounded him and he looked up at her, found her staring at her fingers.

At his blood.

A distant look in her crimson eyes.

"Such power in something so…" She didn't finish that sentence, just lifted her fingers to her lips and tasted his blood, her tongue darting over her fingertips. Her eyes rolled back and she moaned.

That was a first.

She had never tasted his blood before.

He frowned at her, a glimmer of suspicion forming inside his weary mind, pushing through the pain and the fatigue that wracked him.

Her gaze dropped to meet his.

She seemed strangely upbeat. He would go as far as saying she was a little giddy about something. It wasn't there on the surface, on her placid features, but it was there in her eyes as she towered over him.

Something was wrong.

Very wrong.

Nemesis leaned over, her breasts threatening to spill from her black dress, and stroked his cheek.

Daimon stared into her eyes. "Can we get on with this? I have somewhere I need to be."

He knew he was pushing it, but he wanted to be away from her. Far away from her. Something wasn't right about her today. She was always strange, but she had never tasted his blood before and had never been like this. Was it because of Cass?

Or something else?

That feeling that it was about something else only worsened as she smiled.

As she peered deep into his eyes, a sick satisfied edge to hers.

"Oh... sweet Daimon... you are not going anywhere," she murmured, voice dripping honey even as it sent ice skating down his spine.

He reared back, breaking contact between them, and frowned at her. "What do you mean by that?"

Her crimson smile only widened.

"A change of plans, but perhaps for the better."

She raked her scarlet eyes over him, twisted satisfaction and darkness filling them.

"It is such a shame I cannot be there to see your downfall."

She leaned in close and hissed in his ear.

"But I will be here to welcome you with open arms when you return to *my* Underworld."

Daimon stared at her, too stunned to say anything as he realised she was with the enemy. He needed to warn his brothers, but he didn't think he was going to get the chance. He wrestled against the restraints anyway, desperately trying to break them. If he could break the leather straps, he could step back to Tokyo. His pulse pounded faster as the brown leather refused to give.

As Nemesis smiled down at him.

Two Messengers appeared behind her, the black-haired males materialising out of the shadows, their mismatched—one green and one blue—eyes fixed straight ahead of them. Their black tunics bore silver detailing around the cuffs and fastenings.

They served his family.

Or they had served it.

Shock rolled through him as that revelation hit him and he bit out a curse. The enemy had even managed to turn these two males, and the gods only knew how many others, against his father.

Never in all his years had he imagined a Messenger would betray his family.

Nemesis's hand drifted from Daimon's face. "I will await your return, my beautiful slave. You will service me for eternity."

She tilted her head slightly to her left.

"Take him."

CHAPTER 32

Daimon blacked out at some point. When he came around, he was in some kind of loft apartment. Arched windows had been painted black, but as far as he could tell, it was daylight outside.

He twisted on the dusty wooden floorboards, his muscles protesting as he manoeuvred onto his side and realised his arms were bound behind his back. His vision wobbled, blurring and going dark around the edges before it cleared again. He shook his head, trying to shift the heaviness from it.

He felt as if he had drunk a barrel of ambrosia.

The room distorted again as he tried to take stock of his surroundings and figure out where he was being held. The exposed brick walls had been painted white at some point, but the paint was peeling now, and black mould crept across the ceiling from the top corner of the wall nearest the bank of windows.

No furniture either.

It looked as if no one had lived here in a very long time.

Daimon rolled onto his front, pressed his left cheek into the floorboards and pushed his backside up. He wriggled his knees forwards and gritted his teeth as he forced himself into an upright position.

Someone shoved him in the back.

He hit the floorboards face-first and growled at the person.

They weren't powerful.

Not daemon either.

He shuffled around so he could peer over his shoulder at them.

The Messengers.

He glared at the one closest to him, the one who had shoved him, staring right into his mismatched eyes. "My father know you're a traitor?"

The male's eyes brightened dangerously, one glowing emerald as the other shone like a sapphire.

Daimon spat at his feet.

Got a boot in the face as a reward.

He grunted as he was flipped onto his back, his arms twisting painfully beneath him.

The male looked ready to level another blow at him.

Stiffened.

"Now, I do believe we said not to harm him." The soft female voice echoed in the cavernous room.

Daimon's gaze sought the owner of it.

Found her near a metal door a few metres south of his feet.

Her blonde tresses had been twisted into a plait that arced over the front of her hair, and her blue eyes were bright as she gazed at him, her rosy lips curling into the semblance of a smile.

If he hadn't known better, he would have thought it was Marinda.

But he did know better.

He glared at the furie, letting her know exactly what he thought of her. Another traitor. The female didn't react, just kept walking towards him, her eyes never leaving him. Behind her, the second furie entered the room, sighing.

"We will not be able to do anything until nightfall. Evening at the earliest." She didn't sound happy about that.

Daimon was.

It gave him time.

His brothers would be concerned about him by now. Cass definitely would be. He wasn't sure how long he had been out, but he guessed it was a few hours judging by how well the lacerations on his back had healed.

His sorceress didn't seem to be able to let him out of her sight for more than a couple of hours, something he had lamented once but was thankful for now. Providing she hadn't changed that quirk of hers since she had staked a claim on his heart, she would be looking for him. He was sure of it.

"I thought New York in autumn was meant to be dreary." The first Erinyes smoothed her blonde hair, tracing each ribbon of the braid with both hands. "She will not be pleased about the delay."

"A delay is necessary," the second responded as she moved around the room, giving the Messenger who had remained at a distance a slow once-over. She pressed close to him and tiptoed, whispering into his ear, "Can you really not feel things?"

She feathered her fingers down the buttons of his tunic and the way the male reacted when she palmed the front of his trousers said that he definitely could feel things. His mismatched eyes widened and darkened, and edged towards her.

"Such a shame you don't serve me." She gently patted the male's groin.

His pupils devoured the green and blue of his irises.

"Melody," the first furie snapped. "Focus."

"Just trying to find a way to pass the time, Meadow."

Marinda. Melody. Meadow. Three Erinyes. Goddesses of the Underworld that formed a power circle that could be devastating if they put their mind to it and worked together.

Thankfully, Marinda was on his side, weakening the other two Erinyes.

Melody sighed and dragged herself away from the male, coming to stand beside the woman who could have passed as her twin. They were even dressed the same, clad in black corsets and leathers that reminded him of Cass.

But unlike Cass, both of them looked wary of getting too close to him.

Because of his power?

He focused it, keeping his gaze on their faces so they kept looking at him and not at the floor. Ice spread outwards from beneath him.

Meadow was swift to notice and back away, catching Melody's arm and pulling her with her.

The ice formed more rapidly to keep pace with them.

And then it stopped.

He frowned at the wooden floor and cursed. A crudely drawn chalk circle surrounded him, glyphs flowing around the outside of it.

A ward.

Both Erinyes' eyes changed, turning violet edged with black as they glared at him.

"Nemesis wants him kept alive." The Messenger who Melody had groped stepped forwards, his eyes fixed on the female, hunger still shining in them.

Melody's right eyebrow slowly arched as she looked him over and pursed her lips, a sultry pout in his direction that had his eyes darkening further.

Meadow huffed and glared at Daimon. "We won't kill him. Just need to take a little blood."

Blood.

The Erinyes could siphon powers from blood, and had proven in Tokyo that it didn't need to be inside the host for that to happen. If they got their hands on his blood, they would be able to command the gate. One of the gates was bound to him in blood too, and would easily do their bidding.

He bit out a ripe curse, aiming this one at Keras.

His oldest brother should have let him seal the New York gate when he had offered to do it.

Now the enemy planned to use his blood to open it and when it was fully formed and linked this world to the Underworld, they would lock it open with the wards they knew. It could take hours, days to discover which wards they had used through a process of elimination so he could close it again. In that time, the Underworld and this realm would begin to merge. If he couldn't get it closed again, the merging of the worlds could damage the gate to the point where it would remain open no matter what he and his brothers tried to do, and the two worlds would slowly collide, causing catastrophic damage to both sides of the gate.

Forming a new realm.

The mission he had been sent here to fulfil would end in failure.

His home and his family would be destroyed. The enemy wouldn't settle for degrading his father by taking his throne from him. They would kill him and his mother. His brothers would most likely be hunted and slaughtered too.

And all their women.

And Cass.

He wouldn't let that happen.

He narrowed his eyes on the two furies, a battle sparking to life inside him as he thought about what he needed to do.

He couldn't let them get their hands on his blood.

Ice numbed his fingers as he considered what he was on the verge of doing.

It would hurt his family, hitting his parents and Esher the hardest, might even be too much for his brother in his current condition.

And Cass would be furious with him.

But he couldn't let them get their hands on her, and he couldn't let the gate fall. Hurting everyone he loved was better than sentencing them to death.

He pulled down a slow breath, fighting to steady his nerves, to muster the courage he needed—courage that kept slipping through his fingers.

Daimon tilted his chin up.

He had to do it.

He would do it.

He stared into Meadow's eyes.

Let every drop of the hatred he felt towards her and his enemy shine in his eyes, every drop of the rage he felt because they had forced his hand, but hid all the guilt and the pain, the remorse that threatened to devour him and shatter his strength.

He was doing this.

He was going to die here.

Daimon focused on his hands, on his power, but rather than attacking, he turned it inward. His blood was quick to slow in his veins, the cold he always felt growing more intense as his head grew foggy, thoughts blurring together as tiredness rolled through his already weakened body.

Panic sparked, throwing his mind and his heart into turmoil, and he clenched his hands into tight fists as he fought it, kept pushing onwards as his instincts roared at him to stop.

That he would die if he kept going.

That survival instinct battered him, had his ice waning even as he tried to keep it building inside him, spreading through him.

He gritted his teeth and pushed through it, desperately shutting out the voice that screamed in his mind. His feet numbed as ice formed over them, slowly spreading up his calves.

Darkness encroached at the corners of his mind and he gasped for air as the cold invaded his lungs, and his heart slowed.

He was drowning.

Drowning in his own ice.

Momentary blackness washed over him and he tipped forwards, jerked backwards when it released him and shook his head.

"Stop him," Meadow barked as she lunged for him, her violet eyes wild.

He couldn't let them do that.

Ice formed jagged spikes around him, shooting up to the ceiling. The two furies battered it, fracturing and even breaking holes in it in places, but his power was running at full tilt now, was swift to repair any area that took damage. The walls surrounding him slowly turned pale blue as they thickened, inching towards him. They touched his knees first, met with the ice that had formed over them already.

He struggled to breathe, what little air he could get into his burning lungs fogging in front of his face as he expelled it. His teeth clattered, loud in his prison as ice rolled up his stomach and arms, reached his shoulders.

Sapping the last of the heat from his body as it closed over his chest.

His thoughts slowed, his vision dimming.

Ice formed on his cheeks in the path of his tears as he thought of Cass.

He wished he had taken a moment to speak with her before he had gone to Nemesis.

Wished he had told her that he loved her.

Had seen her face one last time.

Said goodbye to her.

Sorrow washed through him as he realised he would never see his beautiful *koldun'ya* again, the last thing he felt as the ice enclosed him.

He had finally found someone he truly loved.

And this time, he was the one leaving her.

CHAPTER 33

Cass stroked Mister Milos, petting the white and ginger cat as she held him in her arms. He purred, the rumbling sound a comfort to her frayed nerves. She tried to focus on him to shut out that unsettling sensation burning inside her heart, but it lingered, tormenting her.

Daimon had been gone too long.

She kept running her right hand over Milos's fur as her bare feet carried her through the Tokyo mansion, towards the voices she could hear in the main living area of the house.

Mari looked over the back of the cream couch, twisting away from Calistos to smile at Cass as she entered the room at the TV area end of it.

"Have you seen Daimon?" Cass paused at the back of the couch.

Calistos set the console controller down on his lap, looked at her and shook his head. When she looked at Valen who lounged on the other couch, twirling a ribbon of his violet hair around his finger with one hand and hammering at the controller he gripped with the other, the god of lightning gave a half-hearted shrug.

"Sometimes penitence is a bitch." Valen glanced at her, looking past Eva where the beautiful Italian assassin sat beside him, acting as his pillow as she cleaned a gun, their black fatigues making them blend together. "Maybe he's chilling out in Hong Kong. Doesn't want you seeing how fucked up he is and going on a bender."

That wasn't a comfort.

She glared at him.

Eva nudged him with her right arm and muttered, "Stronzo."

"What?" He shifted left, so his head landed in her lap, and pulled an innocent and hurt face. "I was being helpful."

"You were being a dick," Cal put in, earning a glare from his brother.

Cass's petting grew more frantic. Milos didn't care. He just purred harder, lapping up the attention. For once, he wasn't even bothered that Calistos was near him.

Her cat had strange tastes. He adored Valen and Esher, and hissed near-constantly at the rest of the brothers.

Of course, he loved every single one of the women.

The little lothario.

Someone stalked into the room to her right, striding from the corridor beside the kitchen.

Esher.

He ran an unsteady hand over his wild black hair, preening it over and over again as he hurried from the bathhouse. Or perhaps the cage. She studied him. Judging by the conflicting feelings his blue eyes held, it had been the cage. Esher had been firmly on edge since coming around, and had almost gone over it when the daemon had died.

After Daimon had left, Esher and Keras had argued.

Rain still poured down outside, creating a melody as it struck the roof of the mansion, a storm that didn't look as if it was going to clear up any time soon.

Ares had tried to keep the peace between the brothers, but Esher was furious about what Keras had done, and Keras was unrepentant.

So the argument continued.

Keras strode in behind Esher, hot on his heels.

"We're done," Esher snarled, throwing a black look over his shoulder.

Keras looked as if he wanted to say differently, but Aiko ran around him, cutting him off, her pigtails and short black ruffled skirt bouncing with each rushed stride. She caught up with Esher and looped both of her arms around his right one.

The feral god slowed and looked down at her, gradually coming to a halt as his face crumpled. He gathered her into his arms and buried his face in her neck, his inky hair blending with hers as he clutched her to him. Aiko wrapped her arms around him and held him, stroked his back through his dark grey shirt and whispered words to him in Japanese.

"He didn't need this shit," Ares muttered as he brought up the rear. "I told you not to do anything."

Keras shot him down with a glare, one that had darkness glittering in his green eyes.

Ares looked as if he was chewing a wasp as he stomped past him, heading for the couches.

"Have you seen Daimon?" She wasn't sure who she aimed that question at as she stroked Milos harder, her nerves getting the better of her again.

Esher lifted his head and looked at her. "He's not back?"

She shook her head.

"It's been hours," Ares muttered with a glance at the drenched garden.

"More like a day," Esher said and straightened, a look crossing his face that had Keras placing a hand on his shoulder.

"You're in no condition to step to Hong Kong." Keras's grip on his shoulder tightened briefly before loosening again when Marek pushed onto his feet on the other side of the low dining table.

"I'll go." The burly brunet glanced down at the pretty caramel-haired woman who paused at the keyboard of a laptop. "Back in a minute. Keep searching."

Caterina nodded and went back to her work as Marek disappeared in a swirl of black smoke.

Cass's gaze drifted to the garden beyond the walkway, focusing on Milos's purring rather than the tense silence that descended as everyone waited.

She scratched Milos behind his ears, rubbed them and tickled his chin.

What was taking Marek so long? Was Daimon seriously hurt and needed his help?

She was on the verge of forming the spell to transport her to Hong Kong when Marek finally reappeared in the middle of the room.

"He's not there." Marek's earthy brown eyes held a lot of concern as he looked at her and only her, his expression so grave that she froze.

Her breath hitched and heart lodged in her throat. "What do you mean he isn't there?"

"He's not there and there's no sign he's been there recently. Bed is made. Everything is clean. No blood. The place is immaculate."

Cass threw a glance at his brothers. "Where can he be?"

Cal slowly stood, coming to face her, and she wanted to lash out at him when he murmured thoughtfully, "What if he never came back?"

"Not possible." Esher was quick to speak before she could, his eyes darkening to navy as he turned on Cal. "Daimon went to pay penitence for me. Maybe it was more punishment than usual. Maybe he's still there."

"For twenty-four hours?" she bit out, her temper fraying as she hugged Milos to her chest.

"It's possible," Esher retorted.

The rest of his brothers looked as if it wasn't. They looked as if they felt the same way as she did.

He was grasping at straws, clinging to hope that Cass couldn't feel as she stared at the garden, as that unsettled feeling condensed inside her into full blown fear.

Something had happened to Daimon.

She looked at each of his brothers in turn.

Keras's eyes verged on black as he twisted the silver band around his thumb, his jet eyebrows knitted hard and his lips compressed into a thin line.

Ares looked equally as troubled, sparks of gold and red lighting his brown irises.

Valen looked ready to rip someone apart.

"You think the enemy might have managed to…" She didn't want to finish that sentence.

"I think the enemy has been in our sights all this time," Ares growled, his face grim and fire raging in his eyes.

She wasn't sure what he meant by that until Calistos spoke.

"Nemesis wouldn't turn against Father… would she?" He didn't look sure about that, his blue eyes turning stormy as he looked between Ares and Keras.

Keras snarled, "Anything is possible."

"I don't like the sound of this," Marek put in. "We need to send a Messenger to Father to ask whether he can feel Daimon in the Underworld. While that's happening, we need to search for him. If he's not in Hong Kong, and he's not here, maybe they took him to one of the old safehouses. We could check there."

"They took him to New York." Keras sounded certain of that.

Everyone looked at Keras. Valen and Eva rose to their feet, giving him the whole of their attention, and Mari pushed to hers at the same time as Caterina stood and went to Marek.

"The enemy attacked Hong Kong when Esher was absent. They know which gate is bound to each of us." Keras looked at Ares, Marek and then Valen. "We head to New York."

"I'm coming too." Esher broke away from Aiko and outside the rain grew heavier again, pelting the earth and filling the air with the scent of it.

"No." That single word fell hard in the room, spoken in a commanding tone that had Esher's shoulders stiffening as he levelled a glare on Keras. Keras didn't give him a chance to argue. "You are in no fit state to step there, let alone fight. On a battlefield, you are a liability right now. I will not risk you."

All of the fight fled from Esher's eyes as the last five words hit him, uttered in a soft tone that had her, and everyone else in the room judging by their faces, aware of the depth of Keras's feelings for his brother.

Keras went to Esher, placed his hands on his shoulders and looked deep into his eyes.

"I know you need to be there, Esher, because it's Daimon… but you are still recovering. You need to sit this one out."

Esher's black eyebrows furrowed, pain dancing in his dark blue eyes as they darted between Keras's.

A need to do something to ease him filled her, had her moving towards him to touch his back. The moment she made contact with him, he turned his face towards her.

"I'll go with them," she said in a low voice, one filled with the compassion she felt inside as she looked into Esher's eyes and saw the conflict in them— the need. The thought of sitting this one out was killing him. Keras was right though. Esher was a liability. He couldn't go into battle, but she could, and she would do it for both of them. "I'll make sure he comes home."

Esher nodded stiffly.

"We'll take care of the ladies," Cal said and came to Esher, slapped him on the back and nodded when Esher looked at him. "Got to keep Megan and the others safe, right?"

Esher's eyes rapidly darkened and he growled as he nodded. "The babe."

Gods help the world if Aiko ever fell pregnant. The beast would probably coddle her to death and kill anyone who so much as looked in her direction.

Ares looked as if he wanted to hug his brother for being so concerned about Megan and the baby, but settled for saying, "Thanks. She'll feel better knowing you're both here."

"I'll kill any bastard who sets foot near here." Eva checked her gun was loaded, her sapphire eyes bright as she stared lovingly at it and then at Valen. "You give them hell."

Valen swept her up into his arms and kissed her. "Always do."

Something deep inside Cass ached, the need to see Daimon was safe and alive burning more fiercely and flooding her with impatience.

"Let us go." Cass walked to Aiko and handed Milos to her.

Her bastard cat continued purring contentedly as Aiko petted him, evidently uncaring about the change of hands. Traitor.

Cass began to form the incantation in her mind.

Stopped when Ares towered over her. "You stay here."

She scowled at him. "I will not."

A few of his brothers looked as if they wanted to voice an objection too, so she glared at them all, making sure they knew she was serious. It didn't matter that the enemy wanted to get their hands on her. All that mattered was bringing Daimon home safe.

"I know the risks, but none of you get a say. This is my decision and no one can stop me from going." She planted her hands on her hips, digging her fingertips into her black leather trousers, and dared them all to speak.

Calistos and Esher both looked as if they wanted her to go, probably for different reasons. Mari looked concerned but unlikely to say something. Valen looked bored.

Marek and Ares looked ready to argue with her about this.

Keras.

Well, he looked as if he was considering tossing her into the cage.

So Cass played her trump card.

She tipped her chin up. "I can use a spell to locate Daimon."

Marek glanced at Ares. Ares huffed.

"You want to find Daimon quickly, you're going to need me." She glared at them all, stoked her magic so it shone in her eyes, making sure they were aware of the hell she would unleash on them if they tried to bench her this time.

Keras's black eyebrows drew down. "The first sign of trouble, and you are off the field."

"I can live with that." She swept her fall of black hair over her shoulder and then held her hand out to Marek. "Shall we go?"

"Wait." Ares looked at Esher as Cal went to the porch, grabbed everyone's shoes and tossed them at them. Ares shoved his feet into his boots. "Summon a Messenger and send it to Father. Tell him to dispatch a legion to Nemesis's domain and secure her. Just in case our hunch is right. We know she can't come here with the gates closed to traffic, so she has to be somewhere in the Underworld. I'd rather she didn't get the chance to run."

The moment Esher nodded, Ares and Keras disappeared. Valen followed them.

Marek took hold of her arm as she finished zipping up her calf-height leather boots and stepped with her, darkness embracing them for a heartbeat before it parted to reveal a shady corner of Central Park.

The humans jogging along the pathway that cut through the enormous park in the heart of New York gave her and the gods at her back strange looks as they stepped out of the trees.

She scowled at them all.

She hadn't been up to any funny business in the bushes with four men if that was what they were thinking.

A few of the female joggers slowed, and one almost tripped over her feet as Keras stepped into the fading light, lifting a hand above his green eyes to shield them as he assessed the position of the sun.

Ares shook his head.

Valen sighed. "I can practically see their panties melting away as they run past him."

Cass looked at Keras. He was beautiful, but only on the surface. Beneath that perfect exterior beat a black, dead heart that was twisted with a need for pain.

He would probably destroy any woman he came in contact with, sucking the light right out of them.

"The light is fading fast. We have perhaps an hour at most before the daemons can walk in it." Keras turned his back on the women, apparently not noticing, or uncaring of, the way they gawped at him.

She supposed he had probably had females fawning over him his entire life, first in the Underworld and now in the mortal one.

"We could wait until it gets dark," Valen put in as he raked his fingers through the longer lengths of his violet hair, pushing it back from his face. "The enemy is bound to want to hit the gate and bring Daimon with them."

He drew a few glances from the women too, ones that rapidly turned to fear as they noticed the scar tissue that ran from the left side of his jaw down his neck. He glared at them, golden eyes dangerously bright.

"Might I remind you that enemy can also draw the power to do just that from his blood?" Cass snapped, fear getting the better of her again.

"She's right." Ares folded his arms, his biceps flexing beneath his tight black T-shirt as fire blazed in his dark eyes. "We're not waiting, leaving Daimon at their mercy."

"If the enemy even has him. Might be a wild goose chase." Valen hiked his shoulders, lifting the hem of his own black T-shirt to flash a toned strip of stomach.

Cass shut them out as they argued about what to do, pressed the fingers of her right hand to her chest and focused as she breathed. Each slow inhale and steady exhale cleared her mind, allowing her magic to come to the fore. It ran in her blood, a comforting presence, power at her fingertips.

The power to save the man she loved.

She focused on that, on him, letting the magic rise inside her and latch onto that desire. It grew stronger, a heady sensation that had her swaying as it began to twine down her legs, twisting around them beneath her skin.

The moment it connected with the grass beneath her boots, she tensed.

Pain bloomed in her heart and she gasped.

"Something is wrong." She flicked her eyes open and looked at Ares, Keras and then Marek and Valen, that bad feeling growing inside her as her magic began to seep outwards, fingers of it stretching in all directions. "I can feel it. I need to find Daimon now."

Keras nodded. "It's best we don't wait for the enemy to approach the gate. If we can get our hands on Daimon, we might be able to avoid the gate coming under fire."

He looked at her.

"Can you sense him?"

She blinked and nodded. "I think so. I'll try a spell."

Cass pieced together the incantation, knitting several different locator spells together in an attempt to make the strongest one she could manage. All the while, the connection between her and nature grew, and the fear she felt grew stronger with it. She could sense the four gods around her so clearly, and sense that Daimon was in deep trouble. She wasn't sure how. She had never experienced anything like this.

Was it because they were born of Persephone's blood and therefore linked to nature? Their powers were all elemental after all. It had to be the reason she could sense a disturbance where Daimon was concerned, felt as if something was terribly wrong. The whole balance of nature felt off in this area and somehow she knew it was because something had happened to him.

"You think the enemy is going to try to use Daimon's blood to open the gate?" Valen muttered.

"Most likely," Keras answered.

"What happens if they want his blood for more than just opening the gate? What if they intend to use him as a sacrifice?" Marek's voice speared her mind, fracturing her focus and scattering the pieces of the spell.

Her gaze snapped to Keras.

His green eyes slid to her and then back to his brothers. "That would be bad. If they kill him, I doubt we would be able to seal the gate. There is a chance it would remain open... and the two worlds—"

"This isn't helping," Cass barked and glared at them all. "Just shut up and let me work."

Her hands trembled and she shook them, trying to stop them. They continued to quiver as nerves rose inside her, fear at the helm, shaking her to her soul. Daimon had to be all right. He just had to be.

She couldn't lose him.

She closed her eyes and built the incantation again, forming the tracking spell as silence fell around her and she banished her fears once more. Fear would only slow her down and Daimon needed her.

As the spell completed, she was instantly connected to everything around her, aware of the world in a way she had never felt before. Every living thing was outlined in the darkness of her mind, a strange echo of each natural object and person built by traces of light. Trees were glittering green silhouettes. Water rippled blue. Rocks shone grey. Humans moving past her were flickering pink outlines.

The four gods watching her shimmered with different colours. Red. Brown. Purple. Black.

Cass pressed her hand to her heart and sought white.

Her eyes scanned the darkness, seeking that absence of colour.

Seeking ice.

She walked forwards with her eyes closed, the spell revealing everything to her in flickers and bolts of light.

"We following her?" Valen's voice warbled in her ears, a distant watery sound.

Cass sensed the power of the four gods buffeting her as they tracked her, keeping a few steps behind her. Their impatience washed over her, mingling with her own to keep her moving forwards.

Seeking the white.

The sensation that something was wrong grew stronger, beating within her, and then weaker again. She backtracked, almost bumping into Ares. His heat washed over her as she moved around him, studying the feeling. It grew stronger again.

Cass tracked it through glittering green fields and around shimmering blue water.

When she neared the other side of the park, she slowed her steps, her eyes lifting to scan the sky beyond the ancient trees.

"He somewhere up there?" Ares's deep voice echoed in her ears.

She nodded. Whispered, "Somewhere."

But all she could see were humans, floating in the air. No shape of buildings.

She moved beyond the park.

Someone grabbed her arm and pulled her back as a car horn blasted.

"You crazy?" Valen barked at her.

Cass opened her eyes and they widened as she saw the steady stream of vehicles darting across the route ahead of her.

"They don't show up," she bit out defensively. "I can see natural things. Nothing more."

Valen dragged her to the nearest crossing. "Now I know that, I'll keep a better bloody eye on you. Daimon would kill us if anything happened to you."

"He's probably going to kill us for letting her come with us anyway," Ares muttered.

She frowned at him. "No one *let* me come."

He just shrugged at that.

She crossed the road and shirked free of Valen's grip, and closed her eyes again. The spell burst back to life, outlining everything for her. She focused on Daimon again, following that feeling in her heart down a side street.

She lifted her head and scanned the buildings around her.

Desperately hoping to see white.

But all she saw was pink humans.

"This place looks familiar," Keras muttered.

"Whole damned world looks familiar these days," Valen grumbled back at him. "Been here way too long."

She frowned and stopped, backtracked a few steps and looked up at the building to her right.

"That's strange." She canted her head at the shimmering forms.

"What's strange?" Keras asked.

"Nothing. Just... those people have two colours." She pointed at them where they hovered high in the air, the only two people in the building.

"Two colours." Ares's gruff voice and the heat of him close to her had her looking at him. "Fucking tell me they're not green and blue."

A shiver chased down her spine and arms.

She nodded.

Ares growled, flashing short fangs, his eyes rapidly darkening. "Bastards."

She wasn't following. She looked at the others.

Shock danced in Valen's golden eyes. "You can't be serious."

Marek and Keras didn't look at all happy.

When she looked back at Ares for an explanation, he bit out, "Messengers."

"Maybe Dad found Daimon before us and sent them to save him?" Valen didn't sound like he believed that.

"Fucking traitors," Ares barked and turned fiery eyes on her. "Is Daimon there?"

Cass shook her head. "I only saw…"

Cold washed through her.

She closed her eyes and looked through the spell again.

Looked more closely this time.

Her heart hitched.

Blood turned to sludge in her veins.

There just beyond the two shimmering blue-green forms was the faintest hint of white, a towering rectangular block of it.

Ice.

"No."

She flicked her eyes open and summoned the spell.

Transported herself before the brothers could stop her.

CHAPTER 34

Rage poured through Cass as she landed in a musty empty loft apartment, fed by despair as her gaze landed on the block of pale blue ice before her.

Daimon knelt in the middle of it, his arms bound behind his back.

"What the—"

The male didn't get a chance to finish that question.

Cass turned on him and screamed as her entire body tensed up, magic sweeping through her in a black blaze. She splayed her fingers into talons and launched them forwards, kept on screaming out her fury as twin twisting orbs of darkness shot from her palms.

Struck the two males.

Crimson rained down on her as they exploded, drenching the peeling white walls of the cavernous room with blood.

Cass kept on screaming, couldn't stop herself as pain burned a path through her, felt as if it was destroying all of her. She leaned forwards, tears streaming down her face, agony ripping her to pieces inside as she broke down. The floor bucked beneath her, the entire building trembling.

"Holy hell," Valen muttered, sounding out of breath. "So much for questioning them."

"Ah, shit." Ares's grave voice pulled a hard sob from her as she stumbled to the block of ice and sank to her knees before Daimon.

Everyone fell silent.

Ares crouched beside her, but she couldn't bring herself to look at him. He growled as he scrubbed at something on the floor and she looked down at it.

At the circle drawn on the wooden boards.

Pain and sorrow twisted inside her as she pieced together what had happened. The enemy had trapped Daimon here. Unable to attack them because of the ward, he had turned his power on himself.

He had sacrificed himself to save the gates, to protect his world and this one.

She cursed him for that.

Pressed her hands to the slick ice and stared at him.

Her beautiful god.

She closed her eyes.

Tensed.

Her breath rushed from her.

She lunged for Ares's hands, muttering a protection spell at the same time. He tried to break free as she grabbed him but she refused to let go, fielding a black look from him.

"She gone crazy?" Valen frowned at her as he leaned towards Marek.

"Maybe," she muttered and brought Ares's hands to the ice, desperate to know that she wasn't imagining things. "Melt it."

Magic never lied though.

She closed her eyes.

Saw the faint, pulsing white outline of Daimon in the centre of the ice.

Each pulse of light was paler than the last, and the time between them was growing.

"Hurry." She shoved Ares's hands harder against the ice.

"Back off then." Ares jerked free of her grip and glared at her. "I'm not doing this with you in the firing line."

She shuffled away from him and everyone else backed off.

Ares closed his eyes and blew out his breath, his dark eyebrows drawing down as he moved his hands over the ice. Heat shimmered over them, starting to rise off his shoulders too as he worked to melt the ice.

"You're doing good," she said, hoping to encourage him, partly because she wanted him to keep going and partly because she didn't want him to burn the building down.

She had never seen him try to control his fire before, hadn't realised how difficult it was for him.

Sweat dotted his brow, fizzled and turned to steam, and his face set in hard lines, concentration etched on it. His shoulders tensed, arms shaking.

She looked at Daimon, more aware than ever of the similarities between him and Ares. Her heart went out to both of them, always having to hold back their powers and fight to keep them in check so they didn't hurt the ones they loved.

She was going to do something about that once this was all over.

If Daimon came back to her, she would move heaven and earth to find a spell that would allow him to have physical contact with his brothers again.

She would do the same for Ares as a thank you for helping her save the man she loved.

The ice creaked and then cracked, great fault lines spreading across it as it gave under the heat of Ares's power. Water pooled around them, slipping between the cracks between the floorboards, dripping into the empty building below them.

The faint pulses of light grew stronger as the ice melted away from Daimon. She swore she wasn't imagining it.

Cass jerked right, towards Ares, as a huge chunk of ice crashed down and tumbled across the floor. More followed it and Marek pulled her backwards as one came right at her. She gasped and looked at Ares, relief washing over her as none of them struck him. They melted as soon as they neared him, falling as water that hissed as it touched his skin.

The moment the ice was gone from Daimon's upper half, she pulled free of Marek's grip and rushed to him. She pressed her fingers to his throat, shivering as the cold numbed them, desperately seeking a sign of life.

She whipped her head around when she found it.

"It's weak," she said, voice wobbling as emotions collided inside her, fear fighting the hope that had dared to rise.

Marek and Valen grabbed Daimon and hauled him from the ice, laying him out on the floorboards. They shook their hands, flexing their reddened fingers. It seemed even when he was close to death, Daimon's power still affected his body.

Ares moved to him and held his hands palm down above his brother, ghosting them over him as Cass joined him. She kept her fingers to Daimon's throat, studying his pulse.

It was too faint for her liking. Slowing again.

He was going to die.

She shoved that thought out of her mind, banishing it as determination flooded her, had her running through every spell she knew.

She had studied the basics of necromancy and she was talented at healing. If she combined the two, would it be enough to pull a living person back from the brink of death?

She looked down at Daimon, heart breaking and tears filling her eyes.

It was worth a shot.

"Hey!" Valen barked as she held her hand out and one of the knives he wore strapped to his ribs shot into her palm.

His golden eyes widened and he lunged for her as she brought it down towards Daimon's throat.

Keras grabbed her before he could, hauling her away from their brother, and she loosed a frustrated grunt when she tried to break free of his grip and couldn't.

"I can save him." She thought she could anyway. "Let me go."

Keras didn't look convinced.

"Let her try." Ares sagged beside her, shaking his head, his dark eyes bleak. "I've done all I can."

Keras kept hold of her, and just as she was about to lash out at him with the knife, he released her.

She twisted back towards Daimon and carefully nicked his bare shoulder, just enough to draw a few drops of blood. She cut the tips of her index and middle finger and pressed them to the blood on Daimon's shoulder. Her eyes slipped shut as she focused on the powerful connection that formed between them.

Cass started with the healing spell first, weaving the strongest one she could manage, and began threading it with incantations she had read in an ancient tome, one that had felt closest to the truth about necromancy to her.

With the tracking spell still active, she could see Daimon as he lay before her, could see Keras as he came to kneel on the other side of him and pressed his fingers to Daimon's throat.

"Is it working?" Ares said.

Keras nodded. "His pulse is getting stronger."

Cass was careful to keep the focus of the spell heavily on the healing side, holding back the darker magic that rose within her, flooding her with cold.

"We need to be ready to move him the moment he's strong enough." Keras's tone had her focus slipping and the hairs on the back of her neck rising. "This was all too easy."

He was right about that.

"Maybe they figured he was dead and useless to them?" Valen sounded hopeful.

"Maybe it's a trap?" Marek offered as a counterpoint.

She was inclined to go with Marek's theory.

Focusing harder, she funnelled the healing spell into Daimon, thawing the ice in his veins with it as the darker magic pooled around his heart and his brain.

"Think he might come back wrong?" Valen whispered.

"Not helping," Ares muttered before she could say it.

"Just asking is all. I want him back as much as everyone else, but what if he comes back with a craving for brains?"

Cass frowned but didn't take her focus away from slowly healing Daimon's vital organs as she bit out, "He wasn't dead."

But he had been close.

His lungs had taken a beating, were slow to respond as she poured the healing spell into them. The darker magic crawled down from his heart, spreading over his lungs, and she did her best to guide it, but it didn't feel entirely under her control. It was like it had a mind of its own. She could direct the healing spell, but the one intended to revive the dead was doing its own thing.

Cass focused on building a tether between her and the spell.

Something it didn't like.

She was beginning to understand why the great covens of the world had banned necromancy.

The spell strained against her, attempting to pull away from her. Not good. She narrowed all her focus down to it, releasing her control over the healing spell, and commanded it to return to her. When it didn't, she worked backwards over the incantation she had used to form it, pulling it apart piece by piece.

Something it *really* didn't like.

Daimon jacked up off the floor and roared.

"Brains?" Valen murmured, a worried note in his voice.

Cass shoved her hands against Daimon's chest to hold him down and pumped another spell into him, one she hoped would contain his ice for at least a few minutes because she couldn't do this alone. "I'm starting to see why witches avoid necromancy. A little help?"

Marek and Valen moved to pin Daimon down for her.

His eyes shot open, irises pure white ringed with glowing blue.

Cass grabbed the sides of his head and leaned over him, stared into those eyes and commanded the spell to release him.

When it didn't, she pressed her mouth to his and breathed in, felt it as the treacherous spell that had been seeping into his lungs was drawn towards her.

She broke away from his mouth and exhaled before covering it again and drawing another breath, stealing the air from his lungs.

She tasted blood.

And then ashes.

She kept sucking in air as she pulled her head back.

"What the—" Valen barked, disgust lacing his voice.

Cass snapped Daimon's mouth closed the moment the twisting black and violet cloud passed his lips and Keras pinched Daimon's nose as the spell lunged for it.

She closed her hands around the spell and gritted her teeth as it fought her, as she muttered a reversal spell intended to erase it.

"Cass?"

The sound of her name had never been so sweet.

She looked down into Daimon's ice-blue eyes, tears filling hers as he stared at her.

"What are you doing here?" Daimon croaked.

Valen began quietly singing 'love is in the air', earning himself a cuff around the back of his head from Marek.

"Saving your sorry ass," Ares offered. "I leave you alone for five minutes and you're off doing heroic shit."

Daimon's eyes edged towards his brothers and he pushed out a single word as a shudder wracked him. "Nemesis."

"We figured as much," Ares said.

Cass wrestled with the unruly spell, closing her fingers tightly around it and trying to contain it as it attempted to leak out of even the smallest crack.

Daimon looked back at her, his weary blue eyes lowering to her hands. "What's…"

"Oh, just a little necromancy." She tried to keep her voice light as she fought it. "It's not happy to leave you."

His eyes widened slightly. "That was *in* me?"

"I refer you back to the part where you were almost dead." She grunted as she hit the spell with another reversal incantation and relaxed a little as this one was effective, had the ball of dark magic losing enough strength that she could contain it.

It grew docile in her hands and she was quick to finish unpicking the spell she had used to create it.

Daimon tried to push up onto his elbows. Keras helped him, gripping his shoulders and easing him into a sitting position, and then quickly releasing him.

"Don't rush it," Cass warned, deeply aware that the healing spell was still at work inside him. "You, ah, this isn't the only spell that I used, but it is the only one that I removed."

Daimon pressed a hand to his stomach and paled. "I thought I felt weird."

"That's probably the brush with death you had," Ares growled. "Last time I'm letting you out of my sight."

"You should rest." Cass vanquished the spell and sagged as she let her hands fall to her lap. She needed a nice rest too.

Daimon nodded and looked around the apartment, and then at her. "Did you deal with the Erinyes?"

"The Erinyes?" Keras said.

"They were here." Daimon frowned at all the blood. "You didn't kill them?"

"Little miss witch here popped two Messengers like they were zits, but no one else was in the building." Valen flipped one of his knives in his hand, his eyes on Daimon the entire time.

That bad feeling Cass had been having since Keras had announced reaching Daimon had been too easy returned full force.

"We should go." She placed her hand on Daimon's arm and looked at Keras.

"But you are exactly where we want you to be."

The female voice rolled across the room.

"And it appears you do have exactly what we need."

A second female voice echoed around her.

Cold shot down Cass's spine.

Marek had been right. It was a trap.

Daimon grabbed Cass, hauling her to him as he growled and bared emerging fangs, his eyes glittering like ice.

Around them, violet-black smoke billowed and twisted, spreading to form five portals that flickered with green and purple lightning.

The two Erinyes stepped from the shadows, melting out of them.

The bitches had been hiding in this room all along, waiting for the right moment to strike.

Waiting for her to reveal she could use necromancy and for Daimon to be free of his ice and revived, his blood ready for them to use against the gate.

Keras seized hold of Ares as the male collared Valen and Valen grabbed Marek.

The moment everyone was in contact, darkness devoured them.

Cass grunted when she was dumped unceremoniously on the damp grass of Central Park and Daimon landed on her, his back slamming into her legs. She rolled as Keras dropped out of the air too, narrowly avoiding being crushed by him. He crashed into the grass, breathing hard, sweat dotting his brow.

Ares bit out a curse and rushed to check on him. "Teleporting so many was dangerous. I had Valen and Marek."

Keras shook violently as he pushed onto his knees, his breath sawing from between his lips. His right hand had burns on it and his left was marred with black bruises, his fingers reddened by cold, telling her that the spell she had used on Daimon had faded but had done its job while it had lasted. That gave her something to go on, built hope that she could do something to help Ares and Daimon with their powers.

Cass touched Keras's arm and funnelled a healing spell into him as she looked up at Ares. "We need to move."

"Can't." That single word leaving Daimon's lips had everyone looking at him and cold stealing through her.

Dread pooled inside her. "What do you mean, can't?"

Remorse shone in his eyes as he glanced at her. "They've been in contact with me. They can open the gate. I can't let them near it."

"You're in no fit state to fight!" she barked and froze, her anger rushing from her as her eyes darted around the dimly lit field.

Portals opened in all directions, daemons spilling from them.

Ares turned his back to her, facing a group of twenty daemons as they charged towards them. Valen moved to stand on the other side of her, his fingers flexing around his blade as lightning arced along the metal.

Keras lumbered onto his feet, shaking his head.

"I'm getting you out of here. Your brothers can handle this." Cass formed the incantation in her mind, heart racing as she hurried to complete it before Daimon could do something reckless like launching into the fray as a fight erupted around them.

"Get her out of here." Daimon pulled her hand from his arm, and she had never heard him so afraid or so desperate.

"You need me here," she snapped and tried to seize him again, determined to stay with him if he wasn't going to let her take him away from the fight.

Before she could grab him, someone grabbed her.

Darkness whirled around her.

Fury poured through her.

No damned way she was being benched.

She hit Marek with the first spell that rose to her fingertips, one that blasted him away from her, and screamed as she fell into the abyss.

Hit something very solid.

Cass wheezed, struggling to get air into her lungs as her entire body ached, and pushed onto her hands and knees.

Was she back in Tokyo?

Or Central Park?

She stood on wobbly legs.

Her blood chilled as she took in her surroundings.

Black lands stretched in all directions, rising into sharp mountains ahead of her.

Beyond an enormous obsidian Greek temple.

Cass swallowed hard.

The Underworld.

She froze as metal clanked and air shifted around her, and edged her hands up in front of her. The four males clad in black armour only jerked the pointed tips of their onyx spears closer to her head.

This wasn't good.

She re-evaluated that thought as a crushing wave of dark power pressed down on her, driving her to her knees on the basalt.

Cass fought the power, resisted it enough to lift her head, and wished she hadn't as her stomach dropped.

Before her towered a man with malice in his crimson eyes, a god whose crown rose in jagged onyx spikes from his black hair. The warm light of his realm reflected off the black metal plates of his armour as he shifted slightly, a breeze catching the heavy blood-red cloak fixed to his shoulders.

He lowered the bident he gripped and pointed it at her chest and then lifted it, so the cold metal kissed her skin and she had to tip her head back to avoid being cut.

Cass stared up at him, her breath lodged in her throat as his scarlet eyes burned with rage.

Hades pressed forwards, his voice a black snarl.

"A life for a life."

CHAPTER 35

Daimon's entire body ached, felt as if a gatekeeper had pummelled him, given him a five minute breather, and then gone in for another round. Memories flickered across his mind as he fought a group of daemons, four adult males who were attempting to breach the barrier he and his brothers formed between the portals and the gate. He remembered the cold. The fear.

The painful thought that he would never see Cass again.

The last thing he could remember was thinking of her, and she had been the first thing he had seen upon being revived.

Gods, he had never beheld a sweeter sight than her sitting beside him.

Fighting to bring him back to her.

He owed her a thousand apologies when they were back together.

And they would be back together.

Lightning crashed down just off to this left, spraying black blood and pieces of daemon across the slick grass. To his right, flames blazed a path through another group of males, filling the air with the stench of burning flesh.

Shadows rushed across the ground, blending with the night before they shot upwards to impale a male and dragged him down as he screamed and writhed, fighting their hold.

Beyond the first wave of daemons, a second wave spilled out of the portals. He cursed.

Marek appeared beside him.

A wall of baked earth rose up, encircling the field, cutting off the daemons he and his brothers were fighting from the next wave. Those daemons growled and snarled on the other side of the ten-foot-high wall. It wouldn't hold them for long, but hopefully it would slow them down enough that Daimon and his brothers could deal with making sure the gate was safe.

He turned towards Marek to thank him.

One glance was all it took to see that something had gone wrong.

"I lost Cassandra," Marek said, guilt and pain shining in his dark eyes. "She broke free of me during the teleport."

Daimon's heart lurched and icy talons formed over his fingers. "What do you mean, she broke free of you?"

"She hit me with a spell that sent me flying. There was nothing I could do."

Daimon couldn't breathe.

He bent forwards, clutching his knees as his mind whirled, thoughts spinning so quickly that he felt sick.

He didn't know what might have happened to her, where she might be.

Gods, he didn't need this.

He was tired, in constant pain as his body tried to complete the healing that Cass's spell had set in motion. Remaining focused on keeping the daemons from the gate had been taxing enough, now that fragile focus was split between the battle and fear for Cass.

What if she had landed somewhere in the Underworld?

If she had, she could take care of herself. She was strong, a powerful warrior, one who had proven she could handle anything life threw at her. He had to trust that she would make it through or at the very least survive long enough for him to finish with these daemons and go after her.

A portal formed on the inside of the wall.

The Erinyes stepped out of it.

Their violet eyes fixed beyond him.

On the point where the gate was hidden.

Could this night get any shittier?

It felt as if the Moirai had answered that question with a mocking laugh as he felt the gate opening behind him.

Impossible.

He twisted to face that direction as Marek joined the fray, teaming up with Ares and Valen.

He glanced at Keras where he fought a few feet away, taking on six daemons by himself.

None of his brothers were close enough to the gate to trigger it.

It shouldn't be opening.

He looked back at the Erinyes. The two blondes stood in front of the portal, an entire legion of daemons forming behind them, at least three dozen strong.

Was it their doing?

He looked his bare chest over, focused on his body, sure that they hadn't managed to cut him and take his blood. Had Nemesis given some to them? Had they taken it before he had tried to kill himself?

Even if they had, he wasn't sure it would be enough for them to trigger the gate from such a vast distance.

It wasn't responding to him and he was standing closer to it.

He backed off, leaving his brothers to deal with the daemons as he turned all his focus on the gate.

A blinding pinprick of violet light burst into existence in the middle of the field before him, spreading rapidly to form the central disc of the gate. It hovered flat above the grass, at least five feet wide, and pulsed brightly, birthing the first colourful ring.

"What the hell?" Ares snarled from behind him. "You doing that?"

"No," Daimon snapped. "It's not me opening it."

But he would be the one to close it.

He focused on the gate, narrowing the world down to it, trusting his brothers could deal with the daemons without him. The gate flashed again and another ring formed, growing outwards. Glyphs shimmered to life around the ring, swirling with colour.

Daimon commanded that ring to shrink.

It grew larger.

Fear threatened to seize him, but he pushed back against it and focused harder, demanding that the gate close itself. His head turned and he pressed a hand to it, squeezed his eyes shut as his vision blurred. He could do this.

He sent another command to the gate.

A third ring formed, rotating slowly counter-clockwise.

Fuck.

"Ares," Daimon hollered. "Can you close it?"

Ares appeared beside him, his face etched in lines of concentration as he stared at the gate. Tense seconds trickled past, filled with the crack of lightning and the sound of grunts and screams as the battle raged behind them.

Ares looked at him out of the corner of his eye, defeat shining in his gaze. "I can't. It's not responding to me. It's like someone is overriding me."

Daimon stared at the gate, that feeling echoing inside him too as he watched another ring form, helpless to stop it. He tried anyway, gritting his teeth and grunting as he exerted all of his will on the gate.

"Go… go!" Meadow yelled, and Daimon sensed the wave of daemons rushing forwards, heard the thunder of their footsteps as they charged across the grass at his brothers.

Daimon fought harder, struggling to focus on the gate and his power over it as his head grew foggy, his body sluggish and slow to respond as he tried to lift his hands.

Ares growled and heat licked at Daimon's back, a wall of fire that wouldn't keep the daemons at bay for long. His brother would need to keep fuelling that wall of fire, draining himself.

Daimon had to get the gate to respond to him.

He raked one of his icy talons over his arm, drawing blood.

"Are you crazy?" Ares lunged for him and Daimon leaped away, placing some distance between them.

"I need more control over it." Daimon dragged another claw over his arm and corrected himself. "I need *some* control. It will respond to my blood."

He wasn't sure that it would.

He had never seen a gate act like this. He had never felt as if it was ignoring him. Sometimes they resisted, but it was as if he wasn't even here.

"Just keep the Erinyes away from it." Daimon glanced at Ares, and the grim look in his brother's eyes said that he was well aware of what might happen if the two furies managed to get closer to the gate.

They were already making it hard enough on him, their control over it something that felt impossible given the distance between them and it.

But it had to be them opening it.

Daimon strode towards the gate, intent on closing it and stopping them.

His vision tunnelled again and he shook his head, waited a moment for it to clear before he continued. Blood tracked down his arm and he grimaced as he raked a third line in his flesh, adding more, aware that he was going to need it.

Lightning rocked the ground and he wobbled, his left knee buckling. He staggered in that direction and managed to remain upright.

Daimon grunted as something smashed into him, knocking him onto his side.

His head whipped towards it.

A growl tore from his lips as the winged scaly daemon lunged for him again, sharp black talons slashing towards him. He rolled across the dewy grass, the scent of his blood growing thicker in the air as he evaded the daemon's blow. Daimon raised his right arm and ice shot up from the earth, tinged red with his own blood.

Huge leathery wings beat the air towards him as the male lifted off, elevating himself away from the reach of Daimon's ice, fading into the night.

Daimon scoured the darkness, remaining still on the grass, anticipating another attack.

When it didn't come, he rolled onto his knees and pushed off, rushing towards the gate.

Air whooshed.

Daimon ducked, sweeping his upper body to his right as the daemon cut across him. Fire streaked across his back and he cried out, the fog in this head growing thicker as blood leaked down his side. He stumbled onwards, eyes locked on the gate as another ring formed.

The daemon swooped again.

A bright explosion of light struck the male and he flew through the air, fire licking over his wings as he tumbled and twisted.

Ares growled and launched another fireball at the daemon. "You all right?"

Daimon managed to nod.

Another two winged daemons plunged from the darkness, both of them aiming for Ares. His brother launched another two orbs of fire, hitting one but missing the other.

Daimon stretched his arm out to the gate as the daemon barrelled into Ares, lifting him off the ground and into the night.

Damn it.

He peered into the darkness, scouring it for his brother, his heart shooting into his throat.

A huge burst of flame flashed about eighty feet above him and then it was gone.

He pivoted on his heel as he heard Ares grunt somewhere behind him, spotted him close to Marek as he tackled three daemons, battling them with spears of solid earth.

Shadows sliced through the daemons, severing limbs, and swirled around Ares, forming a protective wall as he struggled onto his feet.

Lightning blinded Daimon as it forked from the sky, splitting into a dozen jagged white-purple points. Daemons shrieked as the bolts connected, the sound carrying in the still night air.

Mortal authorities would be coming. By now, someone would have reported the sounds of the fight coming from the park.

He had to move quickly.

Keras could freeze time for any human in the vicinity, but he couldn't do it when he was fighting too. His oldest brother would have to focus, and that wasn't going to happen when dozens of daemons were coming at them in waves, forcing him to use his shadows to protect himself, the gate and his brothers.

Daimon wasn't sure Keras could freeze time even if he could concentrate.

Valen had told him about what had happened in the villa outside of Rome, how Keras hadn't been able to completely stop time for the daemons there. Apparently, even Keras had his limits.

Daimon glanced at the daemons surrounding them, doubting his brother would be able to stop them.

Shadows ripped through the ones nearest Keras.

His brother might not be able to stop them in their tracks, but he could stop them in another way.

Agonised bellows filled the night as Keras went to town on the daemons.

Satisfied that the enemy were occupied and he had time, Daimon turned back towards the gate.

Grunted as pain spread across his stomach.

He looked down at the delicate feminine hand close to his hip.

Gripping a blade that sank deeper into his flesh as she pushed forwards.

Daimon swayed towards her, blinking to clear his vision as he struggled to lift his eyes to the woman before him.

"She said not to kill you," Melody hissed as she leaned closer, bringing her mouth to his ear. "She didn't say anything about not maiming you a little."

She yanked the violet blade free of his flesh, jerking him forwards with it, and he staggered and fell into her, was quick to grab her. She screeched as his ice swept over her bare shoulders, shoved him in the chest and broke contact with him. Her purple eyes brightened dangerously as she inspected her reddened shoulders and narrowed as black bruises formed beneath the ice that melted on her skin.

"Bastard." She backhanded him.

Everything went dark for a second and then the world was sideways.

It took him a moment to realise he was on the ground.

Melody grabbed him by his ankle and dragged him.

Towards the gate.

He tried to teleport, but nothing happened. Tried to summon his ice, but his head turned and he almost blacked out. Heat spread through him, a strange sensation that stemmed from the wound on his stomach. He blinked to clear his wobbly vision and looked at the blade she clutched.

The wraith's blade.

Toxin.

She had hit him with the poison that coated it.

If he wasn't healed soon, he would die from it.

He angled his head to his right and stared at the gate as they approached it.

Although he had a sinking feeling that death would come for him before the toxin could kill him.

The furie lifted her arm and he flew over her head, slammed into the earth in front of her and grunted as blood burst from his lips, his vision dimming again before it came back.

"Daimon!" Valen's frantic bellow echoed in his ears and he sought his brother.

His eyebrows furrowed as he spotted him, Marek, Ares and Keras fighting Meadow and the horde of daemons spilling from the portal that had opened between him and them.

Daimon weakly kicked at Melody, trying to break free of her.

She clucked her tongue and leaned over him, backhanded him so hard he blacked out again. He was vaguely aware of the battle that blazed only fifty feet from him, of his brothers as they fought to reach him and called out his name, and of Melody as she gripped his hair and hauled him onto his knees before the gate.

The colourful light of it shimmered across his eyes as they struggled to focus.

Fear and hopelessness washed through him, a cruel combination that left him cold as he stared at the blurry gate.

Were the furies opening it for Nemesis so she could pass into this world and destroy it and his own one?

Melody yanked his head back and poised the blade at his throat.

Ready to cut him the second the gate had fully formed and spill enough blood that it would remain open, causing catastrophic damage to both realms.

Bringing about the calamity the Moirai had foreseen.

He couldn't let that happen.

He couldn't fail.

He summoned the last of his strength, focusing on his power as the final ring of the gate expanded, desperately clawing it together for one more attempt to break free of Melody's hold.

Daimon tried to lift his hand to grab Melody's, intending to freeze her and force her to release him.

His hand refused to move.

He edged his eyes downwards, stared at his hands where they rested on his lap, drenched in his own blood as it pumped from the wound in his side.

The central purple disc of the gate flashed.

Melody pressed the blade into his throat.

It was over.

CHAPTER 36

Cassandra's first instinct was to use her magic to blast Hades and his guards away from her. Probably not a great idea. Her second instinct was to use that same magic to cast a spell that would transport her to Tokyo.

Only when she tried it, nothing happened.

She stared wide-eyed up at the dark god towering over her, despair swift to flood her as she realised there was no escaping him.

It was right there in his cold smile.

In those murderous red eyes.

The bastard knew her magic was useless, which meant he had done something to disable it, or there was something about his realm that stopped it from working.

Hades pressed his bident closer to her throat. She leaned back, tilting her head up further as she swallowed hard, and stared into his eyes as she cast a few prayers to various gods out into the ether just in case one of them was listening.

His lips compressed and twisted into a vicious sneer, his black eyebrows knitting hard above eyes that glowed the colour of blood.

She had thought Keras dark.

Keras looked like a puppy compared to this man.

"A life for a life," he growled again.

Her life, but for whose?

"You... murdered... my... son," he gritted, snarling each word, every pause a punctuation that drove them home.

Made her realise whose life he was talking about.

Daimon's.

"He's alive." She went to jerk forwards as those desperate words burst from her lips and froze in time to stop herself from slitting her own throat on the sharp tips of his weapon.

"He died." Hades pressed forwards and so did his guards.

More than one of their spears nicked her, but she refused to flinch as she faced Hades, refused to show any weakness he could use against her.

"He's alive," she bit out, her eyebrows furrowing as she looked up at him. "I swear it."

"You speak lies, witch." He loomed over her, the very air around him seeming to darken as his eyes brightened further, blazing with the fires of the Underworld.

With pain.

He truly thought his son was dead.

She wanted to shake her head but couldn't without cutting herself. "He's not dead. I brought him back."

"You killed him." He lowered the bident and she glanced down, her eyes widening again as she mentally cursed.

Daimon's blood was on her hands.

"No." She shook her head now that his weapon was away from her throat, leaned forwards and clasped her hands in front of her, opened them again and held them out to him. "I was bringing him back. Blood magic. I would never hurt Daimon. It killed me when I thought I had lost him."

His jaw flexed.

He didn't look as if he believed her.

A delicate pale hand slid over his left shoulder and he stiffened, his scarlet gaze edging towards it. Fingers brushed over the ornate clasps that fixed his red cloak to his shoulders and then drifted lower, skating down his arm.

"The witch speaks true, my love." The softest female voice Cass had ever heard danced in the air, full of light and warmth, and seriously out of place in the dark realm.

A slender female clad in layers of black that formed a flowing dress over her curves stepped around the god, the smile that curled her lips far from fitting given the dire situation. Her green eyes softened as she lifted her right hand and cupped Hades's cheek. Around her bare feet, poppies bloomed, the same colour as her scarlet hair.

Hades began to lean into her touch and then pulled away, drawing a frown from the goddess.

"No," he boomed. "She murdered our son."

"I didn't," Cass snapped and lunged forwards, desperate for him to believe her.

"She did not," Persephone said and touched his cheek again, her caress like black magic, more powerful than anything Cass had at her disposal.

The god softened again, looked unsure for the first time but it was there and gone in the blink of an eye.

"I felt him die," Hades growled and lifted the bident to Cass's throat again, forcing her to lean back.

"He's alive. He's fighting right now to protect the gate. If you'd just listen for five seconds and let me explain." She held her hands up when his eyes darkened, his handsome face twisting in a thunderous look.

Perhaps demanding a god-king listen to her and ordering him around had been a bad idea.

"Let the witch speak, my love." Persephone worked her magic again, stroking his cheek, softening the hard edges of his expression.

When Hades didn't try to kill Cass and didn't speak, she took it as a chance to tell her side of the story.

"Esher was called for penitence and Daimon went. He didn't come back though. I was worried about him." She rushed each word out, unsure how long she was going to be given before Hades decided to go ahead and kill her. Now was not the time for lengthy and detailed explanations. Now was the time for speed. "The brothers… your sons… we feared the enemy had him. The Erinyes know which gate is bound to who so we went to New York, and I used a spell to track Daimon. When I found him, he had encased himself in ice. He was almost dead when Ares got him free, and I used…"

She hesitated. Was it wise to tell a god-king that you used necromancy to save his dying son?

Hades gave her a look that demanded she continue, his bident backing him up as he pressed it forwards, prodding her throat with the sharp tips.

"I used a healing spell and the basic theory of necromancy to—"

"Necromancy?" he barked and she leaned back as he pressed forwards.

Persephone gently placed a hand on his arm and lowered the bident from Cass's throat. "It would explain the sensation of death you felt."

Hades cast her a withering look, one that made it abundantly clear he wanted to argue with her.

Yet he didn't.

He huffed and eased back, scowling at Cass. "Continue."

"Well, he's alive now and he confirmed what we had suspected. Nemesis is involved in this." Cass froze up when Hades's eyes blazed so brightly she was surprised she didn't get burned.

"Nemesis," he growled, and Cass really hoped that murderous look in his eyes was for the traitorous goddess now.

"Why would she?" Persephone looked worried as she gazed at her husband.

"Many reasons," Hades snarled, his deep voice rolling across the land like thunder. "Power. Revenge. She believes I forced her into a life of servitude here after the last rebellion, when the roles of the gods and goddesses in these lands altered. I had her replace the Erinyes as punishment for her disobedience."

"Disobedience?" Cass couldn't hold back that question.

Hades narrowed his crimson eyes on her. "I sent a summons to Nemesis but she refused to answer. Rumours spread that she had sided with my enemy, but when we found her, she was bound and caged, and said that she had been captured by the enemy when she had tried to come to aid me."

Hades growled, the sound a vicious black snarl as his lips peeled back off his fangs.

"You believed her?" Cass said what he wouldn't, because she needed to know what had happened.

He nodded. "The rebellion had been crushed and the realm was safe, but I wanted someone to punish any who would attempt to break one of my rules. I moved her into a position I thought would suit her, allowing her to dispense justice. My justice. At first, she seemed to enjoy it, but then I noticed things. Small things. I began to feel she wasn't satisfied and when I approached her, she spoke of how her small realm felt like another cage. Wanting my people to be happy, I gave her more freedom, allowing her to come and go from that realm as she pleased."

Well, Cass could see why Nemesis hadn't exactly been happy about her new station. Putting someone who had been held captive in a cage into a realm she couldn't leave was just moving her into a new cage.

"Do you think now that the rumours had been true? She had been working with your enemy and when you had been close to discovering it, she had faked it all?" She caught the flicker of confusion in his eyes, there and gone, hidden before anyone could really notice it. This god didn't like to look uneducated. He had pride. Possibly too much of it. That was never a good thing, but she wasn't about to call him on the fact she needed to explain what she meant by 'faked it'. "Maybe she had her people harm her and lock her away to make it look like she was still on your side."

Hades roared, the sound deafening, and the ground bucked and shook so hard that one of the guards to her right landed on his backside and Persephone clung to her husband, casting fearful green eyes around her as fault lines spread across the black earth.

And Cass had thought his sons had serious tempers.

Hades did not like to be crossed.

"I will murder her with my own hands." He raised his right black gauntlet and curled his talons into a fist. He turned a glare on his guards. "Dispatch three legions immediately. She cannot leave these lands with the gates closed. Find her!"

Hades pivoted on his heel, his red cloak swirling outwards with the sharp action, and Cass lunged onto her feet as her heart lurched.

"Wait!" She held a hand out to him, desperation flooding her, making her limbs shake.

He stopped and looked back at her.

"I need to get back to Daimon. Marek tried to take me from the fight but Daimon needs me there… I *need* to be there." Her eyebrows furrowed as she thought about him fighting when he was weak, her mind filling with the reckless things he might do to fulfil his duty.

Like bleeding himself dry to seal a gate.

He wouldn't survive it.

"You worry about him," Persephone said, her voice the first soft kiss of morning light.

"I don't think worry is a strong enough word." Cass shook her head and smiled solemnly. "Daimon is in bad shape, but I know he won't leave. He'll stay and fight and do his duty, and it will get him killed. Valen, Keras, Ares and Marek are there, but… I'm afraid… I don't want to lose him. I need to be there."

Hades turned to face her, a calculating edge to his crimson eyes. "She speaks true. The gate is in danger. I will send you to my son."

Persephone looked pleased to hear that, smiled up at her husband with relief and love glittering in her green eyes. When she turned that same look on Cass, Cass had the feeling it was partly because she had just said without so many words that she was in love with Daimon.

She waited for the restriction on her magic to lift.

When it didn't, she looked at Hades. How was he intending to send her back to Daimon?

He lifted a gauntleted hand above his head.

Between them, a violet pinprick of light sparked to life, and she couldn't believe her eyes as it rapidly expanded into a disc that faced her. It pulsed and a ring appeared around it, growing in size as glyphs shimmered and chased along the curve of it. It rotated swiftly and another ring appeared inside it, this one spinning counter-clockwise, glowing with rainbow colours.

A gate.

This was dangerous.

She felt that in her bones.

The enemy wanted a gate open and Hades was doing it for them.

She looked at him through the shimmering form of the gate. There was a gleam in his eyes as he watched it, fire that shone so brightly that she couldn't miss it. He wanted this opportunity to draw the enemy to him.

He wanted to fight too.

Beside him, Persephone cast him a worried look. Cass was inclined to agree with the goddess. Hades's hunger for battle was not a good thing. It was better that the enemy was kept away from this world and from him, and that he let his sons do their duties and complete the mission he had given to them.

A scream rolled up her throat and she stumbled backwards as the ground shook beneath her and a huge bipedal beast appeared out of the gloom, thundering towards the gate. Mottled stony grey skin stretched tight over the powerful muscles of the five-storey tall monstrosity. It shook its head and roared, the grey-blue horns that covered the top of its head seeming to grow before her eyes as its silver irises glowed brighter.

"Go now," Hades barked and turned towards the beast, grinning at it.

Cass realised that the hunger for violence that shone in his eyes hadn't been about drawing the enemy to him—it had been about preparing to face this beast.

A gatekeeper.

Cass's pulse pounded as she ran for the gate, determined to make it there before the monster could reach Hades.

Daimon needed her.

She leaped into the sparkling violet disc of the gate, screamed as colours twisted around her and she felt as if someone had thrown her into a psychedelic blender. Up and down blurred as she spun. Bile rose up her throat.

Her feet suddenly hit solid ground and she jerked forwards as they stuck to it like glue, flailed her arms to stop herself from falling flat on her face and breathed a sigh of relief when she straightened.

That relief was short-lived as she was lifted upwards.

It turned to horror as the colourful light receded.

Revealing Daimon where he knelt at the edge of the horizontal rings of the gate.

About to have his throat slit.

Cass launched her hands forwards, relief blasting through her when twin orbs of magic shot from her palms.

"Get your damned hands off my man!" she snarled as the spell struck the furie who had been holding him and sent her flying through the air.

Daimon's ice-blue eyes widened, shock dancing in them as he stared at her. His white eyebrows lifted slightly.

She knew what he was thinking.

He was her man.

And she was damned if she was going to let someone take him from her.

His eyes sparkled with warmth as she finished rising out of the gate, as she walked on unsteady legs towards him, trying to ignore the fact she was levitating a good two feet above the rings of the gate.

"How the hell…" He took her hand when she was close enough, helped her down but swept her up into his arms before she could touch the ground. "What happened?"

"I could ask you the same thing." She hugged him and then made him release her, because she hadn't missed the fact he was bleeding everywhere and that he looked tired, on the verge of collapse.

When he loosened his hold on her, she placed her hand over his stomach and funnelled a healing spell into him, stopping the bleeding and destroying the toxin that tainted his blood. She looked into his eyes, caught the fatigue that still laced them, and decided she could spare a little more of her strength to give him a boost. She quickly pieced together another spell, one that would share some of her energy with him, and funnelled that into him too. His eyes instantly brightened, the dark circles beneath them fading, and she felt his strength returning.

"You opened the gate?" He looked at it, confusion shimmering in his eyes, and then at her.

She shook her head. "Not me. Your father."

His face fell, the colour draining from it as he pushed her back and looked her over. "Did he hurt you?"

"No." She kept the fact he had tried to hurt her to herself. "I landed in the Underworld and we had a talk, and then he opened this gate and here I am. I told him about you, and about Nemesis."

Daimon caught her jaw and tilted it upwards as he glared at her throat.

As he brushed thumbs over two sore spots on it.

"Just talked, eh?" He frowned at her.

"There might have been a little growling, some poking, and a few misunderstandings. But I'm safe, unharmed, and this really isn't the place for long conversations." She hurled a spell to her right without looking and the three daemons who had been charging towards them screamed as it struck them.

Tore them to pieces.

"We need to close this gate," Daimon said, a note of worry in his voice that relayed his feelings to her.

She was here with him. Together they could do this.

She pressed a brief kiss to Daimon's lips and then turned her back to him. He pressed his against it as he unleashed a devastating wave of ice spears at a group of daemons. Cass hurled freezing spells at several daemons who were fighting his brothers, picking them off and evening the odds a little for them.

Marek looked at her, relief shining in his dark eyes. She probably owed him an apology.

Cass frowned as she glanced beyond them and spotted more portals opening. How many daemons did the enemy have on their side? She couldn't even guess at the number of dead that lay on the battlefield around them.

Judging by the state of Daimon's brothers, it had already been too many.

Valen, Marek and Ares, and even Keras had multiple injuries, were bleeding from several wounds as they fought the daemons and tried to fight the two Erinyes. The twin blondes were too fast, easily dodging fireballs and lightning, spears of earth and shadows as they attempted to get closer to the gate again.

Daimon's brothers had their hands full.

She looked at the daemons who were piling over the remains of an earthen wall.

Maybe it was time she levelled the playing field a little.

Cass focused on the spell, building the same one she had used in Tokyo, even though she knew it would drain her. Daimon fought at her back, dealing with any daemons who got too close to the gate. Her magic twined around him, drawn to his power, and she held it back, unwilling to draw on him. She could feel he was weak, struggling as it was to fight the enemies and work on the gate.

She muttered the incantation. She clenched her fists as magic surged through her, leaving her trembling in its wake, and exploded from her in a shockwave. It rolled across the land, disintegrating the dead and sending the weaker living daemons flying, leaving only the strongest ones behind. When it neared the wall, it shot upwards, forming a dome over the area.

The daemons outside it immediately began battering it, every strike of their fists feeling like a blow dealt to her. They echoed on her body, faint for now, but if the fight carried on for too long there would be a cumulative effect and she would really start feeling them.

Daimon's brothers didn't miss a beat, kept on fighting as the number of daemons they were facing dwindled, giving them more chances to attack the Erinyes.

Several daemons attempted to make a run for it upon seeing the odds were now stacked against them instead.

They hit the edge of the barrier and bounced off it, landing on their backsides.

She smiled wickedly.

Her barriers worked both ways. Nothing got in.

Nothing got out.

Lightning bounced off the dome, tearing a grunt from her lips and a ripe curse from Valen. When the bright white-purple flash came again, it surged up from below, striking several daemons through their legs.

Ares and Marek switched tactics too, drawing the daemons away from the barrier so their attacks wouldn't strike it.

Keras tore through a group with his shadows and smiled coldly when a feminine shriek pierced the din of battle. Maybe he did resemble his father, had that same darkness within him, as deep and black as an abyss.

The furie he had found shot up into the air, a shadow snaring her leg, and screamed as it twisted with her, bringing her back down in a swift and brutal arc. She smashed into two male daemons, knocking them flying, and rolled across the grass.

Cass launched a spell at her as she struggled onto her feet, and then another and another as the female spotted her and rolled left and right, evading her attacks. The furie pushed onto her knees and then her feet, and sprinted towards her on a low vicious hiss.

The light of the closing gate washed over her face as she thundered towards Cass.

Cass broke away from the gate, hoping to give Daimon time to close it.

She ran at the furie, grunted as they collided and slammed her palm into the female's stomach. The blonde hissed as she flew backwards, violet light sizzling over her skin, and hit the ground hard.

The second furie whipped to face her, bared fangs and growled as she spotted her sister on the ground.

She lashed out at Marek with her claws, driving him back, and made a break for it, charging towards Cass.

Shadows seized her legs and she hit the ground face-first.

The first furie was on her feet and running at Cass again. Cass launched minor spells at her, ones designed to knock her away and do some damage. They were low level and wouldn't drain her. She needed to reserve most of her energy for maintaining the barrier.

The goddess dodged most of the spells that zoomed at her and grunted when one struck her shoulder, spinning her backwards. She found her footing and came at Cass again, faster this time.

Cass bit out a curse in Russian.

She summoned a barrier spell and shoved both of her hands forwards, sending a glowing blue wall at the female.

The furie broke straight through it as if it was paper and barrelled into Cass.

"Cass!" Daimon yelled and she wrestled with the goddess, using her magic to give her a boost in strength.

"I have this," she shouted, not quite sure that she did have it when the furie caught her with her talons, raking them across her side and cutting through her corset. "Take care of the gate."

Because it was almost closed.

The furie threw a desperate look at it.

And then off to her right.

The second goddess was on her feet again, running for Daimon. Shadows chased her and lightning shot up from the ground all around her. She nimbly dodged and rolled, leaped and managed to evade all of the attacks as she closed in on Daimon.

Cass threw a spell at her.

Regretted it when the one she had been using to boost her strength faltered, the drain on her magic proving too much.

The barrier around them shimmered and she focused on it, shoring it back up again, aware that she couldn't let it fall, no matter what happened to her. It was all that stood between the brothers and close to one hundred daemons.

The second furie reached Daimon, lashing at him with her claws, driving him back as he tried to reach Cass.

Cass looked at him as the furie she had been fighting got her in a chokehold and dragged her backwards.

Power vibrated in the air. A portal.

She craned her neck to look behind her as she grabbed the furie's arms, cursed when violet-black clouds billowed outwards from a point only a few feet away. She clawed at the goddess's arm, drawing blood, and pressed her hands to the crimson liquid, forming a connection between them.

The goddess shrieked in her ear as the spell seeped into her and Cass wove it with another, turning it toxic, hoping to weaken the furie enough that she could break free.

She kicked and scrambled with her legs as the bitch pulled her backwards, as the power of the portal grew heavier in the air.

Cass looked at Daimon, awareness washing through her, leaving her cold.

She couldn't stop the furie in time.

He paused as he grappled with the second furie and stared at her, hurt welling in his striking eyes, laced with despair and hopelessness that crashed over her too.

A vicious roar cut through the night as the barrier flickered and faded.

Daimon's head jerked up and he ducked as the furie he had been fighting released him and threw herself to the ground.

Cass stared wide-eyed as a huge lion-like creature with feathered eagle wings and gleaming talons shot past him.

Heading straight for her.

This wasn't good.

Those talons flexed, aimed right at her.

It was going to rip her to pieces.

CHAPTER 37

Daimon ducked and then popped to his feet as the winged lion shot past him, heading for Cass. She froze in the furie's grip, horror shining in her blue eyes as she stared at the beast that was zooming towards her.

Daimon had never been so glad to see the little bastard.

Mister Milos swooped upwards, grabbing the furie with his talons and hauling her up into the night air on hard beats of his feathered wings. The guardian deity growled as he sank fangs into the female's shoulder, as he raked at her with his claws. The goddess fought him as they twisted in the air, scratching at him with her own talons, hissing and snarling the whole time.

Cass sagged to her knees, eyes fixed in a blank stare ahead of her and her skin far too pale for Daimon's liking.

He kicked off, determine to grab her before Meadow could recover from the blow he had delivered when Mister Milos had distracted her with his overly dramatic, and extremely late, entrance.

He left the second furie in the dust as blood rained down from the sky.

The battle that raged there slowly drew Cass's stunned gaze upwards.

Heat licked across his back and he didn't need to look to know Meadow was on her feet and coming after him. Ares grunted as he hurled another fireball at her, and she screamed as this one connected, blasting her towards the gate.

Daimon's breath hitched and he skidded on the grass, twisting towards the gate.

Meadow shot straight through the lingering ring and central violet disc, tumbled across the ground and rolled to a halt.

The ring shrank into the central disc and it began to grow smaller, burning brighter as the power of the gate was condensed down into a single tiny orb.

That orb flashed, the violet light blinding him as it filled the darkness, and then it was gone.

Meadow scrambled onto her feet and glared at where the gate was hidden.

A pinprick of purple light burst back into existence.

"Shit," Ares muttered and raced past him, Valen hot on his heels. "I'll handle this."

Daimon nodded and pivoted, hurried to Cass and helped her onto her feet. She continued to stare up at the sky, watching Mister Milos as he fought the furie. More than just her blood was splattering them now. The guardian was taking heavy damage too. He willed Milos to fight harder, and to survive. As much as he couldn't stand the cat, he had to make it through the battle. Cass would be devastated if something happened to him.

Someone whimpered.

And then Melody plummeted out of the sky, landing hard on her back on the grass, blood bursting from her lips as her body jerked upwards.

Daimon figured the goddess was done for.

She was still for a tense minute and then she coughed and rolled over, pressed her hands and knees into the dirt and shook her head.

Damn.

Twin orbs of twisting green and purple light shot past Daimon and slammed into the goddess, sending her flying.

"Bitch," Cass muttered and sagged in his arms.

He clutched her to him with one arm and raised his other one, and ice shot up from the ground as Melody ran at him. The furie managed to dodge the first shard, but the second caught her calf, and the third pierced her thigh, sending her toppling forwards.

Just as the fourth jagged spear of ice shot up from the ground.

One he had intended to use to block her path to Cass.

The thicker shard impaled her chest, crimson swift to roll down it as it sliced clean through her and the pointed tip emerged from her back.

"Melody!" Meadow yelled, pain and fury in that one word.

Together with fear.

The furie cast one last look at her fallen sister and then spun on her heel, sprinting for a portal that formed just a few feet ahead of her. Ares growled and hurled a fireball at her, and lightning shot up from the ground just in front of her. She threw herself to her left, rolled and came onto her feet, kicked off and leaped.

Straight through the portal.

Keras snarled, a black growl that had Daimon focusing on his brother to see what had him so upset.

The daemons were fleeing.

It was over.

At least for now.

He gathered Cass to him, held her close and pressed a kiss to her messy black hair, a thousand feelings crashing over him as his battle instincts waned. Fear was at the helm, had him clinging to Cass as his mind filled with all the ways things could have gone differently.

Gone wrong.

He had come close to losing her too many times tonight.

When she pulled back and looked up into his eyes, pain shimmering in hers together with tears, he knew that feeling echoed inside her too.

Mister Milos landed as his brothers strode towards him, Keras helping Marek as he pressed a hand to his thigh, and Valen and Ares arguing about who had let the other furie escaped.

Cass slowly turned towards the winged lion, tense at first. Fear ran through her and a glow lit her palm, chasing back the night. He smiled as he realised she didn't know who had been the one to save her.

As the beast limped towards her, blood tracking down his left front leg, and the light of her spell washed over him to reveal scars on his face and the notch in his ear, recognition dawned in her eyes.

"Milos," she breathed, her face crumpling as she broke free of Daimon's grip and hurried to him.

The guardian deity shrank back to his other form as she rushed to meet him, his wings disappearing into his back and white splotches growing on his fur.

By the time Cass had reached him, he was a cat again, purring loudly as Cass swept him up into her arms and fussed over him, using a healing spell on his injuries.

She looked at Daimon. Frowned.

"You don't look surprised." She glanced at his brothers. "None of you do."

Ares and Valen shrugged. Marek grimaced as he applied pressure to his thigh. Keras didn't react at all. He was too busy scouring the darkness, where shadows lashed at the bodies of the daemons, devouring them and leaving nothing more than withered husks behind that broke down in the gentle breeze that swept through the park.

"How long have you known?" Her gaze drifted back to Daimon.

"From the moment I met him." Daimon went to her and rubbed Milos between his ears. The mangey thing hissed at him, baring three yellowing fangs. Daimon let that one slide. "Thanks for taking care of her. You couldn't have hauled arse here a little quicker though?"

Milos meowed, the sound indignant.

He supposed it was a long way between Tokyo and New York when you couldn't teleport great distances. Milos must have teleported close to a hundred times to reach Cass as quickly as he had. He could only imagine how tiring that had been for him.

Daimon made a mental note to treat the beast to some sushi-grade fish later.

Cass turned her frown on the cat. "You have a lot of explaining to do."

Daimon knew she was talking to the cat, but the way she glanced at him made him feel she was talking to him instead.

She was right. He did have a lot of explaining to do.

Or at least a lot of apologising.

"What happened after you slipped my grasp?" Marek finally lifted his head and Cass went to him, crouched before him and tucked Milos against her with one arm.

She held her free hand over Marek's thigh and warm light glowed from her palm.

Beneath the rip in Marek's dark trousers, the long gash in his thigh healed.

Cass stood and gave him a black look. "I landed in the Underworld."

"Shit," Ares muttered.

Marek looked at Daimon.

Daimon shrugged it off. "Not your fault, man. She has a will of her own and apparently a knack for getting into trouble."

"Did you meet Father?" Concern lit Ares's dark eyes.

She nodded and petted the cat. "He was not charming. Has a personality as black as yours."

She flicked Keras a look.

Keras narrowed green eyes on her. "I hope you did not upset him."

Daimon wanted to flash fangs at his brother for being more concerned about their father than her, but he knew where Keras was coming from. Hades in a bad mood was trouble for them all. His father had a short leash on his temper and it snapped more often than not.

"I was delightful. He was not." Cass cuddled the cat and Daimon went to her. Just the thought of her facing his father left his blood cold and filled him with a need to hold her and know she was here now, safe with him again. "I told him what had happened since he thought Daimon had died, and presumed I was responsible because someone dropped me in the Underworld with his blood on me."

"I didn't drop you," Marek grumbled.

"Semantics," she countered, sighed and continued, "I told him everything, and he was... displeased... upon hearing Nemesis is a traitorous bitch."

Ares looked at Keras. "I'm guessing Esher didn't get a chance to send that Messenger."

"For all we know, all Messengers are now working against us." Keras twisted the silver band on his thumb, spinning it around, his gaze locked on it. "What if others are too?"

Those words were spoken so quietly she almost didn't hear them.

Ares ghosted a hand over Keras's shoulder. "You know she wouldn't."

Keras's green gaze snapped to his, rapidly darkening. "Do I? I thought I knew her once. It turned out I was wrong."

He disappeared, leaving black wisps of smoke behind that swirled in the air.

Ares heaved a sigh. "I'll track him down later. Give him five minutes to cool off."

Daimon nodded in agreement. He couldn't remember the last time Keras had actually spoken of Enyo. While he didn't know what had happened between them, he knew it had hurt his brother.

Still hurt him.

Marek scrubbed a hand around the back of his neck. "At least she'll have to come to Tokyo if she wants to pass information to us now. That's me off the hook."

Which sounded a lot like a catastrophe waiting to happen to Daimon.

Valen nudged the dead furie with his boot and jerked backwards when she slid further down the melting ice shard. "One down, eh?"

"I'm not sure this is a good thing." Daimon looked at his brothers. "We have one less enemy, but Nemesis is powerful and the remaining furie is going to want her sister back."

"Mari will be in danger," Cass said, worry shining in her blue eyes. "They'll need her more now than ever."

"You too." Daimon brushed his palm over her cheek, fighting the darker side of his blood as it snarled at him to protect her. "Meadow looked desperate when she left. I have a bad feeling she'll come after both Mari and you. She'll want Melody back."

"So we take the body, stick it on ice. Draw them to us." Ares's eyes glowed in the low light as he growled, "If she wants Melody back, she'll need the body."

"Maybe. I'm not sure. Some forms of necromancy work in other ways, using the soul as the catalyst." Cass leaned into Daimon's side and he rubbed her arm, held her to him and silently offered her comfort he hoped would allay her fears.

No one was going to get their hands on her.

Or Mari.

"We should take it anyway," Valen put in and lifted his gaze to the tree tops and the buildings beyond them. "Just in case. Things are still looking sketchy."

Daimon nodded in agreement as he glanced at the horizon, seeing the otherworld. The sky blazed red, distant screams ringing in his ears, carried on the hot wind that blasted against him and sent flares of gold sparks spiralling up into the sky from the broken burning buildings. He had expected it to look better, but he swore it looked worse. Because the final battle was drawing near?

Maybe they could use Meadow's rage against her, using Melody's body to lure her into the open. Maybe being in possession of the bodies of both one of the furies and the wraith would work in their favour in other ways too. They were two powerful allies that the enemy would definitely try to take back if they were determined to use Cass to revive their fallen.

As far as Daimon could see, his side were holding all the cards.

The enemy would be the one to make the next move.

And it would be the first move of the final battle when it happened.

He could feel it.

"What do we do about Nemesis?" Marek said.

"Your father dispatched legions to hunt for her. He believes she's still in the Underworld." Cass stroked Milos.

"She'll be coming." Ares's hands glowed, flames licking over them as he clenched them into fists at his sides. "Now that she's revealed herself, they're not going to rest. They're going to come at us with all they have to get a gate open and allow her through it, together with whoever else is on her side."

Ares was right.

The enemy were going to make one last stand.

He and his brothers would be ready for them.

He held Cass to him and amended that thought—he and his side would be ready for them. Everyone was a part of this war and everyone was going to want to do all in their power to make sure that when it was over, they were victorious.

"I should close this gate." Daimon glanced over his shoulder in the direction of it.

"Tomorrow," Ares said. "Tonight, we rest and we plan. We go over everything we know and we make sure we haven't missed anything, and we wait for word from the Underworld. If the legions fail to find Nemesis, then we'll call in a favour."

Daimon didn't like the sound of that. "What sort of favour?"

Ares's grim look said it all.

"Shit, man," Valen muttered and pulled his phone from his pocket. Charms dangled from it, one of a sword and shield catching Daimon's eye. "I could just send her a message right now."

Ares shook his head. "Give him time."

Daimon had the feeling that Keras was going to need far more time than they could afford to give him. They needed allies in this war.

What better ally was there than a goddess who had been born for battle?

"Tokyo," Ares muttered.

Marek nodded and disappeared. Valen huffed, grabbed the dead furie and followed him.

Ares hesitated. "Don't linger too long. Esher will want to see you're all right."

Daimon dipped his chin, grateful for a few moments alone with Cass. His brother stepped.

Daimon slipped his hand into Cass's and teleported with her, landing on the terrace of his hillside home in Hong Kong.

All of the strength seemed to leak out of Cass and she looked up at him, tears catching the sunlight as they lined her lashes.

Daimon sighed and brushed them away with his thumbs, turning them into diamonds of ice. "I'm sorry. I never want to hurt you, but I just keep doing it."

She smiled tightly. "I like to think I give as good as I get."

She did. He had lost track of all the scares she had given him and they had only known each other for a few short weeks.

Daimon gathered Cass to him, pressed his forehead to hers and then drew back so he could see her face. Gods, she was beautiful.

And a little bit angry with him.

He smoothed his palm over her cheek, trying not to think about the fact she had somehow ended up facing his father but thankful that she had stood up to him. He could only imagine the hell she had given him. His mother probably adored her for that.

He certainly adored her for it.

He dipped his head and kissed her, savoured the feel of her lips against his and the warmth of her as it chased the cold from his heart, easing his fears and giving him comfort.

She was safe now and he would keep her that way, but not by sidelining her whenever things got rough. He would keep her at his side instead, right where he needed her to be, where they could fight as one, battling to survive and have that forever they both wanted.

A forever he needed with all his heart.

The coming fight wasn't going to be easy, he knew that, but with Cass at his side, together with his brothers and their women, he felt confident that they could win.

They were the guardians of the Underworld, protectors of Hades. Not just him and his brothers, but Cass and the other women too.

Hell, even Mister Milos.

The bastard hissed at him again.

Daimon gave him a black look.

The cat purred louder, vying for attention as Daimon stroked Cass's cheek, as he looked into her blue eyes and saw the love in them, felt that love pouring into him through her caress as she lifted her hand and placed her palm against his cheek, mirroring him.

Daimon drew down a deep breath and found the courage to say something he had wanted to tell her so many times over the last few days.

"You were right," he husked and held her gaze. "You did melt my heart… but you did so much more than that too. You breathed life into it. Into me."

He lowered his head and brought his lips to hers.

"I breathe for you now. Live for you."

He whispered against her mouth.

"I love you, Cass, and I want to be with you. Forever."

Cass brushed her lips across his, sending a shiver rolling through him, heat and light that had the heart she now held in her hands melting as she murmured.

"I love you too."

She kissed him, softly at first, but then passionately, had his head spinning by the time she pulled back and smiled wickedly at him.

"And I'm holding you to that forever. No escape for you now. You're mine, Daimon."

Daimon grinned and gathered her into his arms, careful not to crush Milos or harm the little prick with his ice as the feral beast growled at him.

And breathed against her lips before he kissed her.

"You got me."

The End

ABOUT THE AUTHOR

Felicity Heaton is a New York Times and USA Today best-selling author who writes passionate paranormal romance books. In her books she creates detailed worlds, twisting plots, mind-blowing action, intense emotion and heart-stopping romances with leading men that vary from dark deadly vampires to sexy shape-shifters and wicked werewolves, to sinful angels and hot demons!

If you're a fan of paranormal romance authors Lara Adrian, J R Ward, Sherrilyn Kenyon, Kresley Cole, Gena Showalter, Larissa Ione and Christine Feehan then you will enjoy her books too.

If you love your angels a little dark and wicked, her best-selling Her Angel romance series is for you. If you like strong, powerful, and dark vampires then try the Vampires Realm romance series or any of her stand alone vampire romance books. If you're looking for vampire romances that are sinful, passionate and erotic then try her London Vampires romance series. Or if you like hot-blooded alpha heroes who will let nothing stand in the way of them claiming their destined woman then try her Eternal Mates series. It's packed with sexy heroes in a world populated by elves, vampires, fae, demons, shifters, and more. If sexy Greek gods with incredible powers battling to save our world and their home in the Underworld are more your thing, then be sure to step into the world of Guardians of Hades.

If you have enjoyed this story, please take a moment to contact the author at **author@felicityheaton.com** or to post a review of the book online

Connect with Felicity:
Website – http://www.felicityheaton.com
Blog – http://www.felicityheaton.com/blog/
Twitter – http://twitter.com/felicityheaton
Facebook – http://www.facebook.com/felicityheaton
Goodreads – http://www.goodreads.com/felicityheaton
Mailing List – http://www.felicityheaton.com/newsletter.php

FIND OUT MORE ABOUT HER BOOKS AT:
http://www.felicityheaton.com

Printed in Great Britain
by Amazon